An Alternative History of Britain

 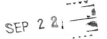

An Attractive History of Britain

An Alternative History of Britain

The Anglo–Saxon Age

Tim Venning

Pen & Sword
MILITARY

First published in Great Britain in 2013 by
Pen & Sword Military
an imprint of
Pen & Sword Books Ltd
47 Church Street
Barnsley
South Yorkshire
S70 2AS

ISBN 978-1-78159-125-3

A CIP catalogue record for this book is available from the British Library.

Typeset in 11pt Ehrhardt by
Mac Style, Beverley, E. Yorkshire

Printed and bound by CPI Group (UK) Ltd, Croydon, CR0 4YY

Pen & Sword Books Ltd incorporates the Imprints of Pen & Sword Aviation,
Pen & Sword Family History, Pen & Sword Maritime, Pen & Sword Military,
Pen & Sword Discovery, Wharncliffe Local History, Wharncliffe True Crime,
Wharncliffe Transport, Pen & Sword Select, Pen & Sword Military Classics,
Leo Cooper, The Praetorian Press, Remember When, Seaforth Publishing
and Frontline Publishing.

For a complete list of Pen & Sword titles please contact
PEN & SWORD BOOKS LIMITED
47 Church Street, Barnsley, South Yorkshire, S70 2AS, England
E-mail: enquiries@pen-and-sword.co.uk
Website: www.pen-and-sword.co.uk

Contents

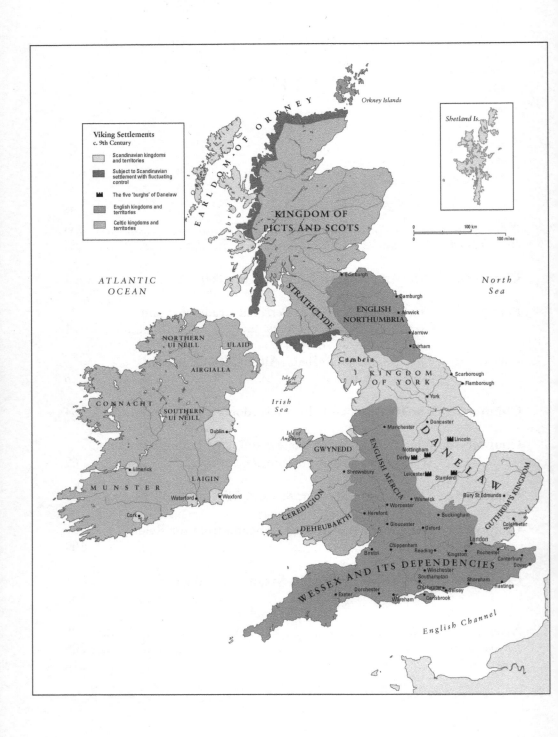

Viking Settlements
c. 9th Century

- Scandinavian kingdoms and territories
- Subject to Scandinavian settlement with fluctuating control
- The five 'burghs' of Danelaw
- English kingdoms and territories
- Celtic kingdoms and territories

EARLDOM OF ORKNEY

Orkney Islands

Shetland Is.

KINGDOM OF PICTS AND SCOTS

ATLANTIC OCEAN

North Sea

STRATHCLYDE

Edinburgh

Bamburgh

ENGLISH NORTHUMBRIA

Alnwick

Jarrow

Durham

Cumbria

NORTHERN UI NEILL

ULAID

AIRGIALLA

Isle of Man

Scarborough

Flamborough

KINGDOM OF YORK

York

CONNACHT

SOUTHERN UI NEILL

Irish Sea

Dublin

Manchester

Doncaster

Lincoln

Isle of Anglesey

GWYNEDD

Nottingham

Derby

DANELAW

Limerick

LAIGIN

Shrewsbury

Leicester

Stamford

MUNSTER

Waterford

Wexford

CEREDIGION

ENGLISH MERCIA

Warwick

Bury St Edmunds

GUTHRUM'S KINGDOM

Cork

DEHEUBARTH

Worcester

Hereford

Gloucester

Buckingham

Oxford

Colchester

London

Chippenham

Reading

Kingston

Rochester

Canterbury

Dover

Bristol

Winchester

Southampton

Shoreham

Hastings

WESSEX AND ITS DEPENDENCIES

Exeter

Dorchester

Chichester

Selsey

Wareham

Carisbrook

English Channel

0   100 km
0   100 miles

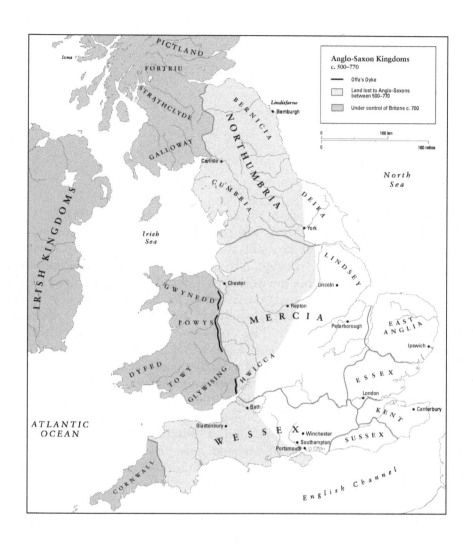

Anglo-Saxon Kingdoms
c. 500–770

— Offa's Dyke

☐ Land lost to Anglo-Saxons
between 500–770

☐ Under control of Britons c. 700

|0   100 km|
|0   100 miles|

PICTLAND

Iona

FORTRIU

STRATHCLYDE

GALLOWAY

IRISH KINGDOMS

Irish
Sea

Carlisle

Lindisfarne
• Bamburgh

BERNICIA

NORTHUMBRIA

CUMBRIA

DEIRA

• York

North
Sea

LINDSEY

GWYNEDD

• Chester

Lincoln •

POWYS

• Repton

MERCIA

Peterborough •

EAST
ANGLIA

Ipswich •

DYFED

TOWY

GLYWISING

HWICCA

ESSEX

London •

KENT

• Canterbury

ATLANTIC
OCEAN

Glastonbury •

• Bath

WESSEX

• Winchester
• Southampton
Portsmouth • •

SUSSEX

CORNWALL

English Channel

Introduction

One of the few dates from medieval British history still firmly in the popular memory is 1066. The end of Anglo-Saxon England and the Norman Conquest are still viewed as major events – England's forcible first 'entry into Europe'. Its somewhat isolated socio-political structure was integrated into the world of Western European Latin-speaking Christendom and what is loosely described as 'feudalism'. The victor, Duke William of Normandy (known, though not to his face, as 'The Bastard' rather than the later sobriquet 'The Conqueror'), had no serious claim on the throne, though he did his best to claim that the late King Edward (not known then as 'The Confessor') had named him as heir and the intervening king, Harold Godwinson, was an oath-breaking usurper. The kings after the Conquest numbered themselves as from 1066, not from English unification in the 920s – Edward 'I' (r. 1272–1307) was in fact the fourth Edward to rule England, starting with the national unifier Edward 'the Elder' (r. 899–924). The work of the unification of England took place with the northwards expansion of the allied kingdoms of Edward's Wessex and his sister Aethelfleda's Mercia into the Danelaw (East Midlands and East Anglia), settled by Danish incomers in the 870s, in 911–18, and by 924 Edward was recognized as overlord by the Danish kingdom of York and the Norse settlers in Lancashire. He secured Mercia too on his sister's death in 918, and York was incorporated into England in 927 though it subsequently revolted and was not finally annexed until 954. Cumbria, independent but linked to Strathclyde in Scotland, was partly overrun in 945 but modern Cumberland only appears to have been annexed in 1092; the shifting Anglo-Scottish border in the east moved south from the Forth to its present position in the 970s.

The creation of a kingdom of England was thus far from straightforward, and there was no tradition of a united Anglo-Saxon kingdom of England so Mercian and Northumbrian regional separatism remained an issue. Edward's annexation of Mercia in 918 was immensely aided by the fact that its heir, his niece Egwynn, was a girl who could not lead armies and there was no male candidate available. Even so, his eldest son, Athelstan, brought up in Mercia and the offspring of a legally questionable marriage, was passed over for Wessex and seems to have been intended to rule Mercia; he only secured Wessex when his half-brother Aelfweard died weeks after Edward in 924. The fact that he was not crowned for a year implies serious resistance to this. Had Aelfweard not died, would England have remained united? Similarly, it is possible that Athelstan's half-brother and successor Edmund intended both his sons, Edwy and Edgar, to rule a kingdom each when they were adult; Edwy succeeded to both in 955 but in 957 Mercia and Northumbria revolted in Edgar's favour. Edwy's death in 959 saw unity restored, but was this inevitable? The succession to Edgar in 975 was disputed between partisans of his two under-age sons, Edward and Aethelred, though division was avoided and in 978 Edward was murdered.

In the 1000s England was gradually overrun by a Viking army under Swein 'Forkbeard', king of Denmark, a war that could have seen England split into two again with him ruling the Danelaw and Northumbria, which were first to accept him. As Wessex rallied against the Danes under Aethelred's son Edmund 'Ironside' in 1016 the latter's defeat at Ashingdon saw England divided between him and Swein's son Cnut, though this was probably only a truce born of exhaustion and Edmund quickly died. A temporary division between the partisans of Cnut's two sons, Harold 'Harefoot' and Harthacnut, followed Cnut's death in 1035, though that was soon reversed as first one then the other took control; and in 1066 King Harald 'Hardradi' of Norway endeavoured to add York (and perhaps more) to his wide-flung domains. After Harald was killed by Harold Godwinson the latter fell in battle against Duke William within weeks – but a less decisive result could have left England divided again, as in 1016.

The triumph of one state in England was far from certain throughout this period, and was due to genetic and military luck rather than 'inevitability'. The 'What Ifs' of English unification are thus many, and pose possibilities of a future for England radically different from reality. And what if the Wessex of Alfred 'the Great' had succumbed to Viking invasion in the 'battle-winter' of 870–1 or the surprise attack of winter 877–8? What if Alfred, a fourth if not fifth son, had never been king? What if two heirs had succeeded in 924, 955–9, or 975? What if Edmund had defeated Cnut in 1016? What if Cnut had not died relatively young in 1035, or both his sons had not died in their twenties? What if Edward 'the Confessor' had had a son, or his nephew and chosen heir Edward 'the Exile' had not died in 1057? Earl Harold Godwinson would have stood little chance of the throne in either case – and Duke William even less. Events cast a long shadow - if the English elite had not been decimated by the wars of the 1000s and Cnut's takeover; King Edward would not have had his political power circumscribed as of 1042 by three powerful earls – all nominees of Cnut – who could call on more military resources than he could. Even if Harold's father, Godwin, had still been chief minister, as in reality, when Edward exiled him in 1051 he would have been unlikely to have fought his way back to power – and again, Harold would never have been in a position to succeed as king in 1066.

The same applies to events before the Viking invasions which began in 865, though here the evidence is less clear – particularly before c.650 – and much has to be guesswork. Basic questions of political and social development have to be asked. Why did pre-850 England consist of so many petty kingdoms, when the incoming Germanic peoples (conquerors or settlers) managed to create one state in Francia? The notion of a stable 'heptarchy' of seven English kingdoms has now been disproved, and it is clear that there were three major states – Northumbria, Mercia and Wessex – plus numerous smaller ones, some of which were temporarily or permanently absorbed by their larger neighbours. But what determined which kingdoms succeeded – geography, greater resources, military structure, or a coherent, dynamic and long-lasting tradition of leadership transmitted successfully from one generation to the next over centuries? The era of settlement and conquest is particularly disputed, and the notion of monolithic 'ethnic cleansing' of Romano-Britons by invading Germans is now thought far too simplistic. Possibly peaceful farmers and traders were as crucial as the traditional picture of war-bands and heroic leaders played up by literary tradition. But it is clear that leadership was crucial – and in the initial century or two of state-formation dynamic war-leaders and 'statesmen' briefly brought leadership of coalitions of smaller kingdoms to states which were later eclipsed, such as Kent, Sussex and East Anglia. Those larger and better-resourced states which soon emerged to prominence, particularly the 'Big Three', had turbulent histories rather than a smooth rise to power, with the dominance of first one and then another, secured and then lost by military means. Wessex, Northumbria, and Mercia all achieved temporary dominance within their regions only to lose it again, by dynastic luck, military misjudgement, or a coalition of their enemies. Northumbria was eclipsed temporarily by Mercia after military defeat in 642–55, and permanently after defeat by the Picts in 685 – which latter battle ended the chance of a 'North English' state encompassing much of Scotland. Wessex, dominant in the South, was eclipsed twice – after 592 and 688. Would Mercia – the leading state through the eighth and early ninth centuries under Aethelbald, Offa 'the Great', and Coenwulf – have lost its dominance to Wessex after 825 if its succession had been more stable? Could a stable Mercia under long-lived rulers succeeded by competent sons have prevented the rise of Wessex under Alfred's grandfather Egbert, and but for the Viking invasions would Wessex have ever united England?

The possible permutations of events given different leadership choices or luck are many – and indeed the limited evidence does not prevent us speculating that Anglo-Saxon rule of all 'England' was not inevitable. What if one or more of the post-Roman British states had held on to more of its territory in the sixth or seventh centuries?

Chapter One

Early Anglo-Saxon Kingdoms to c.800

Part I

The Setting: An Era of Personal Leadership and Creation of New Kingdoms

But what if the fortunes of war and politics had turned out differently?

(a) The problem of the sources

It has become the fashion in recent decades to emphasize the development of the Anglo-Saxon kingdoms of early England in terms of social and economic factors as opposed to their leadership. The nineteenth century historians' enthusiasm for history focusing on the lives of 'kings and queens' has been downplayed, and in school education the old system of learning the names of rulers by rote has been replaced by 'empathizing' with the lives of their subjects – the ordinary peasant-farmers and their families. Assisted by a concentration of resources on archaeology and the excavation of homesteads, the basic details of everyday life have been the mainstay of pre-1066 studies. The complicated details of politics and battles have been neglected, with the additional factor that greater modern understanding of the meagre literary sources poses new questions about them. Just how accurate and reliable are the surviving – often non-contemporary – narratives? To what extent were they written to record details that had been faithfully remembered over generations – and how much were they works of literature and propaganda with a contemporary political purpose?

The issue is particularly acute for the era of 'conquest' – itself a problematic concept at variance with basic archaeology – and settlement, the fifth to seventh centuries. The main semi-contemporary British (Welsh) source, the *De Excidio Britanniae* of Gildas (540s), deals in lurid generalizations of mass-slaughter and polemic about the sins of the British, and its author clearly saw himself as a latter-day Jeremiah inveighing against the moral failings of his sinful countrymen that led to merited punishment. He was not writing as an objective 'historian' in the modern sense (or even as a Roman writer such as Tacitus did), but as a polemicist looking to the Old Testament for inspiration. The post-Roman British of his era had lost the greater part of their land to heathen invaders, just as the Jews of Jeremiah's time had lost Israel and were in the process of losing Judah. The parallel was obvious; the cause of this punishment of God's people must be their sins, and thus Gildas, a devout monk probably writing in southern Britain or Brittany, was bound to play up the extent of the disaster.

But his claims of disaster for the British, with towns sacked and farms abandoned in a systematic and countrywide reign of terror by Germanic invaders, are not backed by the evidence on the ground. The amount of fire-related destruction in towns is limited, and it has been pointed out that not every fire can be attributed to attackers as opposed to accident (which applies to burnt Roman villas too).

Pioneering work on the rural landscape shows a major degree of continuity in occupation from post-Roman to Anglo-Saxon settlement and little sign of devastated farms[1] left vacant for decades.

The first English source, the *Ecclesiastical History of the English People*, was written by another monk, the Venerable Bede, in isolated Northumbria c.731 and sought to describe the inevitable triumph of the Roman Catholic missionaries in converting the English. Bede's monastery of Jarrow on the Tyne in northern Northumbria around 700 was not that remote from events elsewhere despite the geographical location. The kingdom had many contacts with the other English states and bishoprics and the nearer Continent, playing up its role as part of Christendom and its links with the papacy in Rome – particularly under the late seventh century bishopric of the energetic 'Romanizer' St Wilfred. Its elite under King Oswy had made a conscious decision to adopt the Roman religious customs (e.g. in celebrating Easter) at Whitby in 664 to fit in with the Continent, and the Church kept up its international links. Indeed, from 669 the Church in England uniquely had a Greek leader from St Paul's home-town in Cilicia, Eastern Anatolia – Archbishop Theodore from Tarsus. Bede was an assiduous collector of facts and emphasized his use of reliable witnesses. But he had a religious purpose in his writing as much as Gildas had, though he seems to have been less credulous about early history and better informed. His account downplayed both the work of 'Celtic' missionaries from Iona – the defeated faction in 664 – in the conversion of northern Britain and the survival of the post-Roman British Church. If he is to be believed, pre-conversion England was entirely pagan, with no mention of the possibility that Christians using churches (e.g. that of St Martin at Canterbury) had survived in the kingdom of Kent into the sixth century. No Christians were referred to in the British kingdoms of the Pennines annexed to Northumbria in the early seventh century. Nor did he point out that before his hero, St Augustine, and his missionaries arrived from Rome to convert Kent in 597 that King Aethelbert's Christian Frankish wife already had an attendant bishop, Liudhard.

Both Kent and Northumbria were presented as a pagan *tabula rasa* when their Roman Christian converters arrived – Augustine in Kent and Paulinus in Northumbria. In secular matters, Bede's list of the major 'over-kings' in England in the seventh century[2] – the 'Bretwaldas' – notably left out the pagan Penda, ruler of the Midlands from c.625 to 655 and probably more powerful than his Northumbrian contemporaries.

The major secular source for pre-900 history, the *Anglo-Saxon Chronicle*, was not compiled until the later ninth century, 400 years after the early settlements, and concentrates on events in its 'home territory', Wessex. It was probably commissioned by King Alfred's court, at a time of renewed threat from the Vikings, to present an inspiring picture of the struggles of the English peoples against the British (and each other) and to play up the role of Alfred's own dynasty. Much of its early detail is formulaic, with the sparse account of the conquest of Wessex suspiciously similar to that of Kent. The only other southern kingdom covered in any detail is Kent – and that mainly at the time of its conquest in the fifth century and the conversion in the sixth century. Sussex, adjacent to Wessex, so presumably reasonably well known to the latter's annalists, is only mentioned during its conquest in the fifth century and later when its history impinges on Wessex. East Anglia – an important realm, holder of the 'bretwaldaship' in the 620s and location of the major archaeological find of royal treasure at Sutton Hoo – is hardly mentioned, as is Essex. Mercia, crucial in the seventh and eighth centuries and arguably the most powerful kingdom south of the Humber from its unification c.630, is neglected except when its history impinges on Wessex or Northumbria. As with Bede, the career of the pagan Penda is downplayed compared with that of his Christian foes in Northumbria – because Alfred or other 'editors' regarded him with disapproval?

The annals are very much history from a West Saxon point of view – and we must bear in mind that they may have been collected to inspire the readership and listeners about past heroic successes in an era of Viking attacks. As has been pointed out, there is no mention of apparent Saxon disasters such as their defeat by the British at 'Mount Badon' around 500. There is merely a suspicious lacuna in the list of Saxon military successes for the period from 491 to 560, except in Wessex. Again, there are contradictions with the archaeological record – particularly over the early settlement of

Hampshire,[3] the alleged cradle of Wessex. There is no archaeological record of a Saxon settlement in Hampshire around 500, when the 'founder' Cerdic was apparently active. The majority of sixth century settlements are in the upper and middle Thames valley, an area whose warfare is not covered in the *Chronicle* except for a few references in the 570s.

For that matter, even the early Welsh sources have been shown to have contemporary political purposes – as with the *History* attributed to 'Nennius' (c.829), commissioned for a new dynasty in Gwynedd to play up its predecessors' heroism, and the tenth century *Annales Cambriae* compiled at Hywel Dda's court.[4] Sceptics have accordingly had a field day minimizing the reliability of all these sources and limiting the amount of written evidence for the period that can be deemed reliable.[5] It is likely that the sources are not as useless as some historians have implied, and that much detail was copied from non-surviving records without much amendation even if a political 'spin' was put upon it and inconvenient facts were dropped from the record. But it still provides a major note of caution when any assessment of the era of settlement is considered. And for that matter the first, nineteenth century, modern historians to interpret this evidence had their own agenda too. Great 'progressive', 'Whig' historians such as Freeman and Stubbs had a motive for presenting a picture of 'free', racially Germanic Anglo-Saxons creating a distinctly 'English' society, without inconvenient 'Celtic' elements. They looked to emulate their nineteenth century German contemporaries across the 'German Ocean' (North Sea), whence the Anglo-Saxons had come, and to create a founding saga for the British Empire and its democratic institutions. In this respect, the 'Celtic' element in Britain was an irrelevance and any notion of non-Saxon survival in England to be ignored; the argument sometimes took on ominous racial overtones about the innate superiority of the Germanic Saxons to other peoples. In this interpretation, the seventeenth century 'left-wing' notion of the post-1066 ruling class as alien Frenchmen imposing a 'Norman Yoke' on freedom-loving Saxons was revived. A typical interpretation was that of the historical novelist Charles Kingsley of the career of Hereward the post-1066 'freedom-fighter' as 'Last of the Saxons', the epitome of manly English resistance to tyrannous French invaders. Kingsley and Freeman were as much polemicists as Gildas or Bede were.

(b) The importance of leadership – and a culture of Germanic military leadership

The various small kingdoms in post-Roman, Germanic England of the sixth and seventh centuries owed their names to the assorted divisions of the 'Anglian', Saxon, and Jutish peoples settled in the Danish peninsula and the swamps of north-western Germany in the fifth century[6] – the three invading peoples of the mid-fifth century as recorded by Bede. In fact, it is not clear whether there was a clear genetic or geographical distinction between them – did the Jutes come from Jutland, and where precisely was the Angles'[7] homeland? Was it the geographical 'Angle' between Germany and the Jutland peninsula, i.e. modern Schleswig-Holstein? What of the sixth century Eastern Roman account that the 'Frissones' – presumably from the Frisian islands off Holland[8] – were involved in the conquest? Was this another name for one of Bede's peoples, or for those 'Saxons' – not genetically or culturally distinct from the mainlanders – who happened to live on the Frisian islands? Were a distinct 'Frisian' people 'swamped' by numerically superior and more culturally aggressive Saxons and forgotten about by later writers? What of the archaeological evidence of close cultural links between the Jutes of Kent and the Franks, seemingly ignored by Bede?

The question arises of whether the names that we know the new kingdoms by are an accurate memory of the genetic or cultural 'make-up' of the inhabitants, or just 'short-hand' for the self-perceived allegiance of their leadership. The names may reflect the self-perceived identity of the dominant 'people' in an area by the time of Bede, not that of the real-life fifth and sixth century settlers. What he recorded may be myth as much as accurate fact, and at least be distorted by simplification by later generations after the (alleged) settlement. Given the recent discoveries about the makeup of English 'DNA', of which more later, the extent of an influx of settlers from across the North Sea has been questioned. So has the dating of any influx of 'German/Low Countries' DNA – how much of what has been traced was pre-Roman, from the so-called 'Iron Age' when Caesar testifies that some of the tribal 'Belgae'[9] from northern Gaul moved into southern Britain.

Did the identity of 'Angles', 'Saxons', and 'Jutes' reflect the chosen 'creation myths' of the ruling families of family, as recorded by their poets, at the expense of a more muddled and multi-ethnic origin for their followers? So-called 'tribal' identities in post-Roman Europe were sometimes not ethnically monolithic, but consisted of a mixture of warriors and their womenfolk from different regions coalescing around a successful leader – Romans and Germans served in the 'Asian' elite around Attila, for example. Did this apply to England too? Were all the emergent 'kingdoms' as ethnically muddled as that of Attila, which was once assumed to be monolithically of 'Mongolian' stock that had migrated all the way from the borders of China?[10] It is not now certain that they were the 'Hsiung-Nu' Mongolian raiders of Han China in the second and first centuries BC, who had been defeated by the Chinese and were assumed to have migrated all the way to the Black Sea by the time they defeated the Goths there in the early 370s.

By the same definition, some of the 'German' groups in south-eastern England may have been partly British – hence the Romano-British names of the West Saxon 'founder', Cerdic, and some of his kin and of the royal house of Lindsey in Lincolnshire. Both kingdoms had 'capitals' – that is, principal royal residences and bishoprics – in former Romano-British regional capitals, Winchester and Lincoln.

Fifth and sixth century ethnicity is a historical and political minefield, and all that can be said is that the initial approaches of nineteenth century historians were too simplistic and were often influenced by their own contemporary notions of nationhood. Indeed, nowadays some historians even think that the long-cherished differences between archaeological finds for 'Romano-British' and 'Germanic' peoples (grave-goods and methods of burial in particular) reflect cultural fashion as much as ethnicity. Given the likely mixture of ethnic origin for the populace of some kingdoms, were the so-called 'Saxon' territories ever settled 'exclusively' by people from 'Saxony' that is 'Old Saxony' in lower north-west Germany? Or the 'Jutish' territories from Jutland? And how and why did the name of the 'Frisians'/ 'Frissones' become submerged in those of the Angles, Saxons and Jutes?

Creating a sense of identity was important, and the emergence of 'patriotic' legends of identity focussing on a dynasty can be seen in the example of the most successful people of the later fourth and fifth centuries, the Goths; the *Gothic History* (*Getica*) of Jordanes reflects their self-image by c.500 and is centred on the Amal dynasty. The semi-Romanized Goths in conquered Italy are the most visible sign of this tendency, but it seems to apply across many other peoples – as in England with the 'founding myths' of Kent (centred on Hengest) and the Anglian Mercians (centred on their Continental ancestor-king Offa). Crucially, when all this dynastic mythology was created no ambitious literary 'spinner' for a new post-Roman kingship could create a history of ancient ruling royal families who had held power for centuries, giving an impression of antiquity and stability. The post-Roman kingship of the Germanic states in ex-Roman lands was new, and everyone knew it – though some lengthy dynastic 'history' was to be created for non-Roman Denmark by Saxo Grammaticus. The creation of any similar 'foundation myths' and heroic sagas for the English states is more problematic, but it would seem that Hengest in Kent (not even a definitively historical character) benefited from this (see next section). Possibly the arrival and battles of 'Cerdic', founder of the West Saxon kingdom, had a similar heroic saga created about it and this was used by the compilers of the *Anglo-Saxon Chronicle* nearly 400 years later. Given the limited extent of lay literacy in sixth to ninth century England, these stories may have been orally preserved (and possibly embellished). The contrast between post-Roman Britain and post-Roman Gaul is unclear, but the survival of 'sub-Roman' Latinate names for the local Gallic sixth century aristocracy (and its control of Church offices) is apparent. So is literary culture – for Gaul we have the detailed and erudite historical work of Bishop Gregory of Tours but for Britain we have the vague and often obscure *'jeremiad'* of the monk Gildas (whose personal data and location are uncertain). The degree of historical knowledge of the Later Roman period displayed by Gildas is restricted – he mixes up the time and purpose of the building of Hadrian's Wall and thinks that Magnus Maximus, the Western Imperial usurper from Britain who was killed in 388, not Constantine III (407) was the man who took the last Roman troops from Britain.

So clearly the degree of survival of literary history books in his region, as opposed to Gregory's, was limited; he had no access in monastic libraries to fifth century Roman sources such as Orosius and Olympiodorus.

At least in the Mediterranean countries, there was a substantial survival of the Roman population – and even of their urban civilization and traditions, now centred on the Catholic Church. The extent of Romano-'Celtic' survival in 'English' south-eastern Britain has long been disputed, and it cannot be linked conclusively to the eclipse of the Roman 'lingua franca', Latin, as we cannot be sure that all the post-Roman populace spoke that tongue rather than one or more 'Brittonic' languages (presumably including proto-Welsh). There were identifiable people of British origin in Wessex in the 690s as seen from Ine's law-code (though they were treated as second-class citizens and not given the same legal worth as Saxons).[11] The lack of evidence makes it unclear how and where pre-German inhabitants survived as a distinct and resilient culture, but some definitely did in remote and mountainous areas of Gaul and Spain (e.g. the pre-Roman 'Vascones', the Basques). Bede's language would seem to imply a form of genocide of Britons in some conquered areas of Northumbria, but this may be myth or simplification; he was writing over 100 years after the creation of the kingdom across the North by Aethelfrith. The extinction of pre-Anglian Christianity in the North by the pagan Northumbrians, requiring re-conversion by the seventh century Iona and Canterbury missionaries, is also problematic.[12] But Bede, the greatest – and only surviving – English historian of the age was a 'German' in ethnic identity, with limited knowledge of pre-conquest Britain; the Gallic Gregory of Tours was a Romano-Gaul of distinguished noble lineage, looking back to the (Christian) Roman Empire. Bede had little knowledge of Roman Britain, and what he did have was primarily religious – possibly derived from surviving hagiographies of the Romano-British saints such as Alban. Nor did he have a good opinion of the British Church, whose contribution to post-Roman life he minimizes in his history. His Roman missionary hero, St Augustine, comes to evangelize a totally pagan people and has little contact with the 'Welsh' Church, and there is no hint that his heroic King Edwin of Northumbria had lived as an exile in Christian Gwynedd in Wales before he converted to Roman Christianity.

The success of a militarily-organized group of Germans under a dynamic leader in establishing a 'state' depended on the skill and luck of the leaders in carving out – and keeping – a viable territory. Numerous 'peoples' identified in the written records of the fifth century as participants in the invasions (e.g. the Scirians and Heruls) failed to establish a new territory. A few 'states' were personal rather than 'tribal' in their nomenclature, as with the mixed German following of the Scirian warlord Odovacar in Italy who overthrew the last Roman government there in 476 but succumbed to Theodoric the East Goth ('Ostrogoth') in 491/3. The anonymous small-scale 'kingdoms' of the 'Ripuarian' Franks in the Rhine valley were overrun by their 'Salian' rivals under the Merovingian line between c.500 and 540, as was the small kingdom of the Burgundians in Savoy; the small and isolated Suevic kingdom in Galicia (Spain) was overthrown by its more powerful Visigothic neighbours. The Ostrogothic kingdom was overrun by the East Roman armies as they reconquered Italy in 535–9, made a heroic effort to recover its territory under Totila, and finally succumbed in 553–4. (The Gothic officers notably offered their vacant throne at one point to their conqueror, Belisarius, showing their respect for his military skill and honest dealing.) The fact that there was such a prolonged fight against the Eastern Roman armies argues for a substantial 'esprit de corps' and sense of identity by the Gothic military elite, besides the personal charisma and competence of their leader Totila; the war did not end with his death in 552 either. A series of crushing military defeats by the Eastern general Narses, an ageing eunuch despatched west by Justinian in place of the brilliant but distrusted Belisarius, probably crushed the Gothic elite and left the survivors powerless – though the war left Italy economically ruined too. Their state vanished from history, and the next and more long-lasting German kingdom in Northern Italy was created by the new 'wave' of Lombard invaders from 568. In Gaul, the kingdom of the Burgundians – set up in the upper Rhone region by Aetius to settle refugees from Attila in 442 – was overrun by Clovis' sons in the mid-sixth century and vanished as a distinct 'ethnic' entity. The Franks' greater resources and better leadership prevailed, but the notion of a separate kingdom – with the Burgundian name to mark its identity – continued under Frankish royal leaders for centuries. Similarly, the ex-Gothic lands south of the Loire were overrun by Clovis in 507 and politically incorporated into 'Francia'. But an often autonomous sub-kingdom of Aquitaine continued to exist and after the eclipse of the Carolingian state in the later ninth century became a separate, hereditary duchy. In England, the notion of a defeated kingdom surviving as an autonomous entity under kings from the conquerors' royal family can be seen in Deira – conquered by Aethelfrith of Bernicia c.604 to create 'Northumbria' but having separate rulers for much of the seventh century until 679. Did the fact that even powerful warlords Oswald and Oswy of Northumbria, Bernician in origin but with a Deiran mother, felt obliged to retain a Deiran sub-kingdom under their genealogically Deiran cousins reflect a powerful localism in the region? The Deiran sub-kingdom lasted even under the years of Oswy's and his son Ecgfrith's relative security after their defeat of Mercia in 655, until 679 – albeit under their own sons and brothers.

Most of the new mini-kingdoms of the sixth and seventh centuries survived (if only as the names of counties, e.g. Sussex and Essex) though we lose sight of their royal families, whose menfolk were at best sub-kings or governors ('duces' or 'ealdormen') by the eighth century. There was no drastic abolition of the local political entities as they were absorbed by their powerful neighbours, which suggests the 'centralizing' warlords such as Offa and Coenwulf of Mercia had to respect local opinion. Even rebellious Kent, which had broken away from Mercia at least twice before final subjugation in 798, survived as a distinct sub-kingdom under Mercian nominees in 798–825 and thereafter became a sub-kingdom within its next conqueror Wessex.

Both Coenwulf of Mercia and Egbert of Wessex entrusted newly conquered Kent to a close relative (brother and son). East Anglia, whose king – St Aethelbert – was executed in dubious circumstances by Offa of Mercia in 794 and its separate coinage suppressed (a usual sign of political extinction), re-emerged under new kings in the 820s. The division of Northumbria into Deira and Bernicia – aided by the difficulty of one man ruling a large state stretching from Forth to Humber – re-emerged in the 870s, as the Vikings overran and settled Deira but a new Bernician state emerged ruled by the noble dynasty of Bamburgh. Only Hwicce (basically Gloucestershire and Worcestershire) and Magonsaetan (basically Herefordshire and Shropshire), suppressed by Mercia in the eighth century, vanished as distinct sub-regions within their overlord. The eventual success stories were the larger kingdoms among whom two – Mercia and Northumbria – had not existed in the sixth century. Unlike in Francia where the Merovingians of Clovis' dynasty overran the 'Ripuarian' Franks and

Burgundians in the early-mid sixth century and later Bavaria, neither of these kingdoms absorbed all its neighbours. In all these cases, the crucial 'cement' that created and held together a new state in this era of political flux was leadership. But what if these most successful states had not had such a run of good luck in competent leadership?

(c) Identity, founders, and the question of the English sub-kingdoms: the creations of self-made warlords or of a group of settlers?
The question of who founded the English kingdoms has been challenged in the past century. It used to be assumed that the stories in Bede, 'Nennius', and the *Chronicle* of great leaders setting up each kingdom were reasonably accurate – though written down centuries later. The earliest of them, 'Hengest' of Kent was active – if he existed – around the 440s, and our earliest written evidence is nearly 300 years later. Accordingly, modern mythographers and interpreters of post-Roman authors have challenged the reliability of the evidence. Did their informants remember the basic details of the origin of these kingdoms, preserved by oral tradition, or was it all romantic legend 'spun' to give the inhabitants of these kingdoms a sense of identity and a heroic past? Did the creation of a heroic founding ancestor in the sixth or seventh centuries serve to bolster the contemporary claims to authority of their alleged descendants, the current kings? The problem is similar to that of the Trojan War myths in Ancient Greece, where the poems of Homer – whoever he was – were probably composed orally in the eighth century BC but the siege of Troy would have taken place before 1200 BC. In Wales, the legendary warrior-hero 'Arthur' would have been active around AD 500 but the first literary account, by 'Nennius', is dated to the 820s. In Ireland, the mythical heroes of the 'Ulster Cycle' such as Cuchulainn would have been active in the first or second centuries AD and Fionn Mc Cumhaill and the 'Fianna' in the third; nothing was written down for hundreds of years. Accordingly, sceptics have had a field day analysing the political motives of the writers to whom we owe the information and claiming that they had no notion of 'objective' history. The jury is still out on this question, but it is more likely – as with Troy – that some 'originals' lie behind the later myths, however distorted. Political structures such as the new Anglo-Saxon kingdoms are more often created by dynamic individuals than by committees of co-operating delegates. The very nature of the new states – erected in lands formerly ruled by shadowy post-Roman authorities – suggest military activity rather than entirely peaceful penetration by groups of farmers or traders. The latter is more likely where no 'foundation-myth' or clear dynastic founder is recorded, as in Essex.

Some names of 'founders' of new Germanic kingdoms may have been invented by later mythographers as symbols of a precarious national identity, and given impossibly heroic careers that owed much to appropriated legends – e.g. Hengest in Kent. The latter is now often regarded as a mythical figure, with the story of his rise from a minor mercenary captain of British 'High King' Vortigern to a successful rebel and king of Kent taken as a romantic fabrication. His most notorious trick, having his followers hide their long knives up their sleeves at a peace 'summit' and then pulling them out to kill the British delegates, is a staple of contemporary mythology. Indeed, his name means 'Stallion' rather than being a given name – and it probably refers to his standard of the 'White Horse',[13] taken as the Saxon symbol in later myths. 'Horsa' – i.e.' Horse' – is an unlikely name for his fellow-leader, and it is not clear if 'Horsa' or Aesc was Hengest's lieutenant in his early battles. Nor is the date of Hengest's invasion clear – the (ninth century) British sources would indicate that he landed in the late 420s, while Bede places it as 449. But the idea of a hired captain of Germanic 'federates' revolting against his post-Roman royal employer and carving out his own kingdom is logical for the turbulent world of the fifth century, and there are several examples of it on the Continent (e.g. Alaric). Nor should it be assumed that the 'romantic' story of Hengest displaying his daughter Rowena to 'Vortigern', arousing his interest, and craftily giving her to the king as his second wife is just a later literary invention. It may be invented, but it is plausible enough and would account for the breach between 'Vortigern' and his already-adult son and heir Vortimer, who ninth century Welsh writer 'Nennius' cites as the British war-leader who attempted to drive Hengest out of Kent. (The story has Vortimer succeeding but then dying, allegedly poisoned by Rowena on Hengest's behalf, and 'Vortigern' recalling Hengest.) The main problem is that the archaeology of Kent is at variance with the idea of a sudden, unilateral seizure of land by a large force of Germanic immigrants (see later).

The career of Cerdic – a British name, 'Ceredig' – as founder of the West Saxon royal house is equally problematic, and it is probable that the 'Germanic' genealogy that the *Anglo-Saxon Chronicle* (written up c.890) gives him is a literary invention. A founder-hero of a Saxon kingdom claiming to lead all England against the Vikings could hardly be admitted to be a Briton, and there have been claims by recent historians that the consistent pre-eighth century naming of the West Saxon kingdom as that of the 'Gewissae', not the West Saxons, indicates that it was not an 'exclusively Germanic polity in the sixth and seventh centuries. The obscure name 'Gewissae' apparently means 'confederates', which could indicate a multi-ethnic creation by Britons, Jutes (in the New Forest region), and Saxons –

and the archaeology indicates a continuing Romano-British cultural presence in Cerdic's alleged 'heartland' of Hampshire in the early sixth century as well as in Dorset until the seventh century. The first 'Saxon' artefacts from around 500 are found close to the still-occupied post-Roman town of Winchester (Venta Belgarum), implying people (traders or mercenaries and their families?) living there by agreement with the locals. 'British' names of kings continue through the sixth century (Cerdic's 'son' or 'grandson' Cynric, i.e. 'Cunorix') into the later seventh century (Caedwalla, i.e. 'Cadwallon'). The heaviest area of Saxon settlement in the early/middle sixth century was in the Thames valley, which the *Chronicle* does not mention as an area of West Saxon military activity until the 570s. Did the West Saxon 'founders' really set up a Germanic state, or was it a mixed Britsh-Jutish-Saxon state that only acquired a major Saxon ethnic component when it moved into the Thames valley under King Ceawlin after 560?

The role of Cerdic may be different in reality than it is in the patriotic West Saxon legend of Alfred's time – when it would have been unthinkable for the editors of the *Chronicle* to accept that he was not a Saxon by ethnicity as they were seeking to show the heroic past of their kingdom and royal dynasty to inspire a Saxon people threatened by Viking invasion. Alfred could hardly be a suitable leader for the 'national' English resistance, Mercian as well as West Saxon, if his dynasty's founder was not even Saxon – though it is more likely that the notion of Cerdic as a Saxon, not a 'mixed-race' warlord, was already established by Alfred's time, not a deliberate fraud. Given the lack of Germanic archaeological sites in sixth century Hampshire, at the least he ruled a 'mixed' people and he and his British-named successor Cynric (Cunorix) possibly had British mothers and wives.

The *Chronicle* suspiciously gives Cerdic a forty-year career (494–534) as it does Hengest (449–488). Like Hengest, he landed some time before 'taking the kingdom' and was assisted by a younger colleague, the founders' 'sons' being Aesc in Kent and Cynric in Wessex. Is the duplication due to historical fact, or to Saxon poets annexing one man's mythical career for another's?[14]

We do not even have the basic details of the careers of other dynastic founders, as in East Anglia or Mercia, and cannot tell if they were established by one man or by a group of autonomous local warlords whose lands later coalesced into one kingdom. The dating of the first Germanic artefacts in both these states is mid-late fifth century, but the existing royal genealogies only commence with shadowy 'kings' dateable to sometime in the mid-sixth century. Were the many separate 'local peoples' of Mercia originally mini-kingdoms, and ditto the 'North Folk' and 'South Folk' of East Anglia? All that is recorded of Ida of Bernicia is that he took the fortress of Bamburgh in 547,[15] and it is not clear how the succession to this isolated kingdom descended until the early 590s. No kings of the South Saxons are recorded for a century and a half after the founder, Aelle, so did the kingship lapse after the need for a military leader during the conquest passed? But it is probably significant that a mid-sixth century king of Kent, Eormenric, was called after the great Gothic ruler of the 370s destroyed by the Huns and an East Anglian king was called after Totila, the current Ostrogothic war-hero of the 540s.[16] Their parents evidently sought inspiration from the great Continental German heroes, and were aware of their careers – and their perceived cultural identity was Germanic.

The pre-'conquest' names of rulers of assorted peoples were probably manufactured, as with the ancestral Anglo-Saxon dynastic descent from the god Woden, though possibly the pre-conquest Continental Anglian 'king' Offa of Angel was a real person. It is hard to find successful new kingdoms in the fifth to eighth centuries, which have no clear record of dynamic leadership or individual sovereigns. This may not date to the time when archaeology shows the first settlements as occurring – in Mercia there was extensive settlement in the Trent valley in the later fifth century and early sixth century but the ruling kin cannot be dated beyond c.550 and the first known kings of all Mercia only appear in the 580s. There are exceptions where settlement may have been mainly peaceful and there is a degree of continuity of occupation of excavated farmsteads with the post-Roman situation, e.g. East Anglia.[17]

But it is no use assuming from this that there was no tension, eviction, and conquest and thus no need for new, Germanic war-band commanders – if that were so, why is there no major survival of Romano-British names in the area? Why were the 'Welsh', a name equivalent to 'foreigner'/(tenth century) 'slave', which is significant, treated as second-class citizens in the West Saxon law-codes if they had not been conquered by force?

The continuity of land-use may well imply that estates were taken over quickly as coherent, recognizable units and were put into use as agricultural land again with only a short break, with or without some of the original tenants staying on. But they were still taken over, by culturally distinct new owners, as seen by the influx of Germanic goods into the east of England in the years from c.450 to 550 – with most of the earliest artefacts found near the coasts. Crucial decisions of conquest and inter-district warfare were clearly taken by one war-leader to whom warriors could rally (or occasionally two, as with the Goths in 376), though a council of the heads of dominant families could delegate this task to a capable warrior for a short-term crisis if there was no 'on-going' need for military leadership. The fact that the dynastic lists of East Anglia do not include any rulers from the fifth century, when settlement was underway, suggests that there was no permanent kingship – or any unified command? – in the area at this time, unless a leader was forgotten (deliberately by his supplanters?).

Some peoples occupying a specific geographic region lacked kings and seem to have been 'decentralized' under local warlords, such as the Old Saxon lands on the lower Elbe or the new settlements of the Slav peoples in Eastern Europe from the Baltic to the Greek lands. It is possible that the same applies to mini-kingdoms or 'peoples' in Anglo-Saxon England of whom no dynastic record survives, such as the Middle Saxons of Middlesex or the fifth century 'North' and 'South' folks of East Anglia. Bede reckoned that there were 'provinciae' or 'regiones' as a level of administrative organisation below that of the kingdoms; this fits his picture. This would also apply to the smaller local 'peoples' of a district who had a distinct identity but had no need for long-term leadership on account of a largely peaceful history. There may have been no need for leadership except in occasional warfare, and thus when a territory had been conquered its early leadership lapsed into a decentralized network of autonomous communities. It remains at issue whether local 'mini-states', later absorbed into bigger kingdoms, which appear to have been named after one man – e.g. Hastings, East Sussex, as 'Haesta's People' – were named after a conquering war-leader or not.[18]

There are many districts with this distinct '-ingas' terminology in the south-east, e.g. the Rodings and Barking in western Essex and Sonning in the middle Thames valley, and no evidence of sustained local warfare. The concept of their having one founder, the man whose name was used in the area's identification, may be later historians' rationalization of 'conquest' as necessarily being led by a commander, and an artificial creation of the alleged 'founder' from the name of a local grouping. It has been suggested that these regions owed their distinctive identity either to being settled by a coherent group dominated by one 'kin', possibly related families moving in as a group or possibly only co-operating later in self-defence, or to taking over an already distinct post-Roman administrative district[19] (a town, as with Great Chesterford in the Fens, or a rural district, 'pagus').

There is also the question of those 'mini-states', later absorbed into larger ones, whose names seem more clearly to indicate a geographical rather than a personal identity. The greatest number of these are in Mercia, a kingdom only created c.580 according to later royal genealogies and so not coeval with settlement.

Archaeology shows widespread Germanic settlement in the lower Trent valley by the early sixth century, but there is no record of who ruled these areas at the time. As seen from the seventh century *Tribal Hideage*, the kingdom included such distinct peoples based in distinct areas as the

'Pecsaetan' (the Peak District), 'Wreocensaetan' (Wrekin, Shropshire), and 'Arowsaetan' (River Arrow, Warwickshire), along with the 'Hecani' or putative 'West Mercians' of Worcestershire. These appear to be based on geographical identity, which begs the question of whether the locals had seen themselves in that context as a separate 'people' from their arrival or if that identity was created for them by the new kingdom of Mercia for administrative convenience.

In the cases of certain 'provinciae', as Bede calls them, there is an apparent link with a previous Roman unit – e.g. the 'Wreocensaetan', based around Viroconium, which was still inhabited in the sixth century, and the 'Magonsaetan' of Herefordshire based around Magnis (Kenchester). The argument about taking over coherent Roman units (see above) probably applies to their new Anglo-Saxon identity.[20] There is also a question over the surprising names of the kings of the two main West Mercian sub-kingdoms, Hwicce and Magonsaetan. The seventh century kings of Hwicce – based around Winchcombe in Gloucestershire, a long way from Bernicia – have Bernician names, e.g. Eanfrith and Oswald. Is this coincidence, or were they Bernician in origin – refugees from the ruthless state-builder Aethelfrith who sought new lands in a distant kingdom? The first recorded king of Magonsaetan, Merewalh, was supposedly a son of Penda of Mercia but his name means 'noble Welshman'. Was he a son of Penda by his legendary Welsh wife, Heledd of Powys, or a Welsh adopted son or stepson?[21] (The royal charters show that Merewalh's family claimed to be kin to Penda's family, and to the Mercian royals' Kentish 'in-laws'.) The state appears to have centred around a Roman administrative unit (possibly of the town of 'Magnis', Kenchester, near Hereford) and there is no archaeological evidence of Germanic settlers pre-650 so it was probably ethnically mainly British/Welsh.

No lines of rulers, hereditary or otherwise, are recorded for the Mercian sub-states, although they presumably supplied most of the 'duces' – 'governors', not of royal rank, by the normal Latin translation – recorded in the Mercian hegemony by Bede for c.655. Most of the thirty sub-kings who he says fought for King Penda[22] at the battle of Winwaed must have come from within Mercia, given that his non-Mercian allies (e.g. East Anglia) still had full royal status. It may be that they were 'decentralized' local kindreds who only needed a ruler in times of war – as with the earlier Germanic peoples recorded by Tacitus in Germany in the first century who only elected special war-leaders and otherwise relied on 'judges'. Alternatively, the triumphant central kingship of Mercia established c.580 may have suppressed all record of its defeated local rivals, and no lists of kings have survived to be recorded in later books.

However they were governed, such 'mini-states' were at serious risk of being conquered by aggressive, predatory neighbours with larger armies with determined leadership, as the Franks did to the Old Saxons in the mid-late eighth century. The most famed warlord of early Mercia, Penda, may well have conquered his Midlands rivals from the local 'peoples' during his reign from c.625 to 655, and Caedwalla of Wessex similarly suppressed assorted sub-kings recorded for mid-seventh century Wessex during his dynamic reign in 685–8. We know that Northumbria arose from a union of Bernicia (north of the Tees) with Deira (south of it), first imposed by conquest by Aethelfrith of Bernicia c.604 but with the Deirans retaining sub-kings up to 679. Sussex was reduced to a virtual province of its new overlord, Mercia, during the seventh century, and its kings were forced down in rank from 'regi' to 'duces'. Offa and Coenwulf of Mercia endeavoured to force the same subjection on Kent (conquered by force c.785, in revolt 796–8, then a Mercian sub-kingdom up to 807 and absorbed into Mercia from 807 to 825).

The sub-kings of Mercia's south-western vassals, Hwicce (Worcestershire and Gloucestershire) and Magonsaetan (Herefordshire and Shropshire), were abolished some time in the early eighth century. It seems to have been a matter of established royal Mercian policy at the time of Mercia's greatness to reduce these sub-rulers from their original high rank, and it applied to Mercia's distant vassal Sussex too as its kings are referred to as 'duces' after 772. How many more such conquests and annexations of small kingdoms went unrecorded?

The pre-fifth century British: a precedent for the Anglo-Saxon states? Unexpected continuity or similar situations for both?

There is some similarity between the situation of the rival kingdoms of early Anglo-Saxon England and the multiplicity of 'tribal' states that existed before the Roman conquest. Indeed, continuity existed in terms of names – 'Kent' comes from the original British name for the region, recorded by Caesar. Within pre-Roman 'Celtic' Britain, the scant literary evidence is backed up by coinage. It seems that a Germanic-style 'hegemonic' tribal kingdom north of the lower Thames, that of the Catuvellauni, was newly dominant under an aggressive leader – the eponymous Cassivellaunus – when Caesar landed in 55 BC and was still being resisted by its neighbours. Their loyalty could not be taken for granted, and some preferred allying with Rome to preserve their independence. After Caesar's brief expeditions, the Catuvellauni resumed their expansion under Cunobelinus and overran both the Trinovantes of Essex and the Belgae south of the Thames.[23]

The Trinovantian kingdom became a 'sub-kingdom' of the Catuvellauni, given to a prince of the ruling house; and when Cunobelinus died c.40 AD he was succeeded by two sons as joint kings, Caratacus and Tasciovanus. In modern Hampshire (and possibly Sussex), the kingdom of the 'Atrebates' was centred on the large pre-Roman proto-urban settlement ('oppidum') of Calleva (Silchester) in north Hampshire – one of the few pre-Roman and Roman towns not to survive into the Anglo-Saxon era as the centre of an administrative region. The Atrebates and their neighbours, the 'Belgae', had probably fought over control of Hampshire in the first century BC, with the Belgae – new arrivals from the Continent according to Caesar – seizing the south and setting up their principal town at Venta Belgarum (Winchester).

One or two Atrebatic kings took refuge at Augustus' court in Rome in the first decade or so AD according to Roman inscriptions, and it is unclear if he aided them to return by force – there are extensive signs of pre-conquest Roman influence in this region, probably due to trade. Roman pottery is common. The expulsion of the Belgic king Verica, an ally of Augustus who fled to Rome c.40 AD, by the Catuvellauni[24] was one reason for Roman invasion in 43 and shows a fluid British political system with recognizable permanent local kingdoms – such as re-emerged after Roman rule.

In fact, it would now seem that 'Roman conquest' did not lead to the end of all these British kingdoms, even in the south. There is the case of the mysterious king Cogidubnus or Togidubnus, apparently from his location ruler of the 'Regni' around Chichester, who served as a Roman vassal-king for many years after the landings in AD 43 and erected the grandiose palace-style villa at Fishbourne (now believed to be a copy of the Imperial Palace on the Palatine in Rome, built by Domitian in the 80s). Whether he was of the royal house of the 'Regni' , assumed to be the local British people of Sussex, or the Atrebates (or Belgae?) of Hampshire, he was entrusted by Rome with local power within the heartland of the Roman province into the 70s or 80s. The assumption by historians of outright, immediate Roman annexation of all conquered lands is evidently too simplistic – and the extent of usage of Roman 'luxury goods' in the south before the invasion of AD 43 shows that Roman traders were frequent visitors. Some may even have settled in Britain, and there has been recent controversy over a suggestion that Roman troops may have been sent by Augustus to aid the friendly kingdom of the Atrebates around AD 10 (by restoring an expelled allied king?).[25] Were there really some Romans in Britain before their invasion, and ditto Angles and Saxons as mercenaries in fourth century Britain on the so-called 'Saxon Shore' from Hampshire round to Norfolk ? Also, the centre of Atrebatic and Belgic power, in Hampshire, was to be the centre of the kingdom of Wessex by the mid-seventh century – 'Venta Belgarum', the main Romanized settlement of the Belgae, became the Saxon 'capital' of Winchester. The principal settlement of the presumed 'Regni' in western Sussex, Noviomagus, became the South Saxon 'capital' of Chichester, supposedly named after the 'son' of the founding king, Aelle. The continuities may have been greater than the breaks in politico-social affairs in the first and the fifth centuries AD, except at 'elite' level.

Many other Roman settlements that served as the nuclei of local administrative districts became Saxon regional administrative capitals, e.g. Isca Dumnoniorum (of the Dumnonii) as Exeter in Devon and Durnovaria as Dorchester in Dorset. There was clearly some degree of continuity in regional identity, though more in the south than elsewhere else – the kingdom of 'Lindsey' took over the main settlement of the Corieltavi/ Coritani, Lindum (Lincoln), but the main settlement of the Iceni in Norfolk appears to have been near Thetford not the Saxon bishopric site, North Elmham, or Norwich. Deira in Yorkshire took over the main military base and provincial capital of the north-east of Roman Britain, Eburacum, as 'York', but the British tribal capitals of the north-west and West Midlands are unclear. But did any of the – hereditary? – British tribal kingdoms retain a notion of separate identity once they were part of the Empire and controlled directly by Roman governors? Did this notion of a separate identity under their ancient royal families (or nobility) re-emerge after Roman rule ended, and carry over into early Anglo-Saxon England? One argument for this being limited is linguistic – in Gaul the 'native' Gallo-Roman elite, e.g. the Church, served the new Frankish kings and their languages and written culture survived, but in Britain the new regimes were all thoroughly Germanic in language and culture. But the survival of the name of the British 'Cantii' in 'Kent' is clearly no coincidence, and the name would have been transmitted by locals who stayed on under the new dispensation – which argues against the stories in Bede and 'Nennius' of total 'ethnic cleansing' by Hengest and his invading mercenaries.

Roman survival – if in Gaul, why not in Britain?
This does not rule out the possibility that the course of events in Britain could have taken a line more similar to that in Gaul, and that the Romano-British political and cultural elite might thus have survived as a coherent society as it did in sixth century Gaul. The two great historians of the sixth century, Gildas of Britain and Bishop Gregory of Tours in Gaul, were both churchmen – though Gildas, apparently a monk and possibly writing in a monastery library (either in Britain or at Rhuys in Brittany), was only recorded as a senior cleric, abbot of Glastonbury, in his eleventh century hagiography. The Church was the guardian of Roman Christian culture and traditions in Gaul, with its aristocratic bishops – often from a small circle of

families down the generations – based in the towns and with some fourth and fifth century monasteries still flourishing as with Bishop Gregory's Tours, founded by St Martin c.370.

The incoming Franks centred their settlement and their royal itineraries on the north, leaving much of the centre and south of Gaul to the local Romano-Gallic aristocracy and their labourers; and the great break in trade between these urban centres and the Eastern Mediterranean was the Arab conquest in the eighth century, not the German conquest of the fifth century. Britain had at least three urban-based bishoprics by AD 359, one presumably in London and another in York as these were the former capitals of the two pre-Diocletianic Roman provinces. (Geoffrey of Monmouth refers to a bishopric of Caerleon but we do not know what evidence he used, if any.) There was at least one flourishing major Christian shrine in post-Roman Britain, that of St Alban at his eponymous town, which the anti-heretic missionary Bishop Germanus of Auxerre visited around AD 429; there was also a cult of Ss Aaron and Julius, possibly at Caerleon. The loss of functioning shrines to the Saxons in the presumed truce after the battle of Mount Badon c.516 is referred to by Gildas. One of the most original theological thinkers around 400, the 'heretic' Pelagius (active in Italy and North Africa), challenged St Augustine's doctrine of predestination. He was probably a Briton, but need not have learnt his theology in Britain; he had numerous followers there in 420s Britain. Germanus' mission to convert them was at the behest of the worried Gallic Church, and their numbers and episcopal leader Agricola imply an intellectually flourishing (and independent-minded?) Church.[26]

Presumably the upper classes staffed the higher ranks of the Church in Britain as in Gaul, though the only names to survive are probably garbled and unreliable ones in Geoffrey of Monmouth's dubious 'history' written c.1135.

Tradition maintains that there was at least one major monastery in southern post-Roman Britain, of uncertain but venerable date – that of Glastonbury, with its 'Old Church' and its 'twelve hides' of land allegedly granted to the first hermits by 'Celtic' King Arviragus c.63 AD. Britain, as archaeology has shown, had estates with grand villas in the fourth century that were as prosperous as those in Gaul or even Sicily. The precise date of and reasons for their abandonment are uncertain, though it has been suggested that the end of the Roman Army's presence on the Rhine ruined their export trade of corn to the troops and so precipitated economic collapse. But if a coherent, Latin-speaking, Church-led post-Roman society survived Germanic conquest in Gaul, why did it not do so in Britain – and could it have survived? Was the main reason the length of time it took for southern Britain to be 'conquered', at least in terms of a transfer of political power? Central and southern Gaul seem to have had a less prolonged or traumatic transfer of power, with – crucially – less intense Germanic settlement. The region south of the Loire was lost by the Western Roman Empire to the local Visigoths (West Goths) centred at Toulouse in the 470s, but the Goths seem to have been mainly settled in the Garonne valley where they had been granted a third of the land in an orderly transfer of estates by the Roman government in 418.

The region then fell to the Merovingian Franks after Clovis defeated the Goths at the battle for Vouille in 507, but the conquerors remained settled in the north of Gaul where the main estates and interests of their kings lay – the principal royal residences of Clovis' four sons and successors were at Rheims, Paris, Orleans and Soissons.[27] Ex-Roman towns in the south had Frankish 'counts' to supervise the administration and collect food-rents at times, but no intense Frankish settlement.

The south indeed was to retain its own distinct language – that of the *Langue d'Oc* as opposed to the *Langue d'Oeil* – and cultural identity for many centuries. If the post-Roman British polities had been subject to a similar quick transfer of power and a lesser amount of settlement, would British culture and identity have survived in a similar form? Did the 'decentralized' form of settlement in Britain, led by many leaders rather than one dynasty and with many more followers to reward with land, lead to the greater socio-cultural transformation?

It should also be asked whether or not the survival of a post-Roman culture in Gaul was aided by greater urbanization there than in Britain – which feeds into the whole thorny question of how far the British towns were 'self-supporting' and could survive after the end of Roman rule. Were they over-dependent on spending by rural aristocrats who had town houses there to live in while carrying out civic duties as ordered by the Roman state, and on trade from overseas? Did the end of both phenomena after the end of Roman rule cause rapid urban collapse, in the manner in which the coinage vanished? There was overseas trade even in sixth century non-Germnnic Britain, as Mediterranean pottery and jewellery have been discovered – but it came into Britain via isolated minor river-mouth or harbour ports such as Bantham and Tintagel in Dumnonia. There was isolated urban building, but only in the far west principally at Wroxeter/ Viroconium – and in wood not stone; some civic buildings were adapted as craft workshops, which shows priorities. This is far different from the picture in Gaul, which had closer contacts with the Mediterranean world and a vigorous post-Roman aristocracy ruling important towns as bishops. It is possible that greater security under settled political conditions in southern Britain could have enabled towns to survive better, but the evidence and its interpretation are far from clear. In London, as is now evident, the centre of urban settlement shifted from the old walled Roman city to the new trading quarter of the 'Ald Wych' ('old settlement') along the Strand – suggesting at least partial abandonment of the city.

If less piracy at sea and a viable trade in exchanged goods could have kept up trade with Gaul and the Mediterranean through the fifth and into the sixth century, possibly 'incoming' settlers would have faced an extant urban economy in parts of Britain and towns may have survived better. The Germanic kings, as in Gaul, would probably have preferred to live on their rural estates and keep up a traditional itinerant lifestyle, eating up the food-rents due to them from their tenants.

The British and Gallic tribal kingdoms that Rome overran had distinct geographical spheres of influence and separate recognized identities, though of uncertain antiquity. The sub-provincial local rural districts ('pagi') in Gaul kept up the old tribal names after the Roman conquest, and were the focus of revolt by members of the local aristocracy as late as the 20s AD. Logically the same would have happened in Britain – especially as the pre-Roman tribal names re-emerged for the new kingdoms after 410 (see below). It is possible that the unlikely survival of a Romano-British enclave in the Chilterns up to the early 570s – when conquest by Ceawlin's ally Cutha is noted in the *Chronicle* – was due to the existence of a coherent 'state' based on the ancient lands of the Catuvellauni and the town of Verulamium/ St Albans. The former 'state' of the Belgae in Hampshire, based on Venta Belgarum/ Winchester, could have been the nucleus of Cerdic's new West Saxon state, and that of the Regni, based on Noviomagus/ Chichester, been that taken over by Aelle for the kingdom of the South Saxons. One recent suggestion (by Stuart Laycock) that these post-Roman British kingdoms were unstable and constantly in conflict, aiding conquest, is less provable.[28] There is no record of these wars, but the local defensive earthwork of the Wansdyke in the Bath-Bristol area appears to be pre-Saxon and to be defending a kingdom in Somerset from attack from the North-East.

The supposed existence of a multitude of bickering post-Roman kings who only reluctantly united against the Anglo-Saxons under the leadership of 'Arthur' (and earlier Ambrosius?) is a staple of the 'Arthurian' legends from the time of 'Nennius' c.829, who wrote that the kings of the British fought in a coalition led by Arthur though many were more noble in blood than him.[29]

It was then greatly expanded by Geoffrey of Monmouth and the romancers of the twelfth to fifteenth centuries. It is plausible – but apart from Gildas' complaints of tyrannical, unjust, and murderous 'usurper' kings by c.540 there is no contemporary evidence of it.[30]

English 'kingdoms' and leadership: a general overview
In England the question of continuity from the post-Roman 'British' kingdoms (many of which significantly resumed their tribal pre-Roman names, e.g. Dumnonia, Dyfed, and Gwynedd/Venedotia) to the new Anglo-Saxon kingdoms is still a major issue of dispute among historians. The literary evidence, almost all later and containing elements of myth and justificatory propaganda, refers to widespread massacre and conquest by the famous three 'peoples' from north-west Germany and Jutland identified by Bede – the Angles, Saxons, and Jutes. Procopius in Byzantium, working closer to the time but writing in Constantinople not Britain and using some evident legend,[31] refers to the Angles, Saxons, and Frisians. The amount of pre-conquest DNA discovered in the current English population, the lack of archaeological evidence for massacres and the mass-burning of towns, farms, and villas, and the evidence of continuity in estate-boundaries and land-use from post-Roman to Saxon times all suggest a major degree of continuity in many areas. As suggested above, this continuity may explain why many minor 'peoples' or districts have no record of kingship.

However, the written evidence cannot just be brushed aside, and Saxon and Celtic sources are unanimous about the physical conquest of the land by outside settlers – and, crucially, the language used by the population at large (even to name geographical features in most of England) changed from British/Welsh to the Saxon forerunner of modern English. As Norman-French became the language of court and administration following the arrival and seizure of political control by a new elite in 1066, so the change from 'Celtic' to Anglo-Saxon terminology by all classes from the sixth century suggests that at least the leaders of society – the warriors as well as their commanders – were culturally, and presumably ethnically, distinct from the old post-Roman leadership. The survival of Latin terminology in the British/Welsh language, but not in Germanic, would suggest that the former peoples were to some degree linguistically 'Romanized' but the new arrivals after c.400 AD were noticeably not so. (This, however, is not definitive proof of a comprehensive cultural 'break' when the 'Germans' arrived in Britain as we cannot tell when the Latin words entered proto-Welsh – in Roman times or from the post-Roman Church as late as AD 600–900?) The new social and political elite in southern and central Britain saw themselves as Germanic, however many of them married British wives – and the Anglo-Saxon law-codes significantly counted a 'Welshman' (the term was interchangeable for foreigners and slaves, showing the Saxons' low opinion of their neighbours[32]) as worth far less 'weregild' if injured or killed than a Saxon. ('Weregild' is a legal Anglo-Saxon scale of compensation to be paid by a person convicted of an injury to his victim; the higher their rank the more money was paid.) The survival of British names for kings in Wessex (e.g. the founder, Cerdic, and his successor Cynric in the early sixth century and Caedwalla in the 680s) is almost unique, and suggests a degree of inter-marriage by early dynasts. The other exception for kingly dynastic names is in the supposedly 'Germanized' eastern England – Lindsey in Lincolnshire – but their 'Welsh' names (e.g. Caedbad) may reflect local inter-marriage with the post-Roman nobility there.

Names of kingdoms. What do they tell us – establishment by a 'people' or by individuals?
The Anglo-Saxon names for kingdoms reflected those of the dominant people as on the Continent, though usually with a defining geographical context. Thus there were kingdoms of the West Saxons, South Saxons, East Saxons, East Anglians ('North' and 'South' folks), and initially Middle Saxons and Middle Angles. The 'Mercians' took their name from the term for 'border', implying that they were the settlers on the border with the British. ('Mercia' means the 'mark', a name taken up by the distinguished Anglo-Saxon philologist J.R.R. Tolkien for his proto-Anglo-Saxon kingdom of Rohan in his 'Middle Earth'.) A geographical term was also used for the obscure kingdom of Surrey, the 'South Region' – presumably of Middlesex, from which it was divided by the Thames. The first known post-Roman event there, the battle of 'Wibbandun' (Wimbledon?) between Wessex and Kent c.568, presumably indicates these two larger kingdoms fighting over this area.

The names of earlier British kingdoms were taken up for Kent (the land of the pre-Roman 'Cantioi' recorded by Julius Caesar) and Bernicia (the Celtic kingdom of 'Bryniach'). This may reflect the settlers taking over an existing administrative unit in one action, and claiming heirship to their predecessors. The name Deira, which joined with Bernicia c.604 under Aethelfrith to form the geographically-designated land of 'Northumbria', is obscure. (It was based on settlers in the Humber estuary, and expanded to include the local Roman administrative capital of York c.580.) So is that of 'Hwicce' in the south-west Midlands, centred on north-eastern Gloucestershire. 'Magonsaetan' in Herefordshire/Shropshire probably derives from the Roman town of 'Magnis' (Kenchester). The alternative name for early Wessex before the 680s, the obscure 'Gewissae', seems to be dynastic rather than geographical and some Welsh experts have linked it to that of the south-east Welsh kingdom of 'Ewias' to which the founder, the British-named Cerdic, may have been linked.

Founders – real or mythologized?
All the kingdoms whose genealogies have survived (many of their oral records did not survive to be written down by the victorious West Saxon dynasty in their annals) record founding dynasts, evidently war-leaders who established new kingdoms as on the Continent. It is possible that those kingdoms for whom we lack such stories, e.g. East Anglia and Essex, genuinely lacked a history of early conquest and were established by peaceful settlers – but it us equally possible that their founding myths just did not survive. (In East Anglia, one sixth century king was named after the contemporary Gothic military hero Totila – evidence of similar pretensions by his dynasty?) But their names are often obscure and their Germanic ancestors back to the founder-god 'Woden' are clearly mythical. The questions regarding Hengest in Kent and Cerdic in Wessex have already been mentioned. But it is probable that some of the 'founders' were real warlords who set up new kingdoms by force of arms rather than different bands of farmer-settlers coming together at a mutually convenient date to coalesce into an ethnically-defined 'state'.

Not all the 'founder-heroes' of dynasties could have been invented by subsequent generations as a rationalization of a slow politico-economic process into personal terms – the favoured modern explanation of the foundation of Kent. Some strong warlord had to act as cohesive presence to forcefully bring together disparate groups of settlers and 'natives' into one people', with power, resources, and military strength concentrated on a dynasty of warlords – as seen in all the Anglo-Saxon 'states' except small and weak ones that fell prey to their neighbours (e.g. that of the Middle Saxons). In Kent, the dynasty traced its nomenclature from Hengest's 'son' Aesc, who supposedly died in 512; in East Anglia the first of the dynasty to move to Britain (Wuffa) was placed c.520–40; in Mercia the 'founder', Icel, was two generations before king Creoda c.589; in Bernicia the 'founder' Ida landed at Bamburgh in 547. The first recorded kings of the East Saxons were Aescwine in the mid-sixth century, only known to medieval sources, and Sledda c.600.[33]

Were they all artificial creations, based on clear geographic boundaries but not on existing distinct groups of settlers, to turn a disparate group of local settlements into one state? Does the suspicious nature of 'foundation-stories', with those of Kent and Wessex being so similar, reflect the artificial nature of later mythologizing by the ruling dynasty? It is possible that a 'founder-hero' was invented as a point of reference and unity for the ruling dynasties in the sixth century, and that Hengest and Cerdic never carried out their supposed deeds. Possibly the two regional divisions of Kent, East and West, had distinct and unconnected settlers who came together into one kingdom later in the sixth century (under Aethelbert?) and sought to stress their unity by rallying round Hengest's story. Wessex, similarly, was formed of several separate regional districts, not one coherent kingdom under one royal line. It is supposed to have had a number of unnamed 'kings' killed by the raiding Northumbrians c.626, none of them the current senior ruler Cynegils, and jointly-ruling kings after the death of Cenwalh in 674(?) until unity was restored a decade or so later. Were these distinct dynastic 'mini-kingdoms' ruled by separate dynasties and absorbed into an expanding Wessex? Does the highly complex and detailed royal genealogy of Cerdic's family, preserved into the ninth century, reflect an attempt to link all these known local rulers into one family to stress their (imaginary) historical unity?

The alternative possibility for Wessex is that conquest and settlement of these local areas was carried out by different branches of the ruling royal kin, who set up distinct 'sub-kingdoms' but all owed allegiance in war (and possibly tribute in livestock) to the 'over-king'. Thus the line of 'centralized' kings ruling all Wessex, from Ceawlin c.576–92 to Ine in 688–726 – who did not automatically succeed 'father-son' – were the strongest of these princes, elected by agreement by their peers or self-appointed by military conquest. This would fit the turbulent career of one minor prince of the royal lineage, Caedwalla, who had lost his father's lands and was a homeless roving war-leader when St Wilfred first met him but in 685/6 forced his way to ruling the entire kingdom and led its army to conquer Sussex and Kent.[34] The parallel would be with Ireland, where the 'High Kingship' rotated among 'throne-worthy' princes of the 'Ui Niall' dynasty while the various sub-kindreds of this large family proceeded to annex lands for their own local states across central Ireland. Some distinct peoples are known within Wessex – not all of them 'Saxon'. What of the 'Meonware' in the Meon valley of eastern Hampshire, detached from Wessex and given to its neighbour Sussex by Wessex's enemy Wulfhere of Mercia in 661? Or the royal line of (pagan) Wight, descended from the eponymous 'Wihtgar' (who the *Anglo-Saxon Chronicle* alleged to be a nephew of Cerdic) c.530 and terminated by massacre by Caedwalla of Wessex in 686?[35] It has been supposed that the connection with Cerdic was invented later, to legitimize Wessex's conquest. If Wihtgar and his brother Stuf were placed as being Cerdic's nephews, this implied that he was their senior – and thus the kings of Wessex were overlords of Wight of long standing, not alien conquerors.

Part II

The Kingdoms: Real and Alternative Courses of Development

(a) The kingdom of Northumbria
Two choices of development – the dynasties of Deira or Bernicia? The Churches of Rome or Iona?

Thus it appears that the 'family' (dynastically-linked or not) of Ida in Bernicia battled the local British kingdoms through the later sixth century. Its history and kingship then is obscure, but its surviving genealogy and occasional references in the *Anglo-Saxon Chronicle* suggest that it was established by Ida c.547 and based on the coastal rock-fortress of Bamburgh (possibly named after Bebba, wife to his son Aethelric).

Ida and his successors seem to have had short reigns, possibly indicating frequent deaths in battle against Britons or each other; he was supposedly succeeded by Glappa, a kinsman, c.559, and then by a succession of his sons commencing with Adda.[36] (The difficulty of dating is compounded by the uncertain lengths of reigns and the possibility that several kings ruled simultaneously.) From British literary sources it is clear that it came under threat of extinction in the 580s and early 590s from the coalitions built up by its British neighbours, warlords Urien and Owain of Rheged – and that its survival owed as much to its kings' tenacity as to the fortuitous assassination of Urien c.589 by a jealous British rival, Morcant. The string of Germanic coastal settlements from Bamburgh along to the Tees would hardly have defeated the British state commanding the resources of Lancashire, Cumbria, and south-western Scotland (plus occasional outside allies, as seen in the Catraeth campaign c.600) but for determined and skilful leadership. The skill, cohesion, and *esprit de corps* of the warriors of Rheged under Urien and Owain is apparent from the poems of Llywarch 'Hen', and in the *Gododdin* (on the Catraeth campaign) the poet Aneirin presents a picture of a body of heroes from across northern Britain recruited to aid Rheged.[37] The British kings and their warriors were also celebrated by the Welsh poet Taliesin, most of whose 'genuine' poems can be linked to the court of Rheged (later myth also linked him to the court of King Arthur).

There are obvious parallels with other literary assemblies of heroes from a wide area for a 'legitimate' war on the national foe – most obviously the Greek attack on Troy in the *Iliad*. Given the post-Roman heritage of the local British kingdoms based around Hadrian's Wall, a major area of Roman military concentration, it has been speculated that the British had the advantage of cavalry too.

We do not even know the name of Urien's and Owain's Bernician foe, who eventually defeated Rheged – the British sources call him 'Flamdwyn', 'the Flame-Bearer', evidently a nickname, and he was probably the contemporary King Theodric or Aethelric. There was nothing inevitable about the Bernician defeat of Rheged in the mid-590s, when Owain was killed (possibly at Catraeth), or its subsequent defeat of the veteran warlord Aedan of Dal Riada at 'Degsastan' (possibly Dawston in Liddesdale).

The Bernician kings built up a war-machine that Aethelfrith, son of Aethelric, used to take over neighbouring Deira c.604, annex many Northern British kingdoms into one large state, and 'found' Northumbria. The founder of the united state of Northumbria and the first known Anglian king to reach the Irish Sea, he was evidently a talented general and a charismatic leader. He also defeated the British of North Wales at Chester c.616 – notoriously massacring a large party of monks who had come to the battlefield to pray for his opponents. But his ambitions aroused the fears of his southern neighbours, leading to a war with East Anglia with whose king, Raedwald, the refugee Deiran prince Edwin had taken refuge. The two kingdoms were probably also in conflict over the control of the lower Trent valley and Lindsey.

The fearsome reputation Aethelfrith had earned caused the cautious King Ceorl of Mercia, his immediate southern neighbour, to expel Edwin as Aethelfrith demanded rather than face invasion; but Raedwald was made of sterner stuff and chose to fight. The death in battle of Aethelfrith against Raedwald on the River Idle near Doncaster around 617 brought Edwin, brother and son of the kings of Deira he had overthrown, to the united throne of Northumbria.[38]

Edwin secured an even greater empire, including the Isle of Man and Anglesey/Mon so he must have had a fleet. He fully incorporated the eastern Pennine British kingdom of Elmet (around Leeds) in Northumbria, either reduced Rheged to vassalage or annexed it, and as a former refugee in Wales knew enough of Welsh war-tactics and their kings' capabilities to take them on successfully. He temporarily expelled Cadwallon, son of his ex-host Cadfan of Gwynedd, from his kingdom and was probably the first Anglian ruler to march along the North Wales coast as far as the Menai Strait. His marriage to the daughter of Aethelbert of Kent brought a Roman Christian mission under Paulinus, first bishop of York, to his court – Welsh tradition had it that he was first baptized a Christian by ex-king Rhun of Rheged, now a bishop, in exile rather than by Paulinus as stated by Bede.

Whether or not Bede ignored the 'Celtic' Church's contribution to the evangelization of Northumbria in the 620s, Edwin chose to align himself with the Roman Church and its mission in Kent. He thus brought himself into the comity of Christian states linked to the papacy rather than to the surviving, less centralized post-Roman Church in Ireland and Scotland, orientating Northumbria towards the Continent not the Atlantic fringes. His diplomatic as well as religious 'volte-face' from the previous isolated, pagan condition of Bernicia made him the heir to Aethelbert of Kent, his father-in-law, as well as to the great exemplar of an expanding Catholic-orientated Christian monarchy, Clovis the Frank. But, unlike Francia, the Northumbrian state was not able to achieve permanent military supremacy over its local rivals.

Edwin's death in battle against the British king Cadwallon of Gwynedd in 633/4[39] led to Northumbria breaking up temporarily. Aethelfrith's eldest son, Eanfrith, regained Bernicia while Deira, ravaged by Gwynedd, was temporarily kingless and then passed to Edwin's nephew, Osric. Soon the kingdom was reunited by Aethelfrith's younger sons, Oswald (k.642) and Oswy (d.670), who were Christians like Edwin but had been converted in exile in Dalriada. This great power of contemporary Scotland, centred in Argyll, had been founded by Irish settlers c.500 (traditionally led by an Ulster prince, Eric) and was run by a mission following the 'Celtic' Irish Christian customs, which had been set up in the 560s by St Columbcille/Columba at Iona. It was Columba who inaugurated the practice of anointing a king with holy oil to show Divine and Church backing and thus cementing the alliance of Church and State, with his biographer Adamnan recording that he consecrated the Dalriadan king Aedan c.574. This practice – based on the Old Testament anointing of Saul by the prophet Samuel – was now imported to Northumbria and England. But it should be pointed out that the existence of a major Christian mission at Iona, ready to assist Oswald and Oswy, owed a great deal to the minutiae of Irish politics in the 550s. Columba, a great noble from the ruling dynasty of the Irish 'High Kings' (the 'Ui Niall'), had led a coalition of disgruntled local kings to defeat the centralizing 'High King' Diarmait and had apparently been encouraged (or ordered) to leave Ireland and undertake a mission to Dalriada in expiation of the bloodshed that he had caused. But for the revolt against Diarmait, would Dalriada have been Christian and missionary monks been available at Iona?

Contrary to modern nationalist assumptions, the Irish and Dalriadan divergences from Roman Church practices (e.g. the form of the monastic tonsure and the date of celebrating Easter) do not seem to have been deliberately aimed at rejecting Roman authority. The argument of putting traditional usage above conformity to centralized Roman practice was indeed used by the 'Celtic' party, under Bishop Colman, at the crucial Northumbrian Church Council in 664. But this was not why the practices had been adopted in the first place – merely a defensive dislike of change ordered by intruders plus a genuine belief that Rome's practices and Easter calculations were flawed. The 'Celtic' practices had emerged out of local developments in Ireland in an era when it was cut off from close contact with Rome and had no visits from Roman churchmen telling the local clergy what to do.

They had had to develop their own customs, and the papacy – preoccupied with its own problems of Germanic rule to 536 and then wars with Goths and Lombards – did not supervise its distant daughter-churches. Greater papal concern with order and conformity across the West – and bureaucratic zeal for the use of one system of canon law and religious practices – only emerged with the example set by Pope Gregory 'the Great' in the 590s.[40]

But this papal initiative for conformity owed much to current events in Italy, where the secular authority of the traditional aristocratic Senate in Rome had collapsed during the war with Totila in the 540s – the Senate indeed disappeared.[41] Many of the old noble families lost their estates, tenantry, income, and power during the Gothic war, and Rome itself was occupied several times and economically ruined; its population collapsed. Similarly, the exhausted Eastern Empire, preoccupied with its wars of survival in the East against Avars and Persians, could not afford the money or personnel to control the civilian administration of Rome or central Italy, and from the 560s the invading Lombards occupied much territory and cut off Rome from the imperial viceroy's base of power at Ravenna. The Pope became secular as well as religious leader of Rome, with minimal imperial interference and even Ravenna under threat from the Lombards.

By extension, the papacy's prestige (and that of his see as a major pilgrimage centre) brought it to political as well as religious prominence despite the nominal authority of the Eastern Emperor in Italy.

The papacy had already existed as the prestigious Bishopric of Rome, alleged see of St Peter to whom the keys of the kingdom of Heaven had been given by Christ, when fourth century Roman Britain had been converted – officially, by imperial administrative decrees banning 'pagan' beliefs, as much as by missionary work.

As seen by the private 'house church' chapels of villas such as Lullingstone, it had been individual (often rich) families who had converted as a gradual process rather than bishops converting a ruler who then forcibly converted his people. Ireland had then been converted by missionaries (including the British ex-slave St Patrick) despatched from Gaul at the behest of Gallic bishops, backed by the Church in Rome; and from Ireland the missionary expedition of princely Irish bishop St Columbcille /

Columba had founded Iona in the Irish settlers' Scottish land of Dalriada. In none of these instances had there been a specific mission sent solely from and by the orders of the See of Rome, unlike Gregory the Great's mission to Kent in 597; and the errors of clerical tonsure and dates for calculating Easter had crept into religious practice in the remoter parts of the British Isles without attempts at correction by the papacy until 664. Nor had the Irish and Iona Churches made any attempt to impose their own practices on areas following 'Catholic' Roman practices. Thus both Roman initiatives – that of sending Augustine and that of imposing correct religious practices on all the Church – arose from new vigour and centralized orderliness in the Church in Rome, which contrasted sharply with the lack of such concerns before the later sixth century. The popes of earlier times had been more concerned with correcting theological 'heresy' – mainly in the Eastern Church centred at Constantinople, particularly the 'erroneous' doctrines of Nestorianism in the early-mid fifth century and 'Monophysitism' from the 440s to the 520s. (The only Western 'heresy' to be seen as a major threat, in the 410s and 420s, was ironically started by a Romano-Briton, Pelagius.) As late as 536 a pope was deposed by the see's restored secular overlord, the Eastern Emperor – the theologically interfering Justinian, who deported the next pope, Vigilius, to Constantinople in 550 to force him to sign up to his current theological plans. The independence that Gregory and his seventh century successors had to take on initiatives in Britain were thus new, quite apart from the will to do this.

The post-590 papacy under Gregory, a vigorous and morally determined administrator from the old nobility, stepped into the breach in secular and religious leadership in chaotic, Lombard-infested central Italy and added enormously to its power and reputation – and to its bureaucracy. The Eastern Empire was thence preoccupied fighting off the Avars, the Persians, and from the mid-630s the Arabs – though as late as the 660s one emperor, Constans II, briefly campaigned in Italy. Had these Italian crises not occurred after the Eastern Roman reconquest in 536–40, would a reinvigorated papacy have been intervening in England in the seventh century? And without this leadership, would converting 'pagan' England have been left to missionaries coming down via Northumbria from Iona?

The Irish divergences of practice – imported into Northumbria under Oswald and Oswy – served by the mid-seventh century to emphasize a difference in tone from the Roman Church, which the rigid hierarchy and increasing centralization of Rome in the seventh century turned to conflict. The Irish Church, divided into five provinces under loose leadership from Armagh, and its daughter-Church on Iona, had no legalistic central authority issuing directions to its subordinate bishops in the manner which the Pope did from Rome. Indeed, their bishops were not seen as a smoothly-running hierarchy – the religious counterpart of the Late Roman civil bureaucracy, on which the Roman Church had been modelled – under the discipline of their archbishops, who were in turn under the orders of Rome. In the Christianized lands of the former Western Empire the bishops were supposed to be resident in the capital cities of each province, as an essentially urban office – as neatly set out at the Church Council of Nicaea in 325. Ireland had not been a Roman province, had no towns, and had not been Christianized under Roman influence but by post-Roman Britons (and Gauls?) led by Patrick in the second third of the fifth century. Its bishops tended to reside at Royal courts and/or great provincial monasteries, administering the sacraments rather than imposing legalistic discipline, and arguably the leading abbots (often of noble birth) had more prestige. Columba, for example, had been an Irish prince of the line of the Ui Niall 'High Kings' and had run his conversion of Dalriada from the monastery of Iona as its abbot; his role as a bishop was less vital. The bishop's role was to celebrate the sacraments and preside at the royal court as its resident senior cleric, not to run a Church bureaucracy as in urbanized Roman bishoprics (e.g. in Gaul and Italy).

It was the monasteries that were the 'power-houses' of learning, art, and missionary activity – and eager peripatetic missionaries led the way in converting new peoples, not Rome-directed bishops. This extended to 'Celtic' Britain too, as South Welsh monastic trainees such as St Samson and St Paul Aurelian moved into Brittany to set up rural monasteries and convert the locals. Their 'home areas' were, like Ireland, not urbanized – and their monasteries were centred in the 'desert' away from centres of secular power, as in Ireland. (The main South Welsh monasteries were at the Silurian estates of Llancarfan, Llanilltud Fawr and on Caldey Island.[42]) If there were any fifth century monasteries in pre-conquest 'England' they would have been similar, but the only one we have any – problematic – evidence for is the enigmatic Glastonbury, allegedly dating to the first century AD. The British Church did not 'civilize' incoming Germanic leaders, as the Gallic one did to Clovis in France.

This tradition was imported to Northumbria by Oswald's ally Aedan, abbot of Lindisfarne – which was clearly modelled on Iona – as well as bishop of the kingdom. The tradition of the leaders of the 'Celtic' Church in Northumbria as abbots as well as bishops continued with men such as Eata and Cuthbert, and was alien to usual Roman practice – the new monastery and abbot of St Augustine's that the eponymous saint set up at Canterbury, capital of Rome-converted Kent, had no such role. Questions of doctrine and practices in 'Celtic' Church lands were dealt with by occasional religious councils, and the Abbot of Iona did not seek administrative authority over churches established by his missionaries. This has duly made the practices of the so-called 'Celtic Church' seem attractively democratic and non-authoritarian in modern times, and attracted criticism of papal centralization to its activities. In one neat story, the clerics of the British/Welsh Church were fatally offended by St Augustine at their first meeting in c.604 (traditionally at Aust near Bristol) because he arrogantly did not stand up as they arrived. Could they have co-operated? If they had, would Wessex or Mercia been converted earlier? Or were the British clerics, monastery-centred unlike the Roman ones, unambitious for travel except to their kindred in Ireland and Brittany? The importance that Augustine (as related by Bede) gave to matters of Church practice indicates a legalistic insistence on Rome (which he need not have consulted so closely) getting its way.

The Roman proponent St Wilfred appears as an authoritarian centralizer and his opponent Colman to regard winning souls to Christ as more important than squabbling over structures of authority. This has modern overtones. Wilfred, indeed, seems to have been over-confident that Roman backing gave him the right to order kings around, unlike humbler 'Celtic' missionary bishops had done (though he was an abrasive personality by all accounts).

He annoyed Oswy's equally arrogant son Ecgfrith by encouraging his devout wife, (St) Aetheldreda/Audrey, to leave him and become an abbess, and ended up exiled from his bishopric of York[43] – a clash of personalities that would have been unlikely had a less strict and self-confident character been ruling the see. Moreover, given the Irish/ Iona enthusiasm for conversion of 'pagan' kingdoms it is probable that if the Roman Church had not already moved into Kent – and hence the rest of the south – from 597 the Northumbrian Church could have been expected to send successful missions south into those kingdoms had it continued on its pre-664 path. As it was, Northumbrian clerics had some forays into the Midlands and East Anglia in the times of Northumbrian political power in the mid-seventh century.[44] It was crucial that a vigorous and determined figure such as Wilfred chose to adhere to the cause and doctrine of Rome and to take up the notion of an administratively and doctrinally centralized Church promoted by the seventh century papacy. Even when driven out of Northumbria by the irritated Ecgfrith, he was able to settle in and convert Sussex.[45] The wandering and tireless Wilfred was a parallel figure with the adventurous Irish missionaries, some of whom even did missionary work in Gaul and Switzerland, but he was a firm 'Romanist' and his targets for conversion were expected to adhere to the structured Roman Church, not have a vague and unenforced loyalty to distant Iona.

Oswald's successful reconquest of Northumbria from the plundering Cadwallon of Gwynedd in 634 thus had a crucial effect on Northumbria's development. He brought in 'Celtic Church' missionaries from Dalriada and Ireland, most notably St Aedan, the first bishop/ abbot of Lindisfarne, and the Northumbrian Church thereafter showed signs of Irish influence. Paulinus had based his mission in the city of York, former second episcopal see of Roman Britain, according to a papal plan to revive the Late Roman ecclesiastical hierarchy; Aedan, like Celtic bishops in Ireland, was based at the royal court and 'doubled up' as abbot of the new monastery on the island of Lindisfarne. The rural-based abbeys, centres of great estates or placed in the 'wilderness' (often on islands, such as Iona), and their abbots – often from noble kindreds – were the main power in the 'Celtic' Church of Ireland and Dalriada, rather than the urban bishops of the Roman Church. This trend now made itself felt in those areas of northern Britain converted by monks from Iona.

Deira retained enough sense of individuality for its political leadership to be able to insist on a separate kingship, junior to that of all Northumbira, until 679. Initially held by Edwin's relatives, Osric and Oswine, as sub-kings to the Bernician royals Oswald and Oswy in Northumbria, it was transferred by Oswy to junior princes of his own line in 651. However, its first Bernician sub-king, his nephew Aethelwald, promptly joined his Mercian foe, Penda, to attack him in 655 and Deira was to remain a distinct kingdom – now ruled by the heir to all Northumbria, Oswy's sons in succession – from 655 to 679. It was clearly Mercian policy to build up Deira as an ally against Bernicia and so keep Northumbria divided, and in retaliation for this the victorious Oswy tried to split Mercia up in 655–8 (with equal lack of success).

The differences and hostility between 'Roman' and 'Celtic' Churches may have been exaggerated, but the latter followed a number of divergent practices. The divergence became awkward when a king following the 'Celtic' rites married a princess following the 'Roman ' rites and they ended up celebrating Easter on different dates – as when Oswy married Enfleda, daughter of Edwin, who had been brought up in exile in Kent following the overthrowing of her father.[46] Great bishops of the Northumbrian Church under Celtic influence, such as Aedan and Cuthbert, were not based in towns but monasteries and were more involved in travelling evangelization than court politics. The 'Roman' rites and practices were eventually adopted following an ecclesiastical council at the abbey of Whitby in 664, apparently as Oswy was impressed with the political and religious power of Rome.

The official version, by Bede, had it that he said he would not quarrel with St Peter who held the keys of admission to Heaven.[47] The result led to an exodus of Irish monks and their local supporters from Northumbria, some to keep to the 'Celtic' practices at a monastery in exile in Ireland – which shows that many people put their belief in their traditional practices above the unity of the Church and were as obstinate as the 'Romans'. Had the decision gone the other way, the reverse would have happened. But would Rome have granted a 'heretic' York an archbishopric until it reformed? (It did in real life in 735.)

The decision was presented in glowing terms implying inevitability by Bede in the 730s; it was a part of his overall 'narrative thrust' of the – divinely-assisted – triumph of Roman Christianity over its foes. It made political sense for an ambitious Northumbrian kingdom looking outwards to Europe to ally with Continental practice, and it was to make it easier for Northumbrian clerics to undertake missionary work elsewhere with Roman backing. It also implied Northumbrian submission to the will of the southern archbishopric in Canterbury, held at the time by the Greek administrator Theodore of Tarsus chosen by Rome. Theodore of Tarsus was keen to see that the universality of Roman canon law and doctrine was imposed on the Christian kingdoms of Britain, as was enforced by 'centralizing' English Church Councils (e.g. Hertford in 679). This now encompassed Northumbria as well as the south, as planned by Pope Gregory in his instructions to St Augustine in 597.

But had the determined centralizer Theodore, born an Eastern Roman citizen in modern South-Eastern Turkey, not been driven out of his homeland by the Arab wars in the mid-seventh century and taken refuge in Rome he would not have been available for the mission. Presumably some other, Italian, papal bureaucrat would have been chosen – but it was a rare initiative for the Pope to send a Mediterranean cleric to head an existing foreign Church as after the initial conversion sees usually went to local clerics. The sees of much of Gaul, as we have seen, were monopolized by Romano-Gallic clerics, and local figures from the literate post-Roman upper classes also served in the Catholic Church in Spain. The absence of a literate, Latin-speaking local grouping used to monopolizing Church office arguably gave a major boost to papal centralization in England – as it might have not done had more of the pre-English elite survived.

The strength and evident holiness of local clerics trained in the 'Celtic' practices on Iona could easily have led to victory for them in 664, had Oswy – brought up in their traditions – so decided. Did the hostess of this 'summit' at Whitby, the local abbess St Hild (a royal kinswoman), and other prominent observers have a royal hint as to what decision would be most acceptable?

But if Oswy had decided otherwise there could have been an order for the Church in Deira (politically junior to pro-Iona Bernicia) to abandon

'Roman' practices and follow Iona's lead, had its leader, Wilfred, defied Oswy. Had the pro-'Roman' Alchfrith, Oswy's son and King of Deira, not died around 664 it is possible that the ruthless Wilfred would have encouraged him to make war on his father in the name of the See of St Peter. Deiran particularism against rule from Bernicia could have aided their cause. It was unlikely to have been a long-term success given the sheer scale of Rome's administrative power compared with the weaker influence of Iona, an isolated Hebridean monastery with limited manpower and less obsession with 'control' than the papacy, and its supporters. The prospect of the see of Northumbria defying the ecclesiastical authority of the archbishopric of Canterbury would have had a political impact and heightened tension between Northumbria and pro-Canterbury Mercia, converted in the late 650s–660s. The latter was likely to have been backed by the archbishopric (and Rome?) to evict an anti- Roman ruler and his bishops from York. The adoption of Roman practices certainly aided Northumbria's international prestige and its missionaries' role in converting pagans on the Continent, e.g. in Frisia; the eighth century papacy would not have looked so equably on 'heretic' missionaries. The lure of links with the Continent led to close Northumbrian-Frankish relations in the mid-eighth century; the Frankish Church and kingship were both close to the papacy under the Carolingians from 751 and they would have pressurized Northumbria to conform then had it not yet done so.

In political terms, the destruction of Edwin's dynasty in 633/4 also brought major changes. It was not Edwin's dynasty but Aethelfrith's – from Bernicia – which ruled over Northumbria from 633/4 to 729; Edwin's only adult son, Osfrith, was killed with his father, his younger children fled into exile, and their dynasty was not able to secure long-term dynastic stability. Deira was revived as a dependant kingdom for Edwin's cousins Osric and Oswine, subject to Bernician overlordship, though it was later taken over by Oswy for junior members of the Bernician dynasty – some descended from Edwin via his daughter Enfleda. It was incorporated into Northumbria on the death of King Ecgfrith's brother Elfwine in 679, and on several occasions in the meantime its rulers proved less than loyal to the Bernicians. Within six years of the unification Ecgfrith's death in battle against the Picts at Nechtansmere in Fife (685) brought an end to the kingdom's military greatness.[48] The conquest of the east coastlands of Scotland was halted, and Ecgfrith was succeeded by less aggressive or militarily experienced rulers – first the last adult male of the dynasty, his elderly, scholarly half-brother Aldfrith (d. 705), and then the latter's young sons.

The royal house appears to have been extinct with the death of King Osric in 729, leading to decades of usurpations. One noble of unknown descent,

Coenred, had already briefly replaced the tyrant Osred in 716; the first king after the extinction of the main royal house, the mild-mannered and holy Ceolwulf (729–37), may have been his brother. He was deposed briefly and forcibly made a monk, which may not have been unwelcome to him given his enthusiasm for the Church, and he was later induced to abdicate again. It is not known how much of his troubles stemmed from a lack of legitimacy in the eyes of his nobles, as opposed to his weak character or his apparent enthusiasm for giving estates to the Church – which reduced the land available for the king to buy support from his followers, thus weakening the bonds of loyalty. The descent of his successor, the more forceful and successful Eadbert, from the dynastic founder, Ida, was at best remote and may have been invented. The same applies to the two families who then disputed the throne with Eadbert's kin, those of Kings Aethelwald 'Moll' (758–65) and Alchred (765–74). The next half-century saw a notable rash of royal depositions and murders, plus obscure executions or banishments of leading nobles that hint at frequent plots.

The likelihood is that each successful coup encouraged new attempts, and the drastic attempt by Aethelwald's son Aethelred 'Moll' (774–9, 790–6) to stabilize the kingdom by a rash of executions only led to charges of tyranny and his murder.[49] Northumbria's cultural 'leadership' of early-mid eighth century Anglo-Saxon England, as illustrated by Bede's immense scholarship and the *Lindisfarne Gospels*, was not reflected in political power. Its greatest literary export to Charlemagne's Francia in the 790s, Alcuin, thus represented a minor 'power', not a major one.

(b) Mercia and East Anglia – the advantages the former possessed in asserting leadership in southern England

(i) Mercia: rampant centralization?

The pagan warlord Penda achieved a similar ascendancy for Mercia in central England from the 620s to the 650s, as the catalogue of his victories shows, though Bede did his best to downplay his power and importance (no doubt due to religious antipathy[50]). His obscure 'Icelingas' dynasty traced its royal line to a fifth century Continental king called Offa of the Angles, but had not made any impact in the sixth century when Mercia appears to have been a mixture of small groups of settlers identified as 'peoples' by their geographical areas (e.g. the 'Pecsaetan' of the Peak District, 'Wreocensaetan' of the Wrekin, 'Arowsaete' of the Arrow valley, 'Cilternsaean' of the Chilterns, and 'Gyrwe' of the Fens). The creation of Mercian power is obscure but appears to have been mainly Penda's work, given how little is known of his forebears; the nomenclature of his immediate family suggests that their 'power-base' was probably Warwickshire.[51] The south-east Midlands seems to have retained a degree of local self-identification as a separate political unit, the kingdom of the 'Middle Angles', which Penda gave to his eldest son, Peada, in 653.

Penda dominated Central England, aided by the geographical position of Mercia. Little is recorded of his career except his major successes and final downfall, but it is clear that he had a formidable military machine. His armies could strike outwards from a central position to attack any of their neighbours, whereas Northumbrian troops had a long journey south to invade any of their neighbours except Mercia and once they lost control of Lindsey they had no frontier with any other power but Mercia. He repeatedly attacked his main foe Northumbria, and had the manpower and the 'reach' to march right across the kingdom to sack Bamburgh in the far north in the mid-640s. Probably due to his mixture of overwhelming numbers, military skill, and sheer brutality, it seems that Oswy chose to avoid meeting his massive invasion in 655 'head-on' and won his – unexpected – great victory over Penda at the River 'Winwaed' by ambushing his tired army (near Leeds?) in heavy rain on their homeward march. Bede presented this confrontation in religious terms, with the pagan Penda invading Christian Northumbria, and it is possible that after Penda killed the militantly Christian King Oswald (one of Bede's heroes) at Maserfelth/Oswestry in 642 he mockingly subjected his body to a pagan ritual. But Penda had two Christian, British allies in succession – Cadwallon of Gwynedd and Cyndylan of Powys – and allowed his eldest son, Peada, to convert to Christianity.

Oswald's son Aethelwald of Deira preferred to ally with Penda than to his uncle Oswy in 655[52] – possibly hoping for his throne in return. Penda's main aim seems to have been political – to destroy the power of his northern neighbour irrespective of its religious identity. It is notable that even a strong king such as Penda had co-rulers at the height of his power, namely his brother Eowa (killed in 642 at Maserfelth) and in the early 650s his eldest son, Peada. He may well have dominated them, but the scant evidence in the sources may hide a tradition of multiple kingship within Mercia as well as Wessex and Essex.[53] Whether each king had a separate geographical area to rule is more dubious; the only known king ruling a sub-region of Mercia was Peada, Penda's son, as a Northumbrian vassal in 655–8 and in that case he was appointed by his overlord, Oswy, to rule those areas not conquered by Northumbria.

After Penda was killed by Oswy in a massive invasion of Northumbria in 655 at the River Winwaed, the latter temporarily destroyed Mercian power by breaking up the kingdom. He annexed the north and allowed Penda's eldest son, Peada – his own son-in-law – to rule the south, the 'Middle Angles', as his vassal. But the eclipse was temporary, and local particularism and desire for revenge on Oswy was probably unstoppable though he may have miscalculated his strength.

Peada, the likeliest Mercian ruler to act as a loyal vassal of Oswy and keep his people in check, was murdered in 656 in obscure circumstances, probably by his wife and possibly as a 'pre-emptive strike' against revolt ordered by a suspicious Oswy.[54] The crime brought about the feared rebellion, in the name of Peada's refugee brother Wulfhere who had been hidden from Oswy, and Northumbrian power was expelled in 658; Mercia resumed its position as principal power of southern England for the rest of the seventh and eighth centuries, overrunning northern parts of Wessex and permanently annexing the upper Thames valley c.660. Wulfhere's invasion of Wiltshire and probable march to the English Channel in 661 saw Mercia handing over control of eastern Hampshire and the Isle of Wight to Sussex, logically to weaken the power of Wessex, though the latter recovered its power in central southern England two decades later.[55] For the first time Mercia was able to dominate Kent during the regency of its own princess, Eormenhild, for the under-age King Eadric after 673, though a reaction seems to have set in and the king's uncle Hlothere (Lothar, a Frankish name) led a successful anti-Mercian movement when Wulfhere died in 674/5. The latter's brother and successor, Aethelred, sacked Rochester in retaliation, driving out its bishop, though he later became a pious and pacific ally of the Church who renounced such strong-arm tactics.[56]

The advantages of its central position within England and its large resources outweighed Mercia's difficulties about smooth dynastic successions. The abdication of Wulfhere's religious son Coenred in 709 and the suspicious death of Aethelred's violent son Coelred in 716 extinguished the direct line of kings and the next two rulers, remote cousins Aethelbald (d.757) and Offa (d.796), could not found new dynastic lines but the resulting problems over the succession were swiftly resolved in both cases. The lineage of the man who succeeded Offa's short-lived son Ecgfrith in 796, Coenwulf, is even more obscure; and after his brother Ceolwulf was deposed in 823 the lineage of Mercia's last kings is unknown. Offa was accused of eliminating rivals from the royal family by the Northumbrian scholar Alcuin, which probably removed men with strong local resources and support whose 'legitimist' descendants could have rallied the kingdom after the early 820s.

One major point to remember is that the extinction of the dynastic line in 796 did not cause Mercia's decline. Indeed, it went on to subdue its constant irritant Kent in the late 790s under Coenwulf and inflicted serious losses on Gwynedd in the 820s.

Even after Ceolwulf's death, the supposedly shaky non-dynastic ruler Beornwulf led expeditions across Gwynedd as far as Arfon and the Menai Strait; and in the next few decades Powys collapsed under Mercian pressure. Its last king, Cyngen, fled to Rome in 853 after defeat by Burghred of Mercia, with his kingdom having to unite with Gwynedd under his nephew Rhodri 'Mawr' – at a time when Mercia had already been defeated, lost control of Kent to, and briefly been occupied by Wessex.[57]

Burghred, a man with no known links to earlier dynasties, was to be humiliated by the vikings at Nottingham in 868 and in 875 abandoned his kingdom and fled to Rome, like Cyngen. But he was more than a match for Powys in 852–3, albeit with help from Wessex. Mercia's shattering defeat by Egbert of Wessex at Ellandun in 825, followed by the loss of Kent and probably East Anglia as a vassal, must have seriously weakened Mercia.[58] But this was not fatal to the kingdom; Egbert expelled its new ruler, Wiglaf, in 829 but failed to keep control of his kingdom and had to see him return to power in 830. Unlike in Kent or Wessex, a lack of direct 'father-son' descent in the eighth century did not lead to prolonged civil wars or weakened victors. Nor was there repeated rebellion as in post-756 Northumbria. The centralized structure of the kingdom, giving each new king overwhelming military power over his vassals, and the determined and ruthless characters of Aethelbald and Offa were the probable reasons for this. Potential challengers would know that they had little chance of overthrowing the Mercian king, and so be dissuaded from trying. It is possible that the alienation of large amounts of estates from king to Church under Ceolwulf in Northumbria in 729–37 fatally weakened the kingship. In contrast, the equally pro-monastic King Aethelred of Mercia – who also abdicated to become a monk – seems to have kept a strong grip on patronage in both the State and Church.

King Aethelbald (716–57), the first man to claim on his coins to be 'king of the English' and an aggressive warlord and centralizer, apparently confiscated monastic estates for secular use – as gifts for potential supporters? – and lived a life of blatant sexual licence, not bothering to marry or father an heir and infuriating the Church.[59]

Offa in the later eighth century also used the ecclesiastical hierarchy for his own aggrandisement, creating a new archiepiscopal see for his own kingdom under his direct supervision. It is noticeable that from the early 730s archbishops of Canterbury of Mercian origin appear (Tatwine, Nothelm) – logically forced on the Kentish Church by its overlord. But the new archbishopric of Mercia/ Lichfield was abolished as soon as Offa was dead, apparently after intensive and successful lobbying by the threatened Church of Canterbury.[60] Nor could Coenwulf move the archbishopric to

London, now a Mercian city so under his permanent control unlike Canterbury – and envisaged by Pope Gregory as the archiepiscopal see back in the 590s not Canterbury. As in secular matters, local particularism won out over Mercian centralization – and even the aggressive Coenwulf, conqueror of rebel Kent in 798, had to accept it and eventually give in to the Holy See. He did manage to evict the triumphant Archbishop Wulfred of Canterbury c.816 after a dispute over lay appropriation of Church lands, but his successor was forced by the papacy to restore him.[61] The secular powers or the Church in Britain could not just create new sees in suitably loyal towns and rely on the papacy to accept it.

Institutional centralization can also be seen in the *Tribal Hideage*, which as far as we can tell was commissioned within Mercia some time around 680–730 as an administrative record of the amount of land held by and revenues owed by its own people and non-Mercian vassals. The fact that Mercia and its regions amounted to some 66,000 'hides' of land, its largest vassal East Anglia to 30,000, Kent to 15,000, and Essex and Sussex to 7,000 each shows starkly the preponderance of resources in Mercia's favour, which would also show in their relative military weight. The fact that the 'Hideage', centred on Mercia, could be compiled for kingdoms outside its borders shows that the latter's elites had to co-operate with Mercian logistic requirements. (The inclusion of Wessex, at 100,000 'hides', was probably a later addition.) There is a direct route in governmental effectiveness and the concept of a tax-raising administrative structure across southern and central England from the 'Hideage' to the *Domesday Book*, though we cannot tell if the Mercians began a systematic creation or use of the 'hundreds' within each county as a useful administrative tool.[62] The references to Aethelbald and Offa as 'King of the English' ('Angliae') in their new gold coinage – a concept itself of grandiose international origin and based on Arab models – is also problematic. The 'English' who these two men claimed to rule may have been intended as all the kingdoms south of the Humber, which Bede says Aethelbald ruled as overlord, or merely the 'Angles' (i.e. not the West or South Saxons?). Did 'Angles' imply the Angles of Deira and Bernicia, now Northumbria, too?

(ii) East Anglia: too peripheral to succeed?
The dynasty of the 'Wuffingas', again of obscure origin and early history, ruled in East Anglia from the sixth century. The earliest traces of Germanic goods in the area date from early fifth century, which suggests that the earliest settlers were small groups of households without 'royal' leadership.[63] If they were settled by force rather than consent and small 'kingdoms' or chieftainates set up, no memory of the leadership involved survived. Some

sites around Peterborough show signs of apparently seamless transition from Romano-British to Anglian occupation, which may imply a 'peaceful' takeover by invited settlers (or a swift military occupation by unknown warlords). Assuming the apparent existence of massive state-run Imperial estates,[64] not smaller aristocratic landholdings, in the Roman Fenland may explain the absence of local post-Roman 'tribal' nobility or warlords to resist encroachment. The kingdom was coherent and powerful enough by c.616 for Raedwald to be named by Bede as the current 'Bretwalda', an uncertain title but one implying leadership over his neighbours.[65]

The naming of Raedwald's father as 'Tytila', after Totila the great sixth century hero of the Gothic wars in Italy, would suggest grandiose pretensions for his dynasty however they came to power over the (probably politically distinct) 'North Folk' of Norfolk and 'South Folk' of Suffolk. Raedwald seems to have exercised influence over the peoples of south-east England after the death of Aethelbert in 616/18, either before or resulting from his defeat of the era's greatest warlord Aethelfrith of Northumbria. It may well be that he secured control over the small, weak multiple kingship of Essex to his south, along with the minor peoples of the Thames valley; Aethelbert's son and successor Eadbald seems to have been politically weaker than his father. It is also possible that until the rise of Penda, c.626, Mercia did not exercise political control over the peoples of Lindsey and the Fenland and these were under East Anglian control. In any case, the kingdom's pre-eminence was limited to Raedwald's lifetime and did not survive his death c.625. His son Eorpwald converted to Christianity at the behest of his ally Edwin, was soon murdered and the kingdom entered a period of instability under weaker kings, being raided and defeated by Mercia several times in the next decades.[66] In the mid-late eighth century, the identity and length of reign of some kings are unclear; we do not know much about Offa's victim, St Aethelbert, except via his medieval hagiography. Did the East Anglian kinship lapse after his execution in 794, and was it revived by an anti-Mercian revolt? And who were the post-825 kings who twice defeated Mercian armies? Does the similarity of their names with West Saxon princes imply their origin as West Saxon nominees, or even that the mysterious King Athelstan – who disappears from the record at the time of Egbert's death in 839 – was the same man as Athelstan, Egbert's son or grandson, who was then made king of Kent?

(c) Kent: a promising start in the sixth century, falters later

The dynasty of Aesc, presumed to be a son of Hengest (though if the royal house were Hengest's descendants one wonders why they were not named after this illustrious forebear), ruled in Kent from the fifth to the mid-eighth century. The date of their formal settlement in Thanet – given its location, possibly to oppose a Gallo-Roman attack on their employer Vortigern – is given as 449 by Bede, though archaeological data suggests an earlier 'Germanic' presence.[67] This was the heartland of the 'Saxon Shore', dominated by Late Roman coastal fortresses that have been assumed to be bases for troops and ships to deal with Saxon pirates in the Channel.

But were there Saxon settlers here too – 'federate' troops serving the short-staffed Late Roman army? The archaeology suggests scattered – decentralized – settlements using Germanic goods in the early fifth century, rather than one coherent kingdom set up in a defensible unit by 'Hengest'. The Welsh and Saxon legends of the kingdom ('Nennius' c.830 for the Welsh, and Bede c.730 and the *Anglo-Saxon Chronicle* c.880 for the Saxons) agree that the conquest was carried out by Hengest with a long war against his British employers, Vortigern and his son Vortimer.

But modern scholars are more sceptical, given the similarity of some details to those in other Germanic sagas, and it is suggested that both Welsh and Saxon stories derive from a single, post-fifth century 'original' version (probably Kentish) and cannot be used to corroborate each other.[68] Hengest was supposed to have died in 488 after a forty-year rule according to the *Chronicle*, but little is known of his successor, Aesc, and nothing is known of Kentish history from c.500 until the time of Aethelbert in the 590s.

Possibly the kingship lapsed as politically unnecessary in a time of peace, and it is not even clear when Aethelbert assumed power as one version of events gives him a fifty-six-year reign (560–616/17) but the Frankish historian Gregory of Tours only refers to him as the son of a Kentish king, not as the king, c.580.[69]

What is notable is that the prominence given to Hengest as the first Germanic conqueror in Britain by 'Nennius' and the *Anglo-Saxon Chronicle* – the English equivalent of Clovis, though a 'pagan' – did not lead to him establishing a large kingdom and/or a nationally successful dynasty like Clovis did. His lands did not extend beyond Kent as far as is known, and it is not even clear that he rather than Aesc founded the Kentish dynasty. The latter was known as the 'Aescings' not the 'Hengestings'. His success was on a smaller, local scale, whether or not his career (or his existence) was exaggerated by later mythographers; his defeat of the elusive 'Vortigern' the Briton was not as epochal as Clovis' defeats of Syagrius, the post-Roman warlord of Soissons, and Alaric II the Visigoth. He did not create a Germanic kingdom of England, and even if the traditional picture is based on fact and his 'revolt' c.450 led to widespread Germanic attacks on the Romano-Britons his resources seem to have been limited. The first Kentish

'Bretwalda', presumably the acknowledged leader of the Southern English warlords, was Aethelbert.

Events of the initial 'conquest era' in Britain were clearly on a smaller scale than on the Continent – and it is unlikely that any leader of the initial Germanic military incursions could have been as successful as Clovis was in Gaul. Even if 'Vortigern' held authority over a wide area – he was traditionally connected to Gloucester and the ancestor of a sub-dynasty in Powys, yet with authority over Kent – removing him did not lead to the fall of all southern Britain. According to the traditional story (written down in the ninth century) his son Vortimer led a British 'fight-back' and drove Hengest out of Kent on one occasion, then died – and some such resistance could be expected. Probably more martial 'Celtic' traditions had survived in Roman Britain, where the building of typically 'Roman' stone-built mansions in the countryside by a 'Romanized' aristocracy was restricted to the south and east, than in Gaul.

The more upland and less urbanized north-western half of Roman Britain, a separate province from the 210s onwards, was probably less 'Romanized' and retained more of its pre-Roman lifestyles and loyalties – and hence possibly was able to muster more effective warriors after the end of Roman rule. The nature and culture of the local aristocracy as well as the geography may have aided its resistance to post-450 'Germanization'.

Possibly involved in a battle against the expanding power of Ceawlin of the West Saxons at 'Wibbandun' (Wimbledon?) c.568, Aethelbert had some sort of ascendancy over his neighbours in the Thames basin by around 600 and was powerful enough to be known by Bede's time as 'Bretwalda'.[70] Advantages may have accrued from a close cultural and political link with the Frankish kingdom, testified to by archaeological discoveries of Frankish goods in his territories, and his Frankish marriage had brought him a Catholic wife and her chaplain (Liudhard) before the arrival of the missionaries from Rome in 597.[71] His political alliance with St Augustine's mission placed him among the 'civilized' Continental monarchs aligned to Rome, led by the Frankish kings. It brought him the added bonus of the Church relying on royal power and preaching support for a godly king. He also created the first English law code, where the king asserted his power over the localities as guarantor of order and justice and in return could levy fines on malefactors.

The importance of an ex-Roman urban settlement, Canterbury, as Aethelbert's principal residence as well as the new Christian see shows that the King sought to portray himself in Continental terms as a respectable post-Roman ruler, rather than as an uncivilized invader living in isolated rural halls. But it is noticeable that the success Aethelbert had achieved did not make his emergent 'Great Power' a long-term success like Aethelfrith and Edwin's Northumbria or the Francian kingdom of Clovis. He was to be the only 'Bretwalda' of his dynasty, though the latter continued in a stable 'father-son' descent' through the seventh century and survived Mercian assault in the mid-670s.

Ironically, Aethelbert's son Eadbald even contemplated abandoning Christianity on his accession in 616/17; the new archbishop was supposed by Bede to have considered giving up the mission and fleeing but had been scared out of doing so by a visitation from a furious angel. Had Eadbald gone ahead rather than deciding to stay Christian, the kingdom would have had to be re-converted later as 'lapsed' Essex was – from Northumbria? Kent only fell into chaos in the mid-680s (when Caedwalla of Wessex and an Essex ruler each secured temporary control), and then was able to reassert its independence under the rightful heir Wihtred within a few years. The main reason for its failure to continue to overawe its neighbours probably lies in its geography – once it had lost control of the lower Thames basin or Essex it lacked resources. Notably the next major ruler of south-eastern England after Aethelbert's death in 616/17 was Raedwald of East Anglia, not his own son Eadbald; probably the East Anglians had more vassal-rulers and better military leadership.

Bede and the *Chronicle* do not record Eadbald fighting any major wars, so it is probable that Raedwald 'blooded' his military machine in defeating Aethelfrith of Northumbria in 617 and thereafter attracted more local support. Unlike East Anglia, Kent lacked a major regional foe in the 610s – and the concomitant useful military experience for its army.

(d) Other kingdoms: two minor powers, and a temporary success by Wessex in the later sixth century

The small kingdom of Essex, ruled c.600 by Aethelbert's brother-in-law Sledda, never achieved any power outside its own borders despite its possession of the declining town of London, except probably in Middlesex. It may have owned the principal city of southern Roman Britain and thus secured dues from its trade, but this was at nothing like the level of earlier trade and it is not clear exactly what population sixth and seventh century London – a town in steep decline? – possessed. (Some archaeologists have alleged the walled city was abandoned, with a small town at the 'Aldwych' – 'Old Settlement'.) Even if Essex had control over Surrey or the lower Thames this only made it a minor state with few resources. Its only known military success in this period was a brief intervention in disordered Kent around 690.

It was frequently divided among several kings in the seventh century, and saw a succession of Christian and pagan rulers until the 670s, which suggests an inability to complete the conversion as smoothly as in other kingdoms. As the principal see of southern Britain had remained at Canterbury, it lacked the archbishopric that Pope Gregory had intended for it in 597. The three sons of Saebert, who succeeded jointly in c.616, and Kings Sigehere and Saebbi after 663 seem to have been of equal status; the first trio acted jointly to drive out Bishop Mellitus and return to paganism but in the second case one king was pagan, one Christian. Sometimes one king seems to have been senior, at least in terms of military activity where Sigehere took the lead; but in this case Saebbi was a more pacific, holy character who was disinclined for warfare anyway.[72] There was another double kingship after the holy young King Offa abdicated to go to Rome as a pilgrim in 709. The royal genealogy of Essex is as complex as that of Wessex, with notable non-direct successions that logically reflect a rotation or seizure of the kingship by rival lines of descent. It may similarly reflect a 'decentralized' political structure with the kingdom divided among the ruling kindred. Whether each king ruled a separate area is unknown.

The temporary military/political ascendancy of the founder of Sussex, Aelle, c.500, can be assumed from his ranking as a 'Bretwalda' and the West Saxons preserved the basic record of his military triumphs (from his landing in 477 to his conquest of the Roman 'Saxon Shore fortress of Pevensey in 491) in their *Chronicle*.[73] But any leadership he had achieved among south coast settlers was not inherited by his (unknown) successors, and the kingdom had to wait for Christianization until a chance stay there by the exiled Northumbrian bishop Wilfred in the 670s. (The isolation imposed by the Weald probably hindered Sussex's ability to expand.) In the 680s Sussex was a prey for the aggressive young West Saxon king, Caedwalla, who intriguingly had a Celtic name, and in the 700s its rulers declined into sub-kings and 'ealdormen' under the control of Mercia. Geographically, Sussex was as disadvantaged as Kent by its isolation – the Weald inhibited easy movement of armies except on the Downs, and there was only one really fertile strip of coastal plain to achieve a high density of settlement. The emergence of Wessex prevented any post-Aelle kings from adding the resources of Hampshire to its power, although it seems that in the late 660s king Aethelwalh was thrown a 'lifeline' by Mercia when King Wulfhere handed him control of the Meon valley and the Isle of Wight.

Building up Sussex at Wessex's expense was to Mercia's advantage, and Wulfhere was able to campaign in the region and so outmatch Wessex's military power. Sussex could thus have re-emerged as a regional power by courtesy of Mercia, but the revival of Wessex under Centwine and Caedwalla after c.680 ended this possibility. Had Wessex not recovered, then the internal crisis in Kent in the mid-680s could have benefited Sussex not

Wessex and enabled Aethelwalh or his successors rather than Caedwalla to take over Kent.

In the south-west a mixture of Saxon and Jutish settlements and neighbouring British kingdoms were combined into the 'West Saxon' kingdom by the warlord Ceawlin in the 570s and 580s; the archaeology does not suggest any substantial Saxon presence in Hampshire, the supposed base of his dynasty's power from his 'grandfather' Cerdic's time. He may have ruled from the upper Thames valley, where there was more Saxon settlement, or have come from a mainly British and Jutish realm in the South to take over the area. The conquest of Wiltshire is supposed to have occurred in the 550s, moving from south (Old Sarum, 552) to north (Barbury Castle, 556) which suggests an advance from Hampshire.[74] Ceawlin's power extended at least to the Cotswolds and possibly to the Severn valley after his defeat of three British kings at 'Deorham' (possibly Dyrham near Bath) and conquest of Bath, Cirencester and Gloucester c.577. Supposedly acting in alliance with the Saxons who had moved into Buckinghamshire via the Icknield Way under 'Cutha' or 'Cuthwulf', he was probably lord of the Thames valley as well as the central southern counties of England but suffered some sort of military reverse in Oxfordshire c.584. He was driven out of his kingdom by his rebel nephews in 592. Given that his nephew and successor, Ceol, was supposed to have reigned for six years up to 597, the latter either became his accepted co-ruler or seized power in 591 – a sign of impatience by the younger generation with a power-hoarding warlord? The apparent death of Ceawlin's 'son' Cuthwulf, not a king as recorded by the Chronicle genealogies, before his father (in battle?) may indicate an unexpected dynastic setback for Ceawlin.[75] What if his son had lived to succeed him and avert a rebellion in 592 – would Wessex have survived into the seventh century as a major power or broken up in a reaction to Ceawlin's exhaustive use of its manpower on warfare?

The kingdom of the 'Gewissae' then declined under a multiplicity of rulers in the seventh century, with King Cynegils (c.611–43) leading in war with a co-ruler called Cwichelm who did not succeed him. It had many men of royal rank, possibly ruling the later 'counties', and appears from one source to have had no formal 'king' for ten years up to c.683.[76] But there is a major problem with the written history of this state – known as that of the 'Gewissae' rather than as 'West Saxon' until c.680 so possibly originally a multi-racial kingdom named after its dynasty not its people. (The name is of unknown origin, but a link with the south-east Wales kingdom of Gwent has been suggested.[77]) The *Anglo-Saxon Chronicle*'s account of the early years of the kingdom in Hampshire under the 'founder' Cerdic is at variance with the archaeological record, which has the main local Saxon presence in the upper

Thames valley. Cerdic had been given a respectable Saxon pedigree as a descendant of the divine progenitor of Saxon kingship, the god Woden, by the ninth century but had a Celtic name. Accordingly, it is possible that his father, 'Elesa' (or his mother) was a Briton, and that the lack of fifth and sixth century Saxon finds in the area where he landed – probably Southampton Water – reflect his rule over Britons and the New Forest Jutes of 'Ytene'. The basic record in the *Chronicle* is confused, as it has him founding the kingdom twice and ruling for forty years like Hengest, and duplication, legend, and missing details are probable. But it can be assumed that the list of successful battles given to him (in Hampshire) and his successor Cynric (in Wiltshire in the 550s) reflect a dim recall of a gradual military advance Northwards against the British, and that the larger kingdom, from Thames to Selwood, was the creation of three military leaders in the sixth century – Cerdic, Cynric, and Ceawlin.[78] This conquest, as mentioned earlier, did not extend west to include the British of Dorset until after 600, with a victory at 'Beandun' (Bindon, near Wareham or Axmouth) c.614 and one at 'Peonna' (Penselwood near Sherborne) c.658. Probably the sixth century British kingdom of Dumnonia, centred on Devon and Cornwall, served to block major West Saxon success in the south-west – and so reduced Ceawlin's potential acquisition of military resources.

The 'Bretwaldas' – a potential line of permanent 'over-kings'?

In the fluid conditions of sixth to eighth century England, the possibility arose of an outstanding leader from one kingdom imposing his will on his weaker neighbours. The latter's kings would either be retained as dependant kings (or sub-kings) or reduced to governors, the distinction in legal terms being between 'reguli' and 'duces'. Mercia, in particular, was to seek to remove rival royal lines in its dependencies and to call its local governors 'duces' not kings. This appears to be deliberate 'centralization', a policy especially followed by Aethelbald and Offa who went as far as to call themselves 'kings of the English' in charters and coinage – first to be diminished were kings within Mercia, in Hwicce (the North Cotswolds) and Magonsaetan (Herefordshire and Shropshire) in the early-mid eighth century, and later that century in dependencies outside Mercia such as Sussex, Kent, and probably East Anglia. But could such a policy ever have led to permanent amalgamation of several kingdoms in a larger state, as occurred in early sixth century Francia with Clovis' unification?

Temporary local supremacies were reckoned by Bede as the overlordship of a succession of 'Bretwaldas' ('wide rulers'?). They included that of Aelle of Sussex around 500, Ceawlin of Wessex from c.575 to 592, Aethelbert of

Kent[79] (c.592 to 616/17), and Raedwald of East Anglia (c.617 to 625). But they did not last. The small size of the kingdoms of these men suggests a personal ascendancy over weaker neighbours by one energetic king. Indeed, Bede's list of those Anglo-Saxon kings to c.700 who achieved a degree of 'national' recognition across the English states as leaders – the mysterious 'Bretwaldas' – includes kings from many kingdoms. The first is Aelle of the small South Saxon state c.500, a leader whose claim to fame must have relied on war-leadership given the size and lack of resources of his isolated kingdom; his successors are Ceawlin, Aethelbert, Raedwald, and Edwin, Oswald, and Oswy of Northumbria. The cleric Bede notably leaves out the pagan Penda though his power in the south seems to have been greater than the Northumbrian kings' in the early 650s and he could lead thirty sub-rulers to his final battle in 655.

After the death of Oswy in 670 his son Ecgfrith was supreme north of the Humber (also defeating the Picts for control as far north as Fife until 685) while the Mercian kings Wulfhere and Aethelred were powerful south of the river, the two evenly-matched states fighting a drawn battle in 679.[80] But the decline of Northumbria into civil war and rounds of usurpations as the Bernician dynasty died out in the 720s left 'national' supremacy with Mercia under Aethelbald and Offa 'the Great' (716–96). The length of their reigns – forty-one and thirty-nine years respectively – must have been as valuable to Mercian control of their neighbours as was the possession of a strategically crucial central kingdom with large resources. By contrast, only Eadbert of Northumbria (737–58) had a long reign punctuated by notable military successes – and once he died his son Oswulf was soon overthrown. By the 790s Alcuin was lamenting the moral decline and vicious amorality of the kingdom's 'leadership class' and blaming the Viking attack on Lindisfarne in 793 on divine wrath at such backsliding.

Offa was to claim to be king of the English, incorporate Sussex and attempt to incorporate Kent into his realm, execute the king of East Anglia, and deal on nearly-equal terms with Charlemagne in Francia. He was the most powerful king of the English peoples since the conquest, as well as the most autocratic in dealing with his vassals – which in itself was a warning that his death was likely to cause a reaction and his successors would struggle to hold onto his role. The Mercian state's success was not due to institutional advantages over its rivals, but – as with the earlier 'Bretwaldas' – on a personal ascendancy assisted by a powerful army. It does not seem to have been built on anything more solid than Mercia's size and central position, and even in Offa's lifetime he had to fight the West Saxons without notable success and his scheme for a new English Archbishopric at Lichfield was controversial. He was never an imperial ruler in the manner of Charlemagne on the Continent, more a *primus inter pares*, although his state was powerful enough for his immediate successors to suppress the inevitable post-Offa revolt in Kent and bring its line of independent kings to a final end.[81] His brutal execution of his vassal King Aethelbert of East Anglia near Hereford in 794 remains a mystery, supposed by later legend to be an attempted marital alliance that went wrong but more likely linked to suspected disloyalty.[82] But the unusual fact of an over-king suddenly arresting and killing a vassal in peacetime – which clearly made the victim regarded as a martyr – shows Offa's counter-productive brutality and desire to terrorize his sub-rulers. The execution of Aethelbert and the repeated attacks on Kent suggest a reliance on naked force by Offa, and the apparent fondness for poisoning rivals by his daughter, the loathed Queen Eadburh of Wessex, may hint at a family tradition of unscrupulousness.[83]

Offa's plans were frustrated. His son, Ecgfrith, died soon after him, ending his dynasty, and after a revival of Mercian power in the 800s by his cousins Coenwulf and Coelwulf leadership passed to Wessex under Egbert (802–39).

The question arises of why Coenwulf seems to have taken no action to keep his son Coenhelm (St Kenelm) safe from dynastic rivals and so to secure his dynasty – the boy was apparently murdered by retainers of a jealous aunt, according to his hagiography. After Coenwulf died in 821 his brother Ceolwulf staged a major military success against the Welsh but died within two years, and Egbert then defeated the new king of Mercia, Beornwulf, in 825 at Ellandun. The coincidence of this campaign with an anti-Wessex revolt in Cornwall suggests that the Mercians inspired the latter to co-ordinate a joint attack on Egbert but it went wrong. Mercia was routed, and it is possible that the recent wars in Gwynedd had exhausted its manpower and weakened its once-formidable army by 'over-reach' while Egbert had been quietly building up a military machine to challenge them. In 826–7 the Mercians met further humiliation – twice – at the hands of East Anglia, a minor power. Egbert then drove the new Mercian king out of his kingdom temporarily in 829 and marched as far as the Peak District, also taking over the control of sub-kingdoms Kent and Essex from Mercia (and possibly imposing a relative in East Anglia too). Egbert was the first West Saxon leader of the English kingdoms since Ceawlin. But his ascendancy too was temporary, and Mercia regained its independence and could deal with Wessex as an equal ally until the Viking invasions. One sign of Mercian military revival may be that the border-district around Wantage in Berkshire did not pass to Wessex until probably the 840s; as late as 870 the county's 'ealdorman', killed in battle attacking the Vikings at Reading,[84] was of Mercian origin as was shown by his burial in Derbyshire.

The transfer of leadership among the main kingdoms from the sixth century to the 830s shows the fluidity of power in Anglo-Saxon England and the difficulty in any one kingdom – even the largest in resources as specified by the *Tribal Hideage* and the most centrally-placed, Mercia – in maintaining influence over its neighbours. The leadership had included that of smaller kingdoms in the sixth and early seventh century, before Northumbria had achieved its full extent by definitively combining Bernicia and Deira and incorporating the northern British lands from the Mersey and Trent to the Clyde and Forth. This also preceded Mercia's creation in its later form by Penda in the 620s and 630s, as a new state united from a variety of peoples in the Midlands and including the British kingdom of the upper Severn. Penda's powerful kingdom of c.626 to 655, which united the English in Mercia, did not include the enlarged British 'Powys' around Shrewsbury whose ruler, Cyndylan, was remembered in Welsh literature as his ally and brother-in-law. It was broken up after his death in 655 by Oswy; it only permanently reached its full size under his son Wulfhere c.660 and saw successful raids across Wessex (to hand over the Meon valley and the Isle of Wight to Sussex) and into Kent (to sack Rochester).

Until the consolidation of Mercia the smaller kingdoms of the south-east had a greater chance of exerting leadership – Aethelbert of Kent had a degree of influence over his brother-in-law's kingdom of the East Saxons around 600–16, but this would have been likely to be challenged by Mercia had it been powerful. The Kentish king was not powerful enough to annex London to assist the plans of the Catholic mission under Augustine to which he played host from 597, and neither was his successor, Eadbald. London had been the seat of the southern English Christian metropolitanate (archbishopric) under the Romans and as such was Pope Gregory's intended new archbishopric in 597, but the mission to Kent preferred to base themselves permanently at Aethelbert's 'capital', Canterbury, as London was in the territory of the pagan East Saxons. The next 'Bretwaldaship', of the defiantly pagan Raedwald of the East Angles (c.615–25?), was extensive enough to enable him to fight Aethelfrith's Northumbria (successfully) on behalf of the refugee pretender Edwin and install him as its king – and to do so without needing to deal with Mercia first.

Later East Anglia and Northumbria had no common border, so it is implicit that Raedwald's power then extended across the Fens and Lincolnshire towards the Humber – probably involving overlordship of the local 'Gyrwe' and of Lindsey, later clients of Mercia.

Was a 'national' Anglo-Saxon kingdom possible in pre-Viking Britain? Explaining a record of failure

It is possible, but unlikely, that consolidation of several 'peoples' and/or kingdoms into one permanent one could have taken place among the south-eastern kingdoms, particularly Kent or East Anglia, had they had later rulers of the calibre of Aethelbert and Raedwald. Consolidation of multiple post-Roman Germanic states into one kingdom succeeded in Gaul and the Rhineland under the Merovingian dynasty – but why did it not do so in England?

The record of continuity of leadership among Anglo-Saxon kingdoms is not impressive. Aelle was the only 'bretwalda' – if he ever held that honour in contemporary terminology – from Sussex , whether or not his dynasty's power was sapped by the rise of Wessex to the west and Kent to the east. Ceawlin's powerful state of the 'Gewissae' (or West Saxons) apparently collapsed after his expulsion in a revolt in 592, as seen by its limited military record thereafter. Kent was the leading power south of the Humber under Aethelbert from c.592 to 616, though its 'reach' is uncertain – it probably dominated the peoples of the lower Thames, such as the Middle Saxons, but never formally annexed the leading local settlement of London. Aethelbert seems to have been respected or feared enough to ensure a safe passage through southern England to the Severn valley for St Augustine on his journey to meet the Welsh bishops, traditionally at Aust near Bristol, c.604. Canterbury, probably remaining a rare urban centre in Britain from Roman to Saxon times, was adopted as Aethelbert's principal residence and the site of his new Roman Catholic allies' first see – the first 'capital' in post-Roman England. But Kent never held leadership over other kingdoms again after his death, in contrast to other prestigious royal converts to Christianity such as Clovis' dynasty in Francia, although its dynasty survived in a reasonably coup-free patrilinear descent until the chaos of the 680s.

Aethelbert's son Eadbald conspicuously failed to maintain his father's influence over south-eastern England, though he abandoned his initial reversion from Christianity to paganism – probably drawn by the advantages of Church backing for strong kingship – and under his rule a prestigious marital alliance was formed with distant Northumbria. Militarily, the initiative in the south passed to East Anglia and probably some local vassal-kings transferred their loyalties accordingly. In the mid-670s Kent was under serious threat from Mercia after the death of king Ecgbert, and in the 680s it was temporarily overrun by both Essex (a smaller kingdom) and Wessex (a distant one). Nor did East Anglia maintain its supremacy of the late 610s to early 620s, when Raedwald the 'bretwalda' had managed to defeat Aethelfrith of Northumbria, greatest warlord of the north.

Raedwald restored the exiled Edwin of Deira to power and probably regained Lindsey from Northumbria as the price of his aid, yet his power was ephemeral too. His son Eorpwald, converting to Christianity, was promptly murdered – a sign that the East Anglian dynasty had less power to enforce unpopular changes of religion than those of Edwin or Clovis. Within a decade or two of Raedwald's death c.625 his successors were vassals of Penda of Mercia; one (Christian) king, Anna, was driven out of his lands by (pagan) Penda c.649 and his brother and successor Aethelhere fell at the battle of Winwaed as a Mercian vassal (655). In the cases of Sussex, Kent, and East Anglia, although the concentration of early settlers in their areas would have given them an advantage in numbers the emergence of Mercia and Wessex to their west in the seventh century limited the ambitions of their kings – unless a succession of charismatic warrior-kings had been able to absorb the 'border' peoples of the Thames valley and East Midlands into Kent or East Anglia first. The lack of any recorded wars for Kent in the later sixth or early seventh century may be due to loss of evidence not real-life peace, but it is possible that the East Anglians' contrasting position of conflict with Mercia gave their army more experience and attracted ambitious warriors to them. The outstanding example of how military genius and charisma could elevate a minor warlord and eclipsed kingdom to success in a few years is that of Caedwalla of Wessex. Son of a minor ruler within Wessex (identity unclear) and originally operating as a brigand in the western Weald, he rose to conquer Wessex itself in 685, overran the Isle of Wight and eliminated its dynasty, and then used his military machine to overrun Sussex and Kent in 685–6. As brutal as Aethelfrith or Penda but having invaluable support from the powerful Bishop Wilfred (currently in exile from Northumbria for annoying King Ecgfrith), he was halted by a mixture of revolt in Kent and a crippling war-injury. He ended up by abdicating and then dying on a pilgrimage to Rome, aged at most thirty, and left no heirs.[85] But he showed what could be achieved by energy and military competence in an era of fluid power and allegiances.

Geography was crucial. It should be remembered that the England of the sixth and seventh centuries was reliant on a surviving network of Roman roads, not maintained by a single authority since 410 at the latest, and the movement of troops (or traders) was restricted. Nor could kings rely on 'professional' armies who campaigned all year round, except perhaps those bodyguards of their household based at the court who did not spend part of the year on their estates. Quite apart from the difficulties of campaigning in winter, if all kingdoms were like Wessex (whose military structure is known) the royal army was an annual 'levy' of adult males called out for a limited period for a specific purpose. The warrior-class were landholders and their tenants, based on their estates, and the rest of the year was spent farming. The sowing and the harvest had to be considered or the populace would starve – and one advantage the Vikings were able to use in the mid-ninth century was to sit it out inside a fortified camp and wait for their Saxon enemies to have to lift the siege in order to go home for agricultural work.

Geography aided a kingdom based in central England. The limitations of military campaigning by Northumbria into the far south of England restricted its power even under Edwin before the full unification of its southern neighbour, Mercia (c.626), though Oswald of Northumbria had a degree of influence as far south as Wessex whose Christian conversion he assisted in c.635.[86] Logically, Oswald and Cynegils of Wessex had a mutual aim in opposing Penda's Mercia and were natural allies – but Penda was able to defeat both kingdoms separately in the 640s. Thereafter, Mercia blocked Northumbria's southern influence. Even had Oswald not been killed by Penda (Maserfelth/?Oswestry, 642) and Northumbria maintained its military supremacy of the 630s into the 640s, the consolidation of Mercia would have posed problems. Only if Edwin or Oswald had succeeded in killing Penda and breaking up Mercia for a prolonged period would Northumbria have stood a chance of dominating the distant south. After twenty to thirty years of Penda's rule, the Mercian nobility had enough sense of 'national' unity to successfully revolt against the brief ascendancy of Oswy over their leaderless state in 655–8.[87] It is possible that the destruction of Edwin's army by Cadwallon of Gwynedd in 633/4, which led to the re-emergence of Deira as a separate kingdom from Bernicia, and then Oswald's defeat by Penda at Maserfelth in 642 caused major losses to the Northumbrian army and thus dealt a crucial blow to Northumbria's unity and manpower, which gave Penda a military advantage.

Chapter Two

The Post-Roman British Kingdoms

Was a 'Celtic' British resurgence possible?

(a) The era of conquest – fifth and sixth centuries. Our limited evidence

The nature of the evidence for the period of settlement is limited, and this presents problems for considering any alternative scenarios. The basic facts are in dispute, with the archaeological record at odds with the written evidence – almost all of which is from a later date and thus open to mythologizing. Apart from a few scattered references in the fifth century *Gallic Chronicle* – which has Britain passing into Saxon hands in 441/2 – and a reference to surviving but threatened Romano-British cities in c.428 in the *Life of St Germanus*, the nearest written source is the *De Excidio Britanniae* of Gildas in c.540.[1] That monkish writer, later remembered in hagiography as the son of a tribal chieftain (of Strathclyde?) called Caw, was writing a polemic against the sins of his British contemporaries and their deserved punishment, and seems to have seen himself as a condemnatory prophet of doom in the manner of the Old Testament Jeremiah. He was not composing a history but an attack on his fellow Britons and so would be bound to exaggerate their failings and disasters, and indeed where his 'facts' can be checked they are often wrong. His knowledge of the Roman period is hazy; he believes that the Romans had to withdraw due to frequent British revolts, and he ascribes a non-existent 'Wall' in western Britain to Emperor Septimius Severus.

Gildas' apocalyptic account of fifth century events has the deserted Britons of c.410 rallying to drive back the first wave of Saxon attacks, which is in tune with other evidence, but a period of prosperity ending when King 'Vortigern' (a British title, probably 'over-king', not a name) called in Hengest's Saxon mercenaries to fight the raiding Picts and Irish. The mercenaries revolted and ravaged the island 'from sea to sea', a disaster that encompassed all its towns and left an abandoned countryside; many people found their only refuge in the bellies of wild beasts. The survivors then rallied under Ambrosius Aurelianus, a gentleman of noble Roman birth, who led a fight-back that ended with the famous victory over the Saxons at 'Mount Badon' (dated at 516/18 by the tenth century Cambrian Annals). A second period of peace followed, possibly involving a formal division of the island with the remaining Saxons, which left some important Christian shrines (St Albans?) in Saxon hands; this implies a treaty setting geographical frontiers (or 'zones of influence') between leaders able to enforce it. Were these men Ambrosius or the elusive 'Arthur' on the British side and Aelle of the South Saxons and Aesc of Kent – the dynasts of this era in the *Anglo-Saxon Chronicle* – on the Saxon side?

By Gildas' time the Britons were quarrelling again and were ruled by oppressive and extortionate 'tyranni' (probably meaning legally illegitimate rulers, self-appointed military leaders and 'kings' rather than the civilian governors of Roman Britain). The five rulers who Gildas names all seem to have ruled in western Britain, and included 'Maglocunus' i.e. Maelgwyn of Gwynedd, Cuneglasus/Cynglas of Clywd, Vortipor of Dyfed, Aurelius 'Caninus' (Conan?) of Gloucester(?), and Constantine of Dumnonia. Gildas accuses Maelgwyn, greatest in talent but also in evil, of murdering his uncle for the throne and then killing his nephew to take over the latter's wife, plus possibly being homosexual; Constantine had murdered two boy rivals for his throne by sneaking into a church where they were taking sanctuary disguised as an abbot. Aurelius was possibly, given his name, a descendant of Ambrosius Aurelianus; the latter had left descendants who had fallen off from his good qualities.[2] (The existence and approximate dates of Maelgwyn, Vortipor, and Constantine are known from other evidence.) Disaster duly followed with a massive loss of life in the 'Yellow Plague', dated to c.547/9 by the contemporary Irish annals, and in the later sixth century the Saxon advance resumed.

This basic story was in agreement with the Saxon memories used by Bede in the early 730s, with an initial Saxon revolt and rebellion leading to successes that the British halted by a successful campaign in the later fifth and early sixth centuries; he dated Hengest's arrival at 449.[3] Later embellishments by Welsh writers, most notably the Gwynedd bishop 'Nennius' in the 820s, brought in a British campaign of twelve battles leading up to Mount Badon, with the British general being a war-leader of a coalition of kings named 'Arthur' – who Gildas does not mention, except possibly obliquely.[4]

It has been pointed out that 'Nennius' had a contemporary agenda, namely rallying his British countrymen to support a 'fight-back' similar to

Arthur's under the leadership of his employer King Merfyn of Gwynedd, so he had as much reason as Gildas to create a useful myth glorifying the British war effort and building up the mysterious 'Arthur' as a template of leadership. For that matter, Arthur might have been called *dux bellorum* (leader in battles) by 'Nennius' as this was his exemplar Joshua's title in the Old Testament, not because he held this specific office.

Joshua fought twelve battles to conquer Israel – was this why that number had been ascribed to Arthur too?[5] The ninth century West Saxon literary account of their origins, the *Anglo-Saxon Chronicle* (probably written at King Alfred's court), had similar value as 'nationalist' propaganda at a time of Viking attack. It presented a story of gradual West Saxon advance through southern England from the landing of their dynastic founder 'Cerdic' c.495 but notably did not have any major Saxon successes during the 'Arthurian' period in the early-mid sixth century.[6] Its details are almost exclusively southern English for the sixth century, concentrated on Wessex and Kent with a little on the early years of Sussex. But as Aelle of the South Saxons was included in Bede's list of 'Bretwaldas' he must have led a coalition of rulers, presumably in battle against the British, and he would have been contemporary with the Saxon defeat at Mount Badon. (Possibly the editors of the *Chronicle* excised all references to Saxon defeats as politically undesirable.) It is only with the mid-tenth century *Cambrian Annals* – composed at national reunifier King Hywel 'Dda's court in Dyfed – that the dates are set for 'Arthur's success at Badon and death twenty-one years later in battle with Medraut at 'Camlann'.[7] Even so, these so-called 'Welsh' annals included very little detail on other sixth century Welsh rulers and relied heavily on Irish monastic sources.

The literary legend of a fifth century 'High Kingdom' of Britain, governed from c.410 by 'Constantine', the usurper Vortigern, Constantine's sons Ambrosius and Uther Pendragon, and Arthur, was duly turned into terminology suitable for the expanding Anglo-Norman realm by Geoffrey of Monmouth in the 1130s.[8] After this, any serious 'history' of the post-Roman period was replaced with the literary myth of King Arthur and his knights.

Unfortunately, the archaeological record is at odds with this story. There is no evidence of systematic destruction of Romano-British cities by invaders in the fifth century; most buildings seem to have been abandoned to fall into decay not sacked, the few fires that occurred (as with countryside villas) may have been due to natural causes not hordes of invaders, and there are tell-tale piles of bodies only in a few East Coast towns and isolated Yorkshire signal-stations.[9] Some western cities, such as Viroconium, seem to have had building-work (though in wood not stone) into the sixth century.[10] The use of wood suggests that access to quarries and the availability of skilled stonemasons were limited, but the size of the new hall erected in the old forum at Viroconium shows the pretensions of and number of men available to the builder. A concentration of population and resources under 'central' authority thus continued in the west, but without access to the skills of Roman stonemasons.

In some places in the south-east, Saxon-style buildings appear at Late Roman farm sites with no evidence of a break in occupation in between. The nearness of finds of 'Saxon' artefacts, clearly of Continental not Romano-British origin from their styles, in graves to inhabited Romano-British towns in early fifth century south-east Britain suggests that the inhabitants moved in by arrangement with the towns' residents – possibly as mercenaries, possibly as traders or farm-workers.[11] It is now claimed that these 'Germanic' items might have been imported peacefully by trade for use by native Britons after trade with the Roman Empire collapsed, and they are not even a sign of indisputably 'German' owners – only of a change in 'fashion'.[12] This is less likely than a new body of residents from Germany – if it was a change in 'fashion' that brought in Saxon artefacts, why are these not found inside towns? And if the inhabitants were still genetically and culturally British, why did their names change to Germanic ones and their Church decline dramatically by St Augustine's arrival c.600? In a parallel case, the post-Roman aristocracy, its Church, and its cultural identity survived in central and southern Gaul under Germanic rule – though greater Germanic settlement in the (less urbanized) north of Gaul led to its linguistic transformation into a 'Frankish' region.

Valuable work on the ecology of the field-networks of post-Roman Britain has shown no evidence of farmland being abandoned to scrub in the fifth or sixth century as Gildas insists was the norm across Saxon-ravaged Britain. The usual plants that would have grown in abandoned fields do not appear; land seems to have been in use without a break from the Late Roman systems into Saxon times.[13] Some farms showed signs of the existing boundaries of Roman estates continuing in use by the presumed 'new arrivals' – who thus did not have to create new farms in a wasteland.[14] This, and the lack of evidence of destruction, gives us serious doubts about the veracity of Gildas' sweeping claims of disaster. He need not have invented his account, but it was clearly over-simplified for dramatic and polemical effects. Writing around ninety years after the main Saxon 'revolt' and ravages of c.440–50, he may have relied on mostly oral memories from the children of survivors; his exact geographical location is unclear though his family had Strathclyde links and he may have died in Brittany. By eleventh century hagiography he was linked to Glastonbury, but this may have been later annexation of his fame by ambitious monastic writers.

'High Kings'?

With all this in mind, we cannot use the existing sources as evidence of a fifth century Romano-British 'High Kingdom' under a verifiable dynasty of rulers that could have driven back, or contained, Anglo-Saxon settlement. The five provinces of Late Roman Britain had had a unified military force under a 'Count of Britain'[15] according to the contemporary bureaucratic record, the *Notitia Dignitatum*, and some historians have claimed that the post-Roman cities and rural districts could have used this sort of military force to unify their armies.[16] If Britain was governed in the same manner as fifth century Gaul – another patchwork of administrative districts created by Rome out of old 'tribal' territories – there could even have been a 'national' council of senior nobles delegated by the various provinces, meeting (occasionally?) as one body. (The Gallic council met at Arles.) This could have been the shadowy 'council' ascribed by later writers as assisting 'Vortigern' – and it could have employed military leaders, logically post-Roman military commanders from those troops still in Britain and/or local warlords. The obvious men to step into the gap left by the end of the Roman military administration – probably when rebel emperor Constantine III took the army to Gaul in 407 – were local nobles, who could command their juniors' loyalty. Some could even have derived legitimacy from personal links to the old pre-Roman royal tribal dynasties, assuming that family pride and genealogical interests had been kept up; logically those tribal notables who submitted to Rome in the first century AD would have been able to pass on estates to their descendants for generations.

Thus the mysterious 'Constantine' who was later claimed as 'High King' after the Roman withdrawal, being called in from the expatriate British settlements in Armorica, might have been a military commander – Count of Britain? – of noble birth. He could have been connected to the British leadership of the emigration to settle Armorica in the 380s as one story claimed (as the grandson of a South Wales noble, 'Eudaf Hen'?), or even have been the son of the later fourth century Emperor Magnus Maximus as in later legend.[17] (The abandonment of coinage and lack of inscriptions or surviving books means that there is no contemporary proof of his existence.)

Vortigern, later presented as Maximus' son-in-law and founder of the post-Roman tribal kingdom of Powys,[18] could have succeeded to his power over the disparate post-Roman provinces and emerging British kingdoms and called in Saxon mercenaries as 'federates', giving them land in return – a normal Late Roman practice. The legendary linkage of his family to Gloucester – the Roman city whose dependant rural district, 'pagus', formed the nucleus of Powys, which he supposedly ruled – could have been accurate. Similarly, he could have felt insecure due to his dubious 'right' to govern and preferred to rely on foreign troops to using those of potentially rebellious British nobles. By the ninth century he was presumed to have been the enemy of 'Ambrosius', who from his name and from Gildas' account of his noble Roman identity would have represented a 'pro-Roman' faction. Possibly the revival of central Roman governmental control in Gaul in the late 410s and 420s would lead to Vortigern fearing, and Ambrosius' faction hoping for, this outcome in Britain too. Vortigern would thus bring in more German troops to defend himself, as in the story of Hengest – but for local political reasons, not from being 'duped' by a cunning Jute as was later supposed. The mercenaries' revolt and a British 'fight-back' are logical results, and Gildas' account of the British use of hill forts as military bases in this campaign is backed up by archaeology – most notably at Cadbury Castle in Somerset, later associated with King Arthur.[19] The attribution is first attested as late as 1540, but the name of the site – 'Cado's Burgh' – links it to the then current king of British Dumnonia c.500, Cador, father of Gildas' King Constantine and thus the local warlord.

The later accounts from Gildas' time agree that Ambrosius Aurelianus, of Roman noble descent, led the successful British campaign and the invaders could only hold onto Kent. Ambrosius, according to Gildas of 'purple' (Imperial or consular?) blood,[20] which might refer to the legendary descent from Maximus, could have been the first great British commander. Place names with an 'Ambres' element in southern Britain, most notably Amesbury where Geoffrey said he buried the victims of a Saxon massacre of British nobles at Stonehenge, could be linked to his campaigns. Could 'Amber'-named settlements in West Sussex have been established to check Aelle of the South Saxons, and in eastern Oxfordshire to check the Saxons of the middle Thames valley? The British army could indeed have been made up of the forces of rival kingdoms in temporary unity under a 'national leader, as stated by 'Nennius', and Ambrosius' successor as commander could have been 'Arthur' – a 'Celtic' name linked to that for 'Bear'. The emergence of a number of men with this unusual name in the sixth and seventh centuries could suggest a subsequent tradition of kings and nobles naming their sons after a great war-leader of famous memory, and by c.600 the poem *Gododdin* refers to him as a warrior worthy of emulation. Similarly, Gildas refers to Cynglas as 'charioteer of the Bear's fortress'[21] – probably the Clywd hillfort of Dinarth, but a place possibly named after a warlord called 'The Bear', which British word is close to the etymological root of 'Arthur'. The fact that Gildas does not mention Arthur directly adds to the enthusiasm of modern sceptics for declaring that 'Arthur' never existed and that his 'list of battles' in 'Nennius' were mythological or collected from the victories of several men, principally Ambrosius. The latest theory is that

Ambrosius not only commenced the British 'fight-back', which Gildas states, but that he completed it successfully at the elusive 'Battle of Mount Badon' too.[22]

Logically, a successful British army in the fifth century could have continued to use cavalry – part of the Late Roman military forces – against Saxon infantry to devastating effect, and the wide-ranging locations for the elusive 'Twelve Battles' across Britain of 'Nennius' mean that the British army used the still-extant Roman roads to campaign across Britain. The successful war-leader could then have imposed peace between British and Saxons for a generation as implied by Gildas, whose account of his own era concentrates on misrule and civil wars not on external warfare, and the Saxon advance resumed after 'Arthur' was killed in an inter-British war with 'Medraut' and the British lost much of their manpower in the plague of the late 540s.

John Morris' seminal *Age of Arthur* even presented the victorious warlord as a sort of British 'emperor' and national overlord, as recalled in mediaeval Welsh legends, but this is far more contentious.[23] Sceptics would prefer to allege that Arthur never existed, or at best was a successful local commander whose renown led to him being taken up by later propagandists. Some sort of check to the Saxon advance seems to have been achieved around 500, and there is every probability that a major British victory at 'Badon' was the cause of this. But this was later used as the template for enthusiastic Welsh literary portrayals of a 'fight-back' in the early ninth century, intended to inspire contemporaries and so propaganda rather than an 'objective' account of earlier events.

The text of Gildas makes it clear that the British had success in their later fifth century 'fight-back', which culminated at Mount Badon, though the date of the latter was only stated in the tenth centrury *Cambrian Annals* compiled at the court of national leader King Hywel 'Dda' ('the Good') of Dyfed. The date of Badon is given there as 516/18; and twenty-one years later 'Arthur and Medraut fell' (presumably on opposing sides, as in literary legend) at the battle of 'Camlann'.[24] The *Annals* (compiled at St David's in Dyfed) are contentious as evidence, as most of their – scant – data for the sixth century has been copied from Irish sources and the only secular personnel named are Arthur, Medraut and the mysterious 'Merlin' (more accurately, Myrddin), a prophetic bard and probable 'shaman' who went mad after the internecine North British battle of Arderydd near Carlisle in 573. The site of Badon is as contentious as who won it for the British; depending on etymology and logical military strategy there are potential sites in England, Wales and Scotland though if the British were fighting the southern Saxons a site in the south of England is most probable.

Little Solsbury Hill near Bath (a town known as 'Baddon' to the early Welsh), Liddington Castle hillfort near 'Badbury' close to Swindon, and Badbury Rings in Dorset have all been suggested and are possible from a military point of view.[25] (Geoffrey of Monmouth, on uncertain evidence, chose Bath.) Wherever the battle took place and however much Gildas exaggerated the resultant peace and subsequent return to British civil war by the next generation,[26] some sort of British triumph or military stalemate is probable and the *Anglo-Saxon Chronicle*'s list of early sixth century victories for its heroes, Cerdic and his heirs, halts for a generation from c.530.

It is logical to ask if this state of affairs could have continued, and the absence of early and mid-sixth century 'Germanic' artefacts in central or western Britain implies a halt to large-scale settlement, which might have continued had the risks of British counter-attack been too great. Possibly the plague of c.547/9 tipped the balance of manpower against the British and emboldened the Saxons; the British had trading-links with the main area of the plague's activity, the Mediterranean basin, whereas the Saxons did not so the latter probably suffered less. The crucial question here is whether a unified British military command could have continued, with a mobile 'striking force' – cavalry or not – outnumbering the smaller armies of each Saxon kingdom as it attempted to expand. Unfortunately, the evidence is too limited to assess if there was more than a temporary British coalition, under Ambrosius and then possibly 'Arthur', and if legend was correct that the latter was unexpectedly brought down by internal treachery led by 'Medraut'. (The poet Taliesin apparently accused Maelgwyn of treachery to the 'race of Arthur', which may imply that he was involved too.[27]) However, Medraut was not Arthur's illegitimate son by his own sister, a twisted character intent on Oedipal revenge as in legend, as this story only appeared in thirteenth century French romances; and the 'Round Table', a brotherhood of knights defending Britain, is a twelfth century literary invention.[28]

The local British kingdoms

It is impossible to say with any certainty that a unified British command in sixth century warfare extended as far as a 'national' civil government under one leader, or that preserving this polity could have kept the Saxons restricted to eastern Britain through the sixth century and later. The (later) evidence of Welsh genealogies, extant as of the early tenth century, would seem to suggest that the 'founders' of most British kingdoms in the uplands of north and western Britain ruled in the first half of the fifth century, with the arrival of Cunedda, a prince of the Votadini in Lothian, in Gwynedd (to drive out the Irish settlers) and the reigns of Vortigern and his humbly-born supplanter Cadell in Powys, the Irish-descended dynasty of the 'Deisi' in Dyfed, Teithfallt and Teithrin in Siluria, Ynyr (Honorius) in Gwent, Constantine and Erbin in Dumnonia, and Coel 'Hen' in the north.[29] Logically, these men stepped into the breach caused by the end of Roman rule. Gildas' fulminations against 'illegitimate' rulers by the 540s may refer to this plethora of new dynasties, set up by opportunistic warlords rather than by established post-Roman civic authorities. As with the Continent, it was individuals with warbands not councils of civic officials and post-Roman landed nobles who acted as the basis of political power and 'state-building' in the fifth and sixth centuries.

Notably, most kingdoms were created within the boundaries of pre-Roman tribal kingdoms – Gwynedd in that of the North Wales Ordovices, Dyfed in that of the south-west Wales Demetae, the northern kingdom(s) around York in Brigantian territory, and the kingdoms of the Silures (Morgannwg) and Dumnonii in their old lands under their pre-Roman tribal names. As in Gaul, the Romans had preserved the names and identities of tribal areas as a basis for sub-provincial political districts; logically the tribal aristocracies would have survived as 'Romanized' landholders. No dynastic lists survive for the lowland area conquered by the Saxons during the sixth and early seventh centuries, which may mean that this area of more 'Romanized' settlement continued under civic magistrates and councils not tribal-based kings. We know from the archaeological evidence that there was a strong post-400 British settlement in Dorset (particularly around Cranborne Chase), yet there is no mention of the pre-Roman tribal grouping of the 'Durotriges' re-emerging. Does this mean that they had no coherent local aristocracy to take on post-Roman leadership, and their region was subsumed into Dumnonia to the west? The scanty Saxon written evidence indicates that any West Saxon conquest in the early sixth century halted at the Hampshire Avon, where 'Cerdic' allegedly fought in the 520s, and that after Old Sarum in Wiltshire fell c.552 the next recorded battle in this region was near Wareham or Axmouth ('Beandun', i.e. Bindon) c.614.

Alternatively, it may be that the Saxon conquest caused the destruction of records and the end of any reason for surviving Britons there to remember their royal lines. The only such ruler known to later Welsh legend by the ninth century was Gwangon, the king of Kent (i.e. the post-Roman tribal administrative district of the 'Cantii'?) evicted by Vortigern to make way for Hengest. Were these post-Roman 'tribal' rulers all overwhelmed by the Germanic revolt of the 440s? It should be noted that in a comparable ex-Roman region, Gaul, there was a 'council' of the senior notables of the Late Roman provinces – the ex-tribal kingdoms of the first century BC – based at Arles. Was the British equivalent the 'council' who legend says Vortigern consulted over inviting in his Germanic mercenaries?

(b) After the main conquests – later sixth and seventh centuries

Gwynedd and Powys

The limitations of geographical 'reach' for a post-Roman campaign and the emergence of Mercia would have limited the possibility of a resurgence by the most powerful British seventh century kingdom, Gwynedd. Permanent power over a kingdom's neighbours was dependent on a mixture of force and deterrence, with the ability for regular campaigning by an active and successful ruler crucial – potential rebels would thus fear punishment by their overlord's large and well-trained armies. This is most visible in the Germanic states, as with the vigorous Penda's creation of a dominant Southumbrian state of Mercia, but applies to Celtic Britain too. The survival of viable Roman roads as a network for campaigning was one major factor; the existence of a tradition of cavalry warfare in post-Roman Britain is less certain but has been suggested as the origin of the myth of Arthur's 'knights'. There had been cavalry units in the Late Roman army in Britain, as seen from the *Notitia Dignitatum*, with Roman military practice including a mobile 'striking-force' under a 'Count', which could move quickly to deal with emergencies. According to one modern theory, the cavalry units on Hadrian's Wall (with local stud-farms) were the basis of the fifth and sixth centuries' military strength of the local successor-kingdoms (e.g. Rheged), and enabled such wide-ranging campaigns as those of Urien in the 580s. Cavalry might also have been used in the south – the allegedly devastating casualties inflicted by 'Arthur' on the Saxons at Mount Badon (960 men in one assault according to 'Nennius') are more explicable if inflicted by British cavalry charging downhill against Saxon infantry.[30] (The sceptics prefer to write the figure off as myth, boosting the prowess of a 'super-hero'.) Could they have been the military basis for a successful British kingdom to continue – or is the (later) genealogical evidence of political fragmentation a warning that the British were too divided?

Either around 400 or 440 (106 or 146 years before the time of Maelgwyn of Gwynedd, fl. 547) the Late Roman allied British state of the 'Votadini' in Lothian was called upon to supply troops for evicting the Irish from North Wales. The later legends claimed that Cunedda (Kenneth) of the Votadini duly moved to Wales with his multitude of 'sons' and reconquered what became the kingdom of Gwynedd (pre-Roman 'Venedotia'), thence the pre-eminent power in North Wales. Despite the small size and mountainous nature of Gwynedd its military prestige was great in the sixth century when Maelgwyn (r. c.520–47/9) was 'Pendragon', a title implying and remembered subsequently as bringing leadership of the British kingdoms of Wales.[31]

It is notable that this leadership rested with largely highland Gwynedd, not with the kingdom of the Silures in the more fertile and prosperous lands of south-east Wales (which by the archaeological record had large Roman estates and villas). Nor did it lie with Powys, which probably included the upper Severn valley and the large sixth century town of Viroconium (Wroxeter). Did this result from Gwynedd having a better martial tradition, arising from the coherent and war-ready nobility of the 'Votadini' who had been brought there in the fifth century to expel the Irish?

Maelgwyn died in the devastating 'Yellow Plague' of around 549, the local extension of the Mediterranean plague of the early 540s. From the Irish literary evidence, it would seem that losses of manpower were large; it may not be coincidence that the next recorded Anglo–Saxon advances are in the 550s.

Plague spread along trade-routes, and we know that the south-western British had extant ports (Tintagel and Bantham) that imported Mediterranean goods in the early sixth century. Possibly the lowland southern British suffered worse than the isolated kingdoms of the hillier north-west, and this encouraged both Saxon attack and the seizure of British leadership by the less-affected states. Gwynedd continued its wide 'reach' under Maelgwyn's successors; his son Rhun was able to march on one occasion as far as York, and on another to Scotland to assist his brother (?) Bridei mac 'Maelchon', king of the Picts. The kingdom then declined under less aggressive kings such as the pacific Cadfan (fl. 620), and the lowland plains and Mon/Anglesey could be temporarily overrun by Edwin of Northumbria in the 620s. It is possible that a series of less militarily active rulers weakened the military 'machine' and/or the bonds of loyalty in the later sixth century, meaning that the exploits of Maelgwyn and Rhun could not be replicated. Alternatively, the geographical isolation of the heartland of Gwynedd – Anglesey/Mon and the nearby coastal plain of Arfon – may well have put it at a disadvantage in combating the expanding power of Northumbria for control of the crucial region around Chester. It was Powys, not Gwynedd, that faced Aethelfrith of Northumbria in the decisive battle there around 616.

Within Wales, the main military power around 600 seems to have been Powys, then including the upper Severn valley; this ended when King Selyf ap Cynan was killed by Aethelfrith of Northumbria at the battle of Chester c.616. The royal line of Powys was traditionally traced back to the humbly-born Cadell, appointed by St Germanus in the early-mid fifth century on the overthrow of either Vortigern or the unknown 'Benli';[32] Vortigern's line still held a region around Builth. Unlike Gwynedd, Powys included agriculturally prosperous areas of the West Midlands and thus had extra resources; it may have been centred around 500 at the town of Viroconium (Wroxeter), which notably had extensive (wooden) building-works recently found by archaeologists. This rare post-Roman construction work argues for the town and its rulers having both wealth and confidence, and being able to command extensive resources. Hopeful 'Arthurians' have noted that Viroconium had a crucial strategic position close to the main Midlands road-network, enabling easy access by armies to areas across Britain – which they argue 'Arthur' could have used for his successful campaigns.[33] One modern theory makes 'Arthur' the ruler of Powys, which the twelfth century story 'The Dream of Rhonabwy' links to him. Was a strong and successful Powys, a mixed mountain and lowland state, a potential centre of British revival had its cohesion and military successes lasted?

Rheged

The main area of activity in the British-Saxon wars of the later sixth century moved to the North of England, at least as preserved by the surviving Welsh literature. Here the main British kingdom was Rheged (Lancashire/ Cumbria?), leader among a group of states whose rulers were recalled in subsequent genealogies as the 'Gwyr ar Gogledd', 'Men of the North'. They were allegedly descended from the fifth century ruler Coel 'Hen', the original 'Old King Cole', who has been suggested as the inheritor of a powerful post-Roman military force of settler-soldiers based around Hadrian's Wall. The genealogies may express political links in dynastic terms, and the kings have been the political heirs not the 'sons' and 'grandsons' of Coel. But in either case the principal state by c.560 was Rheged, whose ruler, Urien ap Cynfarch, was to be celebrated by poets. His ascendancy was seemingly established by a victory over a rival coalition, led by Gwendolleu of Carlisle, at Arderydd (?Arthuret near Carlisle) c.573,[34] where the bard Myrddin – one of the originals behind 'Merlin' – went insane.

Urien then went on to lead the Northern British against Bernicia in the 570s and 580s, as eulogized by the poet Taliesin.

It is possible that if the main successor to Maelgwyn as chief British warlord from c.560 to 589, Urien, had not been murdered by a rival, Morcant of Bryniach, during the siege of Bamburgh he could have destroyed Bernicia in the 590s.[35] Like 'Arthur', he seemingly fell victim to the endemic jealousy of rival princes. He and his son Owain, patron of the poet Llywarch 'Hen', were evidently charismatic leaders able to attract support, good commanders, and had a long-standing and successful army, including the contingents of the remaining North British kingdoms. It is also possible that they owed their power partly to use of cavalry, and that this was a long-term military inheritance of Rheged (and its allies in Lothian to the east) from the cavalry force used by the Late Roman army on Hadrian's Wall. This would have given them an advantage over the Anglian infantry. In any case the heroic *esprit de corps* of the North British warriors is made clear in the *Gododdin*, the contemporary poem of c.600 commemorating the defeat of a picked force of fighters in an attack on the Angles at 'Catraeth' (possibly Catterick).[36] The main problem for long-term success was the fissiparous nature and rival claims to land of the disparate kingdoms, which could break up a coalition.

It would appear that Urien's assassin during the siege of Lindisfarne c.589 was Morcant, a prince of Rheged's rival kingdom Bryniach (Lothian), and it is logical to speculate that the murderer was jealous of the current domination of the North by his rival and/or the danger of Rheged taking 'his' lands. If legend is accurate the same jealousy of success had given the rebel Medraut support against 'Arthur' at Camlann c.539, possibly including Maelgwyn of Gwynedd.

It is unclear to what extent we can trust the later genealogies that present the Northern British kingdoms, the 'Gwyr ar Gogledd', as originating in a large post-Roman polity founded in the fifth century by Coel 'Hen' – probably based on the local frontier troops settled along Hadrian's Wall and the Roman military base at York.

It was supposedly divided up into kingdoms of Rheged (Lancashire and Cumbria), Bryniach (Northumberland), York, and Elmet (south-west Yorkshire) under Coel's descendants, which may only mean a political inheritance by local warlords not a dynastic relationship with the 'founder'. There were other major British kingdoms in Lothian, the tribal land of the Votadini (i.e. 'Gododdin); at Edinburgh (whose lord, Mynyddog, recruited the warriors who were killed at Catraeth); and in Strathclyde. The lack of one British kingdom may well have hampered the locals' ability to fight off the Anglian settlers, meaning that for most of the fifth and sixth century the latter could tackle one British kingdom at a time and thus Bernicia was able to survive in its coastal footholds. Unfortunately, the virtual absence of written evidence gives us no idea if a viable 'military'-based kingship of the North, centred on the troops defending the Wall and possibly based at the major Roman walled towns of Carlisle or York, was a possibility in the fifth century. In Northern Gaul, a coherent military command centred on the former regional army of the Western Empire was created in the mid-450s by Aegidius, ex-lieutenant of the assassinated commander-in-chief Aetius. Centred at Soissons, this passed to his son Syagrius and was destroyed in battle by Clovis in 486. In Illyria, a similar post-Roman military 'kingdom' was held by another regional commander, ex-Emperor Julius Nepos, until he was assassinated in 480. Could the elusive Coel 'Hen' have done something similar – and if he had had only one son would a coherent kingdom have passed to him? The – much later – genealogies of the supposed dynasty are hugely complex, which in itself may hide a fissiparous regional aristocracy or military command which soon fell apart.

The British were more united later under Rheged's leadership, from Urien's defeat of his rival cousin Gwendolleu of Carlisle at Arterydd/Arthuret around 573, until Owain's death in the mid-590s. If they had destroyed the Anglian settlements of Bernicia, as seems to have been within their military capabilities, the kingdom of Northumbria would have been stillborn. At best the smaller Yorkshire kingdom of Deira would have held on to its lands to face a resurgent British power – which would have been no more of an 'ephemeral' over-kingship of disparate peoples than was that created by Aethelfrith and Edwin of Northumbria.

The fissiparous nature of the British kingdoms means that it is unlikely that the resurgent Rheged would have been able to command its allies or have a run of able leaders for long enough to advance into Mercia and drive out those settlers, but Rheged could have united the North of England from Humber to Forth much as Northumbria was able to do. In this case it would have been Anglian York that was the junior kingdom of an 'alien' people absorbed into a British military overlordship, rather than the Celtic kingdoms of Rheged, Bryniach, and Elmet being absorbed into Anglian Northumbria. The British indifference to the conversion of the pagan Angles – unless it was really Bishop Rhun of Rheged not Paulinus of Kent who baptised King Edwin in the mid-620s – would however have put them at a disadvantage in absorbing their clients. The victorious Angles, Christian from the 620s, faced British clients who were already (Celtic) Christians and of the same distinct religious practices as King Oswald's Celtic evangelizers from Dalriada. British warlords of Urien's line, like the real-life warlords of the Bernician dynasty, would have had to struggle to maintain supremacy over their enemies in Mercia and to the north in the Pictish kingdom. But if Rheged had been the pre-eminent power of the North from the 580s onwards and Anglian settlers been absorbed into it, the political 'fault-line' of the Humber would have assumed a cultural as well as political division between the states to the north and the south. The Humber could have been the boundary between 'Celt' and 'Anglo-Saxon', a northern counterpart of the Wye and Dee in Wales.

Cadwallon of Gwynedd 633 – the final British chance?
Equally spectacular, and equally ephemeral, were the achievements of Gwynedd in the period 633–42. The north Welsh 'war-machine' was used

by Rhun's energetic descendant Cadwallon to defeat Northumbria at the height of its power in 633/4, at a time when it had already absorbed the British north of the Humber. Evidently the recent eclipse of Gwynedd's military power under Cadfan had been temporary, and could be reversed by a competent warrior-king. Possibly the defeat of Powys[37] by Aethelfrith at Chester in 616(?) removed his main local rival, causing north-east Wales chieftains to gravitate to Gwynedd instead. But he had Anglian support as well, showing that seventh century wars were not a clear-cut case of 'Saxon versus Briton'.

Aided by Penda's Mercians as well as his own Celtic allies, Cadwallon killed Edwin and ravaged Deira in 633 or 634 , leaving it leaderless and Northumbria broken in two again.[38] The local British kingdoms of Rheged (Lancashire/Cumbria) and Elmet may have risen against Edwin to aid their fellow-Briton or at least become his allies after his triumph, and Cadwallon had no scruples about allying with a pagan (Penda) aganst fellow-Christians, his ravaging of Deira being notorious and possibly aimed at 'ethnic cleansing' it of Angles in an attempt to turn the clock back to the mid-sixth century.

But the ascendancy of Gwynedd in North Britain, allied to Penda, was brief and was halted by Oswald of Bernicia defeating and killing Cadwallon, near Hexham, after which the British permanently lost control east of the Dee. Gwynedd would have needed a succession of strong and lucky kings to have reasserted itself permanently, and would probably have fallen victim in the 640s to the greater resources of lowland manpower available to Penda and his Mercians. The sheer weight of resources by the 640s was in Mercia's favour, Gwynedd being a smaller and less productive (mainly mountain) state even if it could call on residual British manpower within Rheged and Elmet against war-decimated Anglians. The other principal Welsh state, Powys, was an ally of Mercia in the 640s; it is dubious if its poet-heralded warlord Cyndylan of 'Pengwern'[39] would have been a willing long-term ally of Cadwallon. The rivalry between Powys and Gwynedd seems to have been of long-standing, with co-operation between them a rarity. The picture of 'Briton vs Anglo-Saxon' in the seventh century is far too simplistic, given that Cyndylan fought with Penda – whose apparent 'son', founding king Merewalh of 'Magonsaeatan', had a name meaning 'noble Welshman'[40] and possibly a Welsh mother. Similarly, King Cadfael of Gwynedd, usurping successor of Cadwallon, fought for Penda against Northumbria at the battle of Winwaed[41] in 655 – mutual hatred of Northumbria evidently outmatched what we would term 'ethnic solidarity'.

Chapter Three

Which Anglo-Saxon State could have Triumphed Long Term in the Seventh to Ninth Centuries?

Wessex, Mercia, or Northumbria?

Outline of events and problems

The death or defeat in battle of a powerful warlord could destroy his kingdom's supremacy, as with Ceawlin of Wessex c.592 and temporarily with Northumbria as Edwin was killed in 633/4 and Oswald in 642. A wide-ruling king could be succeeded by heirs unable to maintain his power against the rising military might of his neighbours, as was the case with Aethelbert of Kent and Raedwald of East Anglia.

Aethelbert's son, Eadbald, ruled for over twenty years without apparent challenge, but was eclipsed by the dynasts of Northumbria and Mercia; Raedwald's ephemeral successors suffered repeated defeats and usurpations. In the case of Wessex, unity and military power may have ended with the revolt against Ceawlin and it is clear that a run of military success ended with his deposition in 592. A number of (unnamed) kings were killed by Edwin of Northumbria in punishment for an assassination plot in the 620s and Kings Cynegils (c.611–43) and Cenwalh (c.643–5, 647–74) had other co-rulers including the elusive Cwichelm. Cenwalh was even expelled from his throne for three years by Mercia, and the kingship may have lapsed for a decade after his death as Bede claimed. Interestingly, while the West Saxons were militarily inferior to Mercia they still had the resources and willpower to carry on expanding westwards against Dumnonia. They took over Somerset after a victory at Penselwood(?) in 658 and gaining Exeter soon afterwards (as shown by the local Saxon origins of St Boniface). Major victories over the Dumnonians/Cornish followed in 682 and 710. In 686–8 Caedwalla temporarily overran Sussex and Kent to secure all England south of the Thames, a feat only repeated in 825 by Egbert; at the time this ferocious young warrior was a more dynamic leader than the better-resourced Aethelred of Mercia. Did their kings deliberately attempt to overrun their Dumnonian and Kentish rivals to build up resources ahead of a possible military challenge to Mercia? And would a more long-lived Caedwalla (who abdicated and died at thirty) have had the skill to anticipate Egbert's success of 825 in bringing down Mercian power on the battlefield?

The lack of a strong leader and the existence of a multitude of men claiming royal rank seems to have kept Wessex weak for a century after Ceawlin's death until a series of brutal campaigns by the young Caedwalla temporarily gave it supremacy south of the Thames in c.685–8. Its lack of resources compared with the expanding Mercia (as well as a series of prudent rulers?) seem to have kept it from challenging the supremacy of Aethelbald or Offa except at occasional battles. Wessex indeed lost control of the upper Thames valley to Mercia in the 660s and temporarily saw Wulfhere marching to the Solent to detach control of Wight and the Meon valley[1] from it (they were given to Sussex) to weaken it, and even in the early ninth century Egbert seems to have failed to reannex Northern Berkshire from Mercia. It is possible that Ceawlin, who the *Chronicle* presents as campaigning in the upper Thames valley (a major area of Saxon settlement from c.500) and conquering the Cotswolds with a major victory[2] over three British kings at 'Deorham' (?Dyrham near Bath) in 577, was based in the upper Thames rather than further south. The archaeology of the region shows major Saxon settlement in the Thames basin in the sixth century, and minimal settlement in Hampshire. There is also the mystery of 'Cutha', Ceawlin's alleged brother, and his role in conquering the British of the Chilterns c.571 – was this area also part of Ceawlin's kingdom? A line of strong and victorious West Saxon kings could have maintained the kingdom's supremacy in the area.

As lords of the rich Cotswolds and the Thames valley, they rather than Mercia would then have had the minor kingdom of 'Hwicce' (around Winchcombe in Gloucestershire) as their vassals and would have ruled to the Severn. The first West Saxon royal centre of the sixth to early seventh century appears to have been Dorchester-on-Thames, where the first bishopric was situated after conversion c.635; this would have been a more useful residential centre to control this enlarged kingdom than distant Winchester. The hiatus in our knowledge of political allegiances in early southern Mercia to c.620 suggests that it was open to domination by a successful neighbour.

At this period, it appears that Mercia was disunited preceding the rise of Penda (who apparently ruled for about thirty years before he was killed in

655,[3] some of it with his brother Eowa). The line of Mercian kings appears to commence c.589, probably as a union of various disunited peoples under one chosen war-leader – the name of the kingdom, the 'Mark' or 'Frontier', indicates that it was perceived at the time as embattled. The dates of settlement of different regions are unclear and no military records have survived for the sixth century, but archaeology indicates a gradual 'push' westwards from the thickly settled lower Trent valley and the Fenland. The principal British foe would have been Powys, which at the time included the upper Severn valley with its 'capital' at Pengwern (Shrewsbury or the Wrekin hillfort?) and from surviving Welsh poetry had a strong and cohesive military tradition under a series of aggressive rulers. But Mercia's power was limited in the 600s to the 620s – King Ceorl was weak (or timid) enough to obey Aethelfrith's orders to expel Edwin sooner than face invasion by Northumbria c.616 and in 626 Edwin could march across Mercia to attack Wessex unhindered. The limited royal genealogy noticeably excludes Ceorl, indicating a diversion of the kingship from the 'father-son' line between Pybba's and his son Penda's reigns – perhaps Penda was too young to be war-leader when his father died c.600 and a more experienced noble was chosen as king. It is far more likely that Penda reigned for thirty years (625–55) and died aged fifty than that he ruled for fifty years and died aged eighty, as one (muddled?) source indicates; Ceorl was king in the 610s and Penda's sons were still young in 655.

Mercia and its southern neighbour Wessex first clashed over the Cotswolds (as far as is known) c.628, early in Penda's reign, at Cirencester and then 'came to an agreement'[4] – thus they were more or less militarily equal then. The first king of Mercia noted for major military success was Penda, which gave Wessex a window of opportunity to consolidate its control over the Thames valley and Cotswolds until the mid-late 620s. Assuming that the 584(?) unsuccessful campaign of Ceawlin[5] to the battle of 'Fethan Leah' was in north-western Oxfordshire as suggested by the etymology, could victory and consolidation have given this area to Wessex? The archaeological evidence of settlement suggests a major Saxon presence in the upper Thames valley around Abingdon and Dorchester-in-Thames – the latter was significantly the first episcopal see of the kingdom when it was converted under Cynegils c.635 suggesting that it was close to the royal court. Did Ceawlin's conquest of the Cotswolds c.577 open up the area to full West Saxon control, even as far as the Severn? And could this have permanently weakened Mercia if West Saxon control had continued, making Wessex the dominant power in the South Midlands?

As suggested by historians critical of the 'foundation myth' of Wessex – centred on Hampshire – laid down in the *Chronicle*, the centre of the sixth to early seventh centuries West Saxon power may have been in the Oxford-Abingdon area.[6] This could have continued into the mid-seventh but for Penda's aggressive unification of Mercia, which brought that state's rule into the Thames valley; the major bishopric of the kingdom was only moved south to Winchester (the later capital) under Bishop Wine c.660.[7] But as with Northumbria, Wessex was at a geographical disadvantage in any seventh or eighth centuries attempts to rule central England. The power of a kingdom depended on the 'reach' of its king and his warband, for which a geographically central power-base was important. Northumbria's principal royal centre was at Yeavering in Northumberland, not York – indeed, the York region (Deira) was given to the ruling kings' sub-rulers from 633/4 to 679 not kept by them as their power-base.

After Edwin (son of the king of Deira killed by Aethelfrith c.604) was killed in 633(?), all the kings of Northumbria were from the old royal line of Bernicia in the north and thus had reason to base themselves in that territory. (It was Bamburgh on the Northumbrian coast near Yeavering, not a royal 'vill' in Yorkshire, which was the target of Penda in his greatest raid on his Northumbrian rival Oswy's homeland.[8]) This added to the kings' difficulties in maintaining control in southern England; the royal line of Edwin, based in Deira, would have found it easier but he only left infant sons who never regained the throne. The death in battle of Edwin at Cadwallon's hands in 633/4 thus led to control of the Northumbrian throne by kings based in Bernicia, not Deira, though Oswy carefully married Edwin's daughter Enfleda to shore up his local legitimacy. Arguably Edwin, who was a close ally of Kent and acquired his administratively-organized 'Roman' Christianity thence, would have been more successful as an overlord south of the Humber than Oswald or Oswy were, due to his York capital and use of the Continental Church model. The clerics in the south, led by the archbishopric of Canterbury, would have been his allies – the papal plan of 597 for a second archbishopric at York, aborted by Edwin's fall, was not implemented until 735.

Edwin's dynasty had a problem that was the mirror-image of that facing Oswald and Oswy of the Bernician line after 634 – their ability to be accepted by the nobles of Bernicia, land of Edwin's foe Aethelfrith. In an age of personal loyalty, what hold but fear did he have on the nobles of Bernicia? Under Aethelfrith's rule of Deira c.604–17, Edwin had been in exile (in Gwynedd and Mercia) and been the target of the king who feared his potential as a magnet for dissidents in Deira. Under Edwin's rule of Bernicia c.617–33/4, it was Aethelfrith's sons Eanfrith, Oswald, and Oswy who were in the same position – refugees with the victor's enemies, in this case Dalriada. Would a continuing 'Edwinic' Deiran dynasty in power in

Northumbria after 633/4 have been vulnerable to overthrow by Aethelfrith's heirs Eanfrith, Oswald, and Oswy at the first military reverse, backed by their ally Dalriada? Edwin's 'empire' fell with one defeat by Cadwallon of Gwynedd in real life in 633/4; it could easily have come crashing down in the 640s or 650s after defeat by Penda of Mercia, in the manner that Ceawlin's aggressive Wessex 'imploded' in 592. One major defeat was enough to finish off a post-Roman warlord's 'empire' in Britain, as on the Continent the defeat of Alaric II the Goth by Clovis at Vouille in 507 ended Gothic rule in southern Gaul and in 491/3 the kingdom of Italy fell to Theodoric the Ostrogoth.

One problem for a Wessex based in the upper Thames valley was geography. There was no natural border – hills or rivers – to demarcate their frontier with Mercia, as the Humber and Trent (and Mersey) marked the Mercian-Northumbrian frontier. The latter was so important that the kingdoms and peoples of England could be divided into 'Southumbrians' and 'Northumbrians' in this era.[9] The frontiers of most early kingdoms were in any case problematic, fluctuating with the power of individual kings – as with the case of Lindsey, fought over by Mercia and Northumbria (and probably East Anglia too in the early seventh century). But that between Wessex and Mercia was particularly unclear despite the Thames, even in the early ninth century when it remains uncertain who controlled Berkshire.[10] Lacking a natural frontier to aid them, successful seventh century West Saxon kings would have had to destroy the dynasty of the 'Icelingas' and keep the latter's junior sub-kings as their own vassals to maintain long-term power south of the Trent or north of the Thames. However, the centre of power of the West Saxon kingdom from the 570s to the 640s seems to have been around Dorchester-on-Thames, the site of its first bishopric, with the main manpower of Saxon settlement in that area; a 'super-state' based on that area could have controlled at least the southern part of Mercia under a succession of able kings if Ceawlin's domination of the Cotswolds had continued and a successor had killed Penda. In that case Oxford would have made a logical leading royal residence as it emerged as a settlement in the eighth century, with a local cult (St Frideswide) as an opportunity to create a religious centre, and a unified kingdom of Wessex and Mercia could have been the principal 'Southumbrian' power by the time of the reign of the real-life Offa in 757–96. The later West Saxon capital, Winchester, was only selected as a royal and episcopal centre in the 660s after Wessex had lost control of the Thames valley. Arguably this had long-term consequences for the kingdom of England, as the triumphant early tenth century unifier Wessex was still based in distant Winchester yet had to keep control of the North of England from several hundred miles away in an era of poor roads.

The expanding Frankish state of the eighth century had less of a problem in building an empire, with its kings having major estates in the Rhineland and the Low Countries so they could reach their most turbulent frontiers (in Germany and Austria) quicker.

Northumbria as overlord?

Given this importance of leadership, it is clear that while any Anglo-Saxon leader with the right amount of capability and luck could forge a 'state' and establish a degree of influence over his neighbours in the more fluid sixth century, the emergence of Northumbria and Mercia as powerful kingdoms in the seventh century diminished the options available to leaders of smaller kingdoms. Mercia could revive despite the crushing defeat of 655 and dismemberment of Penda's kingdom by Oswy, and Northumbria survived the killing of both Edwin and Oswald and prolonged ravaging by the alliance of Penda and the Christian British warlord Cadwallon of Gwynedd.

Much of seventh century Northumbria's manpower would have come from its lands in lowland Scotland, where Edwin seems to have overrun British 'Gododdin' in Lothian and the balance of resources was in his favour against the Picts and Dalriada. Given the decline in Northumbrian power after Ecgfrith was killed and his 'empire'[11] north of the Forth lost to the Picts at the battle of Nechtansmere in 685, followed by the extinction of his dynasty in 729 and a series of usurpations, it is arguable that the continuation of Northumbrian rule in Scotland and/or dynastic stability would have improved their position. In real life, no king from 705 was able to pass on the throne to his son and the latter to keep it long-term – Aldfrith's son(?) Osric was replaced by a non-relative in 729, Eadbert's son Oswulf was killed in 759, and Aethelred, the son of Aethelwold 'Moll', was expelled in 779. The latter reigned twice and ended up murdered in 796, despite a marital alliance with Offa of Mercia[12] and apparent attempts to eliminate all possible competitors by violence. The surviving records hint at assorted other rebellions and plots that failed.[13] The mid- and late eighth century throne seems to have been disputed by the families of Eadbert, Alchred, and Aethelwold 'Moll', with a sequence of revolts and no stability. As with the spate of rebellions in fifteenth century England (or twentieth century 'Third World' coups), a chain of successful revolts became endemic and encouraged more ambitious men to try their luck.

By the 790s the émigré monk Alcuin, at the court of Charlemagne, was deploring the moral degeneracy of the declining kingdom and implying that the first Viking raids were God's wrath on the sinful Northumbrians.[14] It is possible that there was one practical reason for this political weakness. Alienation of too many royal estates from the king to the Church in the early eighth century reduced the ability of the sovereign to reward his followers with estates, leading the latter to defect to ambitious would-be rebels. Ceolwulf, the pro-Church king and patron of Bede who abdicated in 735 after an earlier brief deposition,[15] was controversial for this policy. In an age of competitive rewards for restless and acquisitive warriors, a king without the means to secure loyalty was in a weak position – and if the Northumbrian realm had retained control of eastern Scotland conquered lands would have been available to give to royal retainers. The lack of an unchallenged 'legitimist' royal line of descent must have posed an extra problem, in that after Ecgfrith's half-brother, Aldfrith, died in 704 the throne was 'up for grabs' and malcontents dared to stake a claim – which would have been unlikely had each king had an adult and competent brother or son ready to succeed him when he died. Even Aldfrith's son and nephew or sons, Osred (705–16) and Osric (718–29), were not automatic choices as king. The chain of events that weakened Northumbria after Osric's death in 729 need not have commenced had Ecgfrith not been killed – or had he or Aldfrith left an adult and capable son who could rule for decades. What if Ecgfrith and his successors had retained the throne long term – as the male line of the Carolingians did as 'Mayors of the Palace' then as kings in eighth century Francia – and had been able to control the entire eastern lowlands of Scotland as far as Buchan? Would this extended and politically settled kingdom have been viable long term, with plenty of estates to give to restless nobles?

With the added resources of an enlarged kingdom safe from repeated domestic challenges with father still succeeding son, could a continuing line of vigorous legitimate rulers have challenged Aethelbald and Offa of Mercia? Strathclyde, the remaining British kingdom of central/southern Scotland, seems to have been Northumbria's vassal for most of the seventh century and the kingdoms of the Picts and (in Argyll) Dalriada unable to challenge its kings successfully until 685.

The kingships of the latter two seem from the surviving king lists to have passed between men from different lineages, arguing for a lack of stable succession or long-lived warlords able to establish a dynasty.[16] Each succession was thus problematic, though it is possible that strong rulers could designate an acceptable heir in their lifetime and this man then succeed smoothly. (The Irish system of kingship had a term for the designated heir, the 'Tanaist', which survived today as that for Deputy Prime Minister in the Republic of Ireland.[17]) This politico-military disadvantage would have aided Northumbrian power in the seventh century, and if Ecgfrith and his line had continued their ascendancy Northumbria could have retained control of the fertile lands of eastern Scotland and thus had greater manpower into the eighth century.

The crucial problem apart from Ecgfrith's early death in battle was his lack of a son to succeed him – which was arguably due to his (political) choice of wife, the devout Princess Audrey/ Aetheldreda of East Anglia. The daughter of leading Christian enthusiast King Anna, she was allegedly averse to marital relations and left her husband to become founding abbess of Ely; as a result any son that Ecgfrith might have had by a successor would have been under-age when he was killed in 685 so liable to be overthrown. The disaster at Nechtansmere brought in his ageing scholarly half-brother Aldfrith as king in 685 – and the latter's inadequate sons, particularly the tyrant Osred. Osred's murder in 716, while of benefit for his oppressed nobles, began a series of usurpations that added to the lack of a regular dynastic succession from 729 to make Northumbria chronically unstable. Several kings, such as Aethelred 'Moll' and Eardwulf, lost and then regained their thrones and very few were succeeded by their sons; in an age of obsessive interest in genealogical 'legitimacy' their dynastic links to the seventh century dynasty are unclear.[18] In political terms, this aided plotters. The Northumbrian attack on the Clyde by Eadbert c.756 was an isolated example of use of their military power in the North successfully in the eighth century. By the time that the tough and competent Eardwulf (796–806, 808–11) and his son Eanred (811–39) established a new dynasty the kingdom was at risk from the Vikings, whose 'hit-and-run' raids were difficult to tackle without a fleet. Unfortunately, more unrest followed Eanred's death, with Raedwulf's coup (soon nullified by its protagonist's death in battle with the Vikings) around 844 and civil war between Osbert and Aelle in the early-mid 860s.

Due to the geographical isolation of Northumbria beyond the Humber and the block that Mercia provided to advances south to overawe the other kingdoms, the chances of such dominance turning into a permanent Northumbrian leadership of the English are small. Their kings would have had to keep Mercia as disunited as it had been in 655–8 and win all conflicts with local rivals who attempted to reunite the latter. But the Northumbrians, blocked from moving south by the consolidation of Mercia from the late 650s, could still have maintained the favourable position they had achieved in northern Britain from c.600 to 685, and Anglian settlers have moved into Fife and the lowlands to Aberdeen as they did into Lothian. A bishopric was set up at Abercorn before 685, a sign of Anglicization. With the smaller and poorer-resourced mountainous territory of Dalriada unable to challenge the Northumbrian state and the Picts confined north of the Mounth in Moray, the Northumbrian state could have Anglicized the east of Scotland before the outside threat of the Viking invaders challenged them in the 860s. Also, if Ecgfrith's Irish Sea fleet (which raided Ulster in 684) had been kept up it could have met the Vikings at sea.

A stronger Northumbrian kingship would probably have made a greater success of the Viking challenge. It could hardly have fared worse than it did in reality in 866–7, with two kings fighting over the throne as the 'Great Army' – probably intent on settlement – took over York. The invaders were able to entrench themselves in the city, and when Kings Osbert and Aelle finally united to attack them in March 867 both were killed in battle.[19] By this date we do not even know the dynastic legitimacy – if any – of these kings, or the extent of resistance to them from among their nobles.

The last long-reigning king (thirty-two years) to succeed his father, Eanred, had died in 843. Indeed, the ferocity of the Viking assaults on Scotland was such that the kingdoms of the Picts and Scots had recently united permanently under Cinaed (Kenneth) mac Alpin,[20] probably after major losses of the nobility in battle in the late 830s. Given the strong military position of Northumbria in southern Scotland in the mid-seventh century, continuing this dominance could well have led to a Northumbrian king not the Dalriadan Kenneth taking advantage of the Pictish losses. The Dalriadans were also weakened by Viking raids and settlement in Argyll by the 840s and so would have had difficulty interfering – significantly their main religious centre was moved from Iona to inland Dunkeld in Atholl at this time.

Kenneth was supposed to have defeated the Northumbrians in battle in the 830s or 840s, in the mysterious battle that saw the first use of the cross of St Andrew as a sign of victory by the Scots.[21] (This could have been an aerial phenomenon, like the cross seen in the sky before Constantine's victory over Maxentius in 312 or the 'perihelion' at Mortimer's Cross in 1461.) What if it had been Northumbria not Dalriada that had assumed the leadership of war-ravaged Pictland in the 830s?

With strong leadership this Northumbrian war-machine (with Picts and possibly Dalriadans as vassals) would have been able to meet the attack on York in 866–7 on more equal terms. A powerful Northumbrian kingdom could even have taken advantage of the decline of their Viking-afflicted Pictish foe in the early ninth century to reclaim Fife and other lands lost after 685, making the local nobility part of a stronger army in time to meet the Viking attack of 866–7. But their long eastern coastline would have been as vulnerable to systematic raids or several simultaneous descents as was that of Wessex, and the Vikings could also attack from the west from Dublin and the Hebrides. The 'corridor' from the Clyde to the Firth of Forth was to be a major Viking target in the 870s, as a useful means of swift movement from Viking York to Dublin. A ruler with the skill and determination of Alfred would have been needed to avoid defeat at some stage in the decades of Viking raids and settlement that followed. As luck would have it, this role appears to have been taken up by Kenneth and a new 'triple kingdom' of the North (Dalriada, Pictland, and Strathclyde) was forged in the century from the 840s. But this permanent block to Anglian northward expansion was not inevitable.

Mercia as leader of an emerging English state? The case of Offa 'the Great'

The chances of Mercia, a more central kingdom able to attack any of its rivals easily, were greater if it had not fallen victim to dynastic instability in the ninth century – although it is clear that their power was resented enough to be repeatedly challenged even under Offa. Their kings seemed to be en route to Southumbrian pre-eminence from the 660s to 796, with the sub-kings of Hwicce and Magonsaetan being reduced to 'duces' in the mid–eighth century and the kings of Sussex following suit. Offa could not subdue a Kentish challenge in 776, the battle of Otford being at best a draw despite his vast resources, but he seems to have been able to rule Kent without any kings[22] from c.786–96 and to rule East Anglia directly in 794–6. He (or his wife) notoriously killed King Aethelbert of East Anglia at a royal estate in Herefordshire without retaliation in c.794, and the local coinage is absent for several years as if no new king emerged to challenge him. He may have backed the installation of his client and later son–in–law Beorhtric in Wessex in 786, though that kingdom remained at best his junior ally; another daughter was married to the insecure king of Northumbria, Aethelred 'Moll'. But the death without heirs of his son, Ecgfrith, soon after him in 796 ended his dynasty, and his creation of a new Mercian archbishopric and his bold coronation of his son in his own lifetime (a move for stable successions on an Eastern Roman precedent) went for nothing.[23] For all his resources Offa could not ensure stability once he was gone – and indeed his ruthlessness must have antagonized many people, particularly in Kent and East Anglia. Executing a king in peacetime like a rebellious noble was unprecedented, though Oswy had had his defeated foe Oswine of Deira murdered in 651; the Christian cults of both men as 'martyrs' suggests a Church-backed reproach to such unjust excesses. For all his power and bravado, Offa did not impress his Frankish neighbour Charlemagne, who refused to marry his daughter to the Mercian king's son Ecgfrith – which would have implied treating him as an equal. Indeed, the presence of Beorhtric's Wessex foe (and successor) Egbert and the future Kentish rebel Eadbert 'Praen' in Francia confirms that the Frankish ruler deliberately harboured potentially useful rebels who could destabilize Offa's and his successor Coenwulf's overlordship.

The break in Mercian power did not come with the deaths of Offa and his son Ecgfrith in 796, as the new king Coenwulf was able to put down the

Kentish revolts and continue to defeat the Welsh. It came with the deaths of Coenwulf and his brother Coelwulf in 821–3 and a series of defeats for their non-dynastic successors in the mid-820s (not only by Egbert of Wessex but by the smaller East Anglian kingdom). As late as c.824 Beornwulf was able to lead a successful campaign across Powys and Gwynedd as far as Degannwy, and the major victory that Egbert achieved over Mercia at Ellendun in 825 was evidently the most crucial cause or evidence of Mercia's decline with respect to its English rivals. Moreover, when Egbert expelled Wiglaf of Mercia in 829 the exile was able to regain his kingdom within a year, suggesting a revolt by the Mercian nobility once the conqueror had gone back to Wessex[24] or Egbert having to accept that he could not impose direct rule. The West Saxons never returned to Mercia. Mercia continued to devastate Powys, whose king Cyngen[25] fled to Rome in 855 leaving his lands to be absorbed by Gwynedd under his nephew Rhodri 'Mawr'. Even in Mercia's dealings with its fellow-English 'power' Wessex, it appears to have held onto the frontier-district of Berkshire into the 840s. It is uncertain to what extent the fact that the Mercian rulers from 823 had no clear 'legitimate' descent was a problem as in Northumbria, given that there were fewer usurpations than in the latter and so probably less dynastic conflict and insecurity – though no ruler was succeeded by his son. But the post-829 recovery of Mercia suggests its latent potential for success – due to its preponderance of resources if not its stable leadership.

A decades-long rule by Offa's son Ecgfrith from 796 and a continuing line of Offa's – or Coenwulf's – family as kings would not have prevented Kentish revolts, or resistance in East Anglia where the murdered King Aethelbert was regarded as a martyr. Unlike with conquered vassal-regions in Francia, these kingdoms had not been absorbed into their overlord or even provided with members of the latter's royal house as kings – though it is likely that Offa's marriage of two daughters to the kings of Northumbria and Wessex was his substitute for this. Non-local kings substituted for the previous dynasts by a foreign power were likely to have been easier targets for revolt. The only known instance of a Mercian ruling Kent was Cuthred, Coenwulf's brother and nominee after the 798 revolt. Given the lack of evidence, we cannot say definitely that Offa avoided suppressing the kingship in East Anglia in 794 and ruling via 'ealdormen' as he did in smaller Sussex – but if he did the experiment did not last. At the latest, the East Anglian kings were able to issue their own coinage again by 825/7 – as Mercia was preoccupied fighting Wessex?

However, greater stability in Mercia could have preserved Offa's new third English archbishopric, at the Mercian see of Lichfield, which had been intended to replace Canterbury, well into the ninth century had the kings of

Mercia had the diplomatic influence and Frankish support necessary to keep the papacy on their side in the matter. As their kingdom was the most centrally-placed in England, with the smallest amount of coastline, they had a strategic advantage against the Vikings and were not afflicted by recorded raids in the first half of the ninth century. Wessex, the new military power under Egbert, suffered repeated attacks and the latter was apparently defeated at Carhampton/Charmouth in 836, and Kent suffered the first establishment of a winter-long Viking camp (on Sheppey) in the early 850s. The threat only reached Mercia with the major Viking expedition up the Thames in 851, and when the 'Great Army' of Vikings landed in 865/6 its first targets were East Anglia and then Northumbria[26] (two main foes of Mercia). Had the Viking attacks on England been limited to the coastal raids and occasional offshore island camps of the 850s the weakening of Mercia's foes could have benefited its survival as the strongest Saxon kingdom – particularly if it had had more determined leadership than that of Burghred, king from 852. The latter gave up his kingdom in 874/5 and fled to Rome, ironically the same fate as that of the king of Powys afflicted by Mercian invasions twenty years earlier. The survival of a powerful inland kingdom in the face of Viking attacks on its periphery is best seen in Francia, where the kingship survived the repeated Viking incursions up its major rivers and the establishment of the county (later duchy) of Normandy on its northern coast. Burghred's Mercia, like Charles 'the Bald's Francia, could have survived had the Vikings been content to parcel out the land in East Anglia and Deira. Instead, in 874 they moved to inland Repton to take control of half of Mercia and in 878–9 Guthrum was based in the Cotswolds while attacking Wessex.

If the Franks could unite, why not the Anglo-Saxons?

The importance of unity, or of clear central control of resources – was this the reason for English failure?
A note should be made about comparisons with the Continent. There, the evolving and expanding Frankish kingdom under Clovis and his sons absorbed other ('Ripuarian', i.e. Rhine valley) Frankish kingdoms and weaker neighbours such as the Burgundians; even when the kingdom was divided in 511–58 and 561–613 its kings treated it as one unit and usually co-operated. Each king had his own 'capital', or principal residence – after 511 and 561 at Rheims, Soissons/Paris, Orleans and Metz but within one Frankish homeland. Two of the kingdoms, Rheims (which was given in 511 to Clovis' eldest son, Theodoric) and Orleans (which was given to Chlodomir), formed the geographical basis for distinct and long-lasting

'states' – Austrasia and Burgundy, while Paris and Soissons merged into Neustria. As the surviving sons of Clovis given kingdoms in 511 or their heirs died off (some with help from relatives), the kingdoms were reunited under the survivors; in 558–61 only one, Chlotar, was left. A further division among his sons followed in 561, suggesting that either he or his nobles felt it legally apposite to satisfy the claims of all his sons not insist on preserving the unity he had recently forced. (Did local notables of each province prefer a local king of their own, as a controllable source of patronage, to one powerful sovereign in all Francia?) A similar process of attrition reunited the kingdoms under one line of Chlotar's heirs in 613, though the decisive action for reunion in that year, by Soissons/Neustria annexing Austrasia, was complicated by the split among the latter's political elite. (The foes of an over-powerful queen-mother and regent Brunhilde needed Neustrian help to remove her.) Luckily kings Charibert of Paris and Guntramn of Burgundy had died without male heirs (567 and 592) or the split into several kingdoms could have gone on indefinitely, as it did after 843 between (Western) Francia and Germany.

This dynastic co-operation by several equal rulers within one 'family' kingdom implies that in legal terms the entire kingdom was seen as one estate or 'allod'. Within that, there could be several rulers – usually brothers and then their respective sons, each other's cousins – but they shared power and (usually) co-operated. This was present in some smaller English kingdoms with several rulers, e.g. Essex where the coinage shows a division among Saebert's sons (Sexred, Sexbald, and Saeward) in 616 and more divisions in 653(?) (Swithelm and Swithfrith) and 663 (Sigehere and Saebbi). In Kent unknown kings ruled with Aethelbert in his early years c.560–85, the young king Eadric ruled with his uncle Hlothere after 673, the sons of Wihtred ruled after 713, and Heahbert and Egbert ruled in the 760s. In Wessex (where a complex royal genealogy has survived) there are references to many men of royal rank ruling together in the mid-seventh century, with one senior and several junior kings under Cynegils (611–43?) and his son Cenwalh (643–73/4?). Given the disputed length of the reigns of Cynegils' father and uncle, Ceol (591/2–7) and Ceolwulf (597?–611), it is possible that those two brothers – the nephews of Ceawlin – also ruled jointly for a time. Cynegils had a near-equal co-ruler, Cwichelm (his elder(?) but predeceasing son), who is named with him as war-leader in the 620s and 630s. Possibly the central kingship ceased functioning altogether after Cenwalh's death, as Bede implies it was dormant for a decade and was revived by Caedwalla in 685–8 – though the regnal lists of 'central' kings continues, including a unique sovereign queen (Sexburh, c.674–5). What is not clear is the geographical basis for these co-kings, though the division of

Kent into East and West in local administrative tradition may reflect this split and in Wessex the counties may have originally been the patrimonies of local kings. Mini-'states' may have descended from father to son, particularly in Wessex, where Cwichelm (probably buried at 'Cuckamsley Knob' on the Wiltshire Downs) seems to have ruled a geographically distinct area and Caedwalla was reported as having been driven out of his father's lands and turned into a roving plunderer some time before he seized power in 685.

Nor is it clear whether kingly status belonged to the family of Caedwalla's cousin and successor, Ine (688–726); the ninth century 'official' genealogies made him out to be descended from Ceawlin's son but if so this branch had been relegated to junior status before 688. If Ceawlin left a son, why did this prince not succeed him – or did he die before his father? Did Ceol and Ceolwulf 'usurp' rule from this branch of the family? It is not certain that all the sub-kings were related to one central ruling family; but in all cases the notion of one central kingdom survived, as in Francia.

England had recognizably distinct 'ethnic' (or linguistic) groupings according to Bede – Angles, Saxons and Jutes. So why did the Angles north of the Thames never become united under Northumbria or Mercia, or the Saxons under Wessex? If the 'Salian' and 'Ripuarian' Franks could unite, why not the Angles or Saxons? Was Aethelfrith, Edwin, Oswald, Penda, Ceawlin, or Caedwalla a potential Clovis, and if not why not? The difference between the English and the Continental experiences of kingship in the sixth to eighth centuries cannot be put down to the unifying effect of the military struggle against the Western and Eastern Roman Empires and local German rivals on the Continent, though this need for leadership and concentration of resources aided the emerging East and West Gothic and Vandal kingships. This was seen by the careers of the line of Alaric the Goth from c.395 to 476, Theodoric the Amal, and Gaiseric; each carved out a kingdom at the Empire's expense and absorbed local rivals. Each centred their lands within the Empire of 410, and was formally recognized by the Emperor – the West Goths in Aquitaine (granted as a dependant state in 418), the Ostrogoths in Italy from 492/3 (with an Imperial commission to replace the kingdom of Odovacar), and the Vandals in North Africa (recognised formally in 442). Odovacar, the Western Empire's final conqueror in Italy in 476, was recognized as its local lieutenant by the Eastern Empire when he handed over the captured Western Imperial regalia. By the time that Clovis took over most of Gaul from the early 480s onwards, the Empire had no local influence and its recognition was not essential – though he appears to have been granted 'consular insignia' as an ally in 508.[27] The Lombards had a prolonged and continuous struggle against the Eastern Empire in Italy from

568 to 751, but their 'war-leader' kingship of the later sixth century repeatedly broke down and a (fairly) stable polity did not emerge for decades.

Nor did a strong central kingship inevitably emerge from struggles within one 'people'. Clovis and his sons united the Franks in the early-mid sixth century, and that unity survived, although the sources make it clear that 'Salian' (Belgium) and 'Ripuarian' (Rhine valley) Franks had been as diverse in the sixth century as Angles, Jutes, and Saxons.[28] This political disunity of diverse small kingdoms and a large settlement-area were overcome by strong warrior-kings under Clovis' line and no heirs of suppressed states emerged in revolt as the central Frankish monarchy declined into weak *rois faineants* in the seventh century. At most, there was local particularism between the western Franks of 'Neustria' and the eastern ones of 'Austrasia', who often had different kings (if the number of adult male Merovingians and local magnates' ambitions permitted it). Given the young age of many new kings at succession, it is clear that the initiative did not lie with the kings – demanding their rightful share of the kingdom – but with the local nobles. An under-age ruler could serve as a useful conduit for their control of power, and indeed in the seventh century the principal court nobles came to overshadow the Merovingian royal family with 'Mayors of the Palace' controlling the government. Why then could Aethelfrith, Edwin or Penda not unite the Angles in the seventh century or Offa overwhelm his weaker enemies (Kent, East Anglia) permanently in the later eighth century? If the 'Salian' Frankish kingship of Clovis had an overwhelming weight of resources to throw against its rivals, so did Offa. Southern Britain had a network of Roman roads to aid speedy movement of royal messengers and troops, as did Francia, and was smaller than the latter.

The fortunes of war in England

Part of the explanation must lie in the fortunes of war. No English dynasty had the long-lasting run of military success that aided the Merovingians. The mid-fifth century Merovingian kingdom was a small domain in Flanders and Artois, centred on Tournai, but Clovis rapidly expanded it after 481 – initially against the non-Frankish realms of Syagrius (a Roman general left stranded by the end of the Empire) north of the Loire and later against the Visigoths and Burgundians. The details of his campaigns against his fellow-Frankish kings are less well recorded by the only near-contemporary source, Bishop Gregory of Tours (a century later), but no one name or kingdom stands out among them and it seems that Clovis could deal with them piecemeal. Once he had achieved primacy within the lands from the Rhine to the Alps and Pyrenees, roughly modern France and the Low Countries plus the Rhineland, the Frankish kingdom was free from major local foes. This advantage was never secured by any English kingdom. Ceawlin of Wessex, Aethelfrith, Edwin, and Oswald of Northumbria, and Penda of Mercia were all locally predominant in England but fell to coalitions of their enemies (592, 617, 633/4, 642, 655). Caedwalla of Wessex, who temporarily overran Sussex and Kent in the 680s to make Wessex supreme south of the Thames, was crippled and had to abdicate in 688. Ecgfrith of Northumbria, who might have been able to annex eastern Scotland and use its resources for Northumbrian aggression, was killed in 685 and his kingdom's military capability reduced (and hindered by dynastic instability from 704).

No English rulers in one kingdom had the long line of orderly (mostly adult) successions and militarily capable heirs, that the early Merovingians did. Clovis' four sons continued his successes, although they also fought each other; so did his grandsons. In the vacancies between capable adult male rule there was a succession of politically adept Queens as regents, most notably the much-vilified Visigoth princess Brunhilde who married Sigebert II of Metz/Austrasia in the 560s and dominated her son's and grandsons' court until overthrown in 613. (In the mid-seventh century[29] there was even an English, ex-slave Queen, Clovis II's widow Balthildis.)

Once the (usually) orderly control of one dynasty of capable rulers in Francia ended in the mid-seventh century (arguably with Dagobert's sons Sigebert III and Clovis II after 639), the kingdom fell into the hands of equally capable 'Mayors of the Palace' and from 687 was ruled by the Pippinid dynasty. By contrast, weak and disputed rule in post-729 (or post-758) Northumbria and post-592 Wessex led to decades of instability and military decline. It is clear that the mayors in Francia preserved central control of patronage by one political leader – for themselves not the kings, but still for a 'central' government – and so were able to dominate the fissiparous tendencies of provincial elites. This did not happen in England – the Northumbrian kingship in the eighth century was known to have been weakened by giving estates away to the Church and the seventh century Wessex kingship faced powerful local sub-kings.

The English states – too evenly matched for one victor to emerge?
Overall, the impression given by seventh and eighth century inter-state competition is that the English kingdoms were too evenly matched, and too fissiparous, for one 'power' to act as a unifying agent even had it possessed more military luck. Given the geography involved, local dynastic loyalties, and the difficulty of enforcing power by marching armies regularly across the countryside, the best chance for unity lay with Mercia. Its eighth century kings duly used pretentious terminology as 'kings of the English' and Offa

endeavoured to secure dynastic stability by crowning his heir in his lifetime. But it should not be assumed that the deaths of Offa and Ecgfrith in 796, or Coenwulf in 821, prevented a viable and imminent move towards English unity under Mercia.

The advantages that Offa possessed did not enable him to destroy Kentish resistance in 776, and the battle of Otford was presumably a draw or defeat as rebel king Egbert survived. When Offa did annex that kingdom c.785 it revolted again on his death; Coenwulf suppressed it but it rebelled again in 825. Offa fought against the West Saxons on one known occasion (779) without obvious success, and he and Coenwulf had to be content with making its weak late eighth century kings their (subordinate) allies. The Mercians had advanced their Western Wessex frontier in Somerset in the 730s, apparently taking over Bath and Somerton, but could not push any further south. Offa's strong-minded daughter Eadburh, married off to Beorhtric of Wessex in 789, probably acted as his 'agent' in assisting his policies there and inducing her husband to co-operate, but this was not conquest. There was a backlash against her, with West Saxon stories (recorded by Alfred's biographer Asser in the late ninth century) portraying her as an evil serial killer who dominated her husband and ended up accidentally poisoning him in 802; allegedly the title of 'Queen' was banned in Wessex after she was driven out.[30] Nor could Offa's sponsorship of and marriage of another daughter to Aethelred 'Moll' of Northumbria save the latter from murder in 796.[31] At most, Offa could permanently end the kingship of Sussex beyond his borders and Hwicce within them, whose rulers now declined in status to 'ealdormen' (governors). This shows that even the most powerful state in England in the eighth century was unable to hold down its neighbours – a stark contrast to Francia or Spain.

The Welsh factor in Mercia's failure

Is it possible that the constant drain of Welsh raids in the eighth century (leading to the construction of the famous 'Dyke') kept a large part of the Mercian army tied up on that frontier and thus aided Kentish resistance? We have no record of the details of the Anglo-Welsh wars as only the West Saxon *Chronicle* has survived, but the need for a massive earthwork to regulate and defend the Western Mercian border in the mid–eighth century suggests it. It is a logical inference, and would explain the massive scale of Coenwulf's and Beornwulf's assaults on Gwynedd and Powys in the early 820s.[32] Any possibility that ending the Welsh distraction in the 820s would have freed Mercian troops for a successful confrontation with its remaining English rival, Egbert's Wessex, was not implemented; after Coenwulf's death Egbert decisively defeated Mercia in 825 and its south-eastern vassals revolted successfully.

From then on Kent and Sussex passed to kings from Egbert's family – it is possible that his father, Ealhmund, was the eponymous Kentish king of the 760s and he had a dynastic claim there so the local nobles accepted him easily. The identity and lineage of the new kings of East Anglia is unclear, but they appear to have been West Saxon allies.[33] Egbert, like Offa, could not permanently take over his main military rival – and his geographical isolation south of the Thames made matters worse.

Chapter Four

The Vikings and After: 866 and All That

Could the invaders have succeeded across England?

W e can see what might have happened to Anglo-Saxon England in the absence of a large-scale concentrated invasion from the Viking experience in Ireland. There a similar group of large 'native' provincial kingdoms – Leinster, Munster, Midhe (in two divisions), Connacht, and Ulster – had established themselves as fairly stable polities by c.800, with a number of smaller local kindred-based sub-kingdoms. There was no central authority to take on the intruders except a weak 'High Kingship', held by the two lines of the 'Ui Niall' dynasty, which ruled in Midhe (more or less in rotation) and never passed on by father to son in a stable dynasty. Neither of these lines had the resources to dominate the other, or the other major kingdoms. If one king was to attempt to establish a permanent power-base in the 'High Kingship' for his family, his rivals had the resources to bring him down. A powerful central kingship remained an aspiration, and was supposed to have existed in the fifth century under Niall and his successors and been destroyed by provincial revolt in the 550s; it was believed to have originated in the mythical past but modern historians doubt this. At the most, a 'mind-set' among the Irish political and cultural elite recognized the desirability of a central kingship – which was not the case in Anglo-Saxon England.

The Vikings were a constant menace in the ninth and tenth centuries, using the major rivers to plunder far inland and touring the rich monasteries in search of easy loot, and they set up fortified coastal bases on major rivers such as Dublin (meaning 'Black Pool'), Waterford, and Limerick. These became the centres of Viking lordships in the manner of York in England, but never coalesced into one large Viking state. This was partly due to geography – York was more centrally placed to dominate its neighbours, aided by the post-900 Norse settlement in Cumbria, and the sheer size of Ireland inhibited close contact between the Viking port-towns. At times their rulers ventured into neighbouring politics across the Irish Sea (York and the Isle of Man), aided by memories of how Halfdan and Ivarr Ragnarrson had ruled both Dublin and York in the 870s, and at others they were subject to the ambitions of neighbouring Viking warlords such as Sigurd 'the Stout' of Orkney. The geographical problem of controlling both Dublin and York proved too great, though Halfdan journeyed between the two and seems to have used lowland Scotland from Dumbarton to the Firth of Forth as a 'corridor'.

The occasions when Irish Viking forces roamed at will far from their coastal bases, looting and pillaging wherever they wished, did not lead to permanent annexation – the massive Viking attacks on the 'midlands' around the middle Shannon in the 840s did not alter the local political structure in their favour. The lordship of Limerick did not spread inland despite the lack of geographical factors (mountains or bogs) aiding the resistance, and the Vikings never settled the 'midlands'; nor did they move inland from Waterford to overrun Leinster. Unlike in England, the native Irish dynasts of Leinster and Munster survived and fought back – and in the case of Limerick the threat of a nearby Viking lordship stimulated the creation of a dynamic, well-led new sub-province of Munster in Thomond, whose leaders duly took over the entire kingdom. These men, the brothers Mathgamhain and Brian of the 'Dal Cais' dynasty, were notably not from the ancient royal lineage of Munster based around Cashel. By contrast, in England the inland march of the Vikings to Repton in 874 led to the cession of the eastern half of Mercia to them and the settlement of the Danelaw, permanently lost to Mercia. There was, however, some similarity between the cases of Thomond in Munster – the nucleus of resistance to the Vikings within that kingdom – and south-west Mercia in England, where 'ealdorman' Aethelred emerged to lead resistance to the Vikings in the Danelaw. The last king of Mercia, Ceolwulf II, either died heirless or was driven out c.883, vilified in the Wessex-based *Anglo-Saxon Chronicle* as the 'unwise king's thegn' who had collaborated with the invaders and handed over half of the kingdom to them. Mathgamhain and Brian of Thomond took over Munster and reconquered Limerick, and Aethelred and his wife, Aethelfleda, took over western Mercia and later reconquered the east. In both cases, the crisis of partial conquest led to the emergence of new leaders among the invaded peoples.

The pressure of Viking raids weakened but did not destroy the Irish kingdoms, and eventually the most successful provincial warlords – Mathgamhain and his brother Brian of Thomond, from the 960s – led an Irish campaign to defeat and absorb their kingdoms. Brian, like Alfred of

Wessex, went on from defeating the local Viking menace (Limerick) to lead his countrymen beyond the borders of his own state, became the symbol of national resistance, and achieved an ephemeral 'High Kingship' – which in his case did not last. The fact that no Munsterman had held the 'High Kingship' before him was an excuse for his rivals to resist, with the acquiescence of his defeated rivals from the Ui Niall line never certain. The antagonism of Leinster (under Mael Morda), in particular, was a more serious threat to the new Irish unity than anything that Alfred's Wessex had to face from its Saxon neighbours in similar circumstances. The fact that Brian's family, the Munster sub-kings of Thomond, lacked ancient lineage and dynastic legitimacy as 'High Kings' aided their Ui Niall rivals who had held the over-kingship since the fifth century. In England, there was no ancient 'national' kingdom and ancient lineage of kings to be taken over – and thus no claim that Alfred and his son Edward were usurpers.

Why England? Why invade in 865/6?

Why did the Scandinavians invade England in force in 865, in numbers that are unclear but that seem to have been unprecedently large? Infuriatingly, we have no specifics about the invasion. But it was clearly carefully planned – the attackers landed in East Anglia, too small a state to resist them, and blackmailed King Edmund into giving them horses and supplies so they could attack Northumbria. Probably hoping for immunity from conquest in return for encouraging them to leave, he co-operated – and did not assist either Northumbria or (in 868) nearer Mercia to resist. Having disposed of both kingdoms, the Vikings then returned and conquered East Anglia at leisure in 869 before moving on south-west to Wessex, which alone had bothered to come to its neighbours' aid. The numbers of the invaders are unknown, and may have been exaggerated by later myth – nor is it clear if all the Vikings who attacked Wessex in 870 had been with the invasion from 865 or if the latter's success encouraged more land-hungry aspirants to arrive from Scandinavia to join in the later campaigns. The major expedition of 350 ships who invaded eastern Wessex (Kent) in 851 would probably have been smaller than the 'Great Army' – or that nickname would have been used for this earlier attack instead. A total of 350 ships suggests, at around 40 warriors per ship, a force of some 10–12,000 men; the 'Great Army' was probably larger. Their leadership was that of a coalition of warlords, dominated by the three sons of Ragnar 'Lothbrok' – Halfdan, Ivarr, and Ubbe or Hubba.

It is logical that as a major Viking success brought in more warriors (or would-be settlers) to share the pickings, so if Aethelwulf and his son Aethelbald had been defeated in 851 the victorious invaders would have seized London permanently as a riverine base for future aggression as their compatriots did to Limerick and Waterford in Ireland. The news would have led to more Vikings arriving to join in the attacks in 852 and their dispersal across the south-east of England, as the invaders dispersed across central Ireland in the 830s and 840s – with Canterbury as the principal source of monastic loot in the manner of Clonmacnois in the Irish Midlands. Ireland was usefully devoid of a centralized monarchy and large army to lead resistance, so it was an easy target – besides having some long rivers useful for their ships, principally the Shannon. Francia had the rivers, but it also had a powerful and determined central ruler in Charles 'the Bald', experienced in warfare (against his kin) from the early 840s and with the determination of a younger son who had had to elbow his way to power against three elder brothers who had distinct dynastic advantages. The (West) Francian army was used to regular campaigning since the days of Charlemagne, albeit recently against other Franks. Southern England as of the 850s lacked the centralized leadership of Francia, with two kingdoms (East Anglia and Kent) small and a third (Mercia) principally concerned with Welsh wars far away to the west. It had offshore islands (Sheerness and Thanet) and the River Thames to penetrate the interior, and was thus a logical target. The Saxon victory at Aclea postponed the next attack for over a decade, but another attempt to tackle the region was likely – even Alfred's crushing victory in 878 only brought peace for a decade and a half. A new and untried ruler in Wessex – Aethelbert, who succeeded to the full kingdom in 860 – and an apparently young king in East Anglia, Edmund, would have added to the temptation. The civil war between Osbert and Aelle in Northumbria was also useful, though in any case Northumbria was not as militarily powerful as in the eighth century – Egbert of Wessex had had little trouble in securing its submission in 829.

The Army systematically tackled the Anglo-Saxon kingdoms, starting with the weaker ones – but this was standard practice for their roaming bands of warriors on the Continent, who tended to hone in on weaker states. The West Frankish kingdom of Charles 'the Bald' after 840 was their main target there, with its many long and wide rivers providing easy access. As with Wessex in the 870s and early 890s, a determined long-term resistance led to the Vikings leaving – Kings Louis III and Carloman drove the local Vikings out of modern Belgium in the 880s. The size of the Frankish army was larger than that available to either English or Irish provincial kings, which may explain why the latter were more vulnerable to crushing defeat and settlement. The Frankish armies were frequently defeated or were not even able to reach the site of a Viking 'hit-and-run' raid in time; but their state survived as Mercia, East Anglia, and Northumbria did not. The fact that the Vikings were not able to settle in Francia in the mid- and late ninth century as they did in the British Isles may well have owed much to the geographical size of the afflicted kingdom, which in Francia aided long-term resistance. A Viking settlement on a Francian river exposed to easy access from the Atlantic, e.g. at Nantes or Bordeaux, might have defeated the local 'counts' but would still be vulnerable to attack from the central royal army based far inland. In small East Anglia, the local resistance could not retreat out of reach of the Vikings after a major defeat and regroup – and in Northumbria and Wessex the resistance would have to retreat to a remote, infertile area like Bernicia or Cornwall. There was as much fertile land in Francia as in England or Ireland, but the potential Viking settlers could not be so sure that one victory would secure it for them. The action of Hrolf 'the Walker', alias Rollo, the founder of Normandy in securing a grant of Upper Normandy alone from the weak Frankish King Charles 'the Simple' in 911 shows that sensible Viking warlords preferred to devour digestible chunks of land that they could defend adequately. Hrolf, like the Viking annexers of Eastern Mercia in 875 or Deira in 867, took over only part of a region and forced the legitimate sovereign to recognize his acquisition to minimize the risk of counter-attack. The concept of securing local acceptance extended to Kiev in Russia, at least in later legend – invading Swedish warlord Rurik, founding ruler of Novgorod, was supposed to have been accepted as overlord by the local Slavic elders Askold and Dir at Kiev.

It may thus have been military logistics as much as personal vendettas that brought a major Viking force to England in 865. The later Norse sagas, naturally, found the 'revenge' factor – the tale of the warlord Ragnar Lothbrok thrown into a snake-pit by the king of Northumbria and his three sons swearing vengeance – more exciting.[1] It was easier to hold down conquered territory in England, and harder for their foes to regroup inland and fight back; even Mercia was smaller than the West Francian kingdom of Charles 'the Bald'. Using the sagas as evidence is problematic, but it would seem that enterprising pirates such as Ragnar had ventured far and wide across Western Europe (to Spain and Italy?) and could easily assess the size of their enemies' military resources and so select an easy target. It could be myth that the Viking 'Great Army' invasion – evidently intended to conquer land on a large scale across the English kingdoms, which it tackled one by one – was due to personal vengeance by the sons of Ragnar Lothbrok. He was not the only heroic warlord to have allegedly been thrown into a pit of snakes according to myth – the tale is also told of Harald 'Hardradi', king of Norway in the early eleventh century. The Viking saga-writers were fond of explaining campaigns in terms of blood-feuds, and obtaining the maximum amount of land seems to have been the main lure for the participants as they did not satisfy themselves with one fertile Anglo-Saxon kingdom. The question of 'land-hunger' and a population-explosion in the Norwegian fjords or the peninsula of Jutland is usually taken as one cause, with opportunistic would-be settlers testing out the kingdoms of Western Europe to see which would provide least resistance.

There were already large-scale armies, the 'White Foreigners' (Danes) and 'Black Foreigners' (Norwegians), in fertile and divided Ireland, dating from the 840s, and tradition speaks of major warfare with the Picts and Scots in the newly united kingdom of Scotland. Written evidence there is lacking, but the Vikings were settling in large numbers on the Hebridean islands during the mid-ninth century and the recent DNA research shows that the population there has a mainly Norwegian origin. One large force of Vikings attacking England had wintered on Sheppey, moved up the Thames, defeated Mercia, and then been routed by Wessex in 851.[2] It is possible that if the West Saxons had been easier prey then the settlement would have commenced that early. None of the current English kings as of 865 had a prestigious military reputation, although Burghred of Mercia had overrun Powys in 853, and this may well have been a factor in deciding on the attack. Northumbria, as has been said, was in the middle of a civil war; Edmund of East Anglia was young and had few resources. Wessex's co-victor over the Vikings in 851, the young King Aethelbald, had died in 860 and his younger brother, Aethelbert, was to die in midwinter 865–6[3] so the major military power of southern England was in a weak position; the remaining Cerdicing princes, Aethelred and Alfred, were young and untried in war. Is it significant that the Vikings had also attacked Wessex in Egbert's old age (to assist the Cornish) in 838, when his son Aethelwulf was new to the throne in 840, and after Aethelbald's death in 860? Like vultures, they could sense when a king might be weak and ripe for defeat.

Why target Wessex in 870 and 875–8?
The Viking division of conquered Northumbria and Mercia (each left with an Anglian puppet-king ruling part of it) and conquest of East Anglia, all fertile lands able to sustain many settlers, did not satiate the invaders. In 875 Mercia was divided, with the lands west of Watling Street being left to a 'puppet' king (Ceolwulf II) and the east being settled as the Danelaw. After eight years' occupation it appears that Deira was divided for settlement among the conquerors, and less fertile Bernicia was left to the Angles under subordinate local kings. East Anglia had already been settled after the death in battle of King Edmund late in 869 – with a possibility that an obscure local king, Oswald, survived for a few years.[4] There was enough fertile land involved to satiate thousands of land-hungry Scandinavians – yet a second attack on Wessex quickly followed. This new offensive to take over the last

surviving Saxon kingdom is perhaps surprising, considering the limited objectives of earlier attacks on England and of the Viking tactics in Ireland – where no attempt was made to conquer the entire island. The new Scandinavian settlements at major harbours on the coast – Dublin, Waterford, and Limerick – ruled their hinterlands and the fertile central plain was ravaged, but there was no grandiose division of each province among settlers. Nor was it a case of a 'master-plan' by the sons of Ragnar, who appear to have led the first attack on Wessex in the 'battle-winter' of 870–1 and so had experience of the terrain and a stalemate to avenge. By this time Ivarr had left for Ireland to establish himself as king of Dublin, and Halfdan's rule seems to have been centred on York with an eye on events in Ireland; the obscure Hubba was probably in South Wales. None of these three leaders took part in the attacks on Wessex in 875–8, and probably Halfdan, as ruler of York, had already satiated his closest lieutenants with lands there. The settlement of Deira and eastern Mercia in 874–5, plus East Anglia, provided the Vikings who were in the 'Great Army' at those dates with plenty of land.

The kingdom of Wessex had been fought to a standstill in the 'battle-winter' of 870–1, and probably forced to pay tribute. (Alfred's propagandists seem to have covered this up.) The sites of the major battles indicate that the invaders, based at Reading on the middle Thames, had been moving west into Berkshire – to be checked at Ashdown – and then south across Hampshire and Wiltshire. After Ashdown, the main battles were at Basing in northern Hampshire, 'Meretun' (Merton or Marten?) in the Winchester area or western Hampshire, and Wilton in eastern Wiltshire. The death of King Aethelred at Wimborne Minster in eastern Dorset after Easter 871[5] may imply that he had had to move his headquarters there, in retreat westwards – though he apparently owned the local estates as they were inherited by his son Aethelwold. Despite the major West Saxon victory at Ashdown and a number of drawn battles, the defenders seem to have been forced into terms when a second Viking force arrived to assist the invaders. They were no threat to Viking control of eastern England as of 875, so why attack them again? But England was different from the situation in Ireland. Even when the original Viking leadership of 865 – probably Ragnar's sons – were no longer active in southern England in the mid-870s, having turned their attention to York and then Dublin, more Vikings under Guthrum took on Wessex.

The opportunistic attackers were clearly intent on continuing the war until they received a check, as they did in Francia (where their defeats in the 880s sent their main force back to England and in 911 the force led by Hrolf 'the Walker' could be bought off with the grant of Upper Normandy). Given the nature of Scandinavian – as with Germanic – leadership, success depended on a warlord having loot and land to give his followers and thus attracting support over a long period. Possibly each division of a kingdom left some warriors – recent arrivals who had not taken part in the major campaigns of conquest? – without land and they gathered round an ambitious captain who could offer them a new target. Guthrum, not heard of in the 865–71 wars, suddenly emerges as the leader of the attack on Wessex in 875 and would fit this concept of an 'excluded' minor war-leader keen to carve out his own kingdom. His choice of Wareham for his base shows his grasp of strategy – as with York in 866, Nottingham in 868, and Reading in 870, the Vikings took a defensible town with river-access to the sea and proceeded to plunder the hinterland and dare the enemy to attack them. Nor had southern Dorset been involved in the war in 870–1, so there was plenty of fresh loot to seize there.

The leadership of the Viking army was vested with the sons of Ragnar in 865–6, and by the early-mid 870s Halfdan had settled his men in Yorkshire and Ivarr 'the Boneless' had gone on to Dublin; the third brother, Hubba, probably went to Ireland too before he descended on North Devon to aid Guthrum's invasion of 878. But the Viking command at Ashdown in January 871 seems to have been split[6] among various 'kings' and 'jarls', some of whom were killed there. Logically this divided leadership meant that without a clear sign of West Saxon military superiority ambitious Viking commanders were bound to attempt conquest to create a reputation (and larger following) for themselves. The smaller size of the ninth century Saxon kingdoms compared with the Frankish kingdoms of Western Europe made them weaker targets. Even had there not been a 'Great Army' invasion in 865/6, ambitious warlords could have been expected to probe the defences of each kingdom in these decades; any Viking victory would encourage more plunderers to follow suit. It is arguable that the major Viking attack up the Thames in 851, which defeated Mercia but was then destroyed by Aethelwulf of Wessex at Aclea, was such a 'probe' and its defeat put off land-hungry invaders for a decade.[7] As in Ireland but much more rarely, the Vikings occasionally became involved in local politics to back one 'state' against another – in 838 they assisted an unsuccessful Cornish revolt against Egbert and were defeated at Hingston Down.[8] Looking ahead, in 902 the Vikings of York and some in the Danelaw were to back Alfred's disinherited nephew Aethelwold, son of Aethelred, in invading Wessex.

Two chances for a Saxon victory – Nottingham 868 and Reading 870–1
At first the 'Great Army' was able to pick off the Anglo-Saxon kingdoms at leisure, extorting supplies and horses from East Anglia in 866 and moving

off to attack Northumbria, which was usefully in the middle of a civil war. But in 868 the West Saxon King Aethelred, with his brother Alfred, came to the aid of their sister's husband, Burghred of Mercia, to besiege the Viking headquarters on the Trent at Nottingham.[9] In this campaign, control of the Trent was vital to success given that the Vikings clearly preferred to retreat into the town and sit out a siege – possibly as the Saxon army was larger. If the Vikings had received a decisive check from the Anglo-Saxon coalition at the siege of Nottingham, had their supplies cut off, and been starved into promising to leave, this would not have prevented further attacks later. Guthrum's checks at Wareham in 876 and Exeter in 877 (probably involving the tactic of starving out a Viking camp which failed at Nottingham) did not prevent him from attacking Chippenham early in 878. But the combination of Anglo-Saxon kingdoms could have managed to defeat the invaders at Nottingham if they had constructed bridges across the Trent to stop supply-ships coming upstream to the Viking camp – as Alfred succeeded on doing to a camp in Essex on the River Lea in the early 890s.[10] The (larger) Frankish army was able to storm Viking camps in Belgium in the 880s, as the West Saxon chroniclers noted approvingly. But did the West Saxons lack adequate artillery to drive the foe back from the ramparts and set fire to the buildings behind? The Franks, by contrast, had stormed a large fortified camp before – when Charlemagne's men attacked the Avar 'Ring' near the Danube in the 790s. The Franks may have benefited from surviving Roman manuscripts in their monasteries, which included books of military tactics, a factor probably absent in Britain where there was no (known) continuity from Roman to Germanic civilization and storming a walled town was rare (though Aelle had done it in 491).

A Saxon victory at Nottingham would have left the defeated invaders in possession of their first conquest, York, and probably able to recruit enough reinforcements to take over the smaller East Anglia. Even with their real-life successes in 867–70, Halfdan left Bernicia to the local Angles in the 870s and remained content with settling Deira. Alternatively, the West Saxons could have produced a better resolution to the 'battle winter' of 870–1 by following up their victory at Ashdown with more successes and starving out the riverine Viking base at Reading. It is a mystery where the Mercian army was at this juncture, as it could have provided much-needed extra manpower. The help Wessex had given to Mercia in 868 was evidently not reciprocated and Burghred let Aethelred down. There is a hint in the *Anglo-Saxon Chronicle* that the Wessex leadership had been critical of Burghred's caution in 868;[11] was he too afraid of retribution from Halfdan to aid Aethelred? Similarly in 877–8 we do not find Mercian king Ceolwulf II lending any support to the embattled Alfred, even once Guthrum had been defeated.

The extra help provided by Mercia would at least have enabled Wessex to meet the danger of Viking reinforcements outmatching their denuded, war-weary army by summer 871; it seems that the peace (and tribute) that Wessex agreed then followed the arrival of a fresh Viking 'summer army' to aid Halfdan's warriors at Reading. The difficulty of transport in midwinter would have made large-scale Mercian help to Wessex until spring 871 difficult – though the warband of the late ealdorman Aethelwulf of Berkshire, killed attacking Reading in January, took his body safely back to his home near Derby in midwinter.[12] The Anglo-Saxons were also less accustomed than Vikings to fighting all the year round – at Twelfth Night 878[13] Alfred was caught unawares when Guthrum attacked him in Chippenham, so even that flexible commander had not expected attack in that season. But a Mercian army marching to assist Aethelred in spring 871 might well have enabled him or Alfred to win more battles (such as Marten, where Aethelred was probably mortally wounded) and inflict damage on the Vikings. However, that would not have put all attackers off for many years, and Guthrum (new to command in 875 and probably not involved in the 870–1 campaigns) would have been likely to chance an invasion in 875 anyway – the previous West Saxon success in 851 was followed by attack as early as 854–5.

The hard-pressed Vikings at Reading were probably reinforced by a new 'summer army' of invaders in 871, hence their successes in later battles and probable imposition of tribute on Alfred as their terms for leaving his lands that summer. But if the Saxons had defeated and starved the camp out, as they did to Guthrum at Chippenham after Ethandun in spring 878,[14] the main army of invaders might have been more wary of tackling Alfred again in 875–8 or even of taking on and dividing Mercia. The comparable victories of Louis III and Carloman of Francia in Flanders in the early 880s were more ephemeral; the parallel is not exact as the Vikings' return to attack Paris in 887 was aided by the early deaths of the two victors. It was weakness in enemy command that emboldened the Vikings to attack Francia then, and similarly the ageing of Egbert of Wessex in 838, the death of warlike king Aethelbald in 860, and the civil war in Northumbria in 865–6 were followed by opportunistic Scandinavian assault.[15] Viking captains preyed on domestic weakness across Europe, and the fact that Wessex paid tribute in 871 would have encouraged ambitious leaders to chance another assault in 875–6. After his triumph in 878 Alfred was to be left alone until 892, with the new Viking force that arrived at Fulham in 879 deciding not to risk confrontation (possibly on the advice of the defeated Guthrum).[16] Would a decisive success by Aethelred, Alfred, and Burghred (or a bolder Mercian king) in 871, leading to the starving out of the enemy camp in Reading, have saved Wessex from major attack for a decade or two?

A Saxon victory at Nottingham in 868 or Reading in 871 should have saved Mercia from partition in 875, while not enabling the English to drive out the invaders from lands already conquered in the East of England. It would have led to the establishment of a limited Viking settlement-area in East Anglia and York, on a parallel with the coastal Viking lordships of Dublin, Waterford, and Limerick in Ireland – bases that were too powerful to be conquered by a kingdom in the hinterland lacking naval forces to blockade them. This form of Viking settlement was also seen in Francia, where Charles 'the Simple' had to accept a Scandinavian base in the county of Rouen (upper Normandy) in 911. This duly expanded into the duchy of Normandy and acquired Frankish culture and administrative practice – unlike in Ireland (or Eastern England) Scandinavian law and customs seem to have eroded in the generations after settlement though some historians argue that it was the Viking element that gave Normandy its distinctive dynamism and cultural/political ethos in the eleventh century. Had Mercia held out in possession of all its territory, the Scandinavian settlement to its east could have been in the same position in the early tenth century as was the duchy of Normandy with regard to the Frankish monarchy. The case of Danish York would have been different even with a surviving Mercia; it had easy geographical connections to and Lancashire settlers from Dublin to strengthen the Viking element and make it prey to invasion from Dublin. The counts and dukes of Normandy had no close geographical connection to their kin, the jarls of Orkney; but the line of Ivarr 'the Boneless' (co-founder of Viking York) in Dublin could easily cross the Irish Sea to invade York and repeatedly did so in 910–52.

Anglo-Saxon political unity or 'High Kingship' – an option to ensure anti-Viking unity? It worked in Francia and Ireland – why not England?

(i) The parallels – Francia and Ireland
It remains uncertain if the victorious Anglo-Saxons would have been driven to the wise course of combining their armies – or merging the two remaining kingdoms, Wessex and Mercia – for long-term security. But it is unlikely; even in the divided Mercia of 875–918 there was enough local particularism to make the 'sensible' course of absorption by Wessex far from easy. The Frankish kings continued fighting among themselves as the Vikings ravaged their periphery in the mid-late ninth century, even though they had the advantage of a tradition of 'empire' and unity under Charlemagne. The death of Emperor Louis 'the Pious' in 840 had seen his eldest son, the new Emperor Lothar, challenged successfully by the younger ones (Lewis in

Germany and Charles 'the Bald' in Francia); their defeat of him at Fontenoy in 842 split up the empire permanently. Thereafter Lothar only held a nominal primacy and rule of the central Francian lands (Holland, Italy, and the eponymous 'Lorraine'), and none of the rulers bothered to assist their Viking-afflicted kin. The unity imposed temporarily by Charles 'the Bald' in 876 and Charles 'the Fat' in 885 were brief aberrations in the decline of central authority, and ended by local revolt. The ambitions of rival princes with a 'right' to rule came before the need to concentrate resources though the size of the Frankish realms meant that Viking conquest was less of a threat than to Mercia or Wessex. Notably, in the next generation of Frankish princes even the kingdoms of Lothar and Lewis were to be divided among all their sons, not pass to one son in order to maximise their defensive potential. This option of division had been avoided in Wessex on the death of Aethelbald in 860 – though it may be that Aethelred, next brother of the new king, Aethelbert, as well as their youngest brother, Alfred, was too young to govern or fight anyway.

Ireland was similarly afflicted by resident Viking enclaves and endless raiding in the ninth and tenth centuries, and lacked one central power to defeat the attackers. The 'High Kingship' was far older than the new Frankish imperial title, but was equally ineffective. It did not come with a central bureaucracy or army, unlike the empire of Charlemagne. It was more honorary than effective, did not usually pass from father to son as rival lines of the 'Ui Niall' of Midhe disputed it, and could rarely command the support of all the provincial kings. The five Irish provincial states did not unite either in the tenth century, although their resistance to the Vikings made this advisable. The kingdom of Munster under its new 'Dal Cais' dynasts from Thomond, Mathgamhain and Brian 'Borumha', assumed national leadership after driving the Vikings out of Limerick; Brian's military success and wide-ranging campaigns caused many Irish dynasts to rally to his standard. But they were not even the traditional ruling family of Munster, having had to take over power from the ineffective kings based to the south at Cashel. They never secured the loyalty of all the provincial kings in the five major provinces and their sub-divisions, and the south-eastern kingdom of Leinster – traditional foe of Munster – was particularly resentful. Its early eleventh century ruler, Mael Morda, was a personal foe of Brian's and usually preferred allying with the Vikings. Brian's imposed unity as 'High King' from 1002–14 was a personal ascendancy that did not replace the provincial kingdoms but merely made him their temporary leader. The traditional right of the dynasty he had supplanted, the 'Ui Niall' of Midhe, to the 'High Kingship' was restored after he fell in battle against Sigurd's Vikings and their allies at Clontarf; his family had to make do with Munster.

(ii) England

There was no tradition of a Western 'emperor' like Charlemagne as successor to Rome, or a long line of 'High Kings' at Tara, to inspire unity under one leader in ninth century England. The break in cultural continuity between the Late Roman world of fifth century Britain and the Germanic one of the seventh century was thus important. The notion of a British 'emperor' may have survived among the Welsh, as we have seen. We cannot know if the 'bretwaldaship' (a form of supreme military leadership among the kingdoms) meant anything to the ruling class of Wessex and Mercian nobles, as opposed to literary theorists such as Bede (who refers to 'sovereignty' by the overlord) or the later ninth century *Chronicle* compiler. If it was an active source of inspiration to the political leadership it could have served as the 'peg' on which to hang an Anglo-Saxon military 'high command' under a permanent 'overlord', presumably the strongest and most successful king – that of Wessex as heir to the previous 'bretwalda', Egbert? The title was clearly still politically relevant in the later ninth century, or it would not have been mentioned in the *Anglo-Saxon Chronicle* – and its latest holder had been Alfred's grandfather Egbert. But it was not the same as the Imperial title claimed by Charlemagne and his heirs, in which they and their followers were laying claim to the heritage of Rome. (According to one theory it was not Charlemagne but Pope Leo III who thought up the idea of his coronation, for domestic Italian not Frankish political reasons.) Rome was better remembered in Francia than in England, where the post-Roman peoples, culture, and language had been subsumed by a Germanic culture. There was thus no Anglo-Saxon tradition of administrative unity under an Emperor, though Alfred himself valued his (mainly religious) links with Rome and was keen to promote international Latin Christian culture and its values.

Why did Alfred never claim the title of leader of the Angles and Saxons in their resistance to the Vikings as 'Bretwalda'? Was it because there were so few kings left alive at the time of his triumph in 878, or because it was regarded as an antiquarian anachronism? The embattled and then triumphal tone of the *Anglo-Saxon Chronicle* account of his wars shows that he was fully aware of the value of propaganda, and that the pagan nature of the Vikings was played up to make him appear a Christian warrior-hero. He was in the mould of David, the former exile who had returned to triumph over his enemies, and the Israelites who had often been defeated by the Philistines before conquering them. The extent of his links with Rome, the fount of imperial and Church power, was well-recorded, with the *Chronicle* carefully noting his ceremonial recognition (and anointing?) as a small boy by Pope Leo IV – a parallel with the coronation of Charlemagne by Pope Leo III? He had the 'submission' of the southern Welsh princes to his authority – possibly only a military alliance against their foe Gwynedd – played up too. He had every excuse to have claimed an 'imperial' power across Britain by c.890 had such a title been a viable option. But the political 'memory' of an august imperial predecessor was not a factor among the Anglo-Saxons.

There was no plethora of ultra-competitive dynasts (with their own retinues of warriors) in late ninth century England to defy and undermine a temporary unity imposed by a successful war-leader, and Burghred of Mercia had no known heirs. Alfred, however, proceeded cautiously even as the prestigious victor of Ethandun in 878, where he had routed Guthrum's second invasion of Wessex and forced him to 'sign up' to becoming his ally and converting to Christianity. He was a more powerful leader than any king of a Mercia shorn of half its land, and merely co-opted the Mercian leader 'Ealdorman' Aethelred as his son-in-law and ally. Mercia was not annexed until Alfred's son Edward had acquired all the Viking lands south of the Trent in 917–18, and even then it is possible that he had to placate local particularism as he seems to have placed one son (Athelstan) in Mercia – as its next king?[17] – and the designated heir (Aelfweard) in Wessex. The West Saxons seem to have been reluctant to accept a union with Mercia under Athelstan when Aelfweard died just after Edward in July 924, as Athelstan was not crowned their king for another year. Even in 957 the Mercians were to revolt against the unpopular young King Edwy[18] and install his brother Edgar as their sovereign. Given this level of Mercian particularism, it is probable that a union of Wessex and Mercian crowns in the 870s or 880s would have been a fraught option and open to local rebellion.

If Wessex had been militarily dominant and Mercia left without a strong king, the possibility would have arisen of the political choice that Edward seems to have made in 918–24 (and Edmund in 946?) – keeping the Mercian kingdom in existence for a prince of Wessex. It may only have been Wessex heir Aelfweard's early death in 924 that united Wesex and Mercia under Athelstan, not Edward's 'centralizing' plans. The Mercian nobles revolted against Edwy of Wessex in favour of his brother Edgar in 957, and as both were in their teens a long-term division of England might have resulted had Edwy not died in 959. Thereafter, the next death of a strong king with two sons available – Edgar in 975 – did not lead to a division of England, though it is possible that the subsequent armed defiance of the Church's 'excessive' possession of estates in 975–7 was concentrated in Mercia, governorship of its leader Earl Aelfhere, and had an anti-Wessex element. Nor was division of a 'multi-state' English realm among several princes from one dynasty a new policy. Egbert of Wessex had imposed his son Aethelwulf on conquered Kent in 825 to keep the kingdom technically in existence but practically dependent, and in 839 Aethelwulf passed Kent on to his relative (son or brother?) Athelstan when he succeeded to Wessex. Unification only occurred in 860. Mercia, too, had imposed a junior royal relative (Coenwulf's brother, Cuthred) to rule Kent in the 800s; it is possible that the mysterious 'Athelstan' who ruled East Anglia as a Wessex ally from c.825 was a relative of Egbert.

(iii) Wessex's role as unifier – only possible due to the Viking invasions?
The probability of an end to any succession of strong and able leaders able to achieve an unbroken record of military success – if not of dynastic disputes or usurpations – made any kingdom's supremacy ephemeral. In that respect Wessex in the 820s was no more able to impose a permanent military supremacy than any other kingdom had been. In 830 Wiglaf of Mercia regained his lost throne, and thereafter Egbert and his son Aethelwulf at best had control of Essex and some links with East Anglia. No kingdom, not even Offa's Mercia, had been able to produce a stable system of overlordship over its neighbours, although the latter had been able to reduce the rulers of subordinate neighbours (Hwicce as well as Sussex) to the legal rank of governors, 'duces', rather than kings and a succession of strong Mercian rulers with large armies and a sufficient military reputation could have extended this to other smaller kingdoms in the ninth century. A Mercian military genius with an ability to win crushing victories and pretensions as great as Offa's could have defeated Wessex as crushingly as Wulfhere had done and broken it up territorially again, or divided Deira from Bernicia to weaken Northumbria.

Egbert could have defeated Wiglaf or a successor in the 830s and enabled himself and an equally vigorous son to maintain a military supremacy south of the Humber. Given Mercia's size and unity, it is unlikely that Egbert could have controlled it for long via a 'puppet' or divided it into several kingdoms as Oswy had done in 655. Any son or grandson he had intruded into the kingdom as his client – possibly the obscure Athelstan who succeeded his father (?) Aethelwulf as sub-king in Kent in 839 on Egbert's death – would have faced a local challenger. Aethelwulf was not Egbert's equal as a warlord despite his impressive victory over the Vikings at Aclea in 851, allying with Mercia on equal terms in the early 850s and being unable to regain his throne when his son Aethelbald denied him entry back to Western Wessex after his Roman pilgrimage in 855–6. Aethelbald had shared in the glory at Aclea and had enough noble support to take his father's throne successfully in 856, but died in 860 (aged at most in his thirties).

But it was only the circumstances of the Viking invasions that made Wessex the kernel of the new English kingdom by breaking up Mercia (whose eastern half was lost to Viking settlers) in 875 and creating a new Viking kingdom of York, reducing the independent Anglian state of the north-east to the minor power of Bernicia. Indeed, given Wessex's long coastline and susceptibility to invasion from several directions at once (as in 878) the chances of Wessex of surviving a prolonged Viking assault cannot have seemed high to a contemporary observer. Even the weak Mercian ruler of 851–875, Burghred, had been able to continue to defeat the Welsh with West Saxon help.[19] Had he (or more likely a better Mercian general) and his West Saxon allies had the military capability and luck to starve out the Vikings' headquarters at Nottingham in 868–9 and destroy or force out the 'Great Army' Mercia still stood as great a chance as raiding-exposed Wessex of surviving as the major Anglo–Saxon military power. Edmund of East Anglia, whether or not a saintly pacifist in reality as well as legend, had been forced to give aid to the Vikings in 866 and was heavily defeated late in 869 so that kingdom's triumphs of the 820s were long behind it. In Northumbria Kings Osbert and Aelle fought over the throne as the Vikings occupied York, uniting too late to save the kingdom, and in Wessex Aethelwulf's surviving sons after 860 were young and inexperienced. A better general as King of Mercia in the 860s should have been in a good position to maintain the kingdom as a viable separate unit from Wessex, particularly if a Viking defeat at Nottingham led to the opportunistic raiders giving up inland campaigns and returning to the coastal assaults on Wessex of the 830s to 850s.

(iv) Alfred and the Vikings. What if he had lost, and how did he avoid it?
Wessex repeatedly stood on a 'knife-edge' from 871 to 878, and the large Viking armies on the Continent felt it worth returning for another attack in 892. The careful *Chronicle* records of what the Viking army was doing on the Continent in the 880s show that the Wessex leadership was alert to the possibility that the enemy would give up attacking Francia and return to invade them again.[20] In 871 the Vikings could not be driven out of Reading, and a frontal attack on the town after the psychological boost of the victory at Ashdown was heavily repulsed.[21] In 876 their eventual evacuation of their base at Wareham (in the centre of previously unravaged territory, and close to the sea so easy to supply) was probably due to the loss of their fleet in a storm off Swanage. This piece of luck probably then aided Alfred in forcing the land–based Viking expedition, now transferred to another riverine base at Exeter,[22] to agree to terms and promise to leave Wessex in 877. The loss of ships would have prevented the invaders from bringing in adequate supplies. Was the storm the crucial blow that stopped Guthrum from holding out at Exeter as long as he had done at Wareham? Guthrum was forced to swear on his sacred arm-rings to leave Wessex alone and took his army back to Mercia,

but broke his word as soon as a chance for attack arose. Had he not been contained and forced out of Wareham, it had the potential to be a local equivalent of Waterford or Limerick as a Viking base for both trade and conquest; and offshore the Vikings could have used the defensible Isle of Wight as a base, as they appear to have done a century-and-a-quarter later.

Guthrum returned to the attack at midwinter 877–8, probably encouraged by the prospect of catching Alfred unawares at Chippenham close to the Viking bases in south-west Mercia. Attack by land was also less vulnerable to the disruption of supplies than attack by sea, as Guthrum had found – and the fact that Alfred was finally to confront him within a few miles of Chippenham in spring 878 indicates that however much of Wessex had submitted Guthrum had based his army around that town in its north, close to his supply-route to Mercia.[23] It is possible that West Saxon 'spin-doctors' covered up the extent of local submission to him, but Alfred had to hide in the impenetrable Somerset marshes and evidently lacked the ability to fight Guthrum for several months; probably most of Wiltshire, Dorset, and Hampshire were lost. The subsequent landing in north Devon by Hubba implies that that area was holding out, though the uncertain details of the campaign and location of his defeat may imply that 'ealdorman' Odda retreated to a well-defended hillfort (Cynwit/ Countisbury?) and so was nervous of open battle. But within a few months Alfred was able to summon enough men to a rendezvous on the Somerset-Dorset border at 'Egbert's Stone' (near Longleat?) to fight a battle, thus having approximately equal numbers to Guthrum. He then had the time to move up onto the ridge of Salisbury Plain for a battle in the open country there, probably unhindered; the resultant battle was probably on the edge of the ridge at Bratton Down above Westbury. Crucially, after this defeat at 'Ethandun' Guthrum could not sit it out in Chippenham as the sons of Ragnar had done in Reading after defeat at Ashdown in 871 – probably due to not having enough men left to man the walls. Alfred could starve him out as at Exeter in 877, and this time Guthrum was demoralized enough to keep his word to leave permanently – and to take his Christian baptism seriously.

Had Alfred lost a few more battles in the winter-spring of 871, been mortally wounded or succumbed to illness as his brother Aethelred did, or failed to recover from his ignominious flight to Athelney in early 878, the Vikings would have been able to partition his kingdom as they had done to Mercia and Northumbria. The Viking failure to capture or kill him in their surprise assault in midwinter on Chippenham was crucial to Wessex's survival, and the disheartened and disorganized leadership of Wessex clearly had to make a major effort to collect an army to challenge Guthrum at Easter 878. Their victory at Ethandun, probably on the Wiltshire Downs near

Edington, restored the initiative to them and when Guthrum was starved out in Chippenham he luckily chose to abide by the terms of his treaty. His forced conversion to Christianity may even have had a moral effect on him, though his withdrawal to East Anglia in 879/80 still left exhausted Wessex open to attack from new Viking expeditions. Luckily the main Continental army of Vikings was preoccupied in northern Francia through the 880s, giving Wessex a crucial breathing-space to recover and enabling Alfred to build up his defensive system of 'burhs' as local centres of resistance.

When the Vikings next arrived in force to attack Wessex in the early 890s the invaders had to construct their own camps, e.g. Haesten's in Kent, not use convenient Saxon towns. Alfred had a 'rota' system for military service in place so he had a permanent army ready to blockade the invaders who could not wait for the Saxon forces to go home at the end of a regulated length of service.[24] This tactic of 'sitting it out' behind strong fortifications had probably given Halfdan's army success against Burghred in the confrontation at Nottingham in 868, and was Guthrum's plan in seizing Wareham in 875 and Exeter in 876 – both had river-access so the Vikings could bring in supplies while the Saxons had to live off their own people outside the walls. Now the Vikings did not have time on their side.

The invaders were continually harried, reducing their ability to take supplies and thus survive long sieges, and camps at Benfleet and on the Colne and Lea (within reach of the Thames estuary for longships bringing supplies and men) were blockaded and starved out.[25] Significantly the wars became much less static with the invaders marching long distances across country as far as Bridgnorth – presumably to try to find a safe base and easy loot. The repeated Viking 'breakouts' in this last phase of the war suggests that they were running out of supplies and needed to find a new base before they starved, preferably in an unravaged area such as Western Mercia. But once they were out in the open – and unfamiliar – countryside they were at risk of defeat by the local levies, as Edward achieved against the southern Kent Viking army at Farnham in 893. They also had to set up new camps where they could and hope that these were strong enough to withstand siege, as at Buttington and Bridgnorth in the final campaigns; if they were really unlucky they could be caught at a disadvantage and trapped, as the Farnham survivors were north of London on a river-island in 893.

If Wessex had fallen in 871, 876–7, or most likely in 878 it is unlikely that the new Viking settlers from Denmark and Norway would have been interested in the moors of Devon and Cornwall or the forests of the Weald where some minor Saxon lordships could have survived. Wessex would have been as permanently crippled as the other two major kingdoms, and the Danelaw with its Scandinavian settlement, social patterns, and linguistic

affinities extended across the more fertile parts of Wessex. As in the East
Midlands (with the 'Five Boroughs') and at Cambridge, there would
probably have been small political 'units' established around towns as
trading-centres. The likeliest Wessex equivalents of Viking Derby,
Nottingham, and so on would have been towns such as Winchester, Exeter,
Reading, and Wareham – the seaborne Vikings made great use of rivers and
the latter three towns had been used as Viking bases in the wars with Alfred.
Given the strict political control of the *Anglo-Saxon Chronicle*, which
presented an 'authorized version' of the disaster of early 878, we cannot tell
if Guthrum had any discontented princeling – possibly Aethelred's
disinherited young sons, Alfred's nephews – in mind as a 'puppet-king' of
any part of Wessex that was not to be colonized.[26]

It was Alfred's military leadership over decades and his abilities as an
organizer and inspirer that preserved his kingdom to take the lead in the
diffuse world of English, Viking, and Celtic states in the British Isles in the
early tenth century. His scholarly interests, unusual concern both for literacy
among the elite and for the preservation of culture, and personal leadership
in translating useful and inspiring works that lauded Christian leadership
showed his range of talents. As shown by Asser, he was interested in the
wider world of Christendom and sought to build up relations with other
states, received visiting Scandinavian trading explorers and passing holy
men, and worried about the state of learning in a war-ravaged island that had
lost time for the cultivate arts; he was also almost certainly the driving force
behind the creation (or updating?) of the *Anglo-Saxon Chronicle* with an aim
of preserving the inspiring 'authorized version' of his kingdom's and the
Saxon peoples' history to rally his nation in an era of unprecedented threat.
He was the English Charlemagne, with fewer resources so a greater
achievement – and Asser's biography has been seen as inspired by (or
perhaps partially copying ideas from) Einhard's early ninth century life of
that emperor. Some historians have suggested that the surprise double visit
that Asser says he made as a small child to Rome and his anointing by Pope
Leo IV – unusual for a fourth or fifth son not likely to succeed to any throne
– was exaggerated or invented to link him to Charlemagne's coronation by
Pope Leo III.[27] This seems unlikely. But in his multitude of interests and
wide-ranging concerns he gave a coherence and sense of purpose to late
ninth century Wessex, quite apart from his military successes and
administrative reforms. This set the template for the evolution of the
English kingship as it expanded in the early tenth century to take over the
rest of the Anglo-Saxon and Viking kingdoms.

The advantage in that multitude of states lay with the one with the most
determined long-term leadership and the best-organized and led army, and
it was Wessex's good fortune that the new Viking settlements in the East

Midlands and East Anglia had no worthy leadership after Guthrum (d. 890) and rarely acted in co-ordination. The various disunited local jarldoms of Denmark, Norway, and Sweden were able to pursue their own development unhindered and a dynasty of permanent 'centralized' leadership emerged in each (though their traditions spoke of earlier kingship before the ninth to tenth centuries, this is probably only legend). War-leaders united permanent kingdoms. But in England only York served that role for the Vikings, with a distinct and vigorous dynasty linked to that of Dublin though plenty of competition among its rival personnel, and the West Saxons were able to overrun the other Viking 'mini-states' one by one with their superior and unrelenting 'war-machine' under as succession of able adult leaders. The worst possible threat to Wessex was a talented and charismatic Dublin warlord using his battle-hardened Dubliners to take over York and then march into the 'Five Boroughs'; it only faced this from Olaf Guthfrithson in 937 (backed by Scotland) and in 939–41.

By the time the West Saxon kings came up against York in the mid-920s they had built up their resources enough to meet the Dublin-backed York dynasty and their 'wave' of new Norse settlers in Cumbria and Lancashire on at least equal terms. But the repeated succession-crises in faraway Winchester and local particularism enabled the Dublin-York dynastic contenders to stage several successful revolts against Wessex (and fight among themselves). The deaths of Athelstan in 939 and his brother Edmund in 946 caused revolt in York, with the Christian Archbishop notably backing local Viking princes – nominally Christian but culturally linked to the pagan world of Scandinavia – against distant Wessex. Archbishop Wulfstan even backed pagan Vikings rather than Christian kings of Wessex, including the psychopathic Erik 'Bloodaxe' of Norway, though he seems to have encouraged whichever Viking ruled York to convert.[28] The Vikings of York and Dublin were never united for long enough, or on easy enough terms with their previous victims the Scots, to make a sustained challenge to West Saxon power – though the victory of their occasional coalitions, as at Brunanburh in 937, would have halted the consolidation of Wessex-led 'England' at the Humber for many years.

Alfred – an unlikely king?

Indeed, as the youngest of Aethelwulf's four (or five?) sons Alfred had been unlikely to succeed to the throne at all until one brother after another died without male heirs or leaving infants. It is unclear if the mysterious Athelstan, who succeeded Aethelwulf as sub-king of Kent in 839, was a son or a brother.[29] But the eldest (other?) son of Aethelwulf, Aethelbald, the co-victor of Aclea against the Vikings in 851, was at least sixteen or so by then and possibly much older; he was born c.830–5 and Alfred was born in 847/9.[30] He could normally have been expected to survive to his fifties or sixties and to provide sons by the wife he married in 858, Judith the daughter of Charles 'the Bald' – his own stepmother. He was able to win enough local support for a revolt against their absent father in 856 to secure half the kingdom, and when Aethelwulf returned to England he was unable to remove his son from the west and had to make do with co-rule with his next son, Aethelbert, in Kent and Sussex.[31] Accused of unfilial greed and marrying incestuously, Aethelbald may have been controversial but he was not weak; he could have put up as good a fight as Alfred. When he died in 860 Aethelbert succeeded to a reunited kingdom, but died midwinter 865/6 – clearly aged not much over thirty.

Aethelred, Alfred's next brother, was the co-victor of Ashdown over the main 'Great Army' in 871, whatever the truth of the story in Asser's biography of Alfred, that he was prevented from a misjudgement over delaying the attack there by Alfred's greater strategic ability.[32] Aethelred, sidelined by the account of 870–1 in Asser's biography of Alfred, was as much responsible as Alfred for the heroic stand of Wessex in the 'battle-winter'. But the mortality in the House of Cerdic in the 860s and early 870s played a major role in the development of 'England' over the next half-century.

Other kingdoms that emerged from the stimulus of resistance – the case of Scotland

A parallel also exists with the evolution of the kingdom of Scots, traditionally unified in 843 by Kenneth mac Alpin (Cinaed mac Alpin). Here the two separate monarchies of the kingdoms of Picts (the central Highlands and the east) and of the Scots of Dalriada (Argyll) had shared one ruler before, with the Scots prince Constantine mac Fergus (d. 820) ruling the Picts from c.789 and then the Scots too from 811. He was succeeded by his brother Fergus, who died in 834; after this the two kingdoms were separated again. Probably they were the sons of a Pictish princess, like other non-Pictish rulers of the Pictish kingdom, but no Scots princes had been able to succeed to this throne before. One strong Pictish king, Angus, had ruled both kingdoms in the mid-eighth century; this seems to have been a personal ascendancy[33] achieved by warfare rather than a dynastic claim and the Pictish state was probably the more powerful as well as the larger. The details of current Viking attacks are far sparser than for England but the evidence of settlement in the Hebrides indicates a strong Scandinavian presence and Iona was sacked five times in these decades.[34] Logically, the pressure of Viking raids was what impelled the two kingdoms, former foes, to share one king; the permanent union under Kenneth followed a major Pictish disaster c.839 when King Eoganann and much of his nobility were killed in battle by the Vikings near St Fillans.[35] Later myth added that Kenneth invited the surviving Pictish nobility to a banquet and murdered them, but this is unverifiable.

It is probable that this loss of Pictish manpower caused the union, with the Scandinavian settlements in the Hebrides inducing the more exposed Scots communities in coastal Argyll to relocate inland to the Highlands; their 'coronation-stone' was now moved from their main royal residence, the hillfort of Dunadd in Lorne, to inland Dunkeld.[36] Dunkeld was now the royal religious centre for the united kingdom. Kenneth himself did not come from the main royal line of Scots, and indeed his lineage is unclear though strenuous efforts were made to give his obscure connections a respectable link to the ancient royal family and make him a legitimate descendent of the founder Fergus mac Erc. His father, Alpin, may have been the son of Eochaid 'the Poisonous', an obscure eighth century king, and Kenneth appears to have been from a minor line ruling in Viking-afflicted Galloway;[37] he clearly emerged to take over the Scots kingship around 840 as the best military commander available. As in Alfred's and Edward's cases in England, it was military success that determined who now emerged as leader of the local 'resistance' and the surviving indigenous kingdoms united under this leader. The pressure of Viking attack also caused Strathclyde to unite with the new kingship in the 880s, its capital Dumbarton having been sacked in 871 and the sons of Ragnar using the route across Strathclyde as their main route from conquered York to Ireland in the 870s. As with Wessex and Thomond, the stimulus of successful resistance led to the 'national' leadership of a new dynasty. But in this case, as with Alfred's line in Wessex but not with Brian 'Borumha's line in Munster, the new kingdom lasted.

Chapter Five

The Kingdom of Wessex/England from the Reign of Alfred

The overlooked factor of genetic weakness among England's first kings

Fewer early deaths, less instability in the tenth and eleventh centuries?

The ages reached by the first all-English sovereigns in the tenth and early eleventh centuries were notably less than those of comparable Continental dynasties. For example, Alfred died at around fifty-one, Edward 'the Elder' at around fifty-three, Athelstan at around forty-five, Eadred at around thirty-seven, Edwy at eighteen (?), Edgar at around thirty-two, Aethelred 'Unraed' at around forty-nine, and Cnut at around forty or forty-seven. In some of these cases violence was involved or a contributory factor, as with the murdered Edmund I (killed in an avoidable brawl at his hall at Pucklechurch in 946) and the possibly-murdered Edmund II 'Ironside'. In France in the same era, Charles 'the Great' (Charlemagne) lived to around sixty-seven, his third son and successor Louis 'the Pious' to sixty-two, Louis' son Charles 'the Bald' to fifty-four, Hugh 'Capet' (founder of a new dynasty in 987) to around fifty-six, and Hugh's son Robert I to around sixty. In Germany, Lewis 'the German', son of Louis, lived to around seventy and Otto 'the Great' lived to sixty-two; the son and grandson of Otto, Otto II and III, died young but in unhealthy malarial Italy. In Italy/Lotharingia, Emperor Lothar (Lewis' brother) lived to around seventy and Louis' grandson Berengar of Friuli lived to over eighty. In distant Russia, the lengths of their adult reigns would indicate that Vladimir I lived to his fifties and his son Yaroslav 'the Wise' to around sixty. In Denmark, dates are less clear but Gorm 'the Old' ruled for around fifty years in the tenth century and his grandson Swein 'Forkbeard' probably reached his fifties; in Norway the founding king, Harald 'Finehair', traditionally ruled for around fifty years and was probably over seventy when he died. In Scotland, King Constantine II must have been born by 878 due to the date of his father's death, abdicated in 942, and died in 952; Malcolm I (d. 954) probably reached sixty and Malcolm II (d. 1034) probably eighty. Malcolm III was killed aged around sixty-three, and his youngest son, David, lived to around sixty-nine.

When we look at the ages reached by the early English kings, one fact stands out. Among all the 'Cerdicing' line of Wessex from the ninth to eleventh centuries, only Edward 'the Confessor' definitely reached his sixtieth birthday as he was witnessing charters in 1005 and died on 5 January 1066. Egbert of Wessex may have done so, as he was born in the 770s (possibly as early as 772) and died in 839. His son Aethelwulf was probably at least in his mid-50s when he died in 858, being born after his father went into exile in Francia (in c.789 or 799) and married a Frankish princess. The early deaths of the strong rulers and national unifiers Athelstan (born c.894, died 939) and Edgar (born c.943, died 975) were particularly catastrophic in terms of the civil unrest and revolts that followed. When Athelstan died the recently-conquered kingdom of York fell to a Scandinavian challenger, Olaf Guthfrithson, who briefly reoccupied the Danelaw and split the kingdom of England into two; when Edgar died there was a disputed succession between two under-age heirs and the victor (Edward 'the Martyr') was soon murdered. The continuing early deaths of the kings were a major factor for breaks in political continuity given the accession of minors or disputed heirs. Even Cnut, the Danish conqueror of England in 1016, died in his forties (1035) and his two surviving sons died in their twenties, leaving the kingdom to the unlikely figure of Cnut's defeated rival Edmund's half-brother Edward 'the Confessor'. What could the results have been if this level of turbulence had not occurred? And how much of a factor was royal ill-health – perhaps due to genetic weakness – in the repeated crises of tenth century England, which inhibited its smooth development as a powerful monarchy?

(a) King Alfred and the rebellion of Aethelwold

Alfred's mysterious chronic illness, alleged by 'Asser' in his contemporary biography (with the possibility of the latter having been (re?)-written in the early eleventh century according to Alfred Smith[1]), does not seem to have inhibited his effectiveness as a multi-talented ruler of genius and the founder of the Anglo–Saxon kingdom of England. He was able to survive the rigours of the long campaign against the Viking 'Great Army' in 870–1 and his time in hiding in the marshes of Athelney in early 878 without noticeable effects on his health, and it is possible that Asser (or his editor/continuator?) was less concerned with strict accuracy about his condition than a hagiographical picture of a saintly king heroically bearing his God-given affliction. Some modern writers have seen the king's condition as a mixture of piles and psychosomatic breakdown caused by concerns over his sexual desires, and the medieval details are confused. Smith thinks the details were 'lifted' by the monkish historian Byrtferth of Ramsey Abbey c.1000 from a biography of St Odo of Cluny, though most scholars would defend Asser as being the author. Whatever the truth it was not crucial to Alfred's career. It may have been responsible for his elder son, Edward, taking the lead more in campaigns in the 890s, though Alfred was evidently wisely giving him military experience and a chance to build up a reputation as a war-leader ready to take over.

Alfred's main politico-military goal was achieved with the end of the repeated Viking attempts to conquer his kingdom in 896 and the withdrawal of the final raiding army that had crossed from the Continent. Peace followed with little of note mentioned in the *Anglo-Saxon Chronicle*, so if Alfred – apparently aged twenty-three at the time of his accession in April 871, so born between spring 848[2] and spring 849 – had not died at the age of fifty-one or fifty-two in October 899 there would not have been much difference to English political affairs. His nephew Aethelwold, son of his elder brother, Aethelred I, who died during the campaign against the Viking 'Great Army' based at Reading, was excluded from the throne in 871 as an infant in the adult Alfred's favour. On Alfred's death the proven war-leader Edward – victor at Farnham in 893 – was chosen as king rather than Aethelwold, rather than a return to the elder line. As in Kent after the succession of the late ruler's adult second son rather than the young sons of his deceased elder son in 640 (and then the failure of these princes to get the succession the next time round in 664), a prince passed over once could be passed over again. In retaliation Aethelwold tried to raise a revolt at his residence at Wimborne, was besieged by Edward and forced to withdraw, and fled to Viking Northumbria. He returned with an army to challenge Edward in 903, and won over the Viking rulers of East Anglia,[3] but was defeated and killed in the Fens. He would have been likely to do this at whatever point Alfred died – and his being killed in the retreat from his invasion of Wessex was a matter of luck for Edward. The battle was far from easy for the army of Wessex, as seen by the casualty list, and they were far from their border so Aethelwold had a good chance of outmarching them and escaping to stage another attack later.

Only the half of Mercia west of the Watling Street border with the Danes, that part not seized for Danish settlement by the 'Great Army' in 875, had survived the Viking onslaught. A union with Wessex to concentrate resources under one ruler would seem logical but was evidently impractical due to Mercian 'national' pride and a desire for their own rulers, even with the line of kings broken and only a leader of provincial noble rank –

'Ealdorman' Aethelred – remaining as the two surviving Saxon states became stable in the 880s. Alfred, himself married to the Mercian aristocrat Ealswith of the 'Gaini', married off his eldest daughter Aethelfleda – who showed herself to be as competent a ruler as her father and brother over thirty years – to the new ruler as his ally and the two states co-operated closely but did not merge. Alfred and Edward – the latter perhaps more impatiently, considering his speed in annexing Mercia once he had the chance – were wisely content to accept the continuing independence of their weaker Anglo-Saxon neighbour, Mercia, from 886 to 917 under allied rulers (firstly Alfred's son-in-law 'Ealdorman' Aethelred and daughter Aethelfleda and from 911 the latter alone), rather than attempt the politically risky policy of annexing it. That would have run the risk of revolt thereafter from Mercian particularism, which may have led to Edward designating separate sons as rulers of Wessex and Mercia after he did annex Mercia in 918 (Aelfweard and Athelstan) and was notable in defiance of the ruler in Wessex as late as 957. Edward did not try annexing Mercia until he had secured the military resources of the Danelaw and East Anglia and the kingdom had a young and untried female ruler, his niece Ecgwynn, in 918 after the death of her parents.[4] Had Ecgwynn been a boy, local nobles were more likely to have rallied round her as a logical future war-leader.

Accordingly, it is very likely that if Alfred had continued to reign through the 900s there would have been continuing stability between Wessex and Mercia and no challenge from Aethelwold; the two crucial moments for decision were the Wessex succession and then the death of the survivor of the two Mercian rulers. Alfred, a cautious ruler, is less likely than Edward to have taken advantage of the apparent weakening of the Viking kingdom of East Anglia – perhaps only apparent to Wessex with the campaign of 903 that saw the defeat of Aethelwold and his Viking allies – and division of the settlers in the Danelaw to start annexing the Viking lands. He had been acknowledged as the ruler of all the English not under Viking rule, even the nominal suzerain of distant and allied Bernicia where the Angles held out under a local dynasty independent of Viking York, and had high concepts of his duty to his people as a Christian sovereign. But he made no moves to advance into Viking territory and bring the Christian Angles and Saxons there under Christian rule once the final invasion-threat ended in 896. The rulers of East Anglia from Guthrum, Alfred's godson who he had forced to convert after trapping him at Chippenham in the aftermath of the victory at Ethandun in 878, were at any rate nominally Christian and either allowed or joined in the local Christian East Angles' new cult of their late saintly 'martyr' king, Edmund. The end of the long direct Viking challenge to Wessex's independence probably left Alfred believing that his people deserved time to recover and rebuild prosperity and Christian civil society rather than a rash attempt to take advantage of the lack of experienced and/or aggressive military leaders in the Viking kingdoms. In addition, as a devout Christian scholar he may well have also regarded 'unnecessary' – non-defensive – war as a sin.

Whether or not it was his campaign into Viking lands to meet and defeat the challenge of Aethelwold that encouraged Edward to think that his army was capable of taking on and defeating the settlers in East Anglia and Danelaw, he waited another seven years after 903 (with one Viking intervention in the Severn valley in 905). He did not act until the Danelaw settlers had launched an attack on Western Mercia in 910.[5] This challenge, possibly a 'probe' by a new generation of Vikings to see if there were prospects of plunder or land-seizure as 'Ealdorman' Aethelred aged, may well have decided Edward to follow up his action in defeating the raid (at Tettenhall) with an offensive to seize strongpoints while the enemy were weak.

Wessex takes the offensive

The English response to the challenge of 910 – if it was as a result of that rather than a long-prepared plan – had to wait for the death of Aethelred in 911. That fact and the evident co-ordination of the English advance indicate a joint strategy worked out between the brother and sister now in full control of Wessex and Mercia, Edward and Aethelfleda. Their father's defensive strategy of centring troops, supplies, and civil and military control on the principal towns of an area as fortified 'burhs' was now used for an offensive purpose, to seize and control new areas. In 913 Edward crossed the Thames to build new fortresses at Hertford and Witham, securing Hertfordshire and Essex respectively; the *Chronicle* specifically reports the submission of various Danish settlers as sparked off by the building of Witham. In 914 the English built the new fortress of Warwick to control the central-West Midlands near the Anglo-Danish border of Watling Street, and a major Viking attack by sea up the Bristol Channel into Archenfield was driven off by the men of the West Mercian 'burhs' of Hereford and Gloucester. Later in the year Edward moved north to establish new forts on either side of the river at Buckingham, and the leading 'jarl', Thurcytel, most of the leaders of the settlers at Bedford, and many of the leaders of Northampton submitted. In 915 Chirbury, Runcorn, and an unknown site, 'Weardbyrig', were fortified in North-West Mercia; meanwhile, Edward took over Bedford in person with his army. In 916 he fortified Maldon to strengthen his position in Essex, and Thurcytel and other apparent opponents of West Saxon control were allowed to leave the East Midlands for Francia – thus denying the remaining settlers the crucial element of leadership. The following year he built a stronghold at Towcester, which was besieged by the Vikings from Leicester and Northampton but held out; an East Midlander Viking raid on Bedford and a similar assault on a new West Saxon fortress at Tempsford by the Vikings of East Anglia were also repulsed. Later in the summer Aethelfleda took the crucial North Midlands position of Derby and took over Leicester peacefully, and Edward (using two armies in rotation) proceeded in strength across East Anglia, defeating a Viking attack on Maldon and then retaking Colchester and Huntingdon.

The Vikings settled in East Anglia and the separate settler polity at Cambridge then accepted him as their lord. In 918 he moved into the remainder of the 'Five Boroughs' to take Stamford. With Aethelfleda dying that June, he was able to take over her dominions and secure the overlordship she had had over the Welsh kings of Gwynedd (Idwal ap Anarawd) and Dyfed (Hywel 'Dda' and his brother Clydog ap Cadell). He also secured Nottingham, the key to the North-East Midlands and the lower Trent lost to the Vikings' 'Great Army' in 868. In 919 he moved north to secure Thelwall and Manchester and send troops into Northumbria. In 920 he refortified Nottingham and received the submission of the Anglian and Viking lords of the North-East and of King Constantine of the Scots.[6] The whole of England to the dubiously-delineated Scots border was thus actually or nominally gained by the joint forces of Wessex and Mercia in a piecemeal advance from 913 to 920, slowly at first but gathering momentum in 917–18 – when the evidence that the English were winning would have encouraged more leaderless Viking settlers than before to submit and retain their lands.

The English advance had adapted Alfred's tactics rather than inventing new ones, with Edward and Aethelfleda acting in concert and the originator of the strategy unrecorded. (It was the usual practice of chroniclers to give credit to the king.) Alfred's only advance had been to secure London in 885/6, though he had prudently refrained from claiming it as part of Wessex and handed it to the nominal control of his new son-in-law, Aethelred;[7] it and Oxford had never been part of Wessex (unless perhaps in the late sixth century under Ceawlin) and seem to have been Mercian until 899. Alfred had raided East Anglia by sea on occasion, presumably as a pre-emptive strike against warships preparing to land in Kent, and it is possible that his evident strategic concern with the Thames estuary could have induced him too to annex Essex and build forts at Witham and Maldon if the opportunity arose. Essex had been a West Saxon vassal before the 860s, at least from Egbert's time, and control of the estuaries as far north as the Orwell would protect the Wessex coasts from new Viking raiding-bases. But he had never had serious trouble with his ex-foe and godson, Guthrum, in East Anglia after 878, and the *Chronicle* does not indicate any major local Viking aid to the overseas armies that encamped on the Colne and the Lea in the early 890s to raid Wessex.

A new generation of restless young Vikings might not have remained content to farm and so have 'probed' Wessex in the 900s even if the East Anglians had not been appealed to by Alfred's refugee nephew Aethelwold. Aethelred's death in 911 could also have sparked off a major raid westwards by land. But unless given a direct military challenge from East Anglia or Northumbria in the 900s, possibly on an impatient and fleeing Aethelwold's behalf, it is unlikely that an ageing Alfred would have been as willing as Edward was after 913 to run the risk of marching into the Viking lands or build more fortresses than those necessary to defend the existing border (possibly Hertford and Buckingham, to watch the Icknield Way, as well as those in Essex). It is still possible that Aethelwold – born around 870 – could have revolted in his uncle's lifetime and thus precipitated a course of events like that of real-life 900/03 or a war over the Viking lands, but more likely that he would have awaited the chances of the succession with the 'Witan' before giving up hope and revolting. Alfred would have had to live to around sixty-nine to outlive Aethelfleda in 918 and thus face the question of what to do about Mercia, though he is less likely than the more adventurous Edward to have 'cheated' his grand-daughter out of her inheritance.

The situation in 924 – was the preservation of English unity accidental not planned?

It should be remarked that evidence is not adequate to speculate about what would have happened had Aelfweard not died young in 924. The elder of two sons by Edward's second (or first legitimate?)wife, he died within seventeen days of his father in July 924. Edward had died on the Dee while in north-western Mercia and his son seems to have died at Oxford, probably en route to coronation at Winchester or Kingston-upon-Thames. It is not certain that Edward's second marriage followed his accession in 899, but Aelfweard was at most in his mid-20s. His elder half-brother Athelstan was brought up at Aethelfelda's Mercian court, logically as heir to Mercia, and was not accepted as the next king of Wessex well into 925. In turn, Aelfweard's full brother Edwin died mysteriously (apparently drowned in the Channel) in 933, possibly while fleeing the kingdom – twelfth century stories spoke of a plot against Athelstan who had him killed.

Athelstan's refraining from marriage is also unusual, and later it was said that he had promised to stay unwed when he was accepted as king of Wessex in 925 in order not to jeopardize the chances of his half-brothers (Edwin and the two sons of Edward's third marriage, Edmund and Eadred). The antiquity of this tradition is uncertain, but it would explain the mysterious 'stand-off' in Wessex in 924–5 before Athelstan's coronation – which the *Chronicle* carefully avoids mentioning. Had Aelfweard not died suddenly, would the unity of England have ended in 924 and the separate kingships of Wessex and Mercia resumed? This possibility is a warning against assuming that Edward deliberately created a long-term 'united kingdom' in 918. But it is only guesswork to suggest that there was something suspicious about Aelfweard's death, i.e. murder by Athelstan's partisans, given that there is no contemporary evidence and that even later stories are confused. One version has it that Aelfweard was a hermit at Bridgnorth and did not even want the throne,[8] being pressurized into taking it. If he had succeeded his father as king of Wessex in July 924 and Athelstan had been recognized as king of Mercia, the co-operation but separate political leadership of the two states in 886–918 would have continued, and the warlike and politically ambitious Athelstan would have been likely to use the Mercian army to annex York and the Norse settlements of Cumbria in the late 920s. Operating from Tamworth or Chester not from Winchester, he would have had an easier task of keeping the new state unified than the kings of Wessex did in 927–954. But if Aelfweard's early death indicates that the genetic weakness of the Cerdicing line affected him, it is possible that he would have died before either a son of his (born in the late 920s?) or his half-brother Edmund (born 920/1?) became adult. Would Athelstan then have claimed the throne of Wessex and eliminated Aelfweard's full brother, Edwin?

(b) King Athelstan (d. October 939)

The results of Athelstan's early death were a renewed revolt by the Viking settlers in York and the Danelaw in winter 939–40 and the temporary renewal of independence, aided by Dublin Vikings under Olaf Guthfrithson.

Athelstan died c.45 in 939, two years after defeating the great Celtic-Viking coalition of his enemies at Brunanburh and thus preserving the new kingdom he had created with his annexation of York in 927. His date of birth is unclear, but it would appear that he was the eldest son of Edward, by a marriage (?) whose legitimacy could be questioned, and that he was a small boy who was old enough to appear at a public ceremony in Alfred's lifetime (when he was allegedly dressed in a ceremonial outfit with a scarlet cloak that could be taken subsequently as prefiguring his imperial rule). This mysterious incident, related c.1125 by William of Malmesbury and assumed by him to show Alfred's support for his good-looking and talented grandson's future prospects, paralleled Alfred's own ceremonial debut in Rome in 854. Its being remembered and 'highlighted' was probably a conscious act by Athelstan himself to point out the parallels with Alfred's career – assuming that William was using a reliable source for it. At the time of the incidents, both had been boys aged around five, unlikely to succeed to the throne due to the existence of better-qualified brothers.

At the earliest, he may have been born c.892; the story that his mother was a shepherdess who Edward had a 'one-night stand' with is probably later romance. William of Malmesbury is again the source for this, and it is possible that he was using a late Saxon 'saga' poem celebrating Athelstan's career (which would indicate Athelstan's high repute among later generations). Edward seems to have entrusted the boy's upbringing to his sister, Aethelfleda, from c.900, either as her expected heir once it became apparent that she and Aethelred would not have a son or to remove him from the West Saxon court on account of his uncertain dynastic legitimacy. Possibly Edward's new wife's kin (or Edward's parents?) insisted on this to prevent dynastic strife between the partisans of Edward's sons by the two relationships. Even if this preceded the revolt of Edward's cousin Aethelwold in 902 (a warning of what family strife led to) the danger of civil war over the throne on Edward's death was an obvious possibility if he had sons by two wives. It is not known if Alfred decided on sending his grandson to Mercia; one version has it that he approved of the idea of Athelstan inheriting Mercia but the decision may have been finalized after his death.[9]

In the 930s, the new kingdom of England was held together by the personal authority and military force of an adult male ruler. York had been subdued and its northern allies forced to accept vassalage by Athelstan in person with his army, so a revolt could be expected on his death. The pro-Saxon earldom of Bernicia, the last surviving portion of the Anglian kingdom of Northumbria north of the Tees and Alfred's former close ally, and any remaining landholders of Anglian extraction in former Deira were less significant in the control of York than the large number of Danish settlers in Yorkshire and Norse settlers in Cumbria and Lancashire (as indicated by the place-names). They were within reach of the Viking kingdom in Dublin, which in the 870s had been ruled with York by the sons of Ragnar Lothbrok, and the Dubliners – the dynasty dispossessed of York in 927 – could be expected to intervene again once Athelstan died. The first major challenge since the annexation of York in 927 had come in 937, with the British of Strathclyde and the Scots allied to the Vikings of Dublin in what was clearly a concerted Viking-Celtic attempt to drive Wessex out of Northern England. Athelstan and his brother Edmund defeated this at the battle of Brunanburh, which was aptly made the subject of a heroic Saxon poem but is obscure enough for us not to know its site. Yorkshire or the Wirral have been suggested.[10] The importance of the battle was obvious to contemporaries as it was celebrated in verse, including in the *Anglo-Saxon*

Chronicle; it did not end revolts against Wessex in York or Dublin attacks on the North but it did end large-scale anti-Saxon coalitions. The Welsh princes kept out of such plots thereafter, even under the – rare – union of both Gwynedd/ Powys and Dyfed under Hywel in 942–50; though King Edmund's killing of aggressive Idwal of Gwynedd in 942 may have been the decisive military reason for this rather than Brunanburh.

If Athelstan had lived longer the new kingdom of England, recent victor of Brunanburh, would probably not have seen revolt in Northumbria and the Danelaw in 939/40 and a renewed Viking kingdom of York. The local Vikings were clearly ready to rebel at the first chance; notably even the Archbishop (Wulfstan) supported them against his fellow-Christians, which argues for continuing Deiran resistance to rule from Winchester. The dynasty of Athelstan's late brother-in-law, Sihtric, had been dispossessed of York in 927 by Athelstan's first Northern campaign but still ruled Dublin and had the warriors there to launch an expedition across the Irish Sea to join Norse settlers in Lancashire and Cumbria. The current incumbent at Dublin, aggressive young Olaf Guthfrithson, was likely to attack York whenever Athelstan died. If he had lived to c.947/50, i.e. his father's age, or into the early 950s there would still have been revolt then. There is a possibility that Athelstan was considering installing a vassal Viking prince in York as his lieutenant when he died rather than keeping it under direct rule – a sensible precaution given the distance from Winchester to York in the event of a revolt there. But this is only speculation, though a logical move in line with Edward 's policy towards York in 920–4. If Athelstan had lived and handed York to a Viking 'ally', possibly a supposedly repentant Olaf Guthfrithson, there is no guarantee that he could trust them to stay loyal in the event of the Kingdom of England showing weakness at a future date.

Barring Athelstan handing York to a 'loyal' Viking ally, the pretenders to that kingdom would have had to attempt to seize it while the English King was preoccupied elsewhere. The likeliest contenders would have come from Dublin, the kingdom of the heirs of the Ragnarrson dynasty so with a hereditary claim to the loyalty of Yorkshire Danish settlers. The joint kingdom of York and Dublin held by the brothers Halfdan and Ivarr Ragnarrson in the early 870s was the obvious inspiration for such ambitious Dublin-based pretenders. If Olaf Sihtricson, heir to the late ruler Sihtric of York, was not willing to take the risk of invading and his more dynamic cousin, Olaf Guthfrithson, a restless and ambitious warlord, had gone off to try his luck elsewhere – the Hebrides? – the ex-king of Norway Erik 'Bloodaxe' of Norway was the most obvious candidate with a warband available. Already overlord of the Hebrides and an adventurer intent on claiming as wide a lordship as possible, the ferocious Erik would probably have been Athelstan's next major challenger after the Norse-Scots coalition of 937 and have attempted to move on York in the mid-later 940s or early 950s with his Hebridean vassals. He could have invaded the North via Lancashire, from Dublin, or less likely from the east coast – the route of Harald 'Hardradi' in 1066. Either route was possible for a conflict between Athelstan and Erik or between Athelstan and one of the Olafs, and as Athelstan had two adult half-brothers (Edmund and Eadred) by this point one or other of them could have commanded the English army if the king was unavailable due to ill-health or a revolt elsewhere. Accepting a Dubliner Viking vassal-ruler of York in 939, in return for their fighting off rivals, would have served to avoid the risk of an anti-Wessex revolt in York. Edmund attempted this course in 942–5. If Athelstan had considered this in the 940s, Olaf Sihtricson would have been a safer bet than the ultra-ambitious Erik.

Athelstan could have outlived Erik, his probable contemporary, and lived to the age of c.58 like Aethelwulf (i.e. to c.952) and passed the throne to his brother Edmund. It is possible that his success at Brunanburh would have emboldened him to marry and have a direct heir, breaking the compact he had made with his half-brothers' partisans in 925; after all, Alfred had not recommended his elder brother's passed-over son as his own heir but promoted his own son. (The final choice seems to have lain with the royal council, the 'Witan', so technically any private agreement between athelings over the succession could be countermanded.) But a son born to Athelstan c.940 would have been in a weak position as his successor compared with the adult and proven war-leader Edmund, at least until he had gained his own reputation; Edmund's infant sons were superseded by his adult brother in real-life 946; the same could easily have happened to under-age sons of Athelstan in the 950s.

Edmund or his next brother, Eadred, were unlikely to have been passed over when Athelstan died, as England needed an adult war-leader. The likelihood is that there would have been some Viking revolt in York then with or without aid from Dublin, perhaps backed by their 937 allies in Scotland instead; King Constantine (abdicated 942) and his successor, Malcolm I, were experienced warriors keen to defend their border lands of Cumbria, although only Constantine definitely participated in anti-Wessex coalitions to achieve this. Malcolm, whose power Edmund ended in Cumbria in real-life 945, was probably more cautious but may have lacked his predecessor's opportunity to secure aid from a war-minded Dublin Viking state. It is unclear if the Scots aided Erik 'Bloodaxe's attempts to regain York under Eadred (successful in 952), but they or ambitious Viking warlords from Dublin, Man and the Orkneys (the latter Erik's fief) would logically have assisted any attempt by Erik or another leader to seize York.

The timing of the Saxon succession would have been crucial. Had the English king died in the campaigning season – Athelstan died in October 939 so the West Saxon army could not be used for a northwards march until 940 and by then the rebels had spread south to the Danelaw and Edmund had to come to an agreement with them not fight – the new ruler should have been able to march north quickly. The 939/40 revolt in the Danelaw would have been unlikely if a Saxon army could arrive quickly and secure control; so if Athelstan had not died in autumn or winter Wessex was unlikely to have lost control of the region. The temporary disaster to Wessex of winter 939/40 was thus due to timing as much as to any underlying weakness – and as late as 1065 a determined elite revolt in York against the king's unpopular earl could secure practical autonomy with support within Mercia for it. A Viking revolt at York, with reinforcements arriving from Dublin, would still have been serious whenever it occurred and the new English king might well have had to accept York's independence to buy time rather than fight with the Danelaw restive and ready to revolt if he lost a battle against York. Edmund or Eadred, as the new Saxon ruler, would have been likely to accept York's revolt at first, and only move against it later. If Erik or one of the Olafs was the new ruler of York, the chronic divisions among the Viking leadership that led to a swift succession of rulers in the real-life York of the mid-940s could have caused the ruler who had first seized power to be overthrown, which would then give the English king a chance to invade.

(c) King Edmund I – murdered in a brawl at the age of twenty-five (?) in 946.

Results of the death of Edmund: as in (b), renewed independence by Viking York; but not this time revolt in the Danelaw
The early death of Edmund, born around 920/1 and fighting his first battle at Brunanburh in 937, in his mid-twenties was entirely fortuitous. Edmund could easily have avoided his unlucky stabbing (in a chance violent encounter in his hall at Pucklechurch[11]) in 946 and continued to reign for decades, perhaps into the 970s. His death was not even a result of a conspiracy – he apparently recognized a banished felon illegally attending a feast, ordered his steward to throw him out, and when the accused fought back came to the rescue to get stabbed. He had showed his ability in battle at an early age as Athelstan's fellow-commander at the crucial battle of Brunanburh in 937, when he was at most seventeen and probably only sixteen – an earlier age for a serious role in a first battle than Aethelbald (probably around eighteen to twenty at Aclea in 851), Alfred (twenty-three? at Ashdown in 871), and Edward 'the Elder' (around twenty-two at Farnham in 893). Given the high stakes involved in this battle between Athesltan's new kingdom of England

and a coalition of Norse, Scots, and Strathclyders, Athelstan is unlikely to have given him even a nominal role unless he showed military promise.

As king unexpectedly early at eighteen, Edmund had showed caution in tackling the immediate challenge of Olaf Guthfrithson of Dublin, not much older than him but far more experienced from teenage warfare in Ireland, as this veteran of Brunanburh returned in autumn 939 to seize control of York and in spring 940 advanced into the 'Five Boroughs'. Avoiding risky head-on conflict, he had waged a defensive campaign in the eastern Midlands, nearly trapped him and his mixed Dublin Viking – York – Anglo-Danish force at Leicester, and when his foe escaped had conceded control over all the Danish settlements in England to secure a truce, surrendering all that his brother and father had won since 914 (except possibly East Anglia).[12] This was not the usual rash eagerness for battle of a young atheling flushed by triumph at Brunanburh but mature – even excessive? – caution against an experienced foe with potential local aid from fellow-Viking Danelaw residents against the Wessex-based King. It is likely that Edmund saw his first priority to extricate his army, which local Anglo-Danes could betray to the Dubliners, and he was prepared to beat a temporary retreat with every intention of returning to the fray in a year or two. Saving the kingdom's manpower and leadership was better than risking a heavy defeat out of a sense of pride – the loss of many senior leaders at Ashingdon in 1016 and Hastings in 1066 was to paralyse the will to resist invaders and this could have happened at a battle in the Danelaw in 940.

Edmund's caution in 940 might have seemed ignominious, but the likelihood was that Olaf would not be able to control his vast Dublin-York-Danelaw dominion for long. The king had been duly rewarded as Olaf died in a skirmish in Bernicia within a year, and his successor in York, Olaf Sihtricson (son of Athelstan's reluctant vassal, Sihtric of York, d. 927), proved a weaker ruler. Edmund regained the 'Five Boroughs' in 942 and in 943 Olaf had to submit and become his vassal. Having gone back on his word to convert to Christianity, possibly alienating the powerful Archbishop Wulfstan of York (an opponent of English rule who preferred Viking to Wessex rulers in the North), Olaf was expelled from York by a revolt in favour of his cousin, Olaf Guthfrithson's brother Ragnall, who also submitted to Edmund. In 944 Edmund overran York, killing Ragnall, restoring Athelstan's full dominion, and in 945 he drove the refugee Olaf Sihtricson out of Cumbria, defeated its ruler Domnall (Dunmail) of Strathclyde at the pass of 'Dunmail's Rise' by Thirlmere, and forced the land's Scottish overlord, King Malcolm I, to agree to terms.[13] He had thus secured the same dominance that Edward and Athelstan had gained, making up for the inauspicious opening to his reign, and looked set to become as great a ruler as his two forebears.

The revolt that handed York over to the latest external Viking challenger, ex-king Erik 'Bloodaxe' of Norway, in 947 was still possible if Edmund had lived, given Erik's ambitions (and Orkney army to achieve them) and Wulfstan's hostility to English rule. England's misfortune was York's opportunity, and the revolt followed Edmund's death while his successor, Eadred (his younger brother, aged about twenty-three) was new to the throne; had Edmund been alive the revolt and/or an invasion by Erik would probably have been delayed for a year or two at least. The readiness of a strong king, lacking Eadred's probable ill-health, to retaliate quickly to rebellion might have delayed revolt for longer, but not indefinitely given Erik's restless ambition. Taking a risk for great rewards was in the Viking tradition, as taught to generations of future warriors by saga, and even a veteran adult English King such as Harold Godwinson in 1066 (or William in 1069) could face land-grabbing Norse or Danish attempts to retrieve York.

From the sketch of Edmund in the *Life of Dunstan* he would have been less eager for new monasteries and less of a partisan of the 'reforming' abbots and bishops than Edgar.[14] Conversely, it is possible that fewer grants of estates to the Church would have avoided the real-life antagonism to the 'monastic party' apparently in existence by Edgar's death and the resultant backing of one contending prince by nobles hoping for the confiscation of monastic estates. Edmund's relations with Dunstan were apparently wary, and the Saint's hagiography alleged that he had to be divinely[15] impressed into backing him by a near-fatal riding accident in the Cheddar Gorge. But as he had backed this obviously outstanding personality to be Abbot of Glastonbury c.943 he could also have decided that he was the most suitable candidate to be Archbishop of Canterbury in the vacancy of 958/9, possessing the required administrative skills to use the Church to promote national unity with the new ex-Danish lands. He would have passed the throne to one of his two sons – Edwy, b. c.941, or Edgar, b. c.943, as an adult. It is less likely that if Edmund had lived into his forties or fifties he would have been succeeded by his sickly brother Eadred, a year or so his junior, who died in real life in 955 – though without the strain of campaigning as king in the North in the early 950s the latter could have lived longer.

(d) King Edgar – dead at thirty-two? The consequences of another early royal demise

Edgar's rule of a united England from 959 – accident not design?
Edgar died c.32 in 975; he was born some time early in the reign of his father, Edmund, as his second son and was adult enough to be chosen as king by the

Mercians and Northumbrians as they revolted against his elder brother, Edwy, in 957. It has been surmised that his coronation at Bath in 973, intended to formalize the creation of the new kingdom of England (he had been crowned on his accession in 959, at the usual site of Kingston-upon-Thames), took place once he attained the age of thirty to symbolize his legal ability now to perform the functions of a priest as a 'sacral' king.[16] The inspiration was presumably the successful Frankish kingships on the Continent, as their sacral coronation-rite was adapted for the coronation at Bath Abbey. The use of Bath Abbey probably indicates a desire to use a physically impressive venue with Roman remains (the Roman Baths adjoining it were probably partly standing at this date) as an echo of Charlemagne's coronation in Rome in 800.

The reunification of England in 959, which occurred at Edgar's accession, was to prove permanent, except for a brief interval in 1016 when Edmund 'Ironside' had to cede the Danelaw and Northumbria to Cnut after the battle of Ashingdon. (His sudden death weeks later gave the entire country to his rival.) But only two years before the nobles of Mercia and Northumbria had taken Edgar, aged around fourteen, as their king[17] while leaving his elder brother Edwy – aged around sixteen – in control of Wessex. The 'revolt' may not have been as simple as a rejection of the hot-headed Edwy, who has received a poor 'press' due to his short reign, comparisons with his brother, and above all the hostility of Edgar's ally St Dunstan whom he banished from his court. The hagiography of Dunstan painted Edwy as an irresponsible and badly-advised young despot, a lecher who objected to Dunstan telling him off for leaving his coronation-feast in 956 in order to enjoy himself in a back room with his fiancée (?) and her mother. The latter two supposedly influenced Edwy to banish the moralist bishop in retaliation though their dispute may have been due to a struggle for control of patronage rather than something as simple as a quarrel at the coronation.[18] It is possible that the rejection of Edwy's rule by Mercia and Northumbria was not a simplistic 'revolt' against a rash and unpopular king, but an overdue implementation of Edwy's and Edgar's father Edmund's intended plan for the succession. This had been thwarted by his murder when the boys were too young to rule, which gave the crown of all England to his brother Eadred – had Edmund lived until they reached adulthood he would have given Mercia and Northumbria to Edgar. It should be recalled that the same 'post facto' rationalization occurred concerning the plans of Edward 'the Elder'– he may have intended to divide England too, giving the North to Athelstan and the South to the 'legitimate' Aelfweard (see above). Athelstan had been brought up in Mercia, at his aunt Aethelfleda's court; Edgar was brought up, at Edmund's wishes, in the household of Athelstan 'Half-King', 'ealdorman' of East Anglia and most of the East Midlands.[19] Athelstan's son and heir, Aethelwold, who would by this arrangement be the principal governor of local districts under Edgar's rule, was the latter's foster-brother. It would seem that the division of England was thus the implementation of Edmund's long-term plans, and that only the death of Edwy, aged around eighteen, in autumn 959 – unusually young, even for a male of the line of Wessex – prevented the arrangement lasting. The unity of England in the 960s, as after 925, may have been fortuitous and not a 'master plan' by the country's royal leadership.

975 and after – the effects of royal mortality

Edgar, not known for any earlier ill-health, could have lived for another decade or two and passed the throne to one of his sons, Edward (b. c.962) or Aethelred (b. 966/7), as an adult. Alternatively, if Aethelred's older full brother Edmund had not died c.972 he would have succeeded Edgar or Edward.[20] Nor is it clear that the succession was straightforward. Edgar's marriage to Aethelred and Edmund's mother, Elfrida, was his second, or according to one account his third, and the legal status of his earlier unions may have been dubious. The sordid story that Edgar (and Elfrida?) disposed of her previous husband, ealdorman Aethelwold,[21] to make way for their marriage is probably part of the subsequent blackening of Elfrida's reputation due to her alleged part in regicide in 978.

As with the marriage of Edward 'the Elder' and the mother of Athelstan, the king's first marriage may have been irregular – or so backers of his younger sons could claim. The question may revolve around whether a marriage was contracted in church. It is possible that Edgar's marriage to Edmund and Aethelred's mother, Elfrida, involved an agreement that their son Edmund would be his heir, replacing his older son Edward[22] – though this partly relies on a dubious later biography that also puts forward the unlikely claim that Edgar and Elfrida murdered Aethelwold. It is not, however, impossible, given the precedent of Edward 'the Elder' excluding his eldest son, Athelstan, from the succession in favour of the son of a later marriage.

Edgar, like Edwy, was accused of lust and unscrupulous treatment of people who defied him, though this may reflect political opposition rather than reality. All the evidence has to be filtered through the later prism of Elfrida's increasingly hostile portrayal in the sources, with the disasters of her son's reign being regarded as divine punishment for her murder of her stepson. The criticism seems to have rubbed off on Edgar too for marrying her – and, as with Edwy, can be linked to the Church.

It is crucial to remember that if Edgar's son Edmund had lived, the ultimately disastrous Aethelred would have been unlikely to have a chance of ruling, and thus to make the apparent misjudgements of his subordinates that hampered a united resistance to the Vikings in the 1000s. There have been modern attempts to rehabilitate 'Unraed', the 'Ill-Counselled', as the victim of bad luck and hostile literary comments by the editors of the *Anglo-Saxon Chronicle*. But it is clear that at the least he was hesitant about leading his men in battle, the primary duty of a king, and was a disastrous judge of character – the long list of victims of Earl Eadric of Mercia in 1006–16 testifies to that favourite adviser's divisive behaviour.

Edgar (and his predecessors) and Aethelred II: how much of the English failure in war in the 1000s was due to the nature of the current king?

If Edgar had lived into his fifties, i.e. to the 990s, would he have established an even more stable kingdom that survived the Viking onslaught better? He would have been fighting the first Viking raids (from 980 in real life), unlike the weak regency and untried king who faced them after his early death. The latter fact was no doubt an encouragement to invaders - would raiders have dared to challenge an adult ruler with a strong fleet instead of an under-age ruler with his succession tainted by implicit fratricide? Edgar was supposed to have had up to 4000 ships according to later writers, and clearly believed in the value of naval deterrence; the famous 'summit' of kings at Chester in 973 involved a naval demonstration of his fleet in the Irish Sea. At the least, his willingness to use his fleet regularly even in peacetime kept his sailors trained and his neighbours aware of his power – though this would not have prevented 'hit-and-run' raids by Viking captains at a safe distance from his naval bases. (Given events of the 1000s, it would seem that Sandwich was the principal English Channel naval base.) Aethelred's kingdom from 978 was an inviting target; Edgar's was not. Assuming that the more opportunist Viking captains had dared to launch raids on the kingdom, 'hit-and-run' affairs that the English fleet could not deal with adequately, and that in due course larger raids had followed, Edgar should have had the energy and leadership to organize an adequate fleet for patrols and to personally lead the army when a large Viking force landed. Thus, although his military capacity is unknown it is likely he would have been in command of the 'fyrd' in person during major invasions.

In contrast, the *Chronicle* famously complained that frequently when the English army marched to meet the Vikings on land in the later 990s and 1000s battle was avoided and the leadership ended up quarrelling; some commanders even deserted or fled.[23] When they did fight they were almost always defeated. As early as 994, the first major invasion of Wessex since the 890s and a presumed result of the English military disaster of 991, Aethelred failed to meet the invaders in the field. The initiative in paying up instead to ensure the invaders would leave – the first 'Danegeld'[24] – was possibly that of leading Churchmen, but Aethelred still listened.

He did not grasp the point that the ambitious Viking war-leaders needed to see that England was capable of defending itself rather than being a 'push-over', as (in Rudyard Kipling's words) 'Once you start paying the Danegeld/ You never get rid of the Dane'. Mystery also surrounds the question of what he was doing taking his army and fleet to campaign in Cumbria in 1000 (against the Scots of Strathclyde?), when the Vikings should have been his priority.[25] Was he endeavouring to restore his reputation by attacking a foe he was not scared to meet? Unlike in Alfred's last war in the 890s, a Viking attack on a part of Wessex – within reach of Aethelred's main residences, Winchester and London – was not met by the king or his heir marching to confront them. From the *Chronicle*'s casualty lists, it seems that fighting was left to the local notables. Fighting an invader with the royal army was the prime duty of a conscientious king who sought to protect his people, although Aethelred's caution was not unprecedented; even the successful juvenile veteran of Brunanburh, King Edmund, had avoided direct battle with the Dublin warlord Olaf Guthfrithson in the Danelaw in 940 and agreed a treaty giving him the eastern part of England.

Edmund probably feared defeat from a larger enemy army in potentially hostile territory, and Aethelred – as yet untried in battle – had reason to be cautious in 994 against the experienced Olaf of Norway and he succeeded in persuading him to convert to Christianity as Alfred had done with Guthrum. Olaf went back to Norway to seek a kingdom and rule it as a Christian, not troubling Aethelred again – as Guthrum had done with Alfred after 878. But the point is that Alfred negotiated after victory, as a proven battle-winner, and after 940 Edmund (already co-victor of Brunanburh and so respected by his enemies) soon took the offensive again; Aethelred had never won a battle and was never to do so. Significantly, once his second son, Edmund 'Ironside', was leading an army there were more military clashes and the first victories for decades.

The willingness of the English leadership to come to terms and buy off invaders after 991 may have been controversial among the 'Witan' at the time. It had its logic, but the result of a lack of English military success was to embolden further raiders. New expeditions arrived to try their luck, and the *Chronicle* presents a picture of English leaders either shirking battle or being in the wrong place at the wrong time. Whether they were outnumbered by the Vikings is unclear; the latter is more likely when King Swein of Denmark commenced his major invasions after the massacre of Danes in England in 1002, but it should be remembered that the Danish royal army could be beaten by the English in 1014–16. The accounts in the

Chronicle suggest that there was only one major Viking force operating in England before 1002, a 'ship-army' roving around the country ravaging one area at a time.[26] The political threat – as opposed to a search for loot – only emerged when Swein of Denmark took control in person and started over-running provinces one by one, arguably from the attack on East Anglia (which had Danish-descended settlers) in 1004.

There were two separate major Danish armies only after Thorkell's arrival – the English were not caught between two or more foes. Even counting for demoralization after the crushing defeat of Maldon, it is evident that the English were not led inspiringly – for which the king must take ultimate responsibility. Wessex had been defeated repeatedly in 870–1 and invaded and partially occupied in 878, but it fought on; the administrative system for raising and equipping armies set up by Alfred was still in place and the kingdom could raise large armies if the will was there as late as 1016, after twenty-five years of warfare. English armies based on the local county levies and led by their 'ealdormen' and other nobles – are spoken of in the *Chronicle* as marching against and sometimes fighting the attackers; the latter seems to have happened when local leaders rather than the king were in charge, which is suggestive. Defeat was partially blamed on a lack of 'back-up'[27] from the royal army. Similar spirit was rarely shown by the 'central', royal army and the *Chronicle* laments their failure to fight, sometimes implying quarrels among the leadership. There is no such record of quarrels among the military deputies chosen by Alfred, Edward 'the Elder', Edmund, or Eadred in equally crucial campaigns; even if the *Chronicle* possibly covered the events of the 1000s in more detail it is apparent that the king did not choose war-leaders capable of co-operating.

The massive fleet raised in 1008–9 met similar problems, with (Earl Godwin's father?) admiral Wulfnoth who was accused of treason by his co-commander, Earl Eadric's brother,[28] and turning pirate. It was leadership that failed under Aethelred, not the administration of creating armies and fleets. A king accustomed to obedience and respected by his officers should not have faced such chaos, and if Aethelred was let down by his subordinates he could easily replace them. Instead, Aethelred repeatedly failed to choose adequate commanders; his long-term adviser, Eadric, notably failed to co-operate with his fellow-commander, Edmund, in the crucial campaigns of 1014–15 and defected to Cnut.[29] The implication is that Eadric, a Royal favourite, felt able to stand up to the heir to the throne, rather than to accept his orders – and that this insubordination was based on his ability to call on the king to back him up.

Aethelred was clearly capable of stern punishments for his enemies, given the number of mutilations and murders ascribed to him; but it would seem that his military commanders did not fear him enough to mount a competent campaign and to fight at all costs. Given the retention of Eadric in power despite his failings, it is probable that Aethelred was a poor judge of men – though we do not know how biased the hostile editors of the *Chronicle* were against him and his favourites. The fact that Eadric could not co-operate with Edmund 'Ironside' even when there was acute danger to the whole kingdom suggests that he was so self-centred and arrogant that he was incapable of deferring to anyone but Aethelred.

The way in which Aethelred decided to thwart an alleged plot against him by the Danes resident in England – potential partisans of Swein – by organizing a massacre on St Brice's Day in 1002 has often been cited as the outstanding example of his treachery, paranoia, and/or incompetence. As might have been expected, escapees rallied to Swein and the murders – including relatives of the latter – made him more determined to conquer England. But the *Chronicle* makes it clear that Aethelred was following the advice of his councillors rather than acting alone,[30] though that raises questions about their judgement too. The attacks by large-scale Viking armies were already underway, ravaging one area at a time, and did not begin after this atrocity. Nor was it a case of mass-murder across the kingdom, assuming that such counter-productive orders would have been accepted and obeyed by local royal officials in any areas of large-scale Danish settlement. The partially Scandinavian inhabitants of the Danelaw did not desert Aethelred en masse after 1002 – the local army of East Anglia, heavily settled by Danes in the later ninth century,[31] was still fighting for Aethelred in 1010. Therefore they had not been alienated by the – limited – massacre. We do not know to what extent the settlers of Scandinavian origin in the Danelaw – who had been in England for around 130 years – looked on themselves as 'English' by 1002 and how many had close kin in Denmark and/or among the victims of the massacre. The only known mass-killing of Danes on St Brice's Day was the famous incident in Oxford.[32] The most that can be said is that it would have antagonized survivors or their close associates, and that Swein was able to base his campaign of conquest in 1013–14 in the Danelaw – where he died in February 1014, at Gainsborough.

The first major late tenth century Viking challenge – Maldon 991. Was this a 'turning-point' that could have been avoided?

Edgar had the experience of command, if not in battle, to have won at Maldon in 991 as the first major Viking force landed in England to challenge the local authorities. Previous attacks, notably in 980, had been 'hit-and-run' raids; this time the Viking expedition, arriving in Essex, was clearly prepared to fight. The outcome of the battle was clearly going to indicate to opportunist Viking captains if England was a worthwhile target, and its Viking triumph was a boost to the reputation of the victor (presumably Olaf Tryggvason, the future king of Norway). At this point Edgar would have been in his late forties, and even if he had not had the experience of battle that Edward, Athelstan, and Edmund had achieved any moderately competent commander would not have made the elementary mistakes that the real-life Saxon commander 'Ealdorman' Byrtnoth did. The disaster that the over-confident Ealdorman suffered there was avoidable. The *Battle of Maldon*, a contemporary Anglo-Saxon poem on the battle, alleges that the latter over-confidently refused to engage the Danes until they had crossed the Maldon causeway to the battlefield to meet them on equal terms. Worse, he waited at their request after an initial exchange of arrows.

Alternatively, he let them across to force a battle and end a 'stand-off', which would have undermined his men's battle-readiness – a more militarily sensible decision, but still one open to increased risk of defeat. He may have feared that if he refused to let the Vikings cross the causeway unhindered they would sail away and ravage untouched countryside. Allowing them to fight thus gave him a chance to defeat them which might not recur.[33] But in that case it would have been sensible to lure them onto the causeway, wait until the leading files were across and forming up for battle but the rest were still milling around on the causeway, then attack them by surprise. The tactic of a surprise attack on an unprepared enemy had been that of Alfred at Ashdown[34] (according to Asser); it would have given Byrtnoth a vital advantage and trapped the attackers, driving their front ranks back onto the causeway or into the marshes. It was winning that mattered, not fighting chivalrously on equal terms; the Vikings understood reality and were capable of underhand behaviour, as seen by Guthrum's breaking his oath in 877–8 and attacking Chippenham in midwinter. Possibly Byrtnoth, an administrator not a war-leader, had listened to too many heroic sagas and was keener to make a name for himself than to protect his people by winning the battle by any available means.

The impression given of Byrtnoth as a commander is of a warrior eager for glory in a 'head-on' clash, not of a careful general who did not take risks. This may well reflect reality not just the imagination of the recording poet (possibly an eye-witness).[35] Given his age – he was married to the sister of a young queen active in the 950s – he was old enough to know better and to have substantial experience, but the peaceful nature of English politics since the conquest of York in 954 may have denied long-lasting local governors like him a chance to learn tactics on the battlefield.

Even if in his late fifties, he may not have fought in battle before 991. A more ruthless and/or cautious commander would have used the advantage given by the hazard more effectively, and engaged the Vikings at once on the causeway as they crossed – or if they refused to cross it, awaited a safer opportunity of battle. A small number of Saxons locking shields in the 'shield-wall' could have held up any number of Vikings on the causeway, and at least led to a stalemate. The earthen causeway did not have the hazard of a bridge, where (as at Stamford Bridge in 1066) a warrior could climb down underneath the structure and attack the defender(s) from below. The better-disciplined army should have been able to push the opposition back even if they did not have enough archers to thin out their ranks from behind the 'shield-wall', and once over the causeway the Saxons could keep their ranks until the enemy broke.

A victory over the Danes at Maldon in 991 would have shown that the English kings could not be challenged on the battlefield in 991 any easier than in 937 or the 890s, and put the main Viking commanders such as Olaf Tryggvason off returning – at least until after Edgar died. By that date Edgar's eldest son, Edward, born around 962, should have been given his own experience of command and been able to meet the challenge. Olaf would have had to seek success to attract followers elsewhere before commencing his campaign to take over Norway, which in real life was aided by his success in England in 991–4. But if he had been killed at Maldon the impact on Norwegian history would have been small; after his death in a naval battle in 1000 the kingdom broke up again until reunited by his cousin St Olaf around 1015. It is probable that England would still have been open to 'hit-and-run' raids on the coast, particularly once Edgar died, and a lack of swift Saxon responses to them would have encouraged more Viking commanders to try their luck. Ambitious would-be warlords such as Thorkell 'the Tall' and a prestige-hunting ruler such a Swein 'Forkbeard' of Denmark would still have had reasons to launch a major campaign at the first sign of English weakness, as in real life after Maldon. It would be vital that if the invaders managed to gather a large enough army to march across country the English king (or his ealdormen) met them in battle, and the tone of the *Chronicle* for the 1000s shows a mixture of puzzlement and despair at how the Vikings could confidently march far inland unchallenged.[36]

Edward 'the Martyr' and Aethelred – did either have a distorted reputation?

The disaster of the 990s and 1000s makes it difficult to reach an objective opinion about the question of Aethelred's elder half-brother, Edward, being a less disastrous ruler than him had he been in charge. But the outcome suggests that he was unlikely to have been worse. Would an adult Edward, succeeding in the 990s after years of recognition as his father's heir, still have been unpopular on account of his rash and violent temper, as he was apparently in his teens[37] according to the (monastic literary) evidence, or would he have matured? The biased nature of the evidence may exaggerate his failings, but it is apparent that his succession was challenged despite his being the oldest son with no certain question over his legitimacy unlike Athelstan in 924. This challenge in itself did not imply that he was feared to be a poor ruler; his younger half-brother, Aethelred, was aged around eight to his c.13 in 975 and would thus need a regency, and it is probable that ambitious nobles (such as Earl Aelfhere of Mercia) anticipating power in a regency preferred him as king. The location of supporters of Aethelred, e.g. Aelfhere, may also suggest that they hankered after another division of England – with Aethelred as king of Mercia and the North, as Edgar had been in 957. This is not mentioned in the *Chronicle*, but past precedent would suggest that it was one reason for resistance to Edward's rule – the boy's character may have been immaterial, though Elfrida would have played up any defects.

There is also the question of the widespread alienation of estates across England to an ever-expanding group of monasteries in the 960s under Edgar. This was spearheaded by his Church allies at court, led by Dunstan (as archbishop of Canterbury) and Bishop Aethelwold of Winchester. In the lands north of the Thames, the Church was used as an agent of royal control of the localities, with extensive estates being granted to the bishops – led by Archbishop Oswald of York – and abbots. The more land was granted to the Church, the less was available for lay magnates – and a bishop or abbot was a royal nominee who could not pass on his lands to his family, unlike a lay grantee. Relying on the Church and its non-hereditary officials thus aided royal centralization, quite apart from the Church's partnership with the king in ruling it a religious duty to obey authority and regarding rebellion as a sin. This would have aided resistance, particularly in the lands north of Watling Street where the Viking occupation since the 870s had seen probable vacancies in all the bishoprics and all earlier Church estates seized by Scandinavian incomers. Rebuilding Church power there – e.g. the new abbey at Ely with its extensive Fenland estates – threatened local landed interests.

Logically, the close connection of the 'pro-monastic' cause's leader, Dunstan, to Edward's cause would have been used by Aelfhere and Elfrida to rally its opponents (lay magnates) to Aethelred's cause and strengthen their support. Was Edward opposed not for being a potential liability so much as because his age and strength of character implied that Aethelred would be more pliable? Rashness and a hot temper had marked an earlier teenage king, his uncle Edwy (Edgar's elder brother), at least according to the life of his banished opponent, St Dunstan, who had been resented for interfering with his womanizing at the coronation feast – allegedly a 'threesome' with his fiancée (?) and her mother.[38] Edgar too was surrounded by rumours of excessive lechery. Edgar may have indicated a preference for Edward or Aethelred, but the choice of successor lay with the 'Witan'; Edward was the elder and the only contender adult enough to govern in person (unlike the situation of Athelstan vs Edwin in 924–5). Even if Aethelred's full brother, Edmund, had been alive in 975, when he would have been around ten, Edward would have been the elder. The choice of king on Edgar's death might have altered if Edgar had lived until the younger boy(s) were capable of ruling without assistance from a 'regency', i.e. around 982. Even then Edward and the magnates backing him could not be expected to surrender their claims lightly – at best there would have been a 'stand-off' in a divided England as between Harold 'Harefoot' and Harthacnut in 1036.

As Edward's murder in 978 resulted in his sanctification writers after that date had every reason to play down his bad qualities, which sat ill with his reputation. The fact that Edward's personality was not 'whitewashed' to make him a worthy saint victimized by his enemies indicates that the current editors of the *Anglo-Saxon Chronicle* and hagiographers realized there was no point in denying his (well-known?) faults, even when it seemed in the 990s and 1000s as if the renewal of the Viking plague was God's reprimand on the usurper Aethelred and his partisans. The challenge to Edward's succession outside the Church cannot be put down solely to bribery and opportunism organized by his stepmother, Elfrida, and Earl Aelfhere, as Aethelred was only around eight years old in 975 and so was too young for the normal age of succession as a challenger to a teenager. (Edgar, raised up by the Mercian magnates against the incumbent Edwy in 957, had been around fourteen.) If the precedent of Edwy's reign had been followed, it seems probable that the magnates of Mercia and Northumbria – led by Aelfhere? – would have made Aethelred their king when he was in his early-mid teens, in the early 980s. Evidently, Elfrida or other partisans decided not to wait that long, and gambled on securing all England for Aethelred by murdering his brother instead. The possibility that Edward was killed as a result of opportunism rather than a careful plan (see below) does not alter this – whoever killed him knew that it would be backed up by Aethelred's mother and her allies.

Support for Aethelred may have centred on the monastic issue rather than on Edward's character faults. Edgar's large-scale alienation of lands to monasteries caused the bishops and abbots involved to support the 'pro-monastic' Edward, who would guarantee that Edgar's grants would not be reversed. The issue was intense enough for open defiance of the new king and the clergy in 976; aggrieved landowners sacked monasteries and evicted monks, apparently led by Elfrida's ally Aelfhere of Mercia. The fact that the Church had been stripped of lands in the Danelaw (part of Aelfhere's governorship) at the pagan Viking occupation in 875 meant that rebuilding its authority there in the mid-tenth century entailed new grants; the one local bishopric, Dorchester-upon-Thames, was so poor that it was combined with the archbishopric of York under St Oswald. New grants of monastic land was thus a particular grievance in eastern Mercia, and resistance to Edward and his clerical advisers probably centred there due to Aelfhere's involvement; it was safe from quick personal intervention by a king based in Winchester. If Edgar had lived into the 980s, the divisive grants would have continued as he and his clerical advisers built up the local power of the restored Church. Usefully, clerical landowners could not leave their land to dynastic heirs and so build up hereditary power in a region; monastic landowners were safer than lay ones as bastions of royal authority. The grants were thus allied to Edgar's use of abbots and bishops as local royal representatives, e.g. in gathering taxes from their estates to pay for the fleet. Clerics also received special local jurisdictions, as supposedly in the 'hundred' of Oswaldslow in Worcestershire. Could a continuing policy of giving land to monasteries have led to confrontation at the accession of Edgar's successor, even had this person been adult or had 'anti-monastic' leader Aelfhere (d. 983) predeceased Edgar?

Edward 'the Martyr' as king after 978 – what if there had been no regicide?
It should be pointed out that Edward's failure to survive to maturity was not a foregone conclusion, whatever the contentious circumstances of his accession. Other successions had been contentious but not fatal for the new king – Edward 'the Elder' faced revolt from a cousin and Athelstan was not crowned for a year.

Even if Edgar had died in 975, Edward could have been a long-lasting ruler; he had survived the immediate threat posed by Aethelred's partisans in July 975 and his alleged hasty temper need not have been an indicator that he would be a worse king than his father. He was capable of maturing with wise advisors, principally the leading churchmen Dunstan (who lived to 988), Archbishop Oswald of York (who lived to 992) and Bishop Aethelwold of Winchester (who lived to 984). Nor was the association of the king with a 'Church party' an indicator of imminent civil war, though it could have led to embittered, land-deprived Mercian magnates (led by Earl Aelfhere) raising up a rival king in Mercia as their forebears had done in 957.

Aethelred's advisors of the 980s were equally problematic to Edward's, particularly Aelfhere who had defied royal power in organizing monastery-burning in 976. It has been argued that Aethelred contentiously quarrelled with churchmen in the 980s, e.g. when he ravaged the lands of Rochester diocese in 985, and only came to rely on better advisors later.[39] Indeed, it is possible that Edward's murder was a 'spur-of'the-moment' action, not the result of a plot, and was avoidable. If the earliest story of the regicide, in the 'Life' of St Oswald, is correct he called at his stepmother's estate at Corfe (probably Corfe Castle) to seek refreshment or a night's lodging after hunting nearby. If the latter, the date (18 March) would indicate late afternoon ahead of an early dusk. The queen's servants stabbed him while he was sitting in the saddle drinking, and he fell from his horse as it galloped away; only later was it alleged that Elfrida was present and/or a participant.[40] Possibly the king's enemies seized the opportunity to help their mistress' ambitions, and there was no plot – though they knew she would approve of it. Had Edward not exposed himself to attack that day he would have survived – though if Elfrida was known to be likely to reward her men for killing her stepson she may have been openly talking about such an act and have taken a chance to have him killed on another occasion. Possibly, given the precedent of what happened in 957, there was a legitimate hope by Aethelred's partisans that he could secure Mercia and Northumbria as his half-brother's co-ruler once he was a teenager, whether by agreement or by revolt, and Edward was refusing to contemplate a division of his kingdom.

Would the Mercian magnates have raised up a rival king, as they did in 957?
If Edward had been excluded from the succession by Edgar in Aethelred's favour before the reigning king's death in the 980s or 990s, Aethelred (or Edmund had he lived) would have been in a stronger position as he was adult. But Edward could have raised civil war to challenge him, as Alfred's excluded nephew Aethelwold challenged Edward 'the Elder' in 899–902. If Edward was as rash and confrontational as his opponents claimed, he could also have used unwise tactics against the Danes in an over-confident lust for victory like Byrtnoth and suffered his own Maldon-style defeat at the hands of Olaf or another Viking commander.

Would Edgar's large-scale grants of land to monasteries, which caused a reaction and violent reoccupations by secular landowners on his death in 975, have been even more extensive after another fifteen to twenty years of patronage to great monasteries? Edgar would have kept up this policy, affecting landowners in the North and the Midlands in particular as the restored Church became an intrusive presence on the local scene. It could have sparked off a demand by affected nobles for the new king to repossess land on pain of revolt, whether this was Edward or Aethelred. Given the family links between settlers in the Danelaw and their relatives in Denmark and probable regular trading-contracts, it is possible that anger at the alienation of land to monasteries might have coalesced into conspiracy to assist a Viking attack. In real life the transfer of allegiance by the leading men of this region to Danish King Swein 'Forkbeard' in 1013 followed years of incompetent rule by Aethelred, a massacre of English Danes in 1002, and Danish military supremacy over the royal army through the 1000s. The locals fought for the English king against Viking invaders until 1013. But discontent over the loss of land could conceivably have caused a conspiracy in favour of a powerful Viking warlord, most probably a raiding Swein after c.1000, if Edgar had persisted in his transfers of resources to his Church allies in the region for another few decades. Conspirators would have been wary of challenging Edgar himself, a successful war-leader, except in the case of his defeat by a foe such as the Scots, age, or ill-health; but a challenge could have occurred more easily with an untried successor.

Assuming that the chosen heir was well known and adult by this point, would his refusal to return monastic lands to angry landowners have caused a revolt by disappointed nobles, in the name of the excluded candidate – either Edward or Aethelred? Edgar's death, even in the 990s, could have caused a civil war between the half-brothers eligible to succeed him, one with monastic backing and one with the support of alienated landowners. If there had been chaos or stalemate in a prolonged war, perhaps with one brother based in the North or Mercia, which were vulnerable to secession (c.f. their activities in 939/40 and 957 against the West Saxon ruler), would this have given the Vikings the opportunity to attack in force? Aethelred was to prove a poor commander when facing large-scale Viking attacks in the 1000s and never seems to have met even the largest armies of marauders in person, leaving it to his provincial governors. But that need not be an indication that he was more likely to lose a contest for power with Edward, provided that he had adequate senior supporters.

Aethelred's mother, Elfrida's, links with her previous husband's powerful noble family, that of Athelstan 'Half-King' (ealdorman of East Anglia and part of the Danelaw in the mid-tenth century), would logically have made that dynasty his allies. They still held East Anglia until 992 and were the most extensive landowners in the East of England, a useful centre of support for Aethelred, but conversely their foes would have been more likely to back Edward. The ealdorman of East Anglia, Elfrida's ex-brother-in-law Aethelwine, was in fact a keen supporter of monasticism, and leading patron of Ramsey abbey. In real life the reign of Aethelred saw murderous feuds among the senior nobles, the rise of the untrustworthy Eadric 'Streona' of Mercia around 1000, and a series of arrests, exiles, and blindings whose precise political significance is unclear but which testifies to faction-feuds at court. This competition at Aethelred's court would still have added to royal problems had he succeeded Edgar or Edward as an adult in less contentious circumstances.

Would one of the brothers been crowned without immediate objections or a succession-dispute, as the long-appointed heir, but then been vulnerable to a coup? Aethelred could have been vulnerable to the 'anti-monastic' party among the nobles, which backed Edward in real life in 975, and Edward could have been vulnerable to Queen-Mother Elfrida if she was more ruthless than an adult Aethelred in removing rivals. In real life (and subsequent legend) she was believed to be the cause of his murder by her retainers at Corfe in 978, and she was still alive until 1002. Either way, Edgar's kingdom could still have been vulnerable if he died in his fifties in the 990s, if two adult half-brothers and a pro- and anti-monastic split among the courtiers had been ready to cause conflict. Aethelred was less likely than Edward to have had the talent to have brought a civil war to a quick conclusion in his favour, at least as implied by his military failures to tackle the marauding Danish army as it roamed across England after 1002. The resulting possible division of the kingdom, or a particularly bloody series of battles with leading nobles killed, could have enabled Olaf Tryggvason and later Swein 'Forkbeard' to land with large armies and take advantage of the chaos. England would thus still have been afflicted with Viking marauders in the 1000s. Even had Edward succeeded Edgar as an adult and held power successfully, a Scandinavian attempt to meddle with the loyalties of the Danish-descended nobility of York (only incorporated in England in 954) was possible. Dublin Viking invaders had been active there in the 940s and early 950s, and the final Norwegian attack on York was to be in 1066 and Danish attack in 1069.

Ambitious would-be or current kings in Scandinavia were likely to take advantage of any opportunity, such as the accession of a new and untried king in Winchester. Whether or not the English fleet was kept up to its strength of 973 would be vital; in real life there was no English fleet active in the Thames estuary in 991 to drive Olaf off Essex and in 994 to stop him and Swein attacking London. Had Aethelred and his ministers let it decline in the intervening years (due to the cost of paying for it?), and would a vigorous Edgar as king into the 990s have avoided this mistake? Given that Aethelwulf had lived to the age of about fifty-five to fifty-eight, Alfred to fifty to fifty-two, and Edward 'the Elder' to about fifty-three, it was quite feasible that Edgar would have survived into his fifties and passed on the crown and a strong, well-trained fleet to a fully-adult heir c.995.

(e) Edmund II 'Ironside', dead at about twenty-eight – the 'Lost Leader'?

What if Edmund 'Ironside' had won the battle of Ashingdon on 18 October 1016 and killed or driven out Cnut?
Unlike his father, Aethelred, he was an adequate general who had had the skill, luck, and/or charisma to have overcome initially unpromising circumstances in the months since Aethelred's death at London in April. He had already been taking the initiative against the Vikings in Aethelred's lifetime, refusing to go into exile with him in Normandy late in 1013 as Swein 'Forkbeard' received the surrender of most of the English leadership and fighting on. He then made up for one of Aethelred's frequent blunders by marrying the widow of his prominent East Mercian victim, the 'thegn' Sigeferth, and winning over the latter's local support. In addition, in 1015 to early 1016 he campaigned in the North with Earl Uhtred of Northumbria while his father languished in London. He led his troops to assist Aethelred in London in spring 1016, but on his father's death he retreated from the city to raise an army in Wessex, defeated Cnut and his English allies (Earl Eadric Streona of Mercia and Ealdorman Aelfmaer) at Penselwood and Sherston, returned to relieve the siege of London, and defeated the enemy again at Brentford. Driving them out of Kent but receiving the turncoat Eadric into his forces – a decision which the compiler of the *Anglo-Saxon Chronicle* called the worst action taken for England – he eventually confronted Cnut in Essex. This, the *Chronicle* says, was the fifth time he had raised an army in that year's campaign – a testament to his leadership and stamina and his attractiveness as a commander.[41] He was thus in the line of Alfred, Edward, Athelstan, and Eadred as a vigorous war-leader.

It was apparently the treachery of Eadric 'Streona' (again) that caused his defeat at Ashingdon as the latter's Mercians went over to Cnut.[42] This raises the question of why Edmund had trusted this official who had already betrayed his father and been involved in some unsavoury Court faction-struggles and executions in the 1000s. Eadric had failed to co-ordinate the defence of Mercia with Edmund in late 1015 and gone over to Cnut, possibly in fear of Edmund's wife, Edith, influencing her husband to execute him. (Had he been involved with her late first husband's killing?) Eadric had only left Cnut when the latter appeared to be losing. As Cnut was driven out of Kent Eadric returned to Edmund's side and was pardoned.

The accusation of treachery is, however, to assume that Eadric actively deserted to Cnut during the battle according to a pre-arranged plan rather than his troops just running away, possibly due to indiscipline, incompetence, or fear – not treachery. Eadric could have made the most of it to assure Cnut that he had masterminded the manoeuvre. (Cnut temporarily kept him on as Earl of Mercia, but soon found an excuse to execute him.) It is difficult to see what Eadric had to gain from returning to Cnut's allegiance after betraying him, given what Cnut was capable of – the Dane had already mutilated his East Mercian/Anglian hostages after their relatives abandoned his cause for Aethelred's in 1014. Even if Cnut had arranged for Eadric to pretend to defect and then to abandon Edmund at the first battle they fought, the arch-'turncoat' (clearly loathed by the editor of the *Chronicle* but able to command the allegiance of his own Mercians) was capable of deciding to stay with Edmund's cause if Edmund had established a decisive advantage on the battlefield before Eadric took action to desert him. Eadric could have decided not to defect at Ashingdon after all, judging he had more to lose by backing Cnut than Edmund.

What if Edmund had seemed a better 'bet' to Eadric who had remained loyal, or his troops had remained firm – giving Edmund the victory? Timing is vital in battle, and although we do not know the details of what happened at Ashingdon, a critical delay in the Mercians defecting – or running away – could have meant that the Saxon army was able to secure a decisive advantage by that point. Any of the Earl's subordinate commanders who he had instructed to desert the battlefield could have changed their minds to make sure they were on the winning side. One of them could have warned Edmund of what was intended, and he had time to counter it – possibly by luring Eadric away from his 'thegns' and arresting or even killing him.

The massive toll among the English leadership indicates that they did not run away while they had the chance and that the senior nobles stood their ground, possibly in an effort to rescue the battle from disaster; after the battle Edmund was forced to retreat into Western Mercia and was lucky to secure Cnut's grudging acceptance of his retaining Wessex. (He died a month or so later, according to later stories by the hand of Cnut's assassins.) Having inspired his people more in two years than Aethelred had done in thirty, and raised five armies in that time, Edmund could have won at Ashingdon had the timing been different and Cnut been the one to flee.

If Cnut had escaped the battle, Edmund would have been relieved to let him leave England on any terms rather than fight another battle with him and lose more men – and probably Cnut would have cut his losses as in 1014 and sailed back to Denmark to rebuild his forces. His brother Harold was in charge there, probably as king rather than governor though it is uncertain which of the two was the elder son of Swein. Assuming Harold let him land, Cnut would have been in a position to take over Denmark when Harold died in 1018 – but he would have been risking a lot to have another go at England thereafter, though pride and possibly the appeals of Danelaw plotters could have tempted him. He is more likely to have satisfied his need for success to keep his followers loyal by taking on Norway and Sweden, as in real life. The Christianizing rule of 'St' Olaf in Norway was unpopular with some nobles, giving Cnut a potential 'fifth column' there. If he was capable of murdering Edmund to secure Wessex without a fight in November 1016 as one story indicates,[43] he was also capable of murdering his brother Harold. A tenacious warrior who had not given up easily during the long campaigns against Edmund in 1015–16, he would not have sailed tamely into exile as a landless brother of the king of Denmark, a glorified pirate captain. With Denmark behind him Cnut could still have built a Viking empire in Scandinavia, whether or not he had another attempt on England later.

It is even possible that Cnut could have temporarily held onto part of England, such as York, after defeat at Ashingdon. He had put his own man, Jarl Erik, in control of Northumbria after murdering the surrendered Earl Uhtred earlier in 1016, and Edmund lacked the personal connection with York that he had (via Edith) in the Danelaw.[44] Edmund had suffered losses as well as Cnut during the war, and as victor of Ashingdon would have been unwise to leave southern England unprotected while he campaigned up in Northumbria. Cnut would still have had a fleet, unless Edmund had managed 'hot pursuit' after Ashingdon to the coast and burned it. The Danes could have retreated to the Humber and forced the continuation of the war there in 1017, with the need to avoid more bloodshed making more English nobles and clerics advise Edmund to accept a temporary truce. In that case, Cnut is likely to have sailed for Denmark as soon as his brother died in 1018 to secure that kingdom.

Edmund might have been willing to come to a wary agreement with Cnut that each would keep out of the other's territories and cemented it by the (real-life) marriage of his half-Viking stepmother, the ambitious and capable Emma, to Cnut. Emma, daughter of Duke Richard I of Normandy, had been sought by Aethelred as a bride in 1002 as a means of denying her brother Richard II's ports to the Viking fleets, and the ducal line was descended from the Viking warlord Hrolf 'the Walker', cadet of the royal line of Vestfold in Norway and related to the Jarls of Orkney. Emma had her sons' interests to promote in England against those of Edmund's much younger sons as successor to England; her eldest son, Edward, was born in 1003/5 and Edmund had not married until 1015. Edmund could have been glad to get her out of the country even if it meant that she might use the Danish army to invade on her sons' behalf once he died. Or would Edmund not have dared take that risk, and preferred to have kept Emma under his surveillance? The queens of England traditionally had Winchester as the most important part of their landed 'dower' as widows by 1036, when Emma held the town for her son Harthacnut against his half-brother Harold 'Harefoot'; Edward deprived her of her lands in 1043 in apparent fear of a plot against him. It is uncertain if this was already established by 1016, thus making Emma a powerful political player and a possible threat to Edmund and his sons, but as early as 899 Alfred's widow, Ealhswith, had inherited some lands in the district. These estates presumably descended through the line of royal wives.

It is unfortunately unclear if the later hagiography of Edward, Aethelred and Emma's elder son, was correct in claiming that the terms of the marriage allowed Emma's son to be Aethelred's heir.[45] Emma's brother Duke Richard II of Normandy might well have wanted this, but in England the choice of king lay with the 'Witan' and in 1002 Aethelred had at least five sons – the eldest, Athelstan, was around fifteen. Edward would have stood no chance in 1016 as a boy of around thirteen against Edmund, an established commander of troops aged around twenty-eight. But Edmund might have preferred his stepmother, Emma, to re-marry out of England, so that if he died while his sons were under-age they would not suffer from her intrigues on Edward's behalf.

It is possible that Edmund's early death in late 1016 implies that the recent campaigns had undermined his health by the time of Ashingdon. This is more likely than the twelfth century story that he was stabbed on the lavatory by an assassin sent by Cnut[46] or Eadric 'Streona'. The story of a model statue releasing a poisoned spring to gash the king when Edmund touched it is more unlikely.[47] His grandfather, Edgar, and great-uncle Eadred had died in their thirties, and even victory at Ashingdon might have left him with weak health and a need to consider the succession. The marriage of Emma to Cnut in a peace-treaty would have gained Cnut a closer link to Normandy – a useful source of supplies and men if he wanted to attack England again in future. With or without the marriage, if Edmund had died before his sons reached adulthood Cnut was likely to attack England again – possibly using the East Midland links of his mistress or 'common-law' wife, Aelfgifu of Northampton, to start a local conspiracy. It is possible that this liaison dated back to 1015, as the claims of their son (?) Harold 'Harefoot' to England in 1035 would make more sense if he were older than his legitimate half-brother Harthacnut (probably born in 1018). The apparent possibility that Harold was not Cnut's son may have been exaggerated – or invented? – during the 1035–6 crisis by Emma and her followers.

The succession to Edmund – which Edward?
The survival of Edmund as king would have had ramifications as late as 1066. He had two sons by Edith, and the real-life king from 1042, Edward (later known as the 'Confessor' but not in his lifetime), was not his direct

heir. In a restored unified Anglo-Saxon kingdom, Edmund might have lived until his fifties, i.e. after c.1038, and then he would have passed the kingdom to his adult eldest son, Edward 'the Exile', rather than to his half-brother Edward 'the Confessor' – assuming that there was not a coup on the older Edward's behalf. The latter is perhaps likelier if Edward 'the Confessor' had been adult and Edmund's sons still been minors at the time, i.e. until around 1033/5, Edmund's elder son being born at the earliest in winter 1015. What if an unmarried Emma had been in England to promote her sons' cause rather than in Denmark supporting Cnut or her son Harthacnut as king? It is uncertain if the marriage of Aethelred and Emma of Normandy in 1002 contained any clause relating to a son of the marriage as heir to England, thus giving Edward a legal claim at least after Edmund – as Edward's later hagiography claims. But if the ambitious and politically active Emma had not been married to Cnut in 1017 she would have been more likely to press the claims of her sons by Aethelred, as she would not have had Danish nobles or a half-Danish son for her cause. In real life, when Edward landed in England after Cnut died – in Wessex, under Emma's control – he was denied entry and had to sail back to Normandy; his brother Alfred landed in Kent[48] but was intercepted by Emma's ally Earl Godwin and arrested. This then poisoned relations between Edward and Godwin over the latter's responsibility for Alfred's subsequent fatal blinding by Harold 'Harefoot'.

Emma could have pushed for Edward as the new ruler after Edmund, as older and more experienced than Edmund's sons. In terms of English precedent, an adult and experienced brother (Eadred) not an under-age son (Edwy) had succeeded Edmund I in 946. The claim that supporting the half-Norman Edward would assist relations with the Duchy of Normandy, which had been a base for Vikings raiding England in the 990s, was less important after the vigorous adult Duke Robert died on pilgrimage to Jerusalem in 1035 – Normandy was no potential threat to England thereafter. The main focus of English fear of hostile shipping operating across the Channel in the mid-eleventh century was to be Flanders, where Earl Godwin took refuge when driven out of England in 1051 and whence Tostig invaded in spring 1066. Only with the end of years of chaos and civil war in Normandy in 1047, when the now-adult Duke William (born around 1028) defeated his main enemies at Val-es-Dunes, did Normandy become an important international factor again. If Edmund's death had occurred around 1042, when Edmund would have been fifty-four (the approximate age of death of Edward 'the Elder'), Emma's elder son Edward would have been about thirty-nine and his rival, Edmund's elder son Edward (known as 'the Exile'), around twenty-six. If the 'Exile' had been in England from 1016/17 as the son of the reigning king, rather than exiled in Scandinavia as Cnut's enemy, he would have been likelier to succeed to the English throne once he reached his teens (i.e. around 1029/30).

The survival of Edmund 'Ironside' would also have had implications for later dynastic history. His son Edward would not have been married to Agatha, his German wife acquired in exile – probably a close relative of Emperor Henry III, though her exact parentage has been much disputed. Hence there would have been no 'Edgar Atheling' as his son or (St) Margaret as his daughter, and he would more likely have married into the English or Anglo-Danish nobility. There is, however, a chance that Edmund *would* have married him into the German 'Salian' dynasty of Henry III, as Henry was Cnut's southern neighbour and so a valuable ally to threaten war on Cnut should he leave Denmark to invade England again. In real life, Cnut as king of England and Denmark allied himself to Henry's father, Conrad II, in the 1020s and married off his and Emma's daughter, Gunnhilde, to Henry – she died before the latter succeeded as emperor in 1039. Edmund would have been anxious to renew links to the empire, the object of a close marital alliance under Edward 'the Elder' a century before when Otto I married Edward's daughter. Had he not had a daughter available to marry Henry, a German princess would have been a logical partner for his son Edward. The latter would certainly never have ended up living in Russia and later Hungary as he did in real life.

Effects on Scottish history

The long-term ramifications for Edward 'the Exile's family would have been many. Not having to flee England with her brother Edgar 'Atheling' after a revolt against the Normans in 1069,[49] Edward's daughter Margaret would not have been driven into a Scottish harbour and ended up as queen of Scotland as second wife of Malcolm III. The latter's son by his first wife, Ingebiorg of Orkney – Duncan II – would have had no challengers from the children of his father's second marriage when Malcolm died. In real life Duncan, superseded by Margaret's family of at least five sons, was able to seize power in Scotland briefly from his uncle Donald 'Ban' in 1094 but was soon evicted; his family then lost the throne permanently as King William II of England installed Margaret's fourth son, Edgar, in Scotland in 1097.

Had Malcolm not married Margaret, Duncan would have been able to fight over the throne with his uncle Donald 'Ban' without the complication of Malcolm and Margaret's sons – though the English king of the moment might still have backed one candidate against another, as Edward 'the Confessor' did in 1054–7.

But it is not fanciful to suggest that a daughter of Edward 'the Exile' would have been a valuable marital pawn for her father or her grandfather as king. Thus Malcolm III, whether or not he owed his restoration in 1057/8 to

England, would have been a natural partner for an alliance with England in the late 1050s or 1060s and Edward 'the Exile's daughter would still have been a potential wife for him. There had been no marital alliances between the House of Cerdic and the Scots royal family until 1069, Edward 'the Elder' having married his numerous daughters to the principal available candidates in France and Germany and Aethelred marrying his daughters to English nobles. But the Scots succession-dispute among Malcolm II's grandsons from 1034 had led to Macbeth, ruler of Moray, killing his cousin Duncan and exiling the latter's sons Malcolm and Donald 'Ban'. In real life Edward 'the Confessor' gave military backing to Malcolm's claims, and he was restored to the southern part of Scotland (as far as the Firth of Forth?) by Edward's Earl of Northumbria, Siward, in 1054 and took over the North in 1057. Edward 'the Exile', who in real life had the courage to take part in a risky invasion of Hungary from Russia by the exiled prince[50] Andrew in 1046/7, is equally likely to have acted on Malcolm's behalf and more likely to have campaigned in Scotland in person. An Anglo-Scottish marital alliance was still a possibility for cementing ties between Edward 'the Exile' and Malcolm III if the English king had been involved in restoring the Scots prince around 1054.

Effects on Edward 'the Confessor' and the mid-eleventh century kingdom

No great earldoms in existence by 1042 – a stronger monarchy?
Edward 'the Exile' might have ended up exiled after all, though not as a baby by Cnut in 1016/17. He could have lost out in a power struggle with Emma over the succession after Edmund died, particularly if Edmund – weakened by his extensive campaigns against the Vikings – had died before Edward was an adult. Thus Edward 'the Confessor' would have succeeded more easily before c.1031/2 than when his nephew 'the Exile', born around 1016, was adult. He could then have ruled for around 35 to 40 years to 1066. He would not have spent years in exile in Normandy and returned to England as a stranger with a clientele of young nobles and churchmen who he had grown up with, who in real life he rewarded with office after 1042. Indeed, Edward had the first 'castles' in England erected before the Norman Conquest as he brought Norman knights into the border country of Herefordshire to oppose the eastward expansion of Gruffydd ap Llewelyn, the aggressive reuniter of the Welsh principalities in the 1040s and 1050s.[51] His experience of the usefulness of castles in defensive warfare in Normandy would have enabled him to judge them invaluable in protecting the countryside and serving as centres for resistance against the Welsh raids. Had Edward not lived in Normandy in 1016–41, any Norman associations that he promoted would have come via his mother's household and contacts – and also possibly from his sister Goda's French marriages. (His sister's son, Ralph of the

Vexin, was his first choice as Earl of Hereford in the late 1040s but could not hold Gruffydd back.) He would probably have been able to have military experience before his accession as well as building up friendships within the English nobility, and so been less isolated as king.

There would have been fewer deaths in battle, executions, or exiles among the senior political class of Aethelred's England as Cnut would not have won in 1016, meaning fewer of Cnut's Danish followers in senior positions in England in the 1020s and 1030s. Edward would have been in a much stronger position as the new king and able to call on more 'English' ealdormen and courtiers for service than he did in real life in 1042 when he had to take on experienced men inherited from Cnut. By this point England was under the local leadership of three senior Cnut 'loyalists' – Earls Godwin of Wessex, Leofric of Mercia, and Siward of Northumbria – who Edward inherited on his accession and had to continue to use. Cnut – often absent in Scandinavia and in 1027 in Rome – had preferred to rely on a small group of senior earls than a larger political class such as had existed in pre-1016 England, and Edward duly inherited this. Worse for royal power, Cnut had eventually given all Wessex – the heartland of royal power – to one earl (Godwin), making that man rather than the king the focus for loyalty for the Wessex nobility. It did not matter so much for Cnut, a famous warrior who had a large standing army and fleet paid for by extortionate taxes, but it did after 1042 to an untried and probably unmilitary new king. (Edward abandoned this single Wessex earldom in 1051.) The case of Godwin's royal connections in 1042 may have been awkward, given that he had betrayed Edward's brother Alfred to Harold 'Harefoot' after arresting him and murdering his retainers at Guildford in 1036 – Godwin soon gave Edward a present of a splendid warship, which could be interpreted as paying 'weregild' for Alfred.[52] The antagonism between Edward and Godwin until 1051 is unclear, but the new king was in a weak position as he did not have a clientele of personal 'loyalists' as the secular leaders of society.

The granting of Herefordshire to Ralph and (after Godwin's removal) part of Wessex to Odda[53] can be interpreted as an attempt to reassert royal power, and the grants of earldoms to Godwin's (still fairly young) sons and nephew in 1043/7 as forced on the king by Godwin. These young men would have had a weaker claim to earldoms had Edward had a body of noble advisers inherited from Aethelred and/or Edmund to reward. Edward would not have been so beholden to Godwin, and might not have married his daughter Edith in 1045 – which has major implications for the succession in 1066 if Edith was infertile rather than Edward being chaste.

But the senior earls of 1042–51 cannot be written off as a group of 'Danes' (Leofric was genetically West Mercian) whose role in government was inimical to the interests of the House of Cerdic. It should be remembered that prominent East Anglian, East Mercian, and Northumbrian landowners in the early eleventh century were often of 'Danish' or (in the North-West) 'Norse' extraction as far as the Anglo-Saxon chroniclers were concerned, and men of all backgrounds had served Cnut. They often had 'Viking' names and are difficult to distinguish from 'overseas' Danes and Norse new to England in 1016. These 'Viking' Englishmen would have swung back to support Edmund as king from 1016 if he had defeated Cnut as they had abandoned Cnut for the Saxon royal line on Swein's death in 1014 – not least as Edmund had an East Mercian wife. Some 'Danish' nobles would thus have been in prominent positions in 1042 under Edmund as they were in real life under Cnut. Senior figures who had gained rank and power by loyal military service would have been likely to include military leaders such as Siward, the 'Dane' made Earl of Northumbria by Cnut and holding the office to 1055, if not him in person.

A 'southern' English magnate without local ties could have severe difficulties ruling York, as Earl Tostig found as he faced a successful revolt in 1065. Indeed, the unreliability of the local Bernician magnates (the 'House of Ealdred', lords of Bamburgh from the time of the Viking conquest of York in 867) as earls of Northumbria in the early eleventh century would make it logical for a worried king based far to the south in Winchester to use loyal 'Danish' magnates as earls such as Cnut did. Earl Uhtred had eventually backed Edmund against Swein, but his family could not be relied on to remain loyal and intrigued against various appointees of the king to supersede them (most notably Earl Tostig, who may have been linked to the killing of Uhtred's descendant Cospatrick in 1064 and was deposed by rebels in 1065). King William found them no more dependable after 1066.

It is still possible that Edward ('the Confessor') would have been open to Continental influence on his Church – if, for example, he had met Norman clerics in his mother's household or if his half-brother Edmund had trusted him with foreign diplomatic journeys to Germany or Rome. As in real life, Earl Godwin – a leading thane in Sussex by descent, not just a creation of Cnut, and so likely to have been one of Edmund's military officers[54] – would have been a powerful political player; but the earldom of Wessex that Cnut created was unlikely to have been in existence for him. The native-born Edmund is less likely than Cnut to have created this 'super-earldom', not least as he did not have to be out of the country campaigning in Scandinavia for part of his reign as Cnut did. The earldoms of Mercia and Northumbria, however, existed before Cnut – the former possibly divided into several provinces as in the real-life 1030s, not united under one man – and the Saxon-born Leofric would have been ruling at least the West Midlands, which his father ruled before him in the 1030s. The Dane (or Danish Yorkshireman?) Siward would not have received Northumbria from

Edmund unless he had been an exceptionally able and loyal warlord, needed to fight the Scots, who was chosen as a less likely rebel than the local House of Uhtred's menfolk. Earl Uhtred and his kinsmen had monopolized the rule of Northumbria since the time of their ancestors, the independent lords of Bernicia under Alfred, and Edmund and after him Edward 'the Confessor' could have been as eager as Cnut to intrude some trustable officials from outside their dynasty to rule at least part of the region.

The able and military-minded Edmund, who had based his campaign of 1016 in Wessex, was unlikely to have given away his 'heartland' to a semi-autonomous earl. The king of the 1040s and 1050s would thus have had a major advantage over the real-life situation. If Edward – no war-leader except with the fleet in the 1040s – had lacked military experience or interests he might have duly promoted Godwin to rule (part of?) Wessex for him, Godwin's estates being based in West Sussex at Bosham. If it is correct that Godwin had fought in Edmund's entourage in 1016 before joining Cnut when his first commander died, he would still have been a senior figure in the 1040s – though he was less likely to have married a Danish wife.

More senior Saxon thanes, killed in the 1016 defeat or purged by Cnut, would have been available to hold office as 'ealdormen' and earls, and the dominance of the houses of Godwin and Leofric in England by the 1040s is less likely. The structure of government would have relied on a large class of senior officials directly below the king, to the advantage of the latter – though the risky idea of relying on a very few men to hold senior office had been apparent as early as the 950s when Athelstan 'Half-King' had governed the Danelaw and East Anglia. It was not an innovation of Cnut's.

Even if Edward had not yet been married and had chosen Earl Godwin's daughter as his wife when he came to the throne, he would have been less reliant on a small body of powerful provincial 'overlords' and thus would not have been helpless in 1052. Having used Earl Godwin's refusal to punish the inhabitants of Dover for insulting his brother-in-law Eustace of Boulogne and killing his men in a dispute over quarters in 1051 to force a military confrontation, Edward was joined by Leofric and Siward at Gloucester. The outnumbered Godwin was forced into a 'climb-down' and driven out of the country. But when Godwin returned with more men the following year and sailed his fleet up the Thames to Southwark, Edward (stationed in London) found that this time Leofric and Siward were in favour of allowing Godwin and his sons to have their earldoms back and was forced to give in.[55] With more, smaller earldoms and/or some remaining 'ealdormanates' Edward would have been in a better position to secure enough support to outnumber Godwin in 1052 and force a battle, though he could still have been defeated or suffered defections as his father and half-brother had done in battles against Viking armies. In a similar fashion, the royal armies would have been in a better position to resist invasion by the exiled Earl Alfgar, Leofric's son, who was twice dismissed and driven out of England (1055 and 1058) and twice fought his way back to office aided by the Welsh and Norwegians.

Appointing foreigners to senior rank, such as Archbishop Robert of Jumièges to Canterbury, in 1051–2 might have caused defections from Edward's cause in the same manner that his father's unpopular political acts – in his case, including murders and banishments – had caused him in the 1000s. All the resources of the English state could not secure Aethelred's victory over the marauding Viking armies then, and if Edward had alienated sufficient numbers of senior nobles he could still have been humiliated in 1052. But a larger group of senior English office-holding nobles around the king in January 1066 would have made Earl Harold's claim to succeed less plausible. When Edward died his dynastic heir, Edgar Atheling, was at least eleven and at most around fifteen; he is supposed to have been of the same age as William of Normandy's eldest son Robert, born c.1052. Two kings of around fourteen (Edwy and Edward 'the Martyr') and one of around ten (Aethelred II) had succeeded to the throne in the tenth century without attempts to divert the crown to an adult magnate. Accordingly, a surviving substantial 'political class' of English nobles (sharing out the southern ealdormanates?) in 1066 was less likely to accept Harold as king with a viable alternative, even with Normandy and Norway threatening invasion. Unless Edward had chosen to heap lands and offices on Harold as his trusted deputy, that magnate would not have had the overwhelming predominance of lands (as seen in the Domesday Book) and office that aided his cause in securing the throne.

The political situation in January 1066 would have looked much different, with Duke William having to challenge a 'legitimate' sovereign of the line of Cerdic not someone his propagandists could call a treacherous oath-breaker. Indeed, had Edward had a potential Cerdicing heir (Edward 'the Exile'?) on hand in England in 1051–2 as not exiled by Cnut – the mysterious 'visit' of Duke William, which the English sources do not mention, was not likely to have included a promise of the English throne to the Duke. He, like Cnut in 1015–16, would have had to attack England as a predatory neighbour not a 'cheated rightful claimant.'

(f) Cnut and his sons – a Danish rather than a Norman conquest?

Events – three unexpected deaths in six-and-a-half years
Though Cnut and his sons were not of the royal house of Cerdic, their early deaths were vital to the situation of the late Anglo-Saxon kingdom in 1066. Indeed, if they had not all died in the space of a few years in 1035–42 Edward

'the Confessor' would not have been able to return to the throne, having fled to his mother's relatives in Normandy as a boy in 1016 and not returning until 1041. Emma took no political interest in him until Cnut was dead – possibly on the latter's orders – and it has been argued that this psychologically 'warped' him and contributed to his decision to arrest her for alleged plotting in 1043. If the latter story is true, she could be plausibly suspected of preferring Magnus of Norway to Edward as king of England (unless the 'plot' was just an excuse to seize her valuable treasure and lands by an impoverished new king.) The virtual stalemate between Cnut, recognized as king in the Danelaw, East Anglia, and Northumbria, and Edmund 'Ironside' in Wessex in 1016 had been altered in Cnut's favour by the result of Ashingdon but he had still had to accept Edmund as ruler of Wessex in the subsequent truce.[56] Probably he would have returned to the attack in 1017 or 1018 once he had reinforcements, and from his brother Harald's death in 1018 he was king of Denmark and had its resources at his disposal. (Some modern writers even claim that he, not Harald, was king of Denmark already in 1014–18 and that Harald was only his governor.)

However, Edmund died a few weeks after the battle, with the sources unclear if he died of illness or wounds or was murdered – the more lurid stories about an assassin lurking in a privy or a 'booby-trapped' statue are later and so less reliable. Cnut was accepted as king throughout England, thus completing the 'Danish Conquest' on which his father Swein had embarked in the 1000s, and duly acquired Denmark and Norway too. The latter was entrusted to one of his (illegitimate?) sons by Aelfgifu of Northampton, Swein, who was driven out by a revolt shortly before Cnut died in 1035. Cnut had married Aethelred's widow Emma to add more legitimacy to his position. Edmund's brother Edwy and a number of leading Saxon 'thegns' were murdered and Edmund's infant sons driven into exile, ending up in Russia and later Hungary.

The kingship of Cnut – a mixture of Danish and English rule

Cnut was unchallenged throughout his lifetime, and was able to leave the kingdom in the hands of his (mostly Danish) lieutenants while he secured Denmark in 1018 and Norway in 1028, visiting Denmark again in 1020. In 1027 he even ventured south on pilgrimage to Rome as the first reigning English king since Alfred's father, Aethelwulf, to do so. His career of conquest as the greatest warlord in Viking Europe was not without reverses, as his attempt to add Sweden to his dominions was repulsed at the battle of 'Holy River' in 1026. In 1030 the king he had expelled from Norway, (St) Olaf, returned with a small force to instigate or aid a local revolt and was killed in battle by Cnut's loyalists at Stiklestadr, subsequently becoming regarded as the national saint in what was presumably partly a nationalist reproach to his replacement. The Norwegians revolted again even before Cnut died, in the name of Olaf's young son Magnus, and had Cnut lived into the late 1030s his prestige would have required a military response to this. (Luckily for Magnus, the death of Cnut and the resultant lack of English aid to Cnut's son Harthacnut in Denmark in 1035–40 prevented reconquest.) However, Cnut secured his position within the British Isles, invading Scotland in 1031 to reach some form of agreement with King Malcolm II (possibly involving English overlordship) and being watchful and/or suspicious enough to deal ruthlessly with potential rebels within England. The arch-traitor Eadric 'Streona', having been granted Mercia for abandoning Edmund at Ashingdon, was seized and executed as soon as Cnut's regime was secure, and among other great lords who fell foul of Cnut and were exiled was at least one senior 'ealdorman' in his service, Aethelmaer. Cnut's leading Danish lieutenant, 'Jarl' Thorkell, formerly an independent Viking commander who had variously fought for Swein and Aethelred at different times, was left as regent in England in 1018 but was later forced to go abroad to govern Denmark instead – leaving his son as a hostage with Cnut. Cnut's brother-in-law 'Jarl' Ulf, father of Swein Estrithson who was to found the still-reigning royal house of Denmark after Cnut's sons' deaths, may also have fallen foul of Cnut and become involved in a Swedish-backed revolt in Denmark. He was killed in the battle of the Holy River in 1026.[57]

Cnut and William: a tale of two conquerors

(a) An alien ruling a hostile kingdom? The similarities and differences between Cnut in 1016 and William in 1066

It is noticeable that though Danish names predominate in the early charters that give a picture of Cnut's court – and we cannot be certain how many of these were from Denmark, as opposed to being Anglo-Danes from the Danelaw and East Anglia – the king's senior advisers and provincial governors included a number of Englishmen,[58] some of them descended from earlier officials of Aethelred. In particular, Cnut's division of the kingdom among a small group of earls gave places to both English and Danes. The turbulent border province of York, exposed to the ambitions of Scots and Viking Dubliners, was always entrusted to a Dane – though we cannot be certain if Siward, the long-ruling earl from c.1030 to 1055, was from Denmark or a local Anglo-Dane. The grant of Bernicia to the native house of Bamburgh, Uhtred's family, c.1019 was politically necessary but the new incumbent was duly linked by marriage to Siward. The western half of

Mercia went to Leofric, the son of one of Aethelred's local 'earldormen', and the man placed in charge of (eventually all) Wessex was Godwin, son of a senior Sussex 'thegn' called Wulfnoth exiled by Aethelred. Godwin may have married Cnut's sister at one point according to a garbled later legend, and by c.1020 was certainly married to Cnut's sister-in-law Gytha, sister of 'Jarl' Ulf.[59] Cnut's wisdom in keeping Uhtred's powerful northern family loyal and engaged in his service can be compared with the actions of King Edward and Earl Harold in 1055 in handing over Northumbria to a southerner, Harold's brother Tostig, who faced strong local discontent and was eventually driven out by rebels. Incidentally, it should be pointed out that William I – of part-Viking descent – kept on Cnut's policy at first in 1067, installing a local man from the Bamburgh kindred (Copsi) in Northumbria and later risking installing Siward's son Waltheof.

Unlike the similarly foreign conqueror William after 1066 (or 1068/9), Cnut co-opted senior English lords to serve him as well as his own countrymen. Though he was equally harsh in imposing punitive levels of taxation and relying on a substantial army (which this paid for), this was no more than security required. Unlike Edward in 1052, the king had enough troops to face down revolt without relying on his senior earls. Unlike William's reign, there is no evidence of a major alteration in landholding across England in favour of the foreign ruler's countrymen and the culture and terminology of the court remained English.[60] Where Danish terms were used in administration this was not necessarily an innovation from 1016 as many of the Anglo-Danes in eastern England would have spoken Danish anyway. The use of the term 'earl' for a powerful provincial governor rather than 'ealdorman' had become the practice for Mercia, East Anglia, and Northumbria under Aethelred, though Cnut was the first ruler to install an earl in the heartland of royal power in Wessex. The other difference between Cnut and William shows the latter's greater long-term political wisdom; William never granted all Mercia or Wessex to one man, thus risking the latter using his resources to revolt. Where he did create such 'super-magnates' as Cnut did, he faced revolt – as with the Earls of Hereford and East Anglia (one a Norman, one a Breton) in 1075 and allegedly from his own half-brother Odo of Kent in 1083. Cnut could rely on his senior earls through the period 1018–35; William faced more difficulties though it should be noted that both Hereford and East Anglia needed unified military leadership due to their proximity to invaders (the Welsh and Denmark). Usually William preferred to split up a province among several landholders to counter-balance each other, as with Roger of Montgomery and Earl Warenne in Sussex or the separate lordships of the central (Montgomery) and northern (Chester) Welsh Marches. The fact that by 1086 all but one major landholders who were directly responsible to William, the 'tenants-in-chief', were Frenchmen not Englishmen is one crucial difference in the two kings' approaches. But Cnut had not faced widespread revolt from the Englishmen he had given senior office and lands as William did in 1068–70 (as far as we can tell from the *Anglo-Saxon Chronicle*). He had no rival with greater legitimacy abandoning his court to lead a revolt and then fleeing abroad as Edgar 'Atheling' did to William in 1068 – though he was more immediately ruthless by killing his main Cerdicing challenger, Edwy. Both, however, faced some disturbances from lower-class opposition – the enigmatic 1017 rebel Edwy, 'King of the Ceorls', sounds like a prototype for the anti-Norman guerrilla commander Hereward who challenged William in 1069–70.[61]

Cnut also acted as a traditional English king in dealing with the Church, making grants of land and treasure, acting as a devout patron, keeping the Church sees for Englishmen (there were comparatively few Danish churchmen to award posts, unlike the number of French churchmen in the next foreign usurper's entourage), and even visiting Rome and encouraging the veneration of the late Archbishop (Saint) Aelfheah who had been martyred by a Viking army in 1012. Here there was a difference from William's policy, but the latter had a more dynamic and administratively-experienced body of churchmen in his homeland to promote.

Cnut did not replace his Archbishop of Canterbury as William did, but Harold II's Stigand had not been recognized by the legitimate Pope and so was regarded by the Rome-controlled Continental Church lawyers as illegal. (He had, unfortunately, both replaced an illegally deposed living archbishop, the Norman Robert, and received his 'pallium' of office from a pope who was later declared a usurper.) The Norman Church of 1066 was part of the current 'reformist' movement on the Continent, spearheaded by William's ally the papacy, compared to which the traditions and manners of the English Church were outdated. William had talented Norman administrators such as Lanfranc to promote and rely on; the Danish Church in Cnut's time lacked this modernity, dynamism, and usefulness to its secular lord Also, eleventh century English abbots had responsibilities as landlords and leaders of local society, which had led some to fight at Hastings; their administrative role had to be given to Norman 'loyalists' in 1066–70 to govern the localities. William had made much of papal support in his campaign so was bound to back up papal demands for greater order and imposition of Roman standards (and Continental canon law) on the English Church. His choice of archbishop, Lanfranc, was an enthusiast for the current 'reform' being imposed by Rome – though such matters were low enough in William's priorities for him to do nothing until 1070. Even Stigand kept his see for over three years, and the past canon-law-breaking pluralist Archbishop Ealdred of York was allowed to keep his see for his lifetime. (His chances were improved by his having crowned William.) The more military and thuggish Norman bishops appointed to the Northern frontier see of Durham, such as Walcher, were not exactly in the best traditions of the Continental Church, but their combination of religious and military roles was in the usual Norman tradition (as seen by Bishop Odo of Bayeux.) Giving a frontier see with command of troops to a fighting churchman had also been done by King Edward, whose bishops of Hereford had fought the Welsh. By contrast there was no source of scandal in the English Church of 1016 and the papacy at this date was not 'reformist' but still a puppet of local Italian factions.

The 'Danish Conquest' was thus as militarily effective but far less socially and institutionally far-reaching than Duke William's seizure of the throne in 1066, though in any case the culture of Denmark was close to that of the Anglo-Danes settled in Eastern England since the 860s and many of the leading men of the Danelaw had supported Cnut and his father, Swein, in 1013–16. (Cnut had proceeded to mutilate his local hostages in revenge after many supposed supporters abandoned him for Aethelred on his father's death and he was forced to abandon England, which cannot have benefited his reputation.)

(b) Decentralization – the long-term failure of Cnut's system and the success of William's. Why Cnut failed to make as much impact

William was not that dissimilar from Cnut in his initial approach to ruling England, with both men using a mixture of English state administration and law, collaborating English nobles, and ultimate reliance on their own trusted generals and foreign warriors. As of Christmas 1066, William had taken the principal nobles of Anglo-Saxon England – led by Edgar 'Atheling', Earls Edwin and Morcar, Siward's son Waltheof, and the two Archbishops – into his service as Cnut did. In 1069 he was even to hand distant Northumbria to Cospatrick, a scion of the ancient Anglian dynasty of Bamburgh, and later to Waltheof whereas Cnut had killed the then head of the Bamburgh kindred, Earl Uhtred, and installed a Scandinavian as earl. (There were two differences – Uhtred had opposed Cnut's claim in 1014–16 and Cnut, unlike William, was familiar with the North as of his accession.)

Both men divided England up among provincial commands for their senior advisers, with Cnut creating the earldoms that were to last to 1066 – though William created far more provincial magnates (some with titles) and was careful to give fewer blocs of contiguous territory to potential 'overmighty subjects' (except in militarily important border areas such as the Welsh Marches, north-east, and south-east Channel coast).

The record of post-1066 land-grants in the Domesday Book shows that he shrewdly made his senior Norman nobles take smaller blocs of lands in different counties, thus meaning that no one noble would dominate an entire region and so be able to use it as a base for revolt. Other nobles and the continuing royal Anglo-Saxon administration in each county (led by the sheriff) kept each district[62] divided between rival landowners, enabling the king to divide and rule. The exceptions were for militarily important areas where the principal landholder would need larger resources to defeat invaders, and William did his best to ensure (not always successfully) that these lands went to especially close advisers and competent generals – like his half-brothers, Roger of Montgomery, and William FitzOsbern. Roger received the central Welsh frontier (where he built Montgomery Castle) and Pevensey in Sussex; William received the southern part of the Welsh border, based on Hereford. Unfortunately, William was killed fighting for his king in Flanders in 1071, and his son revolted in 1075 in alliance with the Breton Earl Ralph of East Anglia.

Unlike Cnut, William did not 'alienate' provincial government across the country to a small bloc of powerful earls, who Cnut could control – perhaps due to a mixture of personal charisma and energy and his large army – but who after his death were able to take the initiative from weaker kings. By 1042 most of England was governed by a mere three earls – Siward in Northumbria, Leofric in Mercia, and Godwin in Wessex – and this made the new king, Edward, who had long lived in exile and had no political clientage of his own, heavily dependent on their goodwill. The political catastrophe of 1052, where the exiled Godwin family was able to return with an army and link up with the principal remaining earls (Leofric and Siward) to force King Edward to accept their restoration to power, showed the limits of Cnut's system of provincial government by a few powerful men.[63] Again, in 1055 and 1058 exiled Earl Aelfgar was able to force his return to power and office, defying Edward and the Godwin family.[64] Arguably, handing over Wessex – the base of royal power in tenth century England – to one earl, Godwin, some time around 1030 (definitely by Cnut) left the king without a major region where he was in sole control of patronage and landholders looked to him alone for leadership. Edward had to accept this loss of royal power on his accession in 1042 as he was in a weak position, having lived in exile for twenty-five years to 1041 and having no base of local support, though he did attempt to remedy it by dividing Wessex up again after he exiled Godwin in 1051.[65] William divided Wessex up into many smaller lordships, with several rival landholders to balance each other out in each county, and extended this system northwards across Mercia too. This influx of a multitude of small Norman castellans was probably what drove Earl

Edwin into revolt, as the influx of Normans into the Welsh Marches drove Edric 'the Wild' to revolt there and allegedly the seizure of his father's lands at Bourne in Lincolnshire drove Hereward to rebel.

The collection of earldoms in the Godwin family – East Anglia, most of the east and south-west Midlands, and Herefordshire to add to Wessex by 1051, and Northumbria in 1055 – also concentrated power and military resources in one non-royal family. This was a disaster for the monarchy, though it was of Edward's making not Cnut's. Provided that they acted together, they could potentially defy the king; in the confrontation of 1051 Leofric and Siward brought Mercian and Northumbrian troops to aid Edward in exiling them but in 1052 the two stood aside and Edward had to give way to Godwin's return. Leofric's son Aelfgar, as seen above, could similarly invade to demand his confiscated lands back in 1055 and 1058 – presumably Leofric stood aside from aiding Edward to resist him in 1055, as was only natural, but in 1058 Harold and his brother Tostig could not stop Aelfgar.

In 1065 the revolt against Edward's strict Earl of Northumbria, Tostig, was backed up by the rebels' new Earl Morcar's brother Edwin of Mercia and even Harold had to give way.[66] The requirement that he exile Tostig at the rebels' demand is said to have made Edward ill with rage and hastened his demise.[67] Edward's weak position to save his new order in 1051 or to defend Tostig in 1065 could not have been anticipated by Cnut, a man who had a powerful and permanent central army and fleet that Edward lacked after the 1040s. But William was in a similar position to Cnut, and did not make this error of judgement in giving potential power to too few senior lords. The explanation may be that he had seen what 'over-mighty subjects' were capable of in his turbulent minority in Normandy, where great lords had revolted with impunity. There had been no such threat to the king from great lords in Cnut's homeland, Denmark, which was a more egalitarian society with a multitude of medium-ranking farmers (and no castles that rebels could hold out in).

The message for royal power in all this was not comforting – the English king could be defied by a few well-placed senior nobles during Edward's reign. Edward's own nominees to senior provincial office (when he had a free choice in 1051) were largely replaced in 1052; his surviving ally, his nephew Earl Ralph of Hereford (a Frenchman), was militarily unsuccessful in his crucial role of fighting the Welsh, failed to train his men in the new French tactics, lost several crucial battles, and when he died in 1057 was replaced by Harold. If, as seems probable, Edward sought to build him up as a counterweight to Harold he failed. Nobody from outside the two senior families received an earldom after 1052. By 1066 the amount of land that

Harold , Earl of Wessex and now Hereford, owned across southern England made him by far the most powerful man in the kingdom after the king.[68] His relations with Edward were more cordial than Godwin's, helped by the fact that he was a generation younger than the king (they were born c.1003 and c.1022) and lacked Godwin's uncomfortable position as a senior aide of the man who had overthrown Edward's family in 1016 – the man who had betrayed Edward's brother Alfred to his death in 1036. Harold's powerful role in administration and diplomacy by the early 1060s seems to have been perfectly acceptable to the ageing king, whose alleged main interests were religion and hunting,[69] but he was almost a 'Mayor of the Palace' in political terms, which was an unprecedented elevation for an English subject.

William was in an easier position in 1066 than Edward was in 1042, as he had taken the throne by conquest and the two senior southern earls (Harold's brothers Gyrth and Leofwine) and most of the major landholders had been killed at Hastings. Confiscating their vast estates provided him with a ready-made bloc of territory to give to his loyalists in an area vital for defence against Continental attack, without the need for other major seizures. He had to rely at first on the assurances of loyalty by the brothers Edwin of Mercia and Morcar of Northumbria, who led the surrender of the surviving elite to him at Berkhamsted as he advanced on London – but he prudently took them and other senior Englishmen with him in 1067 when he returned to Normandy.[70] He also handed the North-East to a local magnate (Copsi). As he became secure, the senior English office-holders were replaced by Normans; though it is a moot point as to whether it was the defections to rebellions in 1068–9 that caused his drastic purge or if it was always intended. By 1086 only two major landholders in the list of 'tenants-in-chief' in England were English; and most of the English names in the next 'level' of landholders were men who had been connected to King Edward's court or served him in county-level office (and thus could be trusted as servants of any incumbent regime). Some of them, confusingly, were Frenchmen; imported by Edward (exiled in Normandy to 1042) or his nephew Earl Ralph.

William crucially broadened the circle of the senior provincial politico-military elite from the small circle of men endowed with large estates and provincial earldoms in 1016–66. This was partly necessity as he had a large 'class' of his own knights who had come with him in 1066 to reward, but it is probable that he was also aware of the dangers that Edward had faced from having a small group of senior nobles with vast estates. (Had he seen this for himself and discussed it with Edward on his alleged visit to England in 1051, when the king had just dispossessed the worst offenders – the Godwins?)

William followed the landholding system now in use in Normandy, where he had faced defiance from unruly nobles in his minority and had spent his early manhood cutting down 'over-mighty' subjects, powerful provincial lords with their own blocs of territory and private armies of retainers. No subject could now challenge the power of the duke, though some lords on the remote French border (particularly the Belleme family) could still use their territory and retainers to act semi-autonomously if there was a weak duke (as they did later to his son Robert).

The frontier Norman lords also had the advantage over rebels in the island of England in being able to ally with troublemaking foes of William across the border – the kings of France, as lords of the Isle de France, the Counts of Flanders (from 1071), and the Counts of Maine and Anjou. In England, the Welsh and the Scots would hardly make common cause with the alien Normans on their borders – particularly as the latter had 'stolen' land that they claimed, e.g. the upper Severn valley around Welshpool, Clywd, Glamorgan (from the 1070s), Brecon (from the early 1080s), and Northumberland. Rebel noble dynast Aelfgar could call on his daughter's husband, Gruffydd ap Llewelyn of Gwynedd, for aid in 1058; the 1075 Welsh Marcher rebels against William I and the 1102 rebels against Henry I could not call on their Welsh victims for help. William created a senior 'class' of a couple of hundred landholders as tenants-in-chief' , of whom only a small group of men on the Welsh, Scots, and Channel coast frontiers had locally concentrated power in one territory and a large number of troops. Most of the trouble for the king from the landholding class in 1066–1102 came from these men, led by earls who were mostly resident on the borders – the only ones to have the local resources to defy him with hope of success.

The fact that at first (1067–9) William retained as large an earldom of Northumbria as Cnut and Edward had done, divided at most among two men (in 1067) and handed to local Saxon nobles, was probably down to its distance from London. The initial experiment ended when Osulf murdered Copsi, his hereditary foe; William then tried out installing Cospatric, a member of the ancient and locally-accepted Bamburgh kindred who had long held the lordship of Bernicia – which Cnut had also done in Bernicia – and after him the late Earl Siward's son Waltheof.[71] He may have intended this 'devolving' Northumbria to local nobles as a long-term expedient to keep the area quiet while he concentrated his resources on the more important south, following Cnut and Edward's usual solution, and only broken the area up among more, exclusively Norman landholders when the local leadership proved untrustworthy. The massive revolt against his rule in 1069, which destroyed his initial policy, was more due to excessive taxation and ambition by its leaders (who were acting in the name of Edgar 'Atheling' as their candidate for the crown) than 'nationalist' revolt against French rule. No massive confiscations of land had yet occurred; the revolt has more in common with the long history of risings by ambitious local nobles against rule from Wessex, whose kings or nominee earls had been repudiated time after time from 940 to 1065.

In 1069 the new Earl Waltheof of Northumbria joined the revolt in York and a Danish invasion; in 1075 the new Earl of Hereford, son of William's deceased close ally William FitzOsbern, and the Earl of East Anglia revolted. The revolt was complicated by the dynastic claims of William's eldest son, Robert 'Curthose' who was denied the succession to England in favour of his younger brother William II; his principal allies were his half-uncles, Earl Odo of Kent (also Bishop of Bayeux) and Count Robert of Mortain, Lord of Pevensey, with allies in the Marches and the North. In 1095 the rebellion was led by the Earl of Shrewsbury, leading lord on the northern Welsh Marches, and Northumberland.[72] In all these cases revolt was centred in border areas, where the requirements of defence had given large grants of land and armed tenants – military potential – to a few figures. Given the danger of attack and the distance from London, no other course but this 'devolution' of responsibility to a few (hopefully trusted) senior commanders was possible in the Welsh Marches or the Scots border; the king would take time to respond to any crisis in person. The south-eastern coastal command in Sussex and Kent (vulnerable to Continental attack) was entrusted by William I to his half-brothers, Odo and Robert, though he carefully set up 'balancing' magnates in Sussex (Roger of Montgomery at Arundel and William of Warenne at Lewes) to keep check on Robert and in 1083 he arrested Odo.

Elsewhere power and resources were usually more divided, and the potentially dangerous 'bloc' of territory ruled by the Montgomery dynasty in north-east Wales already kept in check by the Earldom of Chester – was to be broken up by Henry I in 1102 after yet another revolt.[73] William's policy of a more extensive ruling elite than Cnut's, with power and resources more divided, was to make the English monarchy that he bequeathed to his heirs stronger than Cnut's.

It should be noted that the scant evidence of revolt against Cnut is no indication that his Danish rule was any more acceptable to the average Englishman than William's French rule, or that he was from the start a 'wiser' ruler who did not cause revolt. The evidence for post-1016 events is minimal due to the far briefer coverage of events then in the *Anglo-Saxon Chronicle* than for post-1066 events, and even so there are hints of serious trouble. The rash of executions of senior nobles in 1017[74] shows that Cnut feared conspiracy to oust him and sought to terrorize opposition. His determination to marry Aethelred's widow, Emma – the sister of the Duke of Normandy, a powerful neighbour and ally of Aethelred with a fleet to hand – can be seen partly as a way to buy off her countrymen from invading. The Norman coast had been a useful base for raiding Scandinavians en route to England in the 1000s, including Cnut's father, Swein, and could be so again. The fact that no new invasion of England from ambitious neighbouring rulers materialized after 1016 does not mean that it was never possible; Cnut's own brother Harald, king of Denmark, had an equal claim to see himself as heir to all Swein's lands but luckily he died in 1018.

After 1066, William faced invasion from King Swein Estrithson of Denmark (Cnut's nephew and Harold II's cousin), who stirred up the Yorkshire revolts of 1068–9 and later landed in Lincolnshire, potentially as serious a challenger as Harald 'Hardradi' had been in September 1066. Swein's son Cnut was still threatening invasion as late as 1085, when William burnt the crops along the East Anglian coast to deny him supplies should he land.[75] There is also the question of popular resistance to Cnut, as to William, among the lower classes in country areas. Who was the mysterious Edwy,[76] the 'ceorls' king' routed by Cnut in 1017, if not some sort of local English guerrilla leader like the 1070 rebel Hereward? The adult sons of Harold II led attacks from Ireland on the West Country in 1068, and Edgar 'Atheling' fled from William's court to join in revolt in the Midlands. When it failed he retired to Scotland where he remained a threat until William's invasion in 1072. Cnut's execution of Edmund 'Ironside's brother Edwy in 1017 was probably carried out to forestall this kind of revolt.[77] The parallels between Cnut's situation and William's are probably greater than are usually realized; and ironically it was Cnut who was the more ruthless – and effective – in his first couple of years in power.

After Cnut: the succession in 1035–42

As analysed by his late twentieth century biographers, Cnut strove to portray a degree of political continuity from Aethelred's reign and stressed in his legal pronouncements of acting in accordance with both justice and tradition.[78] His control of England was total, and after his sudden death in November 1035 the choice of successor for the 'Witan' was divided between his legitimate son by Emma, Harthacnut, aged around seventeen and currently living in Denmark as the heir to that kingdom, and another son called Harold (brother of Swein, ex-ruler of Norway) whose mother, Aelfgifu of Northampton, came from an important East Midlands kindred. It is unclear if Cnut and Aelfgifu were married, though if so it was probably by a local Anglo-Danish 'common-law' arrangement rather than with a Church ceremony and Emma and Harthacnut's partisans treated Harold as a bastard (with some hints that he was not even Cnut's son). Assuming that Cnut had formed his partnership with Aelfgifu while commanding in England under his father, Swein, in 1013–14 or in his unsuccessful war against Edmund in 1015, Harold may have been born c.1015 and so been the older of the youths. In any case he had the support of the Earls of Mercia and Northumbria, the royal fleet, and according to the *Anglo-Saxon Chronicle* almost all the great men north of the Thames. Emma, in charge of the royal treasury at Winchester, naturally backed her son Harthacnut, as did Earl Godwin of Wessex, but Harold was able to control the rest of the kingdom from spring 1036 and due to Harthacnut's delay in sailing to England Wessex eventually capitulated.[79] It is noticeable that there was no support – especially from their mother, Emma – for the legitimate heirs of Aethelred available across in Normandy, Edward and his brother Alfred. The remaining senior English nobles at court and holding land were content to follow the lead of their queen and the senior earls, though given the apparent backing for Harold 'Harefoot' in the Anglo-Danish lands and the adherence of Cnut's fleet and 'Housecarl' bodyguard to Cnut's sons this was less dangerous than staging a hopeless revolt. Possibly the sons of Aethelred would have stood more chance had Cnut had more senior English thegns in his service rather than purging them in 1016–17.

Edward – the senior prince – may have sought to land in Wessex with an armed escort, possibly at Southampton, to stake his claim early in 1036 but was resisted by force and returned to Normandy. Alfred landed in Kent and marched west along the Pilgrims' Way towards Winchester but was intercepted by Earl Godwin. He was lulled into a false sense of security with his host's pretended allegiance, and then arrested suddenly in his lodgings at Guildford while his escort was killed or enslaved. Handed over to Harold, he was blinded with evidently deliberate brutality and soon died of his wounds. Edward was forced to wait abroad until summoned home by the heirless Harthcnut in 1041, and after the latter's sudden death made him king he was then forced to rely heavily on the 'triumvirate' of earls – Godwin, Leofric, and Siward – who had led his election.[80] His succession to his half-brother, aged only around twenty-four, in June 1042 was probably unexpected as there is no indication that Harthacnut had been ailing; normally the latter would have been expected to marry and produce sons. Harthacnut's father had lived to over forty, his grandfather Swein probably to his fifties, and his great-great-grandfather Gorm 'the Old' probably to his seventies. His collapse at a banquet at Lambeth was not ascribed to poison, and alcoholism or diabetes is possible.

What if Cnut had outlived his sons?

Cnut's date of birth is uncertain, but he was in command of troops under his father (i.e. he was at least an adolescent) by 1012/13 and was probably no more than forty or forty-one when he died late in 1035.[81] An alternative suggestion is that he was in command at the Danish attack on Norwich in 1004, which would make him at least fourteen or fifteen then and born c.989, and that a later literary claim that he died at 'fifty-seven' should be read as 'forty-seven'.[82] His failure to react to the expulsion of his son Swein from Norway earlier in 1035 may argue in favour of earlier ill-health, but his death was evidently premature and even in the harsh conditions of Viking life some rulers such as Gorm 'the Old' of Denmark (Cnut's ancestor) and Harald 'Finehair' of Norway could reign as adults for up to fifty years. His control of England, as shown by the events after his death when his young and untried sons had no Anglo-Saxon royal or noble challengers, was such that he should have been able to remain as king for his lifetime – however long that was. It is quite conceivable that he could have lived into his fifties or sixties, putting his death in the 1040s (Emma, at least in her early teens in 1002, lived until 1052), which would have left his stepsons Edward and Alfred with no opportunity to challenge this veteran warrior and his army and fleet for the throne until then. Cnut's son Harold 'Harefoot', having secured all England in 1037 due to Harthacnut's failure to return with a Danish fleet to reinforce his supporters in Wessex, died in March 1040 at the age of no more than twenty-five or twenty-six. His half-brother Harthacnut then died suddenly while attending a banquet in Lambeth in June 1042, aged twenty-three or twenty-four, leaving the male line of Denmark extinct; Harthacnut's full sister Gunnhilde, married to the Holy Roman (German) Emperor Conrad's heir Henry, had also died young in 1038. Swein died mysteriously soon after his expulsion from Norway in 1035, though suicide has been suggested given his ignominious treatment by his subjects and his father's likely fury. Harthacnut might have been poisoned rather than having a fit due to natural causes, possibly exacerbated by excessive drinking, but this spate of deaths suggests that the family of Cnut lacked the sturdier constitutions of earlier kings of Denmark.

If Cnut had outlived all his children by 1042 and been left with an ageing queen unable to bear further children, his likeliest choice as heir would have been within his own family, unless Emma had shown more consideration for her sons by Aethelred than she did in real-life and persuaded him to reinstate them in the succession. Edmund 'Ironside's son Edward 'the Exile', in Russia to 1047 and thence in Hungary, would have had no partisans at court and would have had no reason to trust a summons home; Cnut had already murdered his uncle c.1017. Cnut's nephews Swein, Beorn, and Osbeorn Estrithson were Danes and would have been more likely to have the adherence of Cnut's Danish courtiers, 'Housecarls', and fleet than the half-Norman and long-exiled sons of Aethelred, and their father's sister Gytha and her husband, Earl Godwin, would have been probable supporters given that in real life Godwin secured Beorn an earldom from King Edward in the 1040s. It is possible that Cnut would have been prepared to combine England with Denmark in one kingdom to preserve his 'empire' and reduce the risks of the ruler of one kingdom – both with fleets – attacking the other. In that case Swein Estrithson, the eldest of the trio, would have been Cnut's likeliest successor and would have had to fight off a challenge from Magnus of Norway (as in real life) for control of Denmark. The possession of the English fleet would have given Swein a better chance of victory than he had in real life, where he was losing the war and had had to flee Denmark when Magnus suddenly died in 1047. The combined Anglo-Danish 'empire' of Cnut could thus have survived for another generation, though some division was probable on Swein's own death (1074) given his multiplicity of sons. One of these sons, Cnut, was in real life enough of a threat to England in 1085–6 for King William to pre-emptively burn the crops along the east coast to deny him supplies should he land. England might indeed have suffered the instability that Denmark did from the multiplicity of heirs in the early twelfth century, giving a chance to Edgar 'Atheling' to reclaim the throne (perhaps with Scottish support).

The Godwin family would have been the mainstay of Swein's regime in England as they were of Edward's in real life, with the added advantage of their close kinship. Assuming Cnut had lived to something like his father's age (probably around fifty to fifty-five) and died around 1048, the major military confrontation of the 1050s would have been between Swein and the new King of Norway, Magnus' uncle Harald 'Hardradi' (a veteran of the Varangian Guard in Constantinople and Byzantine-Arab wars in Sicily). Had Swein died or been killed some time before 1074, there is the possibility of the ambitious Earl Harold Godwinson – successor to his father in Wessex c.1053 – fighting Harald of Norway over England as in real life. Harold could have seized the English throne while his cousins, the sons of Swein, were preoccupied in Denmark.

But there would have been no serious possibility of Edward Aethelredson ever returning from Normandy to succeed to England except by the agreement of the clique of senior earls and the still-powerful Emma as a candidate to challenge the family of Swein Estrithson. As Swein was Godwin's kinsman the Godwin family were very unlikely to take that course of action. Edward would have remained an exile in Normandy, as would Edward 'the Exile' and his family in Hungary, and Duke William would never have become a contender for the throne except as an opportunist invader in the manner of Harald 'Hardradi'.

Chapter Six

1066: The Fall of Anglo-Saxon England and its Aftermath

Inevitable or bad luck? What was due to underlying factors, and what was down to luck and timing?

A 'perfect storm' in 1066: the result of a childless king, some convenient deaths, and an unexpected political disgrace?

(a) The path of Harold to the throne in 1066: luck and the removal of rivals

What exactly were Edward's intentions, and was his alleged backing for William in 1051–2 a temporary measure?
The very fact that William was able to plausibly challenge for the throne in 1066 was due to political and dynastic problems in post-1042 England, which acted in his favour. His alleged claim lay on the supposed promise by his cousin Edward in 1051/2, which as we have seen was not the first such promise to a friendly ruler of succession to the English throne – Harthacnut had promised it to Magnus of Norway in 1038/9, if we accept the latter's claim. (This is assuming that Harthacnut's promise referred to England, of which he was not yet king, as well as Denmark.) Of course it is not impossible that Magnus invented the story to justify his intended invasion in 1043–7, which his sudden death (supposedly foreseen by the holy Edward, according to his hagiographer) prevented. But it is probable that the promise was made in an 'open session' of Harthacnut's and Magnus' peace-meeting to end their war over Norway in 1039, which their senior nobles would have attended; it would be risky for Magnus to invent it and be called a liar. Apart from the supposed promise by Edward, William could assert a claim by

naked and unapologetic conquest and subsequent 'election' by coerced local nobles – this was Swein's route to the English throne in 1013. It helped if the alternative claimant publicly renounced their own claim and swore allegiance, which is what Edgar 'Atheling' did for William as he surrendered at Berkhamsted in November(?) 1066. (Aethelred had never abdicated in Swein's favour; he fled and was deposed by his nobles.)

But it is important to remember that naked conquest without a legal claim was a Scandinavian not a Southern European concept, and not common in William's increasingly legalized, Rome-orientated French world. Cnut overran Norway without any legal or hereditary claim in 1028, and Harald 'Hardradi' sought to do this to England in 1066 (though his non-direct ancestor Erik 'Bloodaxe' had ruled York). But the Normans themselves preferred to have a legally recognized claim to lands that they stole from indigenous inhabitants. In 1053 the Norman 'robber barons' who had settled in lands seized from Byzantines and Lombards in Southern Italy and had erected a new 'County of Apulia', led by the sons of William's vassal Tancred de Hauteville, required their captured foe Pope Leo IX to recognize them as his vassals. Like the Hauteville brothers, William preferred to have a legal fiction to cover up naked 'land-grabs'.

As suggested in the previous chapter, the succession of Edward – and thus of William – was in itself an unlikely outcome for England. As of 1016 Edmund Ironside had two sons and a full brother, and after his death his replacement, Cnut, had three sons who reached adulthood. Two kings in succession, Harold 'Harefoot' and Harthacnut, died in their early to mid twenties in 1040–2 to make way for him. And initially in 1042 it would have been assumed that Aethelred's surviving son Edward, in exile since 1016 but returned to England by his half-brother Harthacnut in 1041 and succeeding the twenty-four-year-old king a year later, would have had children. The story of his vow to remain celibate as thanks to God for his unexpected restoration appears in his hagiographical literature, which is not contemporary, and reflects what was expected of a putative saint, not political reality and dynastic duty for a mid-eleventh century king.[1] It may owe something to contemporary gossip, as an explanation for the undeniable fact that he had no children by his (much younger) wife, Earl Godwin's daughter Edith, and have emerged in the light of his religious interests. It is questionable whether the latter have been exaggerated by his admirers, led by the late eleventh and early twelfth century monks of his burial-place Westminster Abbey who hoped to have him canonized and add to their abbey's prestige and tourist-trade.[2] Evidence for his religiosity at the time of his marriage (1045) is limited, and his building of the Abbey did not commence until later; arguably his interest in religion increased with age, in the 1050s, and after his political defeat by Godwin in 1052.[3] Some modern writers have suggested that he did not want to marry his unwelcome patron Godwin's daughter and was pressurized into it – he rid himself of the earl and his family at the first clear opportunity, in 1051 — so he might have remained celibate to deny Godwin the satisfaction of grandchildren on the throne.[4] After her family's exile she was dismissed from court and sent to a nunnery – either the luxurious accommodation of Wilton, a regular queenly 'retirement' residence, or the harsher Wherwell – and her property may have been seized. There was talk of divorce, involving Archbishop Robert of Canterbury,[5] a Norman who was a leading foe of the Godwins – and who thus possibly wanted Edward to have children by another wife, not for his own countryman Duke William to succeed. The king's attitude remains uncertain, and retaining Edith at court would run the risk that she would pass on militarily valuable information to her kinsmen who were to invade in 1052. As of 1051–2 it would seem that the exile of the Godwins would diminish not increase William's chances of inheriting England.

1051 and all that – and the claims of Edward's kin, Earl Ralph and Edgar 'Atheling'
Assuming that William did visit Edward and secure a promise, this has to be seen in the context of how useful his Norman ports would be to an invasion of England by the Godwins – who William might support as his wife, Matilda, was sister to Tostig's wife, Judith. Edward may have promised him the throne to buy him off, and reversed his decision later when he did not need William. He was, after all, the son of the notoriously devious and unreliable Aethelred, and his capacity for turning on an ally can be seen in his exile of the Godwins after eight years of relying on them to lead his government. There is a famous if unproveable claim in one of Edward's biographies that he sarcastically told his ex-minister Godwin in 1051 that he would pardon him if he handed over Edward's brother Alfred and his companions, betrayed to their deaths by Godwin in 1036, alive and well. If true, it presents a picture of a man bringing up an old grudge twenty-five years later and seeking vengeance for his murdered kin like a Scandinavian warlord, not the holy pacifist of twelfth century myth.

As events turned out, the Godwin family were able to invade successfully, secure the backing of Earls Leofric and Siward, and force Edward to restore them to all their lands and offices in 1052. Edith was received back as queen, but there were still no children, though as of 1052 she was probably only in her mid-twenties and Edward around forty-nine. By 1066 she was being referred to by Edward as his 'daughter', rather than in a normal matrimonial context, and the near-contemporary *Vita Aedwardi Regis* of c.1070 (commissioned by Edith herself?) treats them in this manner;[6] it is probable that their relationship in his later years was more filial than sexual. Some modern speculation has even arisen that Edward was homosexual, possibly without knowing it, or had been put off women by his uneasy relationship with his mother, Emma, who had left him to sit out her marriage to Cnut in 1017–35 in exile and does not seem to have hurried to recall him afterwards. (In 1043 he arrested her and temporarily seized her treasure for an alleged plot to replace him as king with his foe Magnus of Norway.[7]) But even if Edward was unlikely to have children, only the Norman chroniclers and no English sources say that he invited his mother's great-nephew William to England after expelling the Godwins in 1051 and named him as heir.[8] If Edward did invite William to England, his priority may well have been the fact that William could give shelter to the exiled Godwin family and their intended invasion-fleet in Norman harbours, as William's grandfather Duke Richard II had sheltered Aethelred's Viking enemies there. It was only a short voyage across the Channel from Norman ports to the Isle of Wight and a landing at Godwin's ancestral home, Bosham on Portsmouth Harbour. The half-Norman Edward, who had sailed from Normandy to Southampton to test the situation in England after Cnut's death in 1035, would have been fully aware of the help William could give to an invasion – and William's wife, Matilda of Flanders, was the sister of Godwin's third son Tostig's new wife, Judith. Edward may have wanted William to ask his father-in-law, Count Baldwin of Flanders, to send Godwin packing from his current refuge in Flanders, and the succession to England – if it was even mentioned – a side-issue at the meeting.

The king's intentions for the succession as of 1051 are unclear, and the whereabouts of his closest male kin – Edmund's sons, his nephews – were apparently unknown as Bishop Ealdred had to seek them out on the Continent when Edward's attention later turned to them.[9] Notably, Edward had made no attempt to find them in the 1040s, even before he married Godwin's daughter. After 1045 Godwin would have opposed such a venture as a threat to his hoped-for royal grandson. But the obvious alternative heir was Edward's sister Goda's eldest son, Ralph, by Count Drogo of the Vexin (William's Seine valley neighbour). Ralph had already been brought to England and succeeded Godwin's disgraced son Swein as Earl of Hereford, either in 1049 or 1051. Granted extensive estates and the command of the crucial South Welsh frontier, Ralph was clearly being built up as a major political player and a potential military commander; unfortunately he was a disaster in the latter role. He introduced castles and Norman cavalry tactics to the Welsh frontier wars, without success, and was backed up by a coterie of Northern French knights (some at least had to flee England on Godwin's return). Unsuccessful both on land and in commanding the fleet as the Godwins returned, he was able to keep his earldom after 1052 but was repeatedly defeated by the Welsh and had to be rescued by Harold, who succeeded him as earl when he died in1057. His son was probably under-age, and retained his lands but not his office; the dynasty lasted into Norman England as lords of Berkeley. Had he been more militarily successful or outlived Edward, and had the Godwins stayed in exile, he was an obvious choice as heir. His accession in 1066 would not have been welcome to William given his lands adjoining the latter's, which he could ally with William's foes (the French king or the Count of Anjou) if William annoyed him. Given that William arrested his brother Walter of Mantes in 1063 (who then conveniently died in prison) and took over his lands, Ralph was an obvious foe for William.

After Godwin's death, Edward sought out the elder (and survivor) of his half-brother Edmund's sons – clearly as his intended heir. This man, Edward 'the Exile', was around his own age at his return to England after a similarly long exile, having been born in 1015/16. He had moved on from Russia to Hungary to assist the successful invasion of an exiled prince, Andrew, in 1046/7 and had estates there; he was duly lured home by Bishop Ealdred and landed in England in 1057. Unfortunately, he died in London before he could meet the king. The lament of the *Chronicle* about the tragedy that he for, whatever reason, was not allowed to see Edward[10] has been interpreted hopefully as a hint that some human not divine agency was responsible for this death, and is implied in the odd wording. Either Harold – accused of poisoning him by some Norman writers – or even William had him killed to remove a rival.[11] Murder remains possible and Edward 'the Exile' was clearly intended as his namesake's heir as of 1056–7, but the wording more probably means that the chronicler was lamenting the unknown reasoning of Providence. The younger Edward would have been no more than fifty-one had he lived to succeed in 1066, and have been home from his exile for far longer than the older Edward had been as of his accession in 1042. Given his apparent adventurousness[12] and military ability in the Hungarian expedition, after a decade to adapt to England he could well have made a capable ruler – though he would have been as overshadowed by a powerful, landed and militarily successful Earl of Wessex (Harold) as the older Edward had been in 1042.

The unexpected death of Edward 'the Exile' left his son Edgar as his heir, and the use of the terminology of 'Atheling' for the latter in contemporary English references[13] shows that he was seen as fully 'throne-worthy' and a probable successor. Born some time between 1052 and 1056 and seen as an exact contemporary of his later friend[14] Robert 'Curthose', who was born in

1051/3, he shared the same fate in that both were the longest-lived of their kin but never secured their father's crowns. He was still alive in 1125 according to William of Malmesbury, and thus lived to over seventy, which was nearly a decade older than the 'Confessor' and far older than most of his male kin.[15] But as of January 1066 he was only aged eleven to fourteen and too young to fight or command at a time of expected invasion by either Normandy or Norway, and was apparently passed over by Edward on his deathbed in favour of the experienced war-leader Harold. (The sources agree that Edward commended his kingdom to Harold[16] – though this might just possibly mean as regent for Edgar, not as king.) In any case, the choice of king as of 5 January 1066 lay with the 'Witan', even if the previous ruler had made a recommendation. They duly accepted Harold as king. The role of the Archbishop of Canterbury, the Godwinson partisan Stigand, would have been crucial if there was any doubt over who should succeed. In that respect it is crucial that Stigand's predecessor, the canonically appointed Norman priest Robert of Jumieges, had been sent packing by the returned Godwin family in 1052 – probably in fear of his life. He had apparently wanted Edward to divorce Edith and marry again[17] and was thus a target of Godwin's revenge as a threat to his dynasty, quite apart from being one of the hated 'Frenchmen' who had to flee London en masse.[18] Edward made no attempt to remove Stigand for the remainder of his reign, despite his appointment being illegal and Archbishop Robert seeking papal support – Stigand managed to secure a papal 'pallium' and recognition from the new Pope Benedict in 1058 only to face more condemnation after this pope was deposed and all his acts nullified.[19] Probably Harold vetoed any attempt to remove Stigand; but if Edward had had a less partisan archbishop would the latter have insisted on Edgar rather than Harold being king after him?

The question of Edward's intentions for the throne in 1057–66 is complicated, and it is not impossible that he changed his mind several times or was hoping to live until Edgar reached adulthood. Tenth century kings had succeeded in their mid-teens, e.g. in 955 and 959. The Norman sources after 1066 claimed that he had kept to his plan of 1051 to make William his heir, and grants of the succession to a foreign ally without a dynastic claim were not unknown if we take Magnus of Norway's claim as Harthacnut's nominee as more than propaganda. There is also the possibility of some hopes being entertained by the second husband of Edward's sister Goda, Ralph's stepfather Count Eustace of Boulogne – who assisted William's invasion in 1066 and fought at Hastings but possibly had his own agenda. A neighbouring ruler with lands on the Channel like William, Eustace had been on a visit to Edward (possibly angling for the throne) in 1051 when his retainers had quarrelled with the men of Dover over lodgings and several had been killed; Edward had ordered Godwin, Lord of Dover, to sack the town in reprisal but he had refused and this had sparked off his confrontation with the king. Eustace was thus hostile to the Godwins and indirectly responsible for their exile in 1051, and after aiding William in 1066 he was later to invade Kent himself – possibly aiming to aid local rebels and seize the throne. He has been suggested as one commissioner for the Bayeux Tapestry, and his motivation throughout the era remains unclear.[20] Did he have hopes from Edward in 1051–66?

The visit of Harold to Normandy in 1064/5

Allegedly the mysterious mission of Earl Harold to Normandy in 1064/5, the opening section of the Bayeux Tapestry, was to confirm the promise of the throne to William. William either persuaded or blackmailed his 'guest' into swearing an oath (on some concealed relics) to uphold his claim. Harold would hand over Dover to William and assist his arrival on Edward's death, and in return he would marry the Duke's daughter (which one is not clear) and be kept on as his leading minister.[21] Harold also took weapons from the Duke on campaign, was knighted, and did homage as his 'man' as seen in the Tapestry – which in Norman legal terminology (which Harold may not have known) obliged him to obey his lord.

He went back on his oath; whether or not he claimed that he had been tricked into it and had not realized that there were holy relics under the table/altar when he swore to assist the Duke's accession is unknown. The terms and location of the oath are unclear, and even the Norman sources cannot agree on them – from which it can be taken that the ceremony was not carried out in public as part of an intended diplomatic mission and that William tricked Harold in front of a limited company of his intimates.[22]

If Edward had ordered Harold to recognize William's claim, it is probable that there would have been a well-known public ceremony whose location could not be disputed. Even by the Norman account where Harold was supposed to be confirming Edward's promise of the throne, it is clear that William felt he could not trust the earl to carry it out and had to resort to an extra precaution – by subterfuge.

Some historians have suggested that the taking of an oath was invented, though it seems somewhat risky to have invented the whole incident, which Wiliam's ill-wishers could then deny with hope of being believed. Certainly it is unlikely that the entire mission was invented by 'Norman propaganda' after 1066 – eleventh century governments did not have that amount of control over their subjects to be able to get away with such a complete fabrication. Not all the post-1066 accounts of the episode were written by obedient writers under direct Norman control, and the silence of the

Chronicle on the incident may be due to it being a minor personal venture by Harold on private business rather than a formal embassy. It is probable that all parties knew that Harold had been in Normandy in 1064/5 if not what he was doing there. It is more plausible to suggest that Harold did not go to Normandy on Edward's behalf, and that this explains the scene in the Tapestry where the King is shown raising a finger of admonition at Harold after he returns.[23] Was he telling Harold off for going? This could be possible if the version of one account is considered – that Harold went to Normandy to negotiate the release of his younger brother Wulfnoth and nephew Haakon, left behind when the Godwins fled England in 1051[24] and handed over by Edward via Archbishop Robert to William. William had recently captured the late Earl Ralph's brother Count Walter of Mantes, a Continental rival but also a potential heir to England as Edward's nephew, and the prisoner had died mysteriously in a Norman prison (perhaps poisoned by William). Was Edward telling Harold that William could not be trusted? If so, it would seem unlikely that Edward intended William as his heir at the time. The scene on the Tapestry clearly had some significance to be included, and its enigmatic nature may be due to the work's creators – commissioned by a Norman such as Bishop Odo, or by William's unreliable ally Eustace of Boulogne? – deliberately leaving its meaning vague. Were Norman spectators meant to think that Harold was being told to be sure to obey orders and assist the Duke's accession, and English ones allowed to derive another meaning from it? One modern theory has it that the Tapestry is not the propagandist piece of Norman 'official history' that used to be assumed, but more subversive and ambiguous.

Aelfgar of Mercia – one crucial absentee from events in 1066
Whatever the truth of the claim that Edward intended William as his heir, the coup that secured the throne for Harold – enabling William to invade in the guise of the outraged party – was assisted by several convenient developments that could not have been foreseen. In the first place, Harold's main domestic rival, Earl Aelfgar of Mercia,[25] had died at an unknown date between 1062 and 1065 – probably closer to the former, as early in 1063 Harold was able to attack his son-in-law and ally Gruffydd ap Llewelyn of Gwynedd without interference. Around the same age as Harold and an experienced warrior, Aelfgar (who initially held East Anglia and then succeeded his father, Leofric, in Mercia in 1057) was a political foe who had been exiled twice, in 1055 and 1058.

Aelfgar had been given East Anglia when Harold was exiled in 1051, had given it up on his return, and had regained it when Harold succeeded to Wessex in 1053; clearly the Godwins had been endeavouring to prevent him succeeding Leofric and thwarting their near-monopoly of power. His exile in 1055 was possibly linked to his opposing Harold's brother Tostig's nomination to Northumbria, and on both occasions he invaded England with his Welsh allies (in 1058 with Norse mercenaries too[26]) and forced the king and Harold to accept his restoration to power. He was thus very unlikely to have accepted his old enemy Harold as king in January 1066 without a fight, and to have backed Edgar instead; his death meant that Harold only had to deal with his young and inexperienced son Edwin, probably in his twenties, in command of Mercia. If Aelfgar had been alive in 1066 it is unlikely that Harold could have succeeded smoothly, and the accession of Edgar would have been more likely; William would have had difficulties in claiming the throne ahead of Edgar, who unlike Harold was the late ruler's close male kin and so a plausible legitimate successor. It would seem unlikely that Pope Alexander II would have backed William against Edward's legitimate kinsman, rather than against a man who may have visited Rome as a pilgrim but had allowed an illegal archbishop to remain in office in defiance of canon law. Edgar's mother, Agatha, was kin to the German emperor (the under-age Henry IV, not yet a papal foe) and his religious mother and regent, Agnes of Poitou, so deposing him would be more objectionable than deposing Harold.

Tostig – one Godwinson against another
Another event that may have emboldened Harold was the deposition of his brother Tostig from the earldom of Northumbria in August 1065. The appointment of Tostig, a rare 'outsider' with no local connections, to succeed Siward (possibly a Yorkshire not overseas 'Dane', and certainly married to a lady of the Bamburgh kindred), in 1055 had been a sign of royal and Godwin family ambition to control the area. Tostig was a strong but unpopular ruler who had to rely on his own bodyguard for support not local kin, and it is possible that he and his sister Queen Edith were linked to the suspicious murder of one of the Bamburgh family, Cospatric, at court late in 1064. This removal of a potential challenger may have sparked off the revolt through the victim's kin seeking justice that they knew the King would not grant, and Tostig was deposed and his guards massacred while he was away from York hunting in Wiltshire with the King. The rebels elected Morcar, the young and inexperienced brother of Earl Edwin of Mercia and thus from the principal dynastic rivals of the Godwin family, as the new earl and marched into Mercia en route to confront the King; Edwin joined them.

As in the invasions by Aelfgar in 1055 and 1058, the family of Leofric and the family of Godwin seemed about to confront each other in arms. Harold, commanding the royal army, gave way and negotiated despite his recent military successes against the Welsh. By the terms of his treaty Morcar was recognized as earl and Tostig had to go into exile.[27] The refusal of Englishman to fight Englishman, which would weaken the realm and aid foreign attackers, was a repeat of the armed confrontations among the elite in 1051, 1052, 1055, and 1058 – but Tostig blamed Harold personally and once the latter was king Tostig sought foreign aid to overthrow him. Based in Flanders with his wife's kin as the entire Godwin family had been in 1051–2, he failed in his initial descent on the south-east in spring 1066 and headed for Scotland to stir up his ally King Malcolm III; he ended up invading in the late summer with Harald 'Hardradi', King of Norway, who was cruising the northern seas with a fleet en route to attack York. In doing so Tostig was following the precedent of Aelfgar's use of the Welsh and Norwegians to challenge Harold, with the added complication that as his wife was sister to William's wife, Matilda, the Duke may have been involved in his schemes (or disappointed his hopes for aid).

But it is possible that Harold's refusal to fight for Tostig's earldom in 1065 had an element of calculation about it, connected to the probability that the ageing king would not live for much longer. Were the Godwinson brothers as united as they seemed on the surface in 1055–65 and would Tostig have opposed Harold' s seizure of the throne?[28] There is a suggestion that Tostig was the favourite of Edith, not of Harold, and his removal in 1065 may have suited Harold's ambitions. Had he still been earl in January 1066, would he have backed Edgar (or even himself) to be king and thus thwarted Harold's succession? There is no indication that his initial attack on south-east England in spring 1066 was in anyone's interest but his own, and in backing Harald of Norway that summer he was having to come to terms with the latter's rival claim to England in return for the usefulness of the Norwegian army in overthrowing Harold.

(b) The timing of events in 1066: William's luck

The result of the battle of Hastings was not inevitable despite the Norman use of cavalry and the exhaustion of the English army, two factors that aided Duke William's chances. Indeed, it was only the luck of a southerly wind at the crucial moment late in September – with Harold away from London in the North – that enabled William's armada to sail from the mouth of the Dives river in Normandy to Sussex and land unchallenged. He had waited for weeks with an adverse wind, at risk of his impatient army breaking up and at least his non-Norman allies (e.g. the Bretons) defying his orders and returning home. In England Harold had had both the 'fyrd' levies and his 'housecarls' stationed along the coast ready to fight, with the English fleet in a position to intercept the Norman shipping.[29] His army, unlike William's, had experience of recent major campaigning against a formidable foe in hostile territory – they had invaded hilly Gwynedd in 1063 to attack Gruffydd ap Llewelyn, dangerous reunifier of the Welsh kingdoms, and had persevered with the war until some desperate Welshmen killed their leader and sent Harold his head to secure peace. In that war, Harold had handled a combined attack by two armies – his own and his brother Tostig's – and had also used a fleet in the Irish Sea. William's experience was limited to small-scale punitive wars against rebellious vassals in Normandy and one major battle against rebels, Val-es-Dunes in 1047, where he had relied heavily on his ally the French king. Harold had personally handled a fleet before, namely during his family's return to power in 1052 when he sailed with an expeditionary force from Dublin via a raid on the West Country to link up with his father, Godwin, at the Isle of Wight; both fleets then advanced to the Thames estuary.[30]

By contrast, William had no known naval experience. The Normans had ironically taken over their Duchy in 911 as seaborne Viking pirates, and their coast was a refuge for Vikings raiding England in the tenth and early eleventh centuries; the last seaborne descent on England by Normans had been in the service of King Edward as he attacked Hampshire from exile in 1035. (He was driven off.) But William himself had never commanded at sea, and once he had decided on an invasion and constructed a fleet (which showed he had few ships permanently ready) he had to wait for a suitable wind. The longer he waited in the estuaries of eastern Normandy, the greater the risk of his bored men declining in efficiency. Had the wind been in William's favour in August or early September he would have had to risk the crossing, in danger of interception at sea or at least of English vessels attacking his ships once they were in harbour.

William chose to land his forces in Pevensey Bay (then a wide estuary around the Levels, not a straight coastline as today). Landing and/or fighting would have been difficult had he not had the advantage of no resistance – as he did once the fleet and 'fyrd' had dispersed in September to bring in the harvest. The remaining troops then had to leave to fight off the landing of Harald 'Hardradi' in Yorkshire – and we can only guess if William had sources of intelligence from resident Frenchmen in England that told him when the Norse army was expected to land. (Or was there a link via his wife with her sister Judith, Tostig's wife?) When he landed on 28 September, he had time to secure the fortified position of Pevensey Roman fortress, forage for food, rest his seasick men and horses, and even to build a rudimentary wooden 'motte' castle at Hastings. He had over a fortnight to wait until the English army returned from its expedition north to defeat the Norwegians and Tostig. Normally a battle-ready English force that had not been exhausted by a march to and from Yorkshire (and diminished by casualties there) would have been available on or near the Sussex coast to attack him within days, though it is not clear where exactly Harold was stationed before he left for York as the Norse invaded. The Normans would not have had weeks in possession of the Hastings peninsula (28 September – 13 October) to prepare for battle, enable their horses to recover from the crossing, and construct a defensive castle. The erection of a castle suggests that William intended to use it to withstand an attack if the 'neck' of the Hastings peninsula was forced, as well as to safeguard his men in a defensible perimeter at night from Saxon raids.

The long delay to William's sailing caused by the adverse winds from July to August meant that the temporary levies in the 'fyrd' and manning the English ships had to be sent home to see to the harvest, and William could land and set up his new base without early interruption. As the Bayeux Tapestry makes clear, his men were able to terrorize the district without Saxon resistance.[31] The burning of villages and expulsion of civilians were probably intended to encourage Harold – whose ancestral home was at Bosham at the far side of the county – back to Sussex quickly to save his people.

Harald 'Hardradi' and Tostig – a crucial English crisis that favoured William
Even if the wind had not changed in his favour until late September, thus depriving Harold of a battle-ready 'fyrd' and fleet, William would have had to meet Harold and his own personal military force quickly if the King had not been called north – and thus faced fresher English troops. The concurrent landing of the Norse army in Yorkshire was co-ordinated to take advantage of Harold's preoccupation in the south, probably by King Harald 'Hardradi's English exile ally Tostig – Harold's disgraced brother, deposed as Earl of Northumbria by local rebels in 1065 without Harold intervening to restore him. Tostig who was married to the sister of William's wife, Matilda of Flanders, had visited William's court since his exile, and may have persuaded Harald to time his attack on Yorkshire to coincide with the expected timetable of William crossing to England. Did Tostig expect his brother to be preoccupied with William's landing at the time of the Norse invasion, and even to have suffered heavy enough casualties to prevent him marching north to fight it?

Tostig had had no success in his earlier raids on the English coast, neither defections to his cause nor victory over the local levies, and the Norse invasion thus gave his cause new hope. Harald 'Hardradi' was already in Orkney when Tostig arrived from his ally King Malcolm's court to join him, probably in mid-summer 1066, and was heading south after asserting the historic Norwegian claim to control over the jarldom of Orkney. It is possible that had the ferocious Jarl Thorfinn 'the Mighty', ruler since 1014, not died recently (1065?) leaving two inadequate sons Harald would not have been there at all. The famous warlord Thorfinn, nicknamed 'Raven-Feeder' from the piles of corpses left from his battles for the birds to eat, would have been a formidable foe; his sons Paul and Erlend meekly submitted when Harald arrived to demand they join his fleet as his vassals.

It may have been Thorfinn's death that emboldened Harald to invade once he and his Scandinavian rival Swein Estrithson had patched up their differences in the early 1060s to end their long war over Denmark – another indirect bonus for William. The restless Harald was not a king to rest on his laurels, and reasserting the tenth century Norwegian overlordship of Orkney was a logical next step once he had fought Denmark to a standstill.

Harald's ancestors in Norway had had a claim as overlords of Orkney, which had been founded as a Viking settlement by Norwegians in flight from Norway's first king, Harald 'Finehair'. (Ironically, its rulers were related to William's own ancestor Hrolf/Rollo, the first Count/Duke of Normandy.) The claim had been sporadically asserted when Norway was strong enough, and was to continue until the sale of the islands to Scotland in 1468. Harald had a claim on (ex-Viking) York as it had been ruled by a former king of Norway, Erik 'Bloodaxe', and his ambitions were limitless quite apart from him needing to keep his restless warriors occupied following peace with Denmark.[32] But Harald need not have attacked England in late summer 1066, and could have pursued Norse claims to Man or Dublin instead. Once he had overrun Orkney, that gave him a claim on Orkney's former interests in Dublin – last asserted by Thorfinn's father, Sigurd 'the Stout', who had come to the aid of the local Norse against 'High King' Brian Borumha in 1014. There was no pre-eminent local Norse warlord in Dublin or Man to defy him with much chance of success. Was it Tostig whose advice was decisive in the timing of his attack on York, and thus in causing King Harold to be absent in the North when William landed?

There are plenty of unanswered questions about the exile of Tostig in 1065, a vital element in William's success in 1066 (see previous section). Is it possible that the acquiescence Harold showed to his brother's exile in 1065 was due to his desire to remove this potential backer of Edgar Atheling as the next king? In any case, it was the Northumbrian revolt of 1065 that meant that Tostig was threatening the North in alliance with Harald 'Hardradi' in 1066.

It was not inevitable that Tostig would invade in alliance with Harald – though his close relationship with King Malcolm indicated that he was liable to seek aid in Scotland. His initial foray from exile in Flanders was aimed at

Kent, where he failed to win support; he then moved north to East Anglia and the Humber, with similar lack of success, before heading to Scotland in summer 1066. Previously, exiles in the Godwin dynasty (their brother Swein in 1047–9 and the whole family in 1051–2) had centred their invasions on the Channel coasts. Possibly Tostig originally wanted William to back his own invasion, and turned to Harald as an ally when the Duke failed to support his plans. His initial raids on the east coasts were logically a 'probe' to see what backing he could muster. If Tostig – unpopular in York, given the extent of the revolt against him in 1065, so unlikely to gain support in his own earldom – had had more success in stirring up local support against Harold he may not have bothered to call on the Norse for help. Harold would then been able to tackle Tostig alone, probably in the summer of 1066, and have had to face the Norse army on its own later – possibly in 1067 if Harald 'Hardradi' had decided to concentrate on the Hebrides in 1066.

Even if Tostig *had* linked up with Harald and their combined army had been the threat that it was in real life, adverse winds could have held the Viking fleet up as it did William's. Thus Harald and Tostig might not have landed in the Humber estuary until after Duke William sailed, and Harold might still have been in the south as the Normans landed and been able to fight them quickly. The later the Norwegians landed, the greater the chance that winter weather would delay an English military response – the way in which the invaders moved off leisurely from York to Stamford Bridge in September 1066 to receive the submission of local thegns shows that Harald and Tostig were not in fear of imminent attack. Tostig's successor in Northumbria, Earl Morcar, probably still in his late teens or twenties, had been routed by Harald and Tostig at Gate Fulford outside York and fled with his brother Edwin of Mercia. The invaders would have been more alert to a counter-attack had they not had an untried young novice commanding the defeated Northumbrian army – in which respect the death of Morcar's father, Aelfgar of Mercia, c.1062 was crucial (see above).

According to Harald's saga, the Norwegians were relaxing on the river-bank at Stamford Bridge when they were caught unawares by the sight of the English army approaching and had to hurry to put on their mail while a solitary warrior held the bridge cutting them off from the attackers.[33] It is quite plausible that if the winds had held the Norse fleet up but October had been reasonably mild, and calm seas beckoned, Harald would still have sailed south then. The invasion could have followed Duke William's landing, and the English could have been able to take on the Normans at Senlac soon after their landing and then faced a Norwegian invasion of York. As viewed by a leader in London in 1066, an overseas Viking ruler in possession of York was not particularly unprecedented – the Dubliner Olaf Guthfrithson had invaded it once and the Norseman Erik 'Bloodaxe' twice in the mid-tenth century and Swein 'Forkbeard' of Denmark had occupied the area in 1013. A weak English government had had to accept temporary Viking reoccupation of York in 939 and 947, and not tackle Cnut's seizure of the area at once in 1015. It would not have been unprecedented – or seen as particularly cowardly – for a cautious English king to leave an invasion force secure in York for the duration of the winter and only tackled them in 1067. Thus it was not inevitable that Harold would challenge the invaders at once; but he was known as a master of swift movement in war, as when he had taken Gruffydd ap Llewelyn of Gwynedd by surprise in midwinter 1062–3. He was thus likelier than another ruler in London to strike back quickly.

The chances of Tostig's replacement as Earl of Northumbria, Morcar the younger son of Earl Aelfgar, and his brother Earl Edwin of Mercia defeating Harald and Tostig at Fulford in September 1066 and not needing King Harold's assistance is smaller. It was their defeat by the invaders that lost York to Harald and Tostig, and resulted in an appeal for help to the English king. But they were unlikely to have won the battle unless perhaps Tostig had been invading alone. Both young men were untried in battle, and Harald was a veteran warrior in his fifties who had first fought against Cnut's men at Stiklestadr in 1030 and served in the Byzantine army in Sicily against the Arabs in the 1030s. Crucially, the early death of their father, Earl Aelfgar of Mercia, aided the Norse chances of success. He was probably under fifty when he died at an unknown date between 1062 and 1064, and he had twice invaded Mercia successfully to retake his earldom in 1055 and 1058; he had also used Norse mercenaries in 1058 so he knew their methods of fighting. This experienced warrior would have been less likely to lose at Gate Fulford – and given his long conflict with Harold Godwinson he would have been as willing as Edwin to see Morcar replace Tostig in Northumbria in 1065. Indeed, it is plausible that Aelfgar's presence in the political crises of 1065–6 would have made it less likely that Harold would have been accepted as king by the magnates on 5 January 1066 rather than Edgar (see above). Having been exiled twice through Godwinson influence, Aelfgar would have been likely to resist the idea of his arch-rival becoming king and thus have backed Edgar. Possibly the timing of King Edward's death at New Year would have been likely to have him celebrating Christmas with his retainers in Mercia not present in London for the election of a new king. Harold could have staged a coup, and had to deal with Aelfgar later – as he did in real life with his sons Edwin and Morcar, who he bought off in an arrangement apparently centred on his marrying their sister.[34] (What she thought of marrying her previous husband's killer is unrecorded.) But the presence of an old rival – a veteran commander – to Harold in England in 1066 would have added a new element to the outcome of events, whether or not Harold had to be content with acting as regent for King Edgar II rather than taking the throne.

(c) The battle of Hastings (or Senlac)

The combat at 'Senlac' on 14 October continued for many hours without resolution. The Anglo-Saxon army, which had taken up its position on a good defensive position on top of a steep ridge on 13 October, had less of a task than William's men on the 14th. Most of them – including the royal bodyguard of 'Housecarls' - had recently marched all the way from London to York to defeat the invading Harald 'Hardradi' and Tostig, and then a few days after their victory had had to march back again and on to Sussex. Precise dates are uncertain for the battle between Harold and the Norse army at Stamford Bridge on 28 September and the English army's arrival at the ridge north of Hastings – which may or may not have been known as 'Senlac Hill', the name ('Sand Lake?') given to the battle-site around 1125 by Orderic Vitalis. The rendezvous for the English was at a prominent landmark, the 'Hoar-Apple Tree' according to the *Anglo-Saxon Chronicle*; this was later identified as a tree on Caldbeck Hill, the next hill inland from the traditional site of the battle at Battle Abbey.[35] The fact that the rendezvous was so close to Hastings, about seven miles away – and thus at risk of a Norman cavalry raid on it if the early arrivals were spotted – suggests that Harold had confidence in being able to gather men there without a immediate counter-attack. Had local Sussex levies already secured the position? It was at the point where the only route out of the Hastings peninsula was narrowed to a ridge a few hundred yards wide, so securing it meant that William could not break out to ravage further. But it would have been risky for Harold to tell his levies to assemble there if it was not already secured, as then a small body of Norman cavalry could easily break up the first English troops to arrive and turn the rendezvous into chaos. Assuming the main Norman army to be at Hastings' new castle, it would not take long for a few hundred horsemen to ride to Caldbec Hill on 13 October. Assembling a few miles inland, perhaps at Robertsbridge, would have been safer – unless Harold guessed that William would not dare to risk a raid as there might be more English troops hiding in the nearby woodland at Caldbec Hill.

If the site of the battle was accurately identified as the hill south of Caldbec – where the Abbey was built on the 'battlefield' in the 1070s and 1080s – it also suggests that William did not hurry to seize this hilltop site before the Saxons moved onto it. They were thus able to draw up a 'shield-wall' at the top of a steep slope and use the geography to their advantage.

They could have done the same at the next hill to the north, Caldbec Hill, had William moved troops onto 'Senlac Hill' (as it is sometimes called), but then William would have held a strong hilltop position rather than being down in the valley below. Was he informed of the English arrival too late on the 13th to send men to take over 'Senlac Hill? Did he fear that they would be ambushed by the enemy, who were more familiar with the area, and so kept all his army together until they could ride out under cavalry protection on the 14th? Or did he think that 'Senlac Hill' was an easier target for a cavalry charge – as it had a gentler slope and fewer trees than Caldbec Hill?

The troops could only have had two or three days' rest in London on returning from York. It was evidently urgent to reach Sussex – Harold's own native county – and seize the road inland from Hastings towards London before the Normans advanced. But they only had to hold off the enemy and keep them penned in the Hastings peninsula until more Saxon reinforcements arrived from London. Once they had seized the high ground around Battle the Normans could not move by land, the marshy and wooded valleys on either side of the ridge being impenetrable, and the English could wait until reinforcements arrived and pen the Normans in territory they had already despoiled of provisions. The English fleet had dispersed in September, before the enemy sailed, for the harvest and would be at risk of storms if it reassembled to prevent Duke William moving by sea to find supplies – but the weather would affect him more. William, operating in foreign territory with limited numbers of horses for his crucial cavalry and only what food he could forage, was reliant on his ships in Pevensey Bay for escape. He had to crush the enemy decisively, wipe out the leadership to prevent them escaping to regroup, and then break out into open country to terrorize all remaining opposition into surrender. In that sense, even an indecisive encounter that left the Saxons in place was no good to William's hopes of the crown as he would have lost irreplaceable men and horses whereas more English reinforcements could be expected from counties further from Sussex as the days progressed. The uncertain nature of the Channel weather also meant that an autumnal storm could occur at any time and cut William off from his homeland. His ships were in reasonable shelter, assuming that he had kept them at Pevensey (then a large bay protected from the prevailing south-west winds not a marsh) rather than moving them to Hastings to support his new garrison there, but if the wind failed and he had to retreat in a hurry he could be becalmed.

The steep nature of the ridge around Battle Abbey shows that William's cavalry were at a disadvantage in charging uphill, and his supporting archers had to fire uphill too with no clear view of their targets. Luckily for him, the geography of the site meant that his archers were firing northwards – if they had had to fire westwards into the setting sun their shooting would have been even more random. All he could hope to do was to break the Saxon line with repeated charges aided by a hail of arrows, or induce the enemy to abandon their strong position and follow his men in a feigned retreat down the hill so that his cavalry could attack them with more success. The Saxons held out on the ridge until quite late in the day, despite the losses of those men who had foolishly left their positions to chase the Normans back downhill and been cut off and killed. William had nearly been killed on one occasion, famously shown in the Bayeux Tapestry, when he had to raise his visor to show his doubtful men that he was still alive. Even if the rain of arrows had accounted for Harold his brothers Gyrth and Leofwine could have remained alive and in charge of a dogged portion of the army still holding the ridge overnight – and the Normans could have been too exhausted or uncertain of success to resume the attack. Within a few days more Saxon militiamen could have arrived. (It is not clear from the narratives at what point the King's brothers fell, though it was apparently before Harold was killed.[36])

Even with all the brothers dead, the Saxon cause was not lost if their line of battle had held. It can be assumed that some local commander or a senior officer of the royal bodyguard (the 'Housecarls') had the authority to keep the army united and the exhausted Normans at bay until a senior commander – Earl Edwin of Mercia? – arrived from London with the Midlands levies. The Saxon army had enough discipline to hold together under lieutenants if its commander fell, as shown by what happened at Maldon in 991. The etiquette of Germanic warrior ethics was that you fought on around your lord's body if he fell, rather than running away; this helped to keep the ranks disciplined even in a crisis. Famously, the bodyguard of West Saxon King Cynewulf in 786 even preferred to stay fighting to the death rather than accepting an offer of a safe retreat when their lord was killed. Harold was the charismatic victor of a major war in Wales in 1063 and clearly capable of inspiring loyalty from his men.

(d) After the battle: was resistance possible, particularly if the Normans had had heavier losses?
Edgar 'Atheling' was available to take the crown as nominal sovereign, though he had been passed over (as too young?) by Edward in January 1066 and was probably around twelve to fourteen. The military command in evicting the Normans could then have been assumed by one of Harold's three illegitimate sons, who were certainly old enough to fight at the head of a fleet from Ireland by 1068 and may well have already been in their late teens or early twenties. Technically Earl Edwin would have been the senior

lord available to lead resistance, though he had only fought one known battle
(Fulford) and then been defeated. Had William killed Harold but won on
less decisive terms, and possibly faced a viable but retreating English army
that Earls Edwin and Morcar could join in London, he would have been in
a difficult position. Like Cnut after Ashingdon, a temporary truce and
division of the kingdom would have been advisable. The lack of military
experience of Edwin and Morcar would then have assisted William's chances
of securing a final victory in 1067 – particularly if he had secured
Winchester, with the Portsmouth area to land reinforcements, or London
with the Thames estuary. It should be remembered that as of 1066 the
English leadership had a hopeful precedent to call on, in spring 1016 when
Aethelred II had died in London and Edmund 'Ironside' had not had the
troops to hold the south-east against the army of Cnut in Kent and East
Anglia. He had retired into Wessex to raise a new army, leaving London
holding out, and had returned later to confront Cnut and drive him out of
Kent. Cnut, like William in 1066, had had a seemingly stronger army, a navy,
and an overseas base to call on for reinforcements (Denmark). Edmund,
however, had enough charisma to raise a new army and return to the attack,
and had secured enough success to cause the notoriously calculating Eadric
'Streona' of Mercia to defect back to his side as Cnut retired into East
Anglia. Could an energetic English leader (one of Harold's sons?) have done
the same as Edmund if William had had worse losses and the Earls of Mercia
and Northumbria not lost many men already at Gate Fulford?

Logically Edwin and Morcar would have been able to protect Edgar
'Atheling' – or Harold's widow, their sister, and her unborn child(ren) – in
Mercia and Northumbria over the winter of 1066–7 if the Normans were
only strong enough to overrun Wessex. The resistance of London to
William's advance from Kent in late autumn 1066 made this a possible
option even after the shattering losses inflicted at Hastings. London, after
all, had held out against Cnut in 1016 and given valuable time to Edmund to
raise a new army. Unable to take London Bridge, William had to move off
south-west to Winchester, which Edward's widow Queen Edith surrendered
to him, and then back north to the Thames at Wallingford.

In 1016 London had defied Cnut and held out for the retreating but intact
army of Edmund 'Ironside',[37] but in 1066 the loss of the Thames 'line' led to
Edwin, Morcar, and Edgar surrendering. Was this a mistake? Or did they
assess that the losses of Mercians and Northumbrians at Gate Fulford and
Stamford Bridge meant that they had no hope of defying William? Had he
had more serious losses, would they have had more confidence? We should
remember that in November 1066 the leading 'players' had no knowledge
that a 'Norman Conquest' was irreversible; their most recent precedent

would have been for Cnut's invasion in 1015–16. Then the conqueror had not secured all the kingdom even with one crushing victory over Edmund (at Ashingdon). There were enough adult males with experience of weapons and reasonable social rank left alive in England after Hastings to fight for Harold's mother, Gytha, at Exeter in 1067–8, for Edwin and Edric in Mercia in 1068, and for Waltheof in Northumbria in 1070. Not all Hereward's men in the Fens may have been local peasants (Morcar joined them) – and a regiment of English warriors was in exile in the Byzantine Empire by 1081, fighting for Emperor Alexius Comnenus against the Italian Normans at Durazzo in Albania. The potential for serious resistance thus existed well after 1066 – and in Yorkshire William resorted to near-genocide to clear resistance out of his way in the 'Harrying of the North' in 1070.

With or without Harold's survival, the Saxon army could well have stood its ground at Hastings (particularly if men had not rushed off downhill after the Normans and been cut off and killed). They held the high ground, and thus had the advantage. The Normans could have lost so many horses in failed attempts to take the hilltop that they could not renew the attack, besides suffering a loss of nerve after hours of unsuccessful charges. William had assorted non-Norman mercenaries (e.g. Bretons) who could resist his orders as they were not vassals in fear of forfeiting their lands. The Norman army would thus have had to withdraw to the coast as English reinforcements arrived from London a few days later, and hope to embark on their ships before the Saxons arrived to burn them. The loss of 'face' that William had suffered would then have been probable to touch off a revolt in turbulent Normandy, particularly on its southern borders or in restive Maine.

(e) And if Harold had won...?

Alternatively, William could have been unhorsed and killed in the melee. His son Robert, aged around fourteen, would have succeeded to a weakened Normandy and Harold have secured his claim on England for his lifetime as Cnut, another 'outsider' from the royal family, had done with military victory and the death of his rival in 1016. Two major victories in the course of three weeks would have cemented Harold's reputation and made it unlikely that he would face a major challenge for years. The Earls of Mercia and Northumbria, Edwin and Morcar, were young and inexperienced in military matters – Edwin had only succeeded his father, Aelfgar, around 1062 and Morcar had been chosen by the Northumbrians in 1065 after they had driven out Tostig. The only important prince now reigning in Wales, Bleddyn ap Cynfyn of Gwynedd and Powys, was Harold's client, imposed after he had destroyed the united principality (or kingdom) of all Wales set up by Bleddyn's half-brother[38] Gruffydd ap Llywelyn with a major offensive in 1063. The king of Scots, Malcolm III, had been restored to his father Duncan's throne by the English under Earl Siward by campaigns from 1054 to 1057 and had been King Edward's dependent ally. The principal Viking overlord of the Northern seas, Jarl Thorfinn 'Raven-Feeder' of the Orkneys, was dead by 1065 and his sons Paul and Erlend were forced to join the English expedition of Harald 'Hardradi' where they had shared in the military losses. Harald's own sons Magnus and Olaf had suffered too heavy losses to challenge the English king again, nullifying the threat from Norway. Magnus was derisively nicknamed 'Barefoot' for fleeing the carnage at Stamford Bridge in haste without his shoes, and Olaf was to win the title of 'Peace-King' for his priorities during his reign to 1093.

Finally, the other major Viking kingdom of Scandinavia was ruled by Harold's own maternal cousin Swein Estrithson, who in real life was to give sanctuary to Harold's female relatives from 1068 and was unlikely to covet his cousin's throne. With William dead Harold would have had no major challengers from October 1066, though the hostility of Counts Baldwin of Flanders (Tostig's brother-in-law) and Eustace of Boulogne (who fought for William at Hastings) was probable. Eustace had been married to King Edward's sister, though as far as is known there were no children to claim the English throne, and he had been a foe of the Godwin dynasty back in 1051 when his retinue was attacked by Earl Godwin's tenantry in Dover and the Earl refused Edward's orders to punish the town.[39]

A few possibilities for the future if Harold had won

Developments in Saxon England from 1066. The comparative strengths and weaknesses of potential Late Saxon and real Norman kings. How to avoid a 'failed state'

Would England have developed more along the lines of the Scandinavian kingdoms, to which it was more culturally kin, than the southern European states? The absence of easily-defendable castles as residences for senior lords would have put the latter at a disadvantage in late eleventh and twelfth century politics if they wished to defy the King. In real-life England William and his sons did their best to prevent the great nobles acquiring geographically contiguous 'blocs' of territory that could become mini-principalities. Men such as the Warennes and Montgomeries had their landholdings spread over several counties, reducing their ability to monopolize the loyalty of tenants in one area and have the manpower to make it a dangerous centre of revolt against the King. The Welsh Marches were the exception, with William first setting up his trusted follower William FitzOsbern as Earl of Hereford in the south (the earldom had to be confiscated from his rebel son in 1075) and then building up the Montgomery family in the centre and North. The large and geographically contiguous blocs of land held by a handful of families were a constant source of turbulence and defiance of royal authority with private 'mini-wars' against each other and the Welsh.[40] The existence of castles gave the advantage to landed defenders defying authority, but after Henry I expelled the Montgomery family in 1102/3 the Norman kings faced no serious political challenge until the disputed succession of 1135 started a civil war.

Would a Saxon king have been stronger or weaker than William?

The main threat facing an adult, active post-1066 sovereign with no dynastic rival was disorder and defiance from locally-entrenched nobles secure in their castles – hence the usual rash of illegal castle-building by ambitious opportunists at each change of sovereign, which a vigorous king such as Henry II dealt with firmly. No one family could appear as strong as the king, or secure a clutch of senior provincial appointments. An earldom did not extend to a whole province (e.g. Mercia) in Anglo-Norman England, with the exception of turbulent Northumbria at first in the late 1060s when William needed a strong and experienced noble with local support and did not dare to bring in a Norman to hold that earldom. (The experiment failed dismally, and William cold-bloodedly resorted to reducing the disobedient populace of the area to starvation to reduce their potential for revolt in 1070.[41]) Thereafter, an earldom only granted practical power in the form of land, patronage, military authority as tenant-in-chief, and sometimes the senior royal administrative office (that of shire-reeve/sheriff) in one county – and in many cases the sheriffdom did not go with the earldom. Royal power meant that an 'over-mighty' minister who had secured enough land and castles from his master to seem a threat to the latter's successor could be dealt with easily, as Stephen did with his predecessor's 'favourite' Bishop Roger of Salisbury. The best hope a rebel had was to use the defensive advantages of his castle to sit out a royal siege until help arrived from elsewhere – if it did not, as with William II's foes at Rochester in 1088, the rebel would eventually run out of supplies and have to negotiate terms.

In Saxon England, by contrast – in the special circumstances of a king who had long lived abroad and had no English clientage – the Godwin family could monopolize the leading southern earldoms and seem as powerful as their sovereign. Godwin was able to advance his young sons and nephews to earldoms from 1045 onwards rather than the King being able to appoint more experienced senior figures, such as those who Edward was to promote when he had a free hand in 1051 (Odda of Deerhurst and his nephew Ralph). It is uncertain if Edward felt compelled to marry Godwin's daughter Edith in 1045, as she was the obvious candidate and Wessex/ English kings had often married into the domestic nobility in the ninth and tenth centuries. It is only speculation that he avoided having children rather than he or Edith being impotent, but once he had exiled her father he sent her to a nunnery (a normal precursor of divorce). Arguably Godwin was as powerful as Edward in secular matters, not least in having far more experience of domestic politics. In 1051 the family were forced into exile when Godwin challenged Edward's orders by refusing to sack Dover after its inhabitants had skirmished with the entourage of Edward's brother-in-law Eustace of Boulogne. The adherence of Leofric and Siward was crucial in providing the King with the manpower to challenge Godwin's levies in the confrontation that ensued, showing that the King could not automatically expect enough loyal supporters to rally to him to see off any challengers; in 1052 Godwin was able to return with a large army and the other earls' defection forced Edward to accept his reinstatement. Edward was undoubtedly weaker for paying off his navy in 1049 once the threat from Norway diminished – but sailors would be useless against an earl's army on land.

That crown weakness would have been inconceivable in Anglo-Norman England where no one family or clique of senior nobles had equivalent power, though the powerful Earl/Bishop Odo was a threat to William I and II in the 1080s and the Montgomeries had to be brought down in 1103. William I had the sense to rely on a 'broad base' of a few hundred tenants-in-chief, usually with their lands scattered over disparate provinces so that they had no solid geographical base for a revolt (the exceptions being the Welsh Marches and, at first, Northumbria). This aided the King's ability to outmatch rebels in terms of geographical 'reach' and resources – though at first, in 1066–9, he did keep on a number of Harold's earls and create new ones in the North so he did not immediately impose a new 'system' of control. But the English governmental system of 1016–66 consisted of a few, large senior earldoms with substantial resources. What did not threaten Cnut, with his large army and his Danish 'power-base', was disastrous for Edward.

Even a strong Anglo-Saxon king with earldoms given to his relatives, such as Harold in 1066, could not monopolize all the provincial governorships – and thus control of military levies – for his family. And would a family always act together? Harold as king would have been weaker than the Norman dynasts, unless he had divided up the major earldoms and so reduced the manpower available to challengers.

The reduced manpower available directly to a pre-1066 English king in a confrontation with 'over-mighty' subjects made it more similar to the French kingship, whose holders only directly controlled the Isle de France, than the Norman state. The French kings indeed held a contiguous 'bloc' of territory, which the pre-1066 English kings lacked – though arguably until the creation of the earldom of Wessex c.1030 they could rely on Wessex. They could also rely on the advantage of a national army and fleet, which the French monarchy lacked, though this was not decisive if its loyalty or morale was poor (as in 1002–14 and 1052). The alienation of Wessex from king to earls after c.1030 was a major threat to the English kingship, as faced by Edward in 1051–2; though it was lesser for a king with a reliable deputy as Earl of Wessex, as Harold had with his brother Gyrth. In the long term, a strong king would have been advised to break up Wessex as Edward had attempted to do in 1051; the heartland of royal power and patronage was safer in the hands of several loyal followers rather than of one man. The one extra advantage that the English monarchy possessed after January 1066 was that the large amount of land alienated from king to Godwin and Harold in 1042–65 had passed back to the crown with Harold's accession, adding to the royal patrimony. As seen by the Domesday Book, by 1066 Harold was by far the greatest landowner in the kingdom and far outmatched the other great landowners, thus posing a threat to the King's control of patronage and resources. Making him king ended this – but the concentration of Harold's estates in the south and east meant that the royal landed presence outside these areas was still small. The king could, however, appoint lay sheriffs as well as the senior clergy, giving him an asset that the Anglo-Norman kings continued to use for their domination of the local nobility (except when hereditary or long-term sheriffs were created, mainly by the weak Stephen). The French kings could not enforce their choices of secular office-holders on distant provinces such as Aquitaine; the English kings could do this on all their lands.

The context of revolt: a new bonus for post-1066 rebels thanks to Norman architecture

But the Anglo-Norman rulers had their own major strategic problem that Harold lacked. Even with no over-powerful provincial governor able to challenge the King's army, they suffered from the fact that rebels could hold out for long periods in their well-defended castles that were increasingly made of stone and had to be starved out by the royal army. Building castles was a 'double-edged' weapon; it provided William I with a network of bases into which his harassed local supporters could retire and sit out rebellion, as during the crises of 1068–71, but if the castellans revolted it left him at a disadvantage. Castles as self-sufficient centres of potential revolt increased the ability of rebels to hold out against Stephen from 1136 to 1153, making it nearly impossible for him to put down a well-supported revolt and meaning that an uneasy stalemate eventually developed between him and Matilda with the supporter of each holding large areas. The threat to the new King William II from Bishop Odo and his supporters, backing his brother Robert, in 1088 would have been serious had Robert invaded quickly to join them. No resolution by a swift military campaign was possible; rather, the changes of allegiance (or capture) of crucial key personnel who held major strategic points could determine the political outcome of a crisis.

This is indicated by the importance of a few key leaders, such as the legate Bishop Henry of Winchester, and their castles in deciding the outcome of the conflict between Stephen and his challenger Matilda in 1141. Matilda could not force her enemies to surrender once she had physical possession of Stephen, and she lost the initiative once some of her own lieutenants had been captured at Winchester/Wherwell.[42] The long duration of the civil war, the 'nineteen winters when Christ and His saints slept', was partly due to the difficulty of either side winning; battles were not decisive if castellans held out in their strongholds, each of which had to be starved out. In 1153–4, the deadlock ended by treaty rather than victory and then Henry II still had to deal with a rash of unlicensed castles that had been erected without royal authority since 1135. That degree of local autonomy and/or defiance would have been impossible in Saxon England, where rebel lords' timber halls surrounded by palisades could be taken more easily. Where a rebellion ended in stalemate or success in pre-1066 England it was due to the amount of military support that the rebels could command, as with Godwin in 1052, Alfgar in 1055 and 1058, and Edwin and Morcar in 1065.

The Church

Would the influx of Continental clerics under King Edward continue under a monarch who showed no particular interest in European religious developments? Harold had made his own religious foundation at Waltham Abbey in Essex, but had not joined in Edward's promotion of Continental clerics in his household or areas of administrative control. There is also the question of the controversial Stigand, a retainer of the Godwin family of long standing whose legitimacy as Archbishop of Canterbury was dubious. Promoted from the bishopric of Winchester (the main bishopric of Godwin's earldom) after Edward's Norman Archbishop Robert of Jumièges fled the country on the Godwins' return in 1052, he did not owe his elevation to a legitimate reason – such as resignation or death of the incumbent – but to vacancy by means of absence. When he finally went to Rome for his recognition by grant of the 'pallium' in 1058, he unfortunately sought the backing of a pope who was soon to be deposed and subsequently declared to have been illegitimate, and his acts invalid. Harold did not dare to have Stigand crown him on 6 January 1066 and used the 'respectable' Archbishop Ealdred of York instead (contrary to Norman propaganda[43]), and the stigma of Stigand's illegality was a major bonus for Duke William in obtaining papal backing from the determined reformer Alexander II.

Would Harold have ultimately abandoned his family client Stigand, and ever have replaced him with a more respectable figure? Lacking any Continental pressure after William's defeat in 1066, he would have been in no haste to placate a pope who had backed his rival and interfered in the English succession. It is more likely that Stigand would have remained as archbishop for his lifetime, and been replaced by another English contender from within the Godwin family's patronage-network.

All bishops were supposed to go to Rome on accession to collect their 'pallia' of office, and the zealously reformist Pope Gregory VII (1073–85) would have been likely to raise questions about the lax practices of the English clergy, which diverged from the new Continental 'norms'. But the English Church, like the Scandinavian ones, was distant from Italy and less amenable to papal pressure and local reforms by Rome-influenced clerics than the Churches of France and Germany whose societies were culturally kin to Southern Europe. Without William's accession there would have been no reformist Italian archbishop (Lanfranc in real life) to head the Church and bring in foreign practices, or an influx of Continental bishops and abbots. The extent to which these men who took over clerical office were 'Norman' is unclear, but their French names show their origins and cultural /legal loyalties.

The quality of the native English episcopate is unclear, with a substantial number of French or Lorrainer bishops having been appointed by Edward and no signs that any English bishops were in tune with the latest reforms on the Continent. The piety or energy in pastoral work of the episcopate in 1066 was not noticeable, with the exceptions of a few individuals such as the holy St Wulfstan of Worcester, but this had been the case for many decades. England had not been involved in a major initiative in monastic reform by a group of talented clerics since the reign of Edgar, and had been distracted by war and unrest for the first few decades of the eleventh century with an undoubted decline in monastic discipline and vigour. Most bishops were probably appointed as effective administrators not for their pastoral role, with the Church helping to run the local administration and provide royal troops from its estates. Some were appointed after royal service in the king's chapel, others as acts of patronage to clerical dependents of great families; much has been made of the unsuitability of some of the Godwins' nominees, such as Stigand (evidently a 'political' cleric loyal to his patrons) or the would-be Bishop Spearhavoc ('Sparrowhawk') of London in 1050/1. The bishopric of Hereford was used by the Godwin family as an auxiliary to the earldom in fighting the raiding Welsh in the 1050s, and one bishop was even killed in battle – though in Normandy too bishops commanded their own retainers in battle. The Normans even appointed royal relatives (Mauger and Odo) as senior clerics, which the English royal family had never done.

Ealdred of York and Worcester was a notable diplomat, but had also been able to govern several bishoprics at once (a practice frowned on in the Continent and technically banned in canon law). His mixing a smaller bishopric in a relatively settled, 'English' part of the country with the main see in the turbulent, Viking-settled North was following the precedent set by St Oswald under Edgar in the 970s, and was an eminently sensible use of the greater wealth of the see of Worcester to support the administration of the larger but poorer York. It was a norm in Late Saxon England after the reconquest of the re-paganized Viking areas, even if it seemed outdated and contravened canon law as far as the stricter Continental Church was concerned. Banning holding more than one see was imposed by the Normans from Lanfranc's reforming synod of 1070. It is apparent that Harold did not appoint any Continentals like his predecessor had done, but he had no opportunity to make any appointments as king and when he was Earl of Wessex in 1053–66 Edward probably used his ecclesiastical interests to maintain control of patronage. (The Godwin family had not removed all Edward's Continental bishops on regaining their major influence in English politics in 1052 – or even replaced all Edward's Normans – so they cannot be presented as hostile to foreign influence as such.) It is unclear if Edward preferred Continentals as bishops out of favour to the sort of men he had been used to from his long period abroad and regarded as being more in tune with 'civilized' developments, and accordingly regarded English clerics as insular and backward. He more definitely preferred Continental religious architecture, as shown by his adoption of the North French style of church for Westminster Abbey.

The English cathedrals were served by bodies of secular canons rather than by fully-professed monks as was the more 'modern' practice on the Continent, while abbeys were also 'secularized' in that their estates served to provide men for the army, some abbots commanding their levies in person at Hastings. The landholding abbots were regarded as part of the local shire administration and ran their estates' courts like secular landowners (c.f. Oswaldslow 'hundred' in Worcestershire). As assessed by Ralph Barlow in his study of the pre-1066 Church, the latter was an integral part of local society with standards and methods that worked well enough but would have seemed outdated or in breach of canon law[44] to zealous French administrators who had absorbed the latest Rome-led innovations. The French and Italian clerics that William brought in were quick to denounce it and all bishoprics and abbacies were occupied by Continentals as they became vacant with one 'purge' of senior clerics in 1070 of which Stigand was the chief victim. But this says as much about a desire to seize and monopolize lucrative patronage as about perceived insufficiency on the part of potential English clerical office-holders. One visibly competent and saintly bishop – St Wulfstan of Worcester – kept his see despite it being a lucrative target for Norman clerics.

The likelihood is that an English Church without a large Norman influx would have continued in the manner of developments before 1066, but without all Edward's foreign appointments. Scions of local landed families and occasional talented monastic trainees of humble birth would have dominated the scene as bishops, with minimal Continental influence except probably in architecture (rather like Scandinavia in the late eleventh century). Given that Edward had used a Continental model (possibly Jumièges in Normandy) for his abbey church at Westminster,[45] even a monarch who had not lived abroad like Harold or his dynastic successor might have been open to employing a similar style of building for royal 'prestige' projects. The style of Harold's one foundation, Waltham Abbey, was as much Continental as English – and there may well have been no perceived sense of making a 'political statement' by Harold in adopting new foreign styles for Waltham (or for any post-1066 projects). Bishops, some already Frenchmen such as Giso of Wells, would have carried on hiring the best architects and masons they could afford from whatever source. The wide-scale rebuilding of local abbeys and cathedrals across England on Continental models is unlikely, with no influx of French clerics to adopt their familiar 'modern' styles. Importantly, the absence of William's new body of clerics would have meant no reorganizing of the Church to move some sees to new sites in 1070–2. The East Anglian see would have stayed at North Elmham rather than being moved (via a temporary stay at Thetford) to Norwich, and the Dorset/ Wiltshire see would not have been moved from Sherborne to Old Sarum. The East Midlands see would not have been moved from Dorchester-on-Thames to the more local and logical Lincoln. Saxon sees were rarely moved for administrative convenience; after the reconquest and re-evangelization of the Danelaw the East Midlands see remained at inconvenient Dorchester without the creation of a new local see, and only a few minor local lapsed sees (e.g. Dunwich) were abandoned. The Norman clerics had no such sense of history, and their new seats of ecclesiastical power duly required new cathedrals.

Similarly, there would have been no incentive for any post-1066 attempt to adopt Continental Church practices and canon law except by some reforming new archbishop who had been educated abroad and had a sympathetic sovereign. The likeliest English king to adopt such a practice would have been the Hungarian-born Edgar 'Atheling', had he ever been restored – his sister Margaret showed an appreciation of Continental Church developments (perhaps picked up abroad or at King Edward's court[46]) as Queen of Scotland in the 1070s and 1080s.

'Devolution' to the earldoms and royal power

Would administrative 'devolution' to the great earls continue under a king more vigorous than Edward, who had inherited the system from Cnut's family – or would Harold and his dynasty ultimately have faced a trial of strength with their long-term rivals the Mercian dynasts? Assuming that the main southern earldoms remained with the Godwin family, and the royal itinerary remained concentrated in southern England so that a king could not physically be in the North often, nevertheless the current arrangements implied a threat to the crown. In 1065 the king's – and the Godwins' – choice of Earl of Northumbria, Tostig, was expelled by the local nobles and the government had to accept it. At some point the king was going to have to move against local particularism in the North, if hopefully without the brutality that William I used to solve the problem in 1069–70. The previous royal initiative to assert central control and end reliance on untrustworthy autonomous earls, by Cnut in 1016–19, had seen the existing earl of all Northumbria – Uhtred, from the Bamburgh dynasty – executed, a loyal Viking (Erik) brought in, and eventually a Bamburgh dynast given half the earldom balanced by a loyalist 'new man' (Siward) in the other half. This solution, with Bernicia and York under two mutually watchful men, was possible; King William was to attempt to divide power in a similar manner, turning the Bishopric of Durham into a new (French-style) semi-secular lordship to hold the balance of power. William briefly resorted to an earl from the Bamburgh kin (Copsi, 1067) but could not trust them long term; neither would Harold have been able to do so. The position of the Bamburgh kin was now complicated by their relationship to the royal family of Scotland, with some of the family holding land in Scotland (the earldom of Dunbar) and having primary loyalty to Harold's foe, Tostig's ally King Malcolm. Cospatrick of Dunbar and his kin would have posed as much of a problem of Scottish claims on Bernicia and Cumbria after 1066 as they did to William's local power. Harold would have needed a local base for royal power, such as William secured by backing the militarized Bishopric of Durham (non-hereditary so immune from dynastic pretensions) and building a castle at Newcastle.

Logically, it would make sense to break up the great earldoms of Mercia and Northumbria (the latter would still need strong military leadership against the threats of Scotland and Norway). Worryingly, Earl Harold and King Edward – at whose initiative is unclear – had twice sought to depose Edwin and Morcar's father, Earl Aelfgar, in the 1050s but had been forced to accept him back after the Welsh and Dublin Vikings had assisted his invasions. This rival dynasty would have had to be tackled and Harold's marriage to the Mercians' sister Edith (formerly married off to her father Aelfgar's ally Gruffydd ap Llewelyn of Gwynedd) was only a temporary solution. Possibly once Edwin and Morcar had been removed as disloyal Harold would have tried to impose one of his own adult illegitimate sons as Earl of Mercia and/or another in Northumbria, with more success than he and King Edward did with Tostig in 1055–65. There was now a militarily active king capable of marching north and repeating his triumph of 1066 against any local Northumbrian revolt. Harold could not be sure of the permanent adherence of Earl Edwin in Mercia or Morcar in Northumbria, even with their sister as queen and thus from late 1066 their nephew(s) as heirs to the throne. But would Harold have been willing to leave Northumbria to its own devices provided it remained loyal as he was too busy dealing with the Welsh and/or watching the Continental powers for a new attack?

In the long term, there would have been a dynastic claim to Northumbria by the late Earl Siward's son Waltheof (still young in 1066[47]) who King William attempted to bring in as a loyal adherent with local support in 1069 but turned into a rebel. Harold, like William, would have been likely to meet trouble from the Siward dynasty as well as the Bamburgh kindred.

The succession to Harold

Who would have succeeded Harold – his son Harold or twins (it is uncertain whether he had one son or twins), born late in 1066, or one of his illegitimate sons? The twins' Mercian dynastic kin, Edwin and Morcar, if they had stayed in power in Mercia and Northumbria as earls, would have been available to back them against the illegitimate sons of Harold and Edith 'Swan-Neck' unless Harold had removed them once his own power was strong enough. The likelihood is that, as with the new dynasty of Blot Sven (from 1090) in contemporary Sweden that ended the long rule of the first ruling house based at ancient Uppsala, the ability and military resources of the new dynasty would have kept them on the throne and kept the old dynasty (Edgar 'Atheling') out. As in Norway with the sons of Magnus 'Bareleg' from 1103, there could even have been a joint kingship of equally-backed claimants such as Harold's twins or older bastards. There was no tradition of equal rule by co-rulers in England, but geographical division had been in existence in the tenth century (924?, 957–9) and had been a temporary solution in 1016. Notably it had failed to win adherents when Harold 'Harefoot' and Harthacnut were rivals for the crown in 1035–6; the half-brothers and their partisans had sought total victory rather than settling on a division into two kingdoms (of Wessex and the North). But could the Scandinavian solution have been attempted had Harold II left a multitude of sons, legitimate and legitimate? As in all three Scandinavian countries, fierce inter-dynastic competition among rival brothers and cousins could have ensued among the twelfth century Godwins involving a period of instability, until one strong ruler established a monopoly for his line. Logically, the fact that Harold's legitimate son(s) were maternal kin of the line of Leofric and Alfgar might have given them a stronger claim on the loyalty of Mercia – as in 1035–6 Harold 'Harefoot' was backed by the Anglo-Danes due to his mother, Aelfgifu of Northampton, coming from the Danelaw.

The military successes of the pre-1066 English kingdom in Scotland and Wales could also indicate that a strong ruler would establish as firm a grip on the British mainland as Athelstan or Edgar had done, and the existence of a fleet opens up the possibility that the Godwins would duly emulate Cnut and intervene in Denmark. Harold's mother, Gytha, was of noble Danish birth and aunt to King Swein Estrithson (r. 1047–74), and though Swein himself may not have dared to attack England after the defeat of Hardradi his sons may have been tempted. In real life there was a Danish invasion-scare in 1085, and with King Harold ageing the Danes could have been tempted to attack. Had Harold died in the 1080s leaving one or both twins as an untried young king, his older illegitimate sons could have sought Danish aid from their cousins. Conversely, one of Harold's grandsons as king of England could have intervened in the strife-torn Denmark of 1134–57 to attempt to re-create Cnut's empire. They would have had a remote claim on local support due to Harold's mother, Gytha. The declining Viking kingdom of Dublin, where Harold had sought refuge from Edward in 1051–2 and which aided his sons in 1068, was another potential target.

Harold was a formidable general and had defeated the united Welsh principality of Gruffydd ap Llewelyn ap Seisyll in a ferocious campaign of ravaging in 1063, attacking in the winter and continuing to ravage until the war-weary Welsh murdered their leader. He had also defeated the most experienced ruler of Scandinavia, Harald 'Hardradi' the veteran of the Varangian Guard in Byzantium, at Stamford Bridge – and in real life marched his exhausted army south very quickly to Sussex and nearly defeated William. With his 'housecarls' and the county levies in the 'fyrd', he was capable of taking on other threats later in the 1060s or the 1070s –

and it is likely that Malcolm of Scotland would duly have resumed his raiding of the 1050s against Northumbria. The new Earl Morcar was young and inexperienced, and Malcolm had been the ally of his dispossessed predecessor Tostig – Harold's estranged brother. So Malcolm was capable of challenging Morcar in the late 1060s with new raids, and Harold could have marched to the Forth and defeated Malcolm, forcing him into vassalage if not on Norman legal terms, as effectively as William did in 1072. Harold had operated a joint land and naval campaign against Gruffydd in 1063, so he could have invaded Scotland by similar means.

Once Edgar 'Atheling' was adult it is not impossible that he would have been as resentful of and keen to seek allies against Harold as he was of William. By the early 1070s Edgar could have decided to leave England to seek foreign allies, using his sister Margaret to arrange a marital alliance with his patron. Could Edgar have married off Margaret to Malcolm as in real life, to get Scots aid for an invasion of Northumbria to detach York from the English kingdom (and if lucky to go further south too) as Harald 'Hardradi' was plotting in 1066? Alternatively, Harold could have sought to remove Edgar and his sister from England in the way that Cnut had removed his potential challengers from the House of Cerdic. It is unclear if Harold (or Duke William's agents?) had murdered Edward 'the Elder', Edgar's father, in 1057 to remove a rival candidate for the throne. If Edgar had been caught plotting against Harold he could have been executed. (Harold, unlike William, did not have secure castles to keep rival claimants as prisoners.) Whether Edgar would have dared challenge Harold is uncertain, given his poor record as a rebel against William; but Harold could have been eager to marry off Edgar's sister(s) to friendly sovereigns and so married Margaret to Malcolm in a peace-treaty following a successful Scottish campaign c.1070.

In that case, the sons of Malcolm and Margaret would have had a 'legitimate' claim to the English throne superior to that of Harold's sons and a civil war among the latter given one of them the chance to invade Northern England in the 1090s or 1100s. Could Harold have foreseen this threat? The English kingdom would then have lacked the superior military tactics of the Normans with their cavalry and castles, giving a Saxon-Scottish prince a chance of victory provided that the sons of Harold were poorer commanders than their father. Much would have depended on whether the Scottish king – still Malcolm, or his eldest son Duncan II? – would have been able to call on the powerful Norwegian king Magnus 'Bareleg', warlord of the Hebrides, for aid in an invasion (via York?) in the cause of overthrowing the House of Godwin. It is possible that a Scottish-Celtic-Viking coalition, in the tradition of Athelstan's foes in the 930s, would have sought to diminish the power of the English crown within the British Isles once Harold was dead and thus provided enough troops to have a chance of victory in defeating the Anglo-Saxon 'fyrd' and imposing one of Malcolm and Margaret's sons as King of England. Scots King Duncan II or Donald 'Ban' might have used this as a way to get the sons of Malcolm and Margaret out of contention for the Scots crown, thus making the eldest son, Edward (killed at Alnwick with his father in 1093 in reality) the new king of England. Any dispute over the English crown between Harold's legitimate and illegitimate sons – a repeat of the conflict between Cnut's sons in 1036–40 – would have given Edgar 'Atheling' and/or the Scots a chance. But in due course, one of the 'Margaretsons' could then have used the resources of England to attack Scotland in return if Malcolm III had been succeeded by his other heirs in the 1090s. His ageing brother Donald 'Ban' (with no known son) was a likelier victim of a successful attack than the younger Duncan who had sons to succeed him if he was killed or incapacitated.

Wales
Harold would not have been colonizing the Welsh Marches with castles like William did, but would have been anxious to keep Wales disunited and would have been likely to maintain the pressure on the Welsh. The kingdom of Gwynedd/Powys had been defeated and divided among princes Bleddyn and Rhiwallon in 1063 and their union with Deheubarth ended, neutralizing the threat posed by the multi-state kingdom built up by Gruffydd ap Llewelyn ap Seisyll from 1055, and Harold would have been determined to keep the Welsh disunited. As the clashes of 1065 had been with Morgannwg in the south-east (over the royal hunting-lodge built west of the Wye at Portskewett) some campaigns there were likely in the late 1060s. Would Harold have wanted to defeat or even kill Caradoc ap Gruffydd ap Rhydderch of Morgannwg as he did the Gwynedd/Powys ruler in 1063, and then advance the English frontier further west? He would not have been building castles to control any new territory as William did, though Edward had allowed his half-French nephew Earl Ralph of Hereford to build a couple of exploratory castles in the area so the idea was not new. The technology was available if Harold was prepared to use it; he would have seen the usefulness of castles for himself in his expedition into Brittany with Duke William in 1064/5. Some advance into Gwent by English settlers was possible and the earldom of Hereford – in existence under Edward – could have been revived for an aggressive military commander to keep the Welsh in order. Given his reliance on his family, Harold could have given it to his youngest brother Wulfnoth – if he had used hostages taken from William's defeated army in 1066 as bargaining-counters to get him back from the Normans – or else one of his own aggressive and now-adult illegitimate sons.

A permanent Godwin dynasty?

Harold was quite capable of living to c.1090, when he would have been in his late sixties and his legitimate son(s) adult. His father, Earl Godwin, was old enough to be considered for a senior administrative role and marital alliance by Cnut soon after 1016 so he was probably around sixty when he died suddenly at a banquet in spring 1053; his mother, Gytha, old enough to have children c.1020, lived until after 1072. Harold could have reigned for longer than Cnut. But would the claims of the 'old' Anglo-Saxon dynasty have preserved enough adherents to make their removal only secure for the lifetime of the immediate supersessor, as it had for Cnut in 1016–35, but not for the reigns of the usurper's sons? Edgar 'Atheling' or Margaret's husband and sons could have been viable contenders in a civil war after Harold died, provided they had military backing. Their claims would have been enhanced if Harold's legitimate and illegitimate sons fought over the throne and/or were inadequate or died young like Cnut's did. Harold's illegitimate sons were determined enough on their rights to challenge William I in the late 1060s in reality, and were able to muster a fleet (probably from Viking settlers in Dublin and Waterford). As in Norway on occasions in the twelfth century (e.g. with Sverker) or in England in 1036–7, an illegitimate son of the late ruler, backed by enough magnates and probably the oldest contender for the throne, could have prevailed over his younger half-brothers to establish a dynasty. One of Harold's sons or grandsons could have then been as powerful a figure on the British mainland as Henry I, acting as overlord of the smaller Welsh principalities and installing a client as king of Scots after Malcolm III's death, with the infantry 'fyrd' and a large body of 'housecarls' acting as the largest army in Britain. Even lacking the Norman advantage of cavalry, this army would have given a strong war-leader the edge over all the other rulers on the island.

Notes

Chapter One

1. See Francis Pryor, *Britain AD* (Harper Collins 2004) , chapters 6 and 7.
2. Bede, *The Ecclesiastical History of the English People*, ed. Judith McClure and Roger Collins (OUP 1999), pp. 77–8; *The Anglo-Saxon Chronicle*, tr. and ed. Michael Swanton (Phoenix 1996), p. 61, sub anno 829 – the Peterborough ('E') version of the text only.
3. See D.P. Kirby, 'Problems of Early West Saxon History', in *English Historical Review*, vol lxxx (1971), pp. 10–29; D. Dumville, 'The West Saxon Royal Genealogical List and the Chronology of Early Wessex' in *Peritia*, vol iv (1985), pp. 21–67; D. Dumville, 'The West Saxon Royal Genealogical Lists: Manuscripts and Texts' in *Anglia* (1986), pp. 1–32; Barbara Yorke, 'The Jutes of Hampshire and Wight and the Origins of Wessex' in *The Origins of Anglo-Saxon Kingdoms*, ed. Steven Bassett (Leicester University Press 1989), pp. 84–96.
4. As seen in the *Annales Cambriae*, probably written up (from earlier texts?) in the early tenth century.
5. See D. Dumville, 'The Historical value of the Historia Brittonum', in *Arthurian Literature*, vol vi (1986), pp. 1–26, and N. Higham, *Arthur: Myth-Making and History* (Routledge 2002).
6. Bede, op. cit., p. 27.
7. F. M. Stenton, *Anglo-Saxon England* (OUP 1989 edition), pp. 11–15.
8. Procopius, *Gothic Wars*, vol iv, p. 20.
9. Caesar, *De Bello Gallico*, tr. S.A. Handford (Penguin 1981), book iv, ch. 12.
10. See E.A. Thompson, *A History of Attila and the Huns* (OUP 1948); E. A. Helfen, *The World of the Huns* (Berkeley, California, 1973).
11. See J. Morris, *The Age of Arthur* (Weidenfeld and Nicolson, 1973), p. 315.
12. See Stenton, pp. 102 and 116 for the background. The question of Christian survival is still unresolved.
13. See J.E. Turville-Petre, 'Hengest and Horsa' in *Saga-Book of the Viking Society*, vol xiv (1953–7), pp. 273–90; K.P. Whitney, *The Kingdom of Kent*, Phillimore, 1982; S.C. Hawkes, 'Anglo-Saxon Kent AD 425–725' in P. Leach (ed.), *Archaeology in Kent to AD 1500* (unknown, 1982), pp. 64–75; S. Bassett (ed.), *The Origins of Anglo-Saxon Kingdoms*, pp. 55–74; Nicholas Brooks 'The Creation and Early Structure of the Kingdom of Kent' in D.P. Kirby (ed.), *The Earliest English Kings* (Routledge 1991), pp. 30–47.
14. See Bassett, op. cit., pp. 84–5, 88–91, 95; Dumville, as n. 3; for general comparison between the Anglo-Saxon, British and Continental kingdoms see Bassett, pp. 28–54.
15. *Anglo-Saxon Chronicle*, pp. 16, 17.

16. See Bassett, p. 64. Tytila's name gives his probable birth-date, i.e. after the Gothic Totila's accession in AD 542 – and thus his son Raedwald's likely approximate birth- date.
17. See M.A. Jones, 'An Early Anglo-Saxon landscape at Mucking', in *Anglo-Saxon Settlement and Lansdcape*, ed. T. Rowley (British Archaeological Reports, British Series no. 6, 1974) pp. 20–35.
18. See Bassett, pp. 21, 78; Stenton, pp. 18, 29; E. Ekwall, *English Place-Names ending in -ing* (Lund, Sweden 1923).
19. See Bassett, p. 25; *Victoria County History: Essex*, vol iii (HMSO 1963), pp. 86–8.
20. See Bassett, pp. 160, 163, 169; Kate Pretty, 'Defining the Magonsaete' in ibid, pp. 171–83.
21. Op. cit., pp. 175–7.
22. Bede, p. 150.
23. Caesar, *De Bello Gallico*, book iv (ed. Handford), pp. 97–102 on 55 BC; book v, pp. 105–21 on 54 BC.
24. See C.E. Stevens, 'Britain between the invasions (54 BC–AD 43): a study in ancient diplomacy' in *Aspects of Archaeology: Essays presented to O. Crawford*, ed. W. Grimes (London 1951) pp. 332–44; B. Levick, *Claudius* (Batsford 1990), pp. 139–40.
25. See Shepherd Frere, *Britannia* (London 1987), p. 30; also note the inscribed 'Res Gestae' of Augustus at Ankara, section 32.
26. Constantius, *The Life of St Germanus*, tr. F. Hoare in The Western Fathers (London 1954), chapter 12; in general, see E.A. Thompson, *St Germanus of Auxerre and the End of Roman Britain* (Boydell 1994).
27. Gregory of Tours, *The History of the Franks*, tr. Lewis Thorpe (Penguin 1974) pp. 153–4, 162, 217.
28. *Anglo-Saxon Chronicle*, pp. 18, 19; Stuart Laycock, *Britannia: A Failed State?* (History Press, 2008).
29. 'Nennius', chapter 56.
30. Gildas, *De Excidio Brittanniae*, tr. M. Winterbotom (1978), chapters 27–33
31. As note 8.
32. Morris, *The Age of Arthur*, pp. 312–13.
33. *The Chronicle of Henry of Huntingdon*, tr. Thomas Forester (Llanerch reprint 1991), p. 49.
34. *Anglo-Saxon Chronicle*, pp. 38–9; Bede pp. 191, 197, 244.
35. Bede, pp. 197–8.
36. See D.P. Kirby (ed.), *The Earliest English Kings*, pp. 69–71; and D. Dumville, 'The Anglian Collection of Royal Genealogies and Regnal Lists' in *Anglo-Saxon England*, vol v (1976), pp. 23–50.
37. J.T. Koch, *The Gododdin of Aneirin* (University of California Press, 1997).
38. Bede pp. 91–4; *The Anglo-Saxon Chronicle*, p. 24.
39. Bede p. 105; *The Anglo-Saxon Chronicle*, pp. 24–5.
40. See J.C. Cavadin (ed.), *Gregory the Great* (Notre Dame, Illinois, 1995); H. Chadwick, *The Church in Ancient Society: from Galilee to Gregory the Great* (OUP 2001), pp. 658–73.
41. See Procopius, *Gothic Wars*, book iii, chapter 20: 18 and chapter 26: 11–14; also Averil Cameon, *Procopius and the Sixth Century* (Routledge 1985) pp. 193–5.
42. See Morris, *The Age of Arthur*, pp. 369–72 (Cadoc), pp. 357 and 370 (Caldey Island), pp. 357–67 (Samson and Pail Aurelian), 350–6 and 372–4 (Ireland); C. Barber and D. Pykitt, *Voyage to Avalon: The Final Discovery of King Arthur*, pp. 79–81 (Blorenge Books, 1993) (Cadoc).

43. Bede, pp. 191, 202–3.
44. Bede pp. 146–7, 163–4, 174–8.
45. Ibid, pp. 192–4.
46. Ibid pp. 153–4; also pp. 154–9 on the Synod of Whitby.
47. Ibid p. 159.
48. Ibid pp. 221–2; Anglo-Saxon Chronicle pp. 38–9.
49. Kirby, op. cit., pp. 141–62; P. Godman (ed.), *Alcuin: the Bishops Saints, and Kings of York* (Oxford 1982).
50. Bede, pp. 120, 135, 136, 138, 144–5, 149–50; Bassett, pp. 159–70 for modern analysis.
51. A. Mawer and F.M. Stenton (eds.), *The Place-Names of Worcestershire* (English Place-Names Society, vol iv, 1927), p. xxii; and Bassett, pp. 163–4.
52. Bede, p. 150.
53. Bassett, pp. 159–70: Nicholas Brooks article on early Mercia.
54. Bede, p. 152.
55. *Anglo-Saxon Chronicle*, pp. 32–3.
56. Bede, pp. 126 and 292.
57. *Annales Cambriae*, sub anno 854: in *Y Cymmrodor*, vol ix (1888), pp. 141–83, ed. and tr. E. Phillimore; *Brut y Tywysogion*, or *Chronicle of the Princes*, ed. and tr. T. Jones (4 vols, Board of Celtic Studies, Cardiff University Press, 1941–7), sub anno 856.
58. *Anglo-Saxon Chronicle*, pp. 60–1.
59. *The Life of St. Guthlac*, ed. B. Colgrave (Cambridge University Press,1956), chapters 48–9.
60. Kirby, pp. 176, 186–7.
61. Stenton, *Anglo-Saxon England*, pp. 295–7, 300–1; Bassett, pp. 119–20, 129–33, 159–61; C.R. Hart 'The Tribal Hideage' in *Transactions of the Royal Historical Society*, 5th series, vol xxii (1971), pp. 133–57.
62. Bassett, pp. 119–20.
63. Bede, p. 77; M. Carver, 'Kingship and Material Culture in Early Anglo-Saxon East Anglia' in Bassett, pp. 141–58.
64. Mattingley, *Britain: an Imperial Possession*, pp. 371, 384.
65. Bede, p. 78.
66. Ibid, pp. 138–8; *Anglo-Saxon Chronicle*, p. 28.
67. Bede, p. 27; S.C. Hawkes, op. cit.
68. See Bassett, pp. 55–74; Kirby, pp. 30–47; Dumville, 1986 (in *Arthurian Literature*), op. cit.
69. Gregory of Tours, book ix, ch. 26.
70. Bede, p. 77.
71. Ibid p. 41.
72. Ibid pp. 189–90.
73. *Anglo-Saxon Chronicle*, pp. 14–15.
74. Ibid, pp. 16–17.
75. Ibid, pp. 19, 20, 40.
76. Bede, p. 191. But does the 'ten years' imply revival of central power by Centwine not by the Church-promoted Caedwalla?
77. See Barber and Pykitt, pp. 102–5; H.E. Walker, 'Bede and the Gewissae' in *Cambridge Historical Journal*, vol xii (1956), pp. 154–86. Geoffrey of Monmouth refers to fifth century British 'High Kings like 'Vortigern' as rulers of the 'Gewissae', which would imply a South Welsh not West Saxon context.

78. *Anglo-Saxon Chronicle*, pp. 14–19 for 'official' version of the conquest.
79. Bede, *The Ecclesiastical History of the English People*, ed. Judith McClure and Roger Collins (OUP 1999), pp. 77–8; *The Anglo-Saxon Chronicle*, tr. and ed. Michael Swanton (Phoenix 1996), p. 61, sub anno 829 – the Peterborough ('E') version of the text only.
80. *Anglo-Saxon Chronicle*, pp. 38–9; Bede p. 207.
81. Kirby, p. 179.
82. *Anglo-Saxon Chronicle*, pp. 54–5; William of Malmesbury, *The Kings Before the Norman Conquest*, tr. Joseph Stevenson (Llanerch reprint 1989), p. 68; lurid version of events in Roger of Wendover, *Flowers of History*, tr. J.A. Giles (Llanerch reprint 1993), pp. 158–9.
83. Asser, *Life of King Alfred*, chapters 14–15.
84. Aethelweard, *Chronicle* (ed. A. Campbell, 1962), p. 37.
85. Bede, pp. 244–5.
86. Ibid, p. 120.
87. Ibid, p. 152.

Chapter Two
1. *Life of St. Germanus*, chapter 12: Gildas, op. cit.
2. Gildas, chapters 28–33.
3. Bede, pp. 26–7.
4. 'Nennius', chapter 56; Gildas, chapter 32.
5. See D. Dumville, 'Sub-Roman Britain: History and Legend' in *History*, vol lxii, pp. 173–92; O. Padel, 'The Nature of Arthur' in *Cambridge Medieval Celtic Studies*, vol xxvii (1994) , pp. 1–31; N. Higham, *Arthur: Myth-Making and History* (OUP 2002).
6. See D.P. Kirby, 'Problems of Early West Saxon History', in *English Historical Review*, vol lxxx (1971), pp. 10–29; D. Dumville, 'The West Saxon Royal Genealogical List and the Chronology of Early Wessex' in *Peritia*, vol iv (1985), pp. 21–67; D. Dumville, 'The West Saxon Royal Genealogical Lists: Manuscripts and Texts' in *Anglia* (1986), pp. 1–32; Barbara Yorke, 'The Jutes of Hampshire and Wight and the Origins of Wessex' in *The Origins of Anglo-Saxon Kingdoms*, ed. Steven Bassett (Leicester University Press 1989), pp. 84–96.
7. *Annales Cambriae*, sub anno 516, 537.
8. Geoffrey of Monmouth, *History of the Kings of Britain*, tr. Lewis Thorpe (Penguin, 1966), pp. 151–2 (Constantine), 152–4 (Constans), 186–201 (Ambrosius), 202–11 (Uther), 212–61 (Arthur).
9. See *Archaeological Journal*, vol lxxxix (1932), pp. 203 ff.
10. See P. Barker, *Wroxeter: Roman City Excavations, 1960–80* (Worcester 1981) and *From Roman Viroconium to Medieval Wroxeter* (Worcester 1995). Some sceptics now regard the theory that the discoveries imply a major sixth-century town at the site to be exaggerated.
11. See Morris, *The Age of Arthur*, pp. 106–10.
12. See Catherine Hill, *The Origins of the English* (Duckworth, 2003); also discussion in F. Pryor, *Britain AD*, chapter 7.
13. See Pryor, op. cit.
14. See N. Higham, *Rome, Britain and the Anglo-Saxons* (Routledge,1992); David Brown, 'Problems of Continuity' in Trevor Rowley (ed), *Anglo-Saxon Settlement and Landscape* (British Archaeological Studies, no. 6, Oxford 1974).
15. J.H. Ward, 'The Notitia Dignitatum' in *Latomus*, vol xxxiii (1974), pp. 397–434.
16. R.L. Collingwood and J.N. Myres, *Roman Britain* (OUP 1932). The theory originated in Germany in 1896.

17. See 'The Dream of Macsen Wledig' in *The Mabinogion*, ed. Jeffrey Gantz (Penguin 1976), pp. 118–27, and the placing of Maximus at the head of South Welsh genealogies in the collection edited by P. Bartrum, *Early Welsh Genealogical Tracts* (University of Wales Press, 1966).
18. 'Nennius', chapters 31, 36–8 and 47–8 on Vortigern, also chapters 37–9 on Rowena and 43–4 on Vortimer. For the 'Pillar of Eliseg' with Vortigern's genealogy, see Barber and Pykitt, pp. 103–4.
19. L. Alcock, *'By South Cadbury is that Camelot...'* (Thames and Hudson 1972) and Cadbury Castle, Somerset (University of Wales Press 1995). The ferocity of the attacks on Alcock's perfectly logical deductions is surprising, though the name of the site would make it more plausible that Cador of Dumnonia, father of Gildas' opponent King Constantine, was the post-Roman builder not 'Arthur'.
20. Gildas, chapter 25.
21. Morris, p. 100. Sceptics prefer to believe the similarity of names is a coincidence.
22. See Padel, op. cit.
23. Morris, pp. 116–17.
24. *Annales Cambriae*, sun anno 537 (i.e. 539?).
25. See K. Jackson, 'The site of Mount Badon' in *Journal of Celtic Studies*, vol ii (1953–8), pp. 152–5; R. Castleden, *King Arthur: the Truth Behind the Legend* (Routledge 2003), pp. 91–6; discussions in M. Ashley, *The Mammoth Book of King Arthur* (Constable 2005), pp. 148–53 and T. Green, *Concepts of Arthur* (Tempus 2007) pp. 204–7, 212–17, 245–6 with mention of a Lincolnshire site at 'Baumber'. T. and A. Burkitt, 'The frontier zone and the site of Mount Badon: a review of the evidence for their location', in *Proceedings of the Somerset Archaeological and Natural History Society* (1990) pp. 81–93, favour Bath; so do Barber and Pykitt, pp. 128–30. K. Jackson, op. cit., and M. Gelling, 'Towards a Chronology for English Place-Names' in D. Hooke (ed.), *Anglo-Saxon Settlements* (Oxford 1988) think it could be any site with the element 'bad' in its name. Baram Blackett and Alan Wilson, in *Artorius Rex Discovered* (Pontyridd, 1995), pp. 86–7 and 116–20, veer between Mynydd Baedan near Bridgend and Bouden Hill near Linlithgow in Scotland.
26. Gildas, chapter 26; he notably implies a formal partition of the island between Briton and Saxon.
27. Quoted in Blackett and Wilson p. 94.
28. Wace, *Roman de Brut*, E. Arnold (ed.) (2 vols, Paris 1938–40).
29. British Library, Harleian Mss. 3589, collection of genealogies; also see Bartrum, op. cit., for collections from the 'Bonedd y Saint' , pedigrees 44, 45 and 55 (South Wales) and the 'De Situ Brecheniauc' pedigree 10 (Silures). The 'Book of Llandaff' material is more problematic as it was compiled c.1100.
30. 'Nennius', chapter 56. Higham and Crowne regard this as a typical Nennian 'miracle' entry for a supernatural hero, not a factual account of an achievement by Arthur's men.
31. Implied in Gildas, chapter 33.
32. 'Nennius', chapters 31, 36–8 and 47–8 on Vortigern, also chapters 37–9 on Rowena and 43–4 on Vortimer. For the 'Pillar of Eliseg' with Vortigern's genealogy, see Barber and Pykitt, pp. 103–4; Barber and Pykitt, pp. 98–9.
33. *Annales Cambriae*, sub anno 573.
34. Quoted in Ashley, p. 51–2.
35. 'Nennius' chapter 63; Morris pp. 233–4.
36. J.T. Koch, *The Gododdin of Aneirin* (University of California Press, 1997).
37. *Annales Cambriae*; and see *Anglo-Saxon Chronicle*, pp. 22–3 and note.

38. Bede, pp. 105, 110–11.
39. Morris, pp. 241–5.
40. Op. cit., pp. 175–7.
41. 'Nennius', chapter 65.

Chapter Three
1. *Anglo-Saxon Chronicle*, pp. 32–3.
2. Ibid, pp. 18–19.
3. See Nicholas Brooke's article in Bassett, pp. 165–7.
4. Wendy Davies, 'Annals and the Origin of Mercia' in *Mercian Studies*, (ed.) A. Dornier (1973), pp. 17–29; Bassett, pp. 162–4; *Anglo-Saxon Chronicle*, pp. 24–5.
5. *Anglo-Saxon Chronicle*, pp. 20–1.
6. J.N. Myres, *The English Settlements*, pp. 149–62 (Clarendon Press/ Oxford University Press 1986); R.G. Collingwood and J.N. Myres, *Roman Britain and the English Settlements* (Clarendon Press/ Oxford University Press 1937), pp. 403–4; D.P. Kirby, 'Problems of Early West Saxon History' in *EHR*, vol lxxx (1975) pp. 10–29.
7. Bede p. 121.
8. Ibid p. 135.
9. Ibid pp. 77–8.
10. D.P. Kirby, *The Earliest English Kings*, pp. 191–2, 195.
11. Bede p. 221; see also entry in *Annals of Ulster* for '686'.
12. *Anglo-Saxon Chronicle*, pp. 56–7; Kirby pp. 152–5.
13. Kirby pp. 147–55.
14. *Epistolae Karoli Aevi*, vol ii, nos. 16 and 18.
15. Kirby, pp. 147–8.
16. See Marjorie Anderson, *Kings and Kingship in Early Scotland* (Edinburgh 1973) ; A. Boyle, 'Matrilinear Succession in the Pictish Monarchy' in *Scottish Historical Review*, vol lvi (1977) pp. 1–10; Alfred Smyth, *Warlords and Holy Men*; Scotland AD 80–1000 (Edward Arnold 1984) pp. 72–6 and 177–81.
17. See Gerard McNicoill, 'The heir designate in early medieval Ireland' in *Irish Jurist*, vol iii (1968), pp. 326–9, and Donnchaidh O'Corain, 'Irish Regnal Succession: a Reappraisal' in *Studia Hibernica*, vol xi (1971) pp. 7–39.
18. Se Kirby, pp. 142–58.
19. *Anglo-Saxon Chronicle*, pp. 68–9.
20. Smyth, pp. 180–1.
21. The story first appears in Buchanan's sixteenth century Scots history and is supposed to have occurred at Athelstaneford.
22. Kirby, pp. 165–70.
23. *Anglo-Saxon Chronicle*, pp. 54–5.
24. Ibid pp. 62–3.
25. *Annales Cambriae*, sub anno 854.
26. *Anglo-Saxon Chronicle*, pp. 68–9.
27. Gregory of Tours, p. 154.
28. Ibid, pp. 155–8.
29. Ian Wood, *The Merovingian Kings AD 450–751* (Longmans 1994), pp. 198–201.
30. Asser, chapters 13–15: presumably derived from King Alfred himself.
31. *Anglo-Saxon Chronicle*, pp. 55–7.
32. Kirby, pp. 187–8; *Annales cambriae*, sub anno 817, 818, 822.
33. Kirby, pp. 190–2.

Chapter Four

1. *Anglo-Saxon Chronicle*, pp. 64, 65, 66–7, 68–73. For Ragnar, see Margaret Schlauch (tr.). *Saga of the Volsungs: the Saga of Ragnar Lodbrok Together with the Lay of Kraka* (New York 1965); also Alfred Smyth, *Scandinavian Kings in the British Isles* (Oxford 1977) pp. 169–213 on the Ragnar dynasty and the invasions.
2. *Anglo-Saxon Chronicle*, pp. 64–5.
3. Ibid pp. 66–7 (860) and 68–9 (865–6).
4. Ibid pp. 70–1; Aethelweard, *Chronicle*, p. 36.
5. *Anglo-Saxon Chronicle*, pp. 72–3.
6. Ibid, pp. 70–1; Aethelweard, p. 40. See general discussion of the 871 events in Alfred Smyth, *Scandinavian Kings in the British Isles*, pp. 240–54.
7. *Anglo-Saxon Chronicle*, pp. 64–5.
8. *Anglo-Saxon Chronicle*, pp. 62–3.
9. Ibid pp. 68–70
10. Ibid pp. 87, 89.
11. Ibid, pp. 70–1.
12. Aethelweard, p. 37.
13. *Anglo-Saxon Chronicle*, pp. 74–5.
14. Ibid, pp. 76–7.
15. As implied by Simeon of Durham's statement of the lengths of their reigns, which must overlap: in *Symeonis Monachi Opera Omnia*, (ed.) T. Arnold (2 vols, London 1882–5). See also D.P. Kirby, 'Northumbria in the Ninth Century' in *Coinage in Ninth Century Northumbria: the Tenth Oxford Symposium on Coinage and Monetary History* (British Archaeological Reports: British Series no.180, Oxford 1987) pp. 11–25.
16. *Anglo-Saxon Chronicle*, pp. 76–7.
17. See Sarah Foot, *Athelstan: the First King of England* (Yale UP 2011) pp. 37–9.
18. *Anglo-Saxon Chronicle*, p. 113.
19. Ibid, pp. 70–1.
20. Ibid, pp. 76–9 (anno 880–3), 78 (anno 884), 82 (anno 891).
21. Ibid, pp. 70–1.
22. Ibid, pp. 74–5.
23. Ibid, pp. 76–7.
24. Ibid, p. 89.
25. Ibid, pp. 85, 86, 89.
26. Ibid p. 85; Aethelweard, pp. 49–50. See also R. Abels, *Alfred the Great: War, Kingship and Culture in Ango-Saxon Engand* (Longmans 1998) pp. 152–62 on the war between Alfred and Guthrum in 878.
27. Asser, chapter 8; discussion in Abels, op. cit., pp. 57–67.
28. *New Dictionary of National Biography*, article on Arhcbishop Wulfstan; also Claire Downham, *Viking Kings of Britain and Ireland: the Dynasty of Ivarr to AD 1014* (Dunedin Academic Press, Edinburgh 2007).
29. See discussion in T. Venning, *The Anglo-Saxon Kings* (Amberley, 2011) pp. 123–4, 132.
30. See D. Dumville, 'The West Saxon Genealogical Regnal List: manuscripts and texts' in *Anglia*, vol civ, p. 25.
31. Asser, chapter 12.
32. Ibid, chapters 37–8.
33. Smyth, *Warlords and Holy Men*, p. 178.
34. See S. Oppenheimer, *The Origins of the British* (Constable and Robinson, 2006).
35. Smyth, pp. 180–1.

36. *The Scottish Chronicles*, anno 849, in A.O. Anderson (ed), *Early Sources of Scottish History* (2 vols, Stamford 1990).
37. Smyth, pp. 181–2.

Chapter Five
1. See Alfred Smyth, *Alfred the Great* (Oxford 1995); also J. Campbell, 'Asser's Life of Alfred' in C. Holdsworth and T.P. Wiseman (eds.), *The Inheritance of Historiography AD 350–900* (Exeter 1986) pp., 115–35. On the question of Asser's authorship, also: V. Galbraith, 'Who Wrote Asser's Life of Alfred?' in his *An Introduction to the Study of History* (1994), pp. 127–8.
2. Asser states that Alfred was aged forty-four at the completion of his book in 893. For Alfred's illness, see G. Craig, 'Alfred the Great: a diagnosis' in *Journal of the Royal Society of Medicine*, vol lxxxiv (1993), and Ables, op. cit., pp. 96–8.3. *Anglo-Saxon Chronicle*, pp. 92–3.
3. *Anglo-Saxon Chronicle*, pp. 92–3.
4. Ibid, p. 103; Henry of Huntingdon p. 168.
5. *Anglo-Saxon Chronicle*, pp. 94–5.
6. Ibid, pp. 96–104.
7. Ibid, pp. 80–1.
8. Ibid, pp. 96–104.7. Ibid, pp. 80–1.8. See S. Keynes, 'Anglo-Saxon Entries in the Liber Vitae of Brescia' in Alfred the Wise, (eds.) J. Roberts, J. Nelson and M. Godden (Cambridge 1998) pp. 19–22. For Edwin's alleged plot, see later version in William of Malmesbury, pp. 123–4.
9. Ibid p. 116. The dispute over his veracity depends on whether he obtained his information from a then extant tenth century source, perhaps a heroic saga poem about Athelstan. This is backed by Michael Wood, e.g. in his *In Search of England* (Viking 1999) pp. 149–68, but opposed by Michael Lapidge.
10. *Anglo-Saxon Chronicle*, pp. 106–10; for the sites of Brunanburh, see Sarah Foot, op. cit., and Wood, op. cit.
11. *Anglo-Saxon Chronicle*, p. 112; Henry of Huntingdon p. 172; Roger of Hoveden, Annals, (tr.) Henry Riley (Llanerch reprint 1994) p. 65.
12. Roger of Hoveden p. 65. *The Anglo-Saxon Chronicle* plays down the English problems in 940–1 by virtually ignoring them.
13. If Dunmail was the king of Strathclyde, he was not killed at the battle and buried in a nearby tumulus as said by local legend.
14. See discussion in *St Dunstan: His Life, Times and Culture*, (eds.) N. Ramsey, M. Sparks and T. Tatton-Brown (Boydell 1992).
15. Roger of Wendover, *Flowers of History*, pp. 250–1.
16. *Anglo-Saxon Chronicle*, pp. 118–19.
17. *Anglo-Saxon Chronicle*, p. 113 (minimal reference as embarrassing?); Florence of Worcester, *Chronicon ex Chronicis*, (tr.) J. Stevenson in his *Church Historians of England* (1853–68), vol ii, p. 137.
18. Roger of Wendover, p. 257; see also *New Dictionary of Nat. Biography* articles on King Edwy/Eadwig and St Dunstan.
19. Roger of Hoveden, p. 71; Roger of Wendover, p. 258.
20. Roger of Wendover, p. 261.
21. See also William of Malmesbury, pp. 140–1 on later legends of Edgar's lechery.
22. Edmund precedes his older half-brother Edward in charter witness-lists and is specifically called 'legitimus', which both indicate his superior rank.

23. *Anglo-Saxon Chronicle*, p. 119; Henry of Huntingdon, pp. 175–6. Roger of Wendover (pp. 263–4) is the first to mention the kings rowing Edgar on the Dee.
24. See *New Dictionary of National Biography* article on Archbishop Aelfheah.
25. *Anglo-Saxon Chronicle*, p. 133.
26. Ibid, pp. 131–3.
27. Ibid, pp. 133, 135, 139.
28. Ibid, p. 138.
29. As n. 27, especially the reference on p. 139; also pp. 146, 147, 150–1.
30. Ibid pp. 128, 133, 134–5, 137.
31. Ibid p. 140.
32. See *The Cartulary of St Frideswide's*, (ed.) S.R. Ingram, vol 1, pp. 2–9.
33. 'Song of Maldon', lines 84–90. See D. Scraggs (ed.), *The Battle of Maldon 991* (1991).
34. Asser, chapters 37–8.
35. See *New Dictionary of National Biography* article on Byrhtnoth.
36. *Anglo-Saxon Chronicle*, pp. 133, 135, 136, 137.
37. See NDNB article on Edward 'the Martyr'.
38. See Ramsay, Sparks and Tatton-Brown, op. cit. The identity of the woman Edwy was misbehaving with at his coronation feast as his fiancée is not certain.
39. *Anglo-Saxon Chronicle*, p. 125; also A. Campbell (ed.), *The Charters of Rochester* (London 1973) pp. 42–4. For the anti-monastic backlash in 975, see D.J. Fisher, 'The anti-monastic reaction in the reign of Edward the Martyr', in *Cambridge Historical Journal*, vol x (1950–2), pp. 254–70.
40. *Anglo-Saxon Chronicle*, p. 123; The Life of St Oswald entry is in *Historians of the Church of York and its Archbishops*, (ed.) J. Raine (Rolls Series, vol lxxxi, London 1879–94) vol I, pp. 449–50. For further elaborations later: e.g. William of Malmesbury p. 143.
41. *Anglo-Saxon Chronicle*, p. 151; on 1015, see pp. 145–6; on 101, see pp. 146–52.
42. Ibid, pp. 152–3.
43. Ibid, pp. 152 and 153; see notes 46 and 47 on the assassination.
44. Ibid p. 148.
45. *Vitae Aedwardi Regis*, (ed.) F. Barlow (Nelson's Medieval Texts 1962) pp. 7–9.
46. Henry of Huntingdon, p. 196; William of Malmesbury p. 168; Roger of Wendover p. 292.
47. Geoffrey Gaimar, *Histoire des Engles*. Adam of Bremen says Edmund was poisoned.
48. *Anglo-Saxon Chronicle*, pp. 158–60.
49. Ibid pp. 200–01.
50. See G. Ronay, *The Lost King of England* (Boydell 1989).
51. *Anglo-Saxon Chronicle*, p. 176; F. Barlow, *Edward the Confessor*, p. 94.
52. *Vita Aedwardi Regis*, (ed.) Barlow, pp. 13–14.
53. *Anglo-Saxon Chronicle*, p. 177; Barlow, *Edward the Confessor*, pp. 89, 93.
54. Ian Walker, *Harold the Last Anglo-Saxon King* (Sutton, 1995) pp. 1–5; E. Freeman, 'The Origins of Earl Godwin' in his *The Norman Conquest*, vol I (1874), pp. 719–31; A. Anscombe, 'The Pedigree of Earl Godwin' in *TRHS*, 3rd series , vol vii (1913) pp. 129–32; F. Barlow, The Godwins (Sutton 2003) p. 18. Lundie Barlow, 'The Antecedents of Earl Godwine of Wessex' in *New England Historical and Genealogical Register*, vol. lxi (1952) p. 32.
55. *Anglo-Saxon Chronicle*, pp. 174–82.
56. Ibid pp. 152–3.
57. As recounted in the 'Saga of St Olaf' by the Icelander Snorri Sturlason.
58. M.K. Lawson, *Cnut: England's Viking King 1017–35* (History Press 2011) pp. 161–3.

59. Walker, op. cit., pp. 9–10.
60. See discussion in M.K. Lawson, *Cnut: England's Danish King* (Longmans 1993).
61. *Anglo-Saxon Chronicle*, pp. 154–5; K. Mack, 'Changing Thegns: Knut's Conquest and the English Aristocracy', in *Albion*, vol xvi (1984) pp. 375–80.
62. F. Barlow, *The Feudal Kingdom of England 1042–1216* (Longmans 1976) pp. 109–10
63. Roger of Hoveden, p. 103.
64. *Anglo-Saxon Chronicle*, pp. 184–7 (1055) and 188–9 (1058).
65. Ibid, p. 177.
66. Ibid, pp. 190–3.
67. *Vita Aedwardi Regis*, p. 53.
68. Walker, pp. 54–73.
69. As stated by Osbert of Clare in his version of the *Vita Aedwardi Regis* in the 1120s – exaggerating to press his hero's claim to sainthood?
70. *Anglo-Saxon Chronicle*, p. 200; William of Poitiers, *Gesta Guglielmi Ducis*, (ed.) R. Foreville (Paris 1952) pp. 268–71.
71. Simeon of Durham, sub anno 1072; and see Ann Williams, *The English and the Norman Conquest* (Boydell 1995) pp. 17, 27.
72. *Anglo-Saxon Chronicle*, pp. 203–4, 210–11, 230–1.
73. Ibid, p. 237.
74. Ibid, pp. 154–5.
75. Ibid, p. 216.
76. *Anglo-Saxon Chronicle*, pp. 154–5; K. Mack, 'Changing Thegns: Knut's Conquest and the English Aristocracy', in *Albion*, vol xvi (1984) pp. 375–80.
77. Ian Walker, *Harold the Last Anglo-Saxon King* (Sutton 1995) pp. 1–5; E. Freeman, 'The Origins of Earl Godwin' in his *The Norman Conquest*, vol I (1874), pp. 719–31; A. Anscombe, 'The Pedigree of Earl Godwin' in *TRHS*, 3rd series, vol vii (1913) pp. 129–32; F. Barlow, The Godwins (Sutton 2003) p. 18. Lundie Barlow, 'The Antecedents of Earl Godwine of Wessex' in *New England Historical and Genealogical Register*, vol. lxi (1952) p. 32.
78. A. Rumble (ed.), *Cnut*, pp. 157–9.
79. *Anglo-Saxon Chronicle*, pp. 158–61.
80. Barlow, *Edward the Confessor*, pp. 56–7, 88–9.
81. As presumed from his being a capable leader by 1014. *The Knytlinga Saga*, (eds.) H. Palsson and P. Edwards (Copenhagen 1986) says he was thirty-seven when he died but this seems a little young.
82. Ottar the Black, in his *Knutsdrapa* (ed. D. Jonsson), says he was present at the attack on Norwich in 1004, which implies that he was in his early teens then at least.

Chapter Six

1. *Vita Aedwardi Regis*, pp. lxx ff, 112 ff; Osbert of Clare's version in pp. 14–15.
2. Barlow, *Edward the Confessor*, pp. 267–84.
3. See discussion in ibid, pp. 132–4.
4. Ibid, pp. 80–1.
5. *Vita Aedwardi Regis*, p.23.
6. Ibid, pp. 41–2 and 59–60.
7. *Anglo-Saxon Chronicle*, pp. 162–3. The later legend of her having to undergo an ordeal to prove her innocence or being reduced to poverty appears to be part of a hagiography for her alleged saviour St Swithun.

8. William of Poitiers, (ed.) Foreville, pp. 30–2, 100, 158, 168, 174–6; William of Jumieges, (ed.) J. Marx (Rouen and Paris 1914) p. 132; see also Barlow, *Edward the Confessor*, pp. 107–9. If the alleged 'diplomatic mission to promise William the throne' by Harold in 1064/5 was a formal royal offer to the Duke, on usual precedents William would have been given hostages – but he was not.
9. William of Jumieges, pp. 120–1; William of Poitiers, pp. 4–6; Florence of Worcester, vol I (ed. B. Thorpe. 1848–9), pp. 191–2.
10. *Anglo-Saxon Chronicle*, p. 188 – Worcester version only.
11. See comments in the edition of the *Chronicle* (ed.) by D. Whitelock, D.C. Douglas, and S. Tucker, at p. 133 note.
12. See G. Ronay, *The Lost King of England* (Boydell 1989).
13. See N. Hooper, 'Edgar the Atheling: Anglo-Saxon Prince, Rebel and Crusader' in *Anglo-Saxon England*, vol xiv (1985).
14. *Oderic Vitalis*, (ed.) M. Chibnall (13 vols, Oxford 1969–78), vol v, p. 272.
15. As noted by William of Malmesbury – which might make Edgar aged seventy-three.
16. *Vita Aedwardi Regis, p. 80.*
17. As note 5.
18. *Anglo-Saxon Chronicle*, pp. 180–2.
19. Walker, p. 137.
20. See D.R. Bates, 'The Character and Career of Odo, Bishop of Bayeux (1049/50– 1097' in *Speculum*, vol 1 (1975) pp. 1–20; A. Bridgeford, *The Hidden History of the Bayeux Tapestry* (London 2004) and D. Bernstein, *The Mystery of the Bayeux Tapestry* (London 1986) on Odo and the Tapestry.
21. *Oderic Vitalis*, vol iv p. 351; see F. Barlow, *William Rufus* (Yale UP 2000) pp. 441–2 on who Harold's fiancée was.
22. William of Poitiers, p. 118 (Bonneville-sur-Toques); Oderic Vitalis pp. 134–6 (Rouen); and the Bayeux Tapestry (Bayeux). Commentary, Walker pp. 100–01.
23. The incident can be interpreted as admonitory or reproach depending on understanding of the contemporary meaning of such a gesture.
24. William of Poitiers, p. 21. This would imply a William/Edward treaty.
25. Walker, p. 87, for best estimate of the date, i.e. after the election of Bishop Wulfstan of Worcester in spring 1062.
26. *Anglo-Saxon Chronicle*, pp. 188–9.
27. Ibid, pp. 192–3.
28. Florence of Worcester, vol I, p. 222, on Edith and the killing of Cospatric at Court. See also *Vita Aewardi Regis*, p. 31 and Barlow, Edward the Confessor, pp. 234–9.
29. Walker, p. 150.
30. *Anglo-Saxon Chronicle*, pp. 178–9.
31. As seen on the Tapestry – presumably around Hastings, where there was still land laid waste noted in the Doomsday Book twenty years later.
32. *King Harald's Saga*, (eds.) M. Magnusson and T. Palsson (Harmondsowth 1966) pp. 62–6.
33. Ibid, p. 150; *Anglo-Saxon Chronicle*, p. 198 ('C' version only).
34. Walker, pp. 138–9; date probably spring 1066.
35. *Anglo-Saxon Chronicle*, p. 199 (Worcester version only).
36. Walker, pp. 176 and 180.
37. *Anglo-Saxon Chronicle*, pp. 148–50.
38. Ibid, p. 191.

39. Ibid, pp. 172–3.
40. See R.R. Davies, *Conquest, Co-Existence and Change: Wales 1063–1415* (University of Wales Press 1987) pp. 82–107.
41. Roger of Hoveden, pp. 142–3.
42. Florence of Worcester, vol ii, pp. 134–5.
43. *Three Lives of the Last Englishmen*, (tr.) M. Swanton (London 1984) p. 105; John of Worcester, *Chronicle* (eds.) R. Darlington and P. McGurk (Oxford 1995), vol 2 sub anno 1066.
44. F. Barlow, *The English Church 1000–1066* (London, Methuen, 1963).
45. Barlow, *Edward the Confessor*, p. 231.
46. P. Rex, *Harold II* (Tempus 2003), following the version that there was only one child, not two.
47. Peter Rex, *Harold II* (Amberley 2000) p. 263.

Bibliography

Fifth to eighth centuries

Original sources

The Annales Cambriae, (ed.) E. Phillimore, in *Y Cymmrodor*, vol ix (1888), pp. 141–83.

The Annals of Ulster, (ed.) S. McAir and G. McNiocaill (Dublin 1983).

Bartrum, P. C. (ed.), *Early Welsh Genealogical Tracts* (University of Wales Press 1966).

Bede, *Ecclesiastical History of the English People*, (ed.) Judith McClure and Roger Collins, Penguin Classics, 1999.

Brut y Tywysogion, or *Chronicle of the Princes*, (ed. and tr.) T. Jones, 4 vols (Board of Celtic Studies, Cardiff Univ., 1941–71).

Canu Llywarch Hen, (ed.) Ifor Williams (Cardiff, University of Wales Press 1945).

The Chronicle of Aethelwaerd, (ed.) A. Campbell (Routledge 1962).

The Anglo-Saxon Chronicle, (ed. and tr.) Michael Swanton (Dent 1996).

Julius Caesar, *De Bello Gallico*, (tr.) S.A. Handford (Penguin 1981).

Constantius, *Life of St Germanus*, in (ed.) F. Hoare, *The Western Fathers* (New York, Sheed and Ward 1954).

Eddius Stephanus, *The Life of Bishop Wilfrid*, (ed. and tr.) B. Colgrave (Cambridge University Press 1927).

Geoffrey of Monmouth, *History of the Kings of Britain*, (tr.) Lewis Thorpe (Penguin 1966).

Gildas, *The Ruin of Britain (De Excidio Britanniae) and Other Works*, (ed. and tr.) Michael Winterbottom (Phillimore 1978).

Koch, J.T., *The Gododdin of Aneirin* (University of Cardiff Press 1997)

Gregory of Tours, *History of the Franks*, (tr.) Lewis Thorpe (Penguin 1974).

The Chronicle of Henry of Huntingdon, (ed. and tr.) Thomas Forester (Llanerch reprint 1991).

'Nennius', *British History (Historia Brittonum) and the Welsh Annals*, (tr.) John Morris (unknown 1980).

Procopius, *The Gothic Wars* in *The Wars of Justinian*, 7 vols, (ed.) H.B. Dewey (Harvard UP 1914–40).

Roger of Hoveden, *Annals of English History*, vol. I, (tr.) Henry Riley (Llanerch reprint 1994).

Roger of Wendover's Flowers of History, (ed. and tr.) J.A. Giles, vol. I (Llanerch reprint 1993).

Symeoni Monachis Opera Omnia, (ed.) T. Arnold, 2 vols (London 1882–5).

The Life of St. Guthlac, (ed.) B. Colgrave (Cambridge University Press 1956).

Two Lives of St Cuthbert, (ed.) B. Colgrave (Cambridge University Press 1940).

Wace, *The Roman de Brut*, (ed.) E. Arnold, 2 vols (Paris 1938–40).

William of Malmesbury, *History of the Kings of England: the Kings Before the Norman Conquest*, (ed. and tr.) Joseph Stevenson (Llanerch reprint 1989).

Secondary sources

Alcock, Leslie, *'By South Cadbury is that Camelot...'* (Thames and Hudson 1972).
Alcock, Leslie, *Cadbury Castle Somerset* (University of Wales Press, 1995).
Alcock, S., *Alcuin of York* (Oxford University Press 1984).
Anderson, M., *Kings and Kingship in Early Scotland* (Edinburgh University Press 1973).
Ashley, M., *The Mammoth Book of King Arthur* (Robinson 2005).
Blackett, Baram and Alan Wilson, *Artorius Rex Discovered* (Pontypridd 1985).
Barber, C. and D. Pykitt, *Journey to Avalon: the Final Discovery of King Arthur* (Blorenge Books 1993).
Barber, R., *The Figure of Arthur* (London, Longmans 1972).
Barker, P., *Wroxeter: Roman City and Excavations, 1960–80* (Worcester, HMSO 1981).
Barker, P., *From Roman Viroconium to Medieval Wroxeter* (Worcester 1995).
Bassett, Steven (ed.), *The Origins of Anglo-Saxon Kingdoms*, (Leicester University Press 1989).
Boyle, A., 'Matrilinear Succession in the Pictish Monarchy', in *Scottish Historical Review*, vol lvi (1977), pp. 1–10.
Bromwich, Rachel, 'Concepts of Arthur', in *Studia Celtica*, vols. 10–11 (1975–6), pp. 163– 81.
Brooks, N.P., *The Early History of the Church of Canterbury* (Leicester University Press1984).
Brown, D., 'Problems of Continuity' in T. Rowley (ed.), *Anglo-Saxon Settlement and Landscape* (British Archaeological Studies, Oxford 1974).
Cameron, A., *Procopius and the Sixth Century* (Routledge 1985).
Castleden, R., *King Arthur: the Truth Behind the Legend* (Routledge 2003).
Cavadin, J.C. (ed.), *Gregory the Great* (Notre Dame, Illinois, 1995).
Chadwick, H., *The Church and Society in the Ancient World: From Galilee to Gregory the Great* (OUP 2001).
Chadwick, N. K., 'The Conversion of Northumbria: A Comparison of Sources', in *Celt and Saxon: a Study in the Early British Border* (1963), pp. 138–66.
Coates, R., 'On Some Controversy surrounding Gewissae/Gewissei, Cerdic and Ceawlin', in *Nomina*, vol xiii (1989–90), pp. 1–11.
Collingwood, R.G. and J.N. Myres, *Roman Britain and the English Settlements* (Oxford University Press 1937).
Collingwood, W.G., 'Arthur's Battles', in *Antiquity*, vol iii (1929), pp. 262–98.
Dark, Ken, *Civitas to Kingdom: British Political Continuity 300–800* (Leicester U.P., 1994).
Dark, Ken, 'Centuries of Roman Survival in the West', in *British Archaeology*, vol xxxii (March 1998).
Dumville, David, 'The Anglian Collection of Royal Genealogies and Regnal Lists', in *Anglo-Saxon England*, vol v (1976), pp. 23–50.
Dumville, David, 'On the North British Section of the Historia Brittonum', in *Welsh Historical Review*, vol viii (1976–7), pp. 334–54.
Dumville, David, 'Sub-Roman Britain: History and Legend' , in *History*, new series, vol. lxii (1977), pp. 173–92.
Dumville, David, 'The Welsh Latin Annals', in *Studia Celtica*, vol xii-xiii (1977–8), pp. 461–7.
Dumville, David, 'The Historical Value of the Historia Brittonum', in *Arthurian Literature*, vol. vi (1986), pp. 1–26.

Dumville, David, 'The West Saxon Regnal Genealogical Lists: Manuscripts and Texts', in *Anglia*, vol civ (1986), pp. 1–32.

Dumville, David, *Histories and Pseudo-Histories of the Insular Middle Ages* (Ashgate 1990).

Ekwall, E., *English Place-Names ending in –ing* (Lund, Sweden 1923).

Finberg, H.P., 'Mercians and Welsh', in *Lucerna* (collection of articles by author/editor) (ed.) H.P. Finberg (publisher unknown 1962), pp. 62–82.

Finberg, H.P., 'The Princes of the Magonsaete', in his *The Early Charters of the West Midlands* (publisher unknown 1962).

Frere, S., *Britannia* (London, Routledge 1987 edition).

Gelling, M., 'Towards a Chronology for English Place-Names', in D. Hooke (ed.), *Anglo-Saxon Settlements* (OUP 1988).

Godman, P. (ed.), *Alcuin: the Bishops, Saints and Kings of York* (Oxford , Oxford University Press1992).

Green, T., *Concepts of Arthur* (Tempus 2007).

Hanning, R.W., *The Vision of History in Early Britain* (New York and London, Routledge 1966).

Harrison, K., 'The Reign of Ecgfrith', in *Yorkshire Archaeological Journal* vol 43 (1971), pp. 79–84.

Hart, C.H., The Tribal Hideage,', in *Transactions of the Royal Historical Society* , 5th series, vol xxi (1971), pp. 133–57.

Hawkes, S.C., 'Anglo-Saxon Kent AD 425–725', in *The Archaeology of Kent to AD 1500*, (ed.) P. Leach (publisher unknown 1982).

Higham, N., *Arthur: Myth-Making and History* (Routledge 2002).

Hill, C., *Origins of the English* (Duckworth 2003).

Hunter Blair, P., 'The Origins of Northumbria', in *Archaeolia Aeliana*, 4th series, vol xxv (1947), pp. 1–51.

Hunter Blair, P., 'The Northumbrians and their Southern Frontier', in *Archaeolia Aeliana*, vol xxvi (1948), pp. 98–126.

Jackson, K., 'The Site of Mount Badon' in *Journal of Celtic Studies*, vol 2 (1953–8), pp. 152–5.

Kirby, D.P., 'Problems of Early West Saxon History', in *English Historical Review*, vol lxxx (1965), pp. 10–29.

Kirby, D.P., *The Earliest English Kings* (Routledge 1991).

Lapidge, M. and D. Dumville (eds.), *Gildas: New Approaches* (Boydell 1994).

Laycock, S., *Britannia: A Failed State?* (Sutton 2008).

Leeds, E.T., 'Early Saxon Penetration of the Upper Thames Area' in *Antiquaries Journal*, vol xiii (1933), pp. 229–51.

Levick, Barbara, *Claudius* (Batsford, 1990).

Lindsay, Jack, *Arthur and His Times: Britain in the Dark Ages* (F. Muller, 1958).

Matingley, D., *An Imperial Possession: Britain in the Roman Empire* (Penguin 2007).

McNiocaill, G., 'The heir designate in early medieval Ireland', in *Irish Jurist*, vol iii (1968), pp. 326–9.

Moisl, H., 'Anglo-Saxon Genealogies and the German Oral Tradition', in *Journal of Medieval History*, vol vii (1981), pp. 219–23, 231–6.

Morris, John, *The Age of Arthur* (Weidenfeld and Nicolson 1973).

O'Corrain, Donnchaidh, 'Irish regnal succession: a reappraisal', in *Studia Hibernica*, vol xi (1971), pp. 7–39.

Pelling, R.A., 'The Concept of Wessex', in *A Survey of Southampton and its Region* (British Association for the Advancement of Science, 1964) pp. 174–6.

Padel, Oliver, 'The Nature of Arthur' in *Cambrian Medieval Celtic Studies*, vol xxvii (1994), pp 1–31.

Phillips, G. and M. Keatman, *King Arthur: the True Story* (Century 1992).

Pryor, Francis, *Britain AD* (Harper Collins 2004).

Ridyard, S.J., *The Royal Saints of Anglo-Saxon England* (Cambridge Studies in Medieval Life and Thought 1988).

Sims-Williams, P., 'The Settlement of England in Bede and the Chronicle', in *Anglo- Saxon England*, vol xii (1980),pp. 1–40.

Sims-Williams, P., 'Gildas and the Anglo-Saxons', in *Cambridge Medieval Celtic Studies*, vol vi (1983), pp. 1–30.

Smyth, A., *Warlords and Holy Men: Scotland AD 80–1000* (Edward Arnold 1984).

Stenton, Sir Frank, *Anglo-Saxon England* (OUP, 1989 edition).

Stenton, Sir Frank, *Preparatory to Anglo-Saxon England: Being the Collected Papers of Sir Frank Merry Stenton*, (ed.) M. Stenton (Clarendon Press/OUP 1970).

Stevens, C. E., 'Britain between the invasions: 54 BC to AD 43' in *Aspects of Archaeology: Essays Presented to O. Crawford*, (ed.) W. Grimes (London, H.W. Edwards 1951), pp. 332–44.

Thompson, E.A., *St Germanus of Auxerre and the End of Roman Britain* (Boydell 1994).

Turville-Petre, J.E., 'Hengest and Horsa' in *Saga-Book of the Viking Society*, vol xiv (1953–7), pp. 273–90.

Walker, H.F., 'Bede and the Gewissae: the Political Evolution of the Heptarchy and its Nomenclature', in *Cambridge Historical Review*, vol xii (1956), pp. 174–86.

Wood, Ian, *The Merovingian Kingdoms AD 450–751* (Longmans 1994).

Wormauld, P., 'Bede, the Bretwaldas and the Origin of the Gens Anglorum', in Wormauld (ed.), *Ideal and Reality in Frankish and Early Anglo-Saxon History*, (publisher unknown 1983).

Whitney, K.P., *The Kingdom of Kent* (Phillimore 1982).

Yorke, Barbara, *Kings and Kingdoms in Early Saxon England* (Seaby 1990).

Yorke, Barbara, 'Fact or Fiction? The written evidence for the fifth and sixth centuries AD', in *Anglo-Saxon Studies in History and Archaeology*, vol vi (1993), pp. 45–50.

Ninth and tenth centuries to 978

Primary sources
Abbo of Fleury, *Passio Sancti Edmundi: Three Lives of English Saints*, (ed.) M. Winterbottom (University of Toronto Centre for Medieval Studies 1972).

Aethelweard, *Chronicle*, (ed.) A. Campbell (OUP 1962).

Annales Cambriae, (ed.) D. Dumville (Cambridge University Press 2002).

The Anglo-Saxon Chronicle (trans. and ed.) M. Swanton (Phoenix Press 1996).

Asser, *Life of King Alfred*, (eds.) S. Keynes and M. Lapidge (Penguin 1983).

Anderson, A.O. (ed.), *Early Sources of Scottish History*, 2 vols (Stamford 1990).

Henry of Huntingdon *The Chronicle of Henry of Huntingdon*, (tr. and ed.) T. Forester (Llanerch Press reprint 1988).

Historians of the Church of York and its Archbishops, (ed.) J. Raine (Rolls Series, vol lxxi, London 1879–94).

Roger of Hoveden, *Annals of Roger of Hoveden, part One: AD 732–1154*, (tr.) H. Riley (Llanerch Press reprint 1994).

Roger of Wendover, *Roger of Wendover's Flowers of History*, (tr.) J. Giles (Llanerch Press reprint 1993).

Saga of the Volsungs: the Saga of Ragnar Lodbrok, Together with the Lay of Kraka, (tr.) Margaret Schlauch (New York, American Scandinavian Foundation 1964).

Stevenson, J. (ed. and tr.), *Church Historians of England*, vol 2 (unknown publisher 1868).

Symeoni Monachis Opera Omnia.

William of Malmesbury, *History of the Kings of Britain: Part One, the Kings Before the Norman Conquest* (Llanerch Press reprint 1989).

Secondary sources

Abels, R., *King Alfred: War, Kingship and Culture in Anglo-Saxon England* (Longmans 1998).

Beavan, M.L., 'The Regnal Dates of Alfred, Edward the Elder and Athelstan', in *EHR*, vol xxxii (1917), pp. 517–31.

Beavan, M.L., 'King Edmund and the Danes of York', in *EHR*, vol xxxiii (1918).

Brooks, N., 'England in the ninth century: the crucible of defeat', in *TRHS*, vol xxix (1979), pp. 1–20.

Campbell, A., 'The End of the Kingdom of Northumbria', in *EHR*, vol lvii (1942), pp. 91–7.

Campbell, F. (ed.), *The Battle of Brunanburh* (Heinemann 1938).

Craig, G., 'Alfred the Great: a Diagnosis', in *Journal of the Royal Society of Medicine*, vol lxxxiv (1991).

Davis, R.H.C., 'King Alfred: Propaganda and Truth', in *History*, vol lvi (1971).

Downham, Claire, *Viking Kings of Britain and Ireland: the Dynasty of Ivarr to AD 1014* (Dunedin Academic Press, Edinburgh 2007).

Dumville, D., *Wessex and England from Alfred to Edgar* (Boydell 1992).

Enwright, M.J., 'Charles the Bald and Aethelwulf, the Alliance of 856 and strategies of medieval succesion' in *Journal of Medieval Studies*, vol v (1979), pp. 291– 302.

Fisher, D.G., 'The Anti-Monastic Backlash in the Reign of Edward the Martyr', in *Cambridge Historical Journal* vol x (1950–2), pp. 254–70.

Foot, Sarah , *Athelstan: the First King of England* (Yale UP 2011).

Galbraith, V., 'Who Wrote Asser's Life of Alfred?' in his *An Introduction to the Study of History* (OUP 1864), pp. 88–128.

Higham, N. and D. Hill (eds.), *Edward the Elder* (Routledge 2001).

Holdsworth, C. and TP Wiseman, *The Inheritance of Historiography AD 350–900* (Exeter University Press 1987).

Jones, Gwyn, *A History of the Vikings* (OUP 1984).

Keynes, S., 'The control of Kent in the ninth century', in *Medieval Europe*, vol ii (1983), pp. 111–32.

Keynes, S., 'On the authenticity of Asser's Life of King Alfred' in *Journal of Ecclesiastical History*, vol xlvvii (1996), pp. 526–51.

Kirby, D.P., 'Northumbria in the ninth century', in D.M. Metcalf (ed.), *Coinage in Ninth Century Northumbria* (British Archaeological Reports: British Series no. 180, Oxford 1987).

Kirby, D.P., 'Asser and his Life of King Alfred', in *Studia Celtica*, vol vi (1971), pp. 12– 35.

Loyn, H. R., *The Governance of Anglo-Saxon England, 500–1087* (Stafford 1984).

Loyn, H. R., *The Vikings in England* (Batsford 1994).

Nelson, J., *Charles the Bald* (publisher unknown 1992).

The New Dictionary of National Biography , (ed.) Colin Mathew (OUP 2001).

Peddie, J., *Alfred the Good Soldier: A History of his Campaigns* (Bath 1989).

Pratt, D., 'The Illnesses of King Alfred', in *Anglo-Saxon England*, vol xxx (2003), pp. 39– 90.

Ramsay, N., M. Sparks and T. Tatton-Browne (eds.), *St. Dunstan: His Life and Times* (Boydell 1997).

Ridyard, J., *The Royal Saints of Anglo-Saxon England* (Cambridge University Press 1988).
Roberts, J., J. Nelson, and M. Gooden (eds.), *Alfred the Wise* (Cambridge University Press 1998).
Scraggs, D. (ed.), *The Battle of Maldon 991* (Boydell 1991).
Smyth, Alfred, *Scandinavian Kings in the British Isles* (OUP 1977).
Smyth, Alfred, *Warlords and Holy Men: Scotland AD 80–1000* (Edward Arnold 1984).
Smyth, Alfred, *Alfred the Great* (Oxford 1995).
Stafford, Pauline, 'The King's Wife in Wessex, 800–1066', in *Past and Present*, vol xci (1981), pp. 7–27.
Stenton, F.M., *Anglo-Saxon England* (OUP 1971 edition).
Wood, Michael, *In Search of England* (Viking 1999).

978 to 1066

Original sources
Ailred of Rievaulx, *The Life of St Edward, King and Confessor*, (tr.) J. Bertram (St Austin Press 1990).
The Anglo-Saxon Chronicle.
The Carmen de Haestingas Proelio of Guy Bishop of Amiens, (ed. and tr.) F. Bass (Oxford 1999).
Eadmer, *Historia Novum in Anglia*, (ed.) M. Rule (Rolls Series, HMSO 1884, 1965 reprint).
The Ecclesiastical History of Oderiv Vitalis, (ed. and tr.) M. Chibnall (1969–80).
Encomiae Emmae Reginae, (ed. and tr.) A. Campbell,Camden Society, 3rd series, vol lxxii (Camden Society 1949).
The Gesta Guglielmi of William of Poitiers, (ed.) R. Foreville (Paris, publisher unknown 1952).
The Gesta Normannorum of William of Jumieges, Oderic Vitalis and Robert of Torigny, (ed. and tr.) E. van Houts , 2 vols (OUP 1992–5).
King Harald's Saga, (ed.) M. Magnusson and H. Palsson (Harmondsworth 1966).
Henry of Huntingdon.
John of Worcester, *Chronicle*, (ed.) R.R. Darlington and P. McGurk, vol 2 (Oxford 1995).
Ottar the Black, *Knutsdrapa*, (ed.) F. Jonsson (Copenhagen, date and publisher unknown).
Knytlinga Saga, (ed.) H. Palsson and P. Edwards (Odense, publisher unknown 1986).
The Life of King Edward Who Rests at Westminster, (ed. and tr.) F. Barlow (OUP 1992).
Snorri Sturlason, *Heimskringa: the Olaf Saga*, (tr.) S. Laing (Reykjavik, publisher unknown 1964).
Roger of Hoveden, *Annals of Roger of Hoveden, Part One: AD 732–1154*, (tr.) H. Riley (Llanerch Press reprint 1994).
Roger of Wendover, *Roger of Wendover's Flowers of History*, (tr.) J. Giles, (Llanerch Press reprint 1993).
Simeon of Durham, *Symeoni Monachis Opera Omnia* (Rolls Series).
Three Lives of the Last Englishmen, (tr.) M. Swanton (London, Routledge 1984).
Vita Aedwardi Regis, (ed.) F. Barlow (Nelson's Medieval Texts 1962).
Vita Haroldi: the Romance and Life of Harold, King of the English, (ed. and tr.) W. de Gray (Birch 1883).
William of Jumièges, *Gesta Normannorum*, (ed.) J. Marx (Rouen and Paris, publisher unknown 1914).
William of Malmesbury, *History of the Kings of Britain: Part One, the Kings Before the Norman Conquest* (Llanerch Press reprint 1989).

Secondary sources

Anderson, T.M., 'The Viking Policy of Ethelred the Unready', in *Scandinavian Studies*, vol lix (1987), pp. 287–97.

Anscombe, Alfred, 'The Pedigree of Earl Godwine', in *TRHS*, 3rd series, vol vii (1913), pp. 129–50.

Barlow, Frank, 'Edward the Confessor's Early Life, Character and Attitudes' in *EHR* vol lxxx (1965).

Barlow, Frank, 'Cnut's Second Pilgrimage and Emma's Disgrace in 1043' in *Medieval Scandinavia*, vol iv (1971) , pp. 66–79.

Barlow, Frank, 'Emma, Reine d'Angleterre: mere denature ou femme vindictive?' in *Annales de Normandie*, vol xxiii (1973) pp. 97–114.

Barlow, Frank, *Edward the Confessor* (Methuen 1979).

Barlow, Frank, *The English Church 1000–1066* (Methuen 1979).

Barlow, Frank, *William Rufus* (Yale UP 2000).

Barlow, Frank, *The Godwins* (Sutton 2003).

Barlow, Lundie, 'The Antecedents of Earl Godwine of Wessex' in *New England Historical and Genealogical Register*, vol lxi (1957), pp. 30–8.

Bates, D., 'The Character and Career of Odo, Bishop of Bayeux (1049/50–1097)' in *Speculum*, vol l (1975) pp. 1–20.

Bates, D., *William the Conqueror* (Sutton 2001).

Bernstein, D., *The Mystery of the Bayeux Tapestry* (Weidenfeld and Nicolson 1986).

Bridgeford, A., *1066: the Hidden History of the Bayeux Tapestry* (Fourth Estate 2004).

Brown, R. Allen, *The Normans and the Norman Conquest* (Constable 1969).

Campbell, M., 'Earl Godwine of Wessex and King Edward's Promise of the Throne to Duke William', in *Tradition*, vol xxviii (1972), pp. 141–58.

Davies, R.R., *Conquest, Co-Existence and Change: Wales 1063–1415* (University of Wales Press 1987).

Douglas, David, 'Edward the Confessor, Duke William of Normandy and the English Succession', in *EHR*, vol lviii (1953).

Douglas, David, *William the Conqueror* (Methuen 1964).

Hill, D., *Ethelred the Unready: Papers from the Millenary Conference* (Oxford, British Archaeology Reports 1978).

Hooper, N., 'Edgar Atheling: Anglo-Saxon Prince, Rebel and Crusader' in *Anglo-Saxon England*, vol xiv (1983).

Kappelle, W.E., *The Norman Conquest of the North: the Region and its Transformation, 1000–1135* (University of North Carolina Press 1979).

Keynes, S., 'The Declining Reputation of Ethelred the Unready', in D. Pelteret, (ed.), *Anglo-Saxon History: Basic Readings* (Routledge 2000) pp. 157–90.

Lavelle, R., *Aethelred II, King of the English 978–1016* (History Press 2002).

Lawson, M.K., *Cnut: England's Danish King* (Longmans 1993).

Mack, K., 'Changing Thegns: Cnut's Conquest and the English Aristocracy' in *Albion*, vol xvi (1984) pp. 375–80.

Mason, Emma, *The House of Godwine: History of a Dynasty* (Continuum 2004).

Maund, K.L., 'The Welsh Alliances of Earl Aelfgar of Mercia and his Family in the Mid-Eleventh Century' in *Anglo-Norman Studies*, vol xi (1988), pp. 181–90.

Morillo, S., *The Battle of Hastings 1066: Sources and Interpretation* (Boydell 1996).

Ronay, G., *The Lost King of England: Edward the Exile* (Boydell 1989)

Rumble, A. (ed.), *The Reign of Cnut* (Leicester Univ. Press 1994).

Stafford, Pauline, *Queen Emma and Queen Edith: Queenship and Power in Eleventh Century England* (Wiley Blackwell 1997).

Walker, Ian, *Harold: the Last Anglo-Saxon King* (Sutton, 1997).

Williams, Ann, 'The King's Nephew: the Family and Career of Ralph, Earl of Hereford' in C. Harper-Bill et al. (ed.), *Studies in Medieval History for R. Allen Brown* (Boydell 1989), p. 330–8.

Williams, Ann, *The English and the Norman Conquest* (Boydell 1995).

Wilson, D.M., *The Bayeux Tapestry* (London 1985).

Wisselik, R.D., 'The Saxon Statement: Code in the Bayeux Tapestry' in *Annuale Medievale*, vol xix (1979), pp. 81–8.

Index

COMING SOON FROM
PEN & SWORD BOOKS...

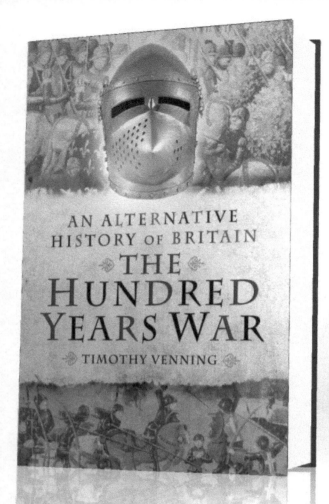

9781781591260 •
240 pages • HB • £19.99 •
Available February 2013

Continuing his exploration of the alternative paths that British history might so easily have taken, Timothy Venning turns his attention to the Hundred Years War between England and France. Could the English have won in the long term, or, conversely, have been decisively defeated sooner?

Among the many scenarios discussed are what would have happened if the Black Prince had not died prematurely of the Black Death, leaving the 10-year-old Richard to inherit Edward III's crown. What would have been the consequences if France's Scottish allies had been victorious at Neville's Cross in 1346, while most English forces were occupied in France? What if Henry V had recovered from the dysentery that killed him at 35, giving time for his son Henry VI to inherit the combined crowns of France and England as a mature (and half-French) man rather than an infant controlled by others? And what if Joan of Arc had not emerged to galvanize French resistance at Orleans?

While necessarily speculative, all the scenarios are discussed within the framework of a deep understanding of the major driving forces, tensions and trends that shaped British history and help to shed light upon them. In so doing they help the reader to understand why things panned out as they did, as well as what might have been in this fascinating period that still arouses such strong passions on both sides of the Channel.

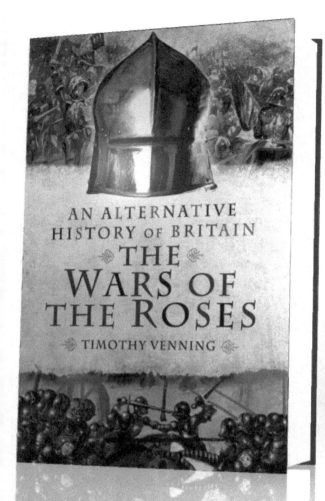

9781781591277 •
240 pages • HB • £19.99 •
Available March 2013

Timothy Venning's exploration of the alternative paths that British history might easily have taken moves on to the Wars of the Roses. What if Richard of York had not given battle in vain? How would a victory for Warwick the Kingmaker at the Battle of Barnet changed the course of the struggle for power? What if the Princes had escaped from the tower or the Stanleys had not betrayed their king at Bosworth? These are just a few of the fascinating questions posed by this book.

As always, while necessarily speculative, Dr Venning discusses all the scenarios within the benefit of a deep understanding of the major driving forces, tensions and trends that shaped British history. In so doing, he helps the reader to understand why things panned out as they did, as well as what might have been in this tumultuous period.

TO PRE-ORDER THE
NEXT INSTALLMENTS IN THE
ALTERNATIVE HISTORY OF BRITAIN SERIES
AT **20% OFF** THE COVER PRICE
PLEASE CALL 01226 734222

OR PRE-ORDER ONLINE VIA OUR WEBSITE:
WWW.PEN-AND-SWORD.CO.UK